DARK DISCIPLE

EVER DRIVEN BY his lust for power, Marduk, aspiring Dark Apostle of the Word Bearers Chaos Space Marine Legion, strives to unlock the secrets of an ancient and deadly artefact. This quest throws him and the Word Bearers into a deadly warzone and a desperate battle between their Imperial enemies and the alien tyranids. Amidst the carnage and the attentions of a third enemy faction, the piratical dark eldar, the Word Bearers must act quickly lest the object of Marduk's desire be lost forever. Surrounded by foes, this could be the Dark Apostle's sternest test yet.

A WARHAMMER 40,000 NOVEL

Word Bearers

DARK DISCIPLE

Anthony Reynolds

To Lady, my constant companion through the writing of this book (though a few less of the fur-balls next time would be appreciated).

A BLACK LIBRARY PUBLICATION

First published in Great Britain in 2008 by
BL Publishing,
Games Workshop Ltd.,
Willow Road, Nottingham,
NG7 2WS, UK.

10 9 8 7 6 5 4 3 2 1

Cover illustration by Klaus Sherwinski.

A CIP record for this book is available from the British Library.

ISBN13: 978 1 84416 607 7
ISBN10: 1 84416 607 4

Distributed in the US by Simon & Schuster
1230 Avenue of the Americas, New York, NY 10020, US.

See the Black Library on the Internet at
www.blacklibrary.com

Find out more about Games Workshop
and the world of Warhammer 40,000 at
www.games-workshop.com

Printed and bound in the US.

IT IS THE 41st millennium. For more than a hundred centuries the Emperor has sat immobile on the Golden Throne of Earth. He is the master of mankind by the will of the gods, and master of a million worlds by the might of his inexhaustible armies. He is a rotting carcass writhing invisibly with power from the Dark Age of Technology. He is the Carrion Lord of the Imperium for whom a thousand souls are sacrificed every day, so that he may never truly die.

YET EVEN IN his deathless state, the Emperor continues his eternal vigilance. Mighty battlefleets cross the daemon-infested miasma of the warp, the only route between distant stars, their way lit by the Astronomican, the psychic manifestation of the Emperor's will. Vast armies give battle in His name on uncounted worlds. Greatest amongst his soldiers are the Adeptus Astartes, the Space Marines, bio-engineered super-warriors. Their comrades in arms are legion: the Imperial Guard and countless planetary defence forces, the ever-vigilant Inquisition and the tech-priests of the Adeptus Mechanicus to name only a few. But for all their multitudes, they are barely enough to hold off the ever-present threat from aliens, heretics, mutants – and worse.

TO BE A man in such times is to be one amongst untold billions. It is to live in the cruellest and most bloody regime imaginable. These are the tales of those times. Forget the power of technology and science, for so much has been forgotten, never to be re-learned. Forget the promise of progress and understanding, for in the grim dark future there is only war. There is no peace amongst the stars, only an eternity of carnage and slaughter, and the laughter of thirsting gods.

PROLOGUE

It FELT LIKE his body was on fire. Every nerve ending was awash with agony. He had never dreamed that such excruciating torment could be possible.

A shadow leant over him, the image of death itself: skeletal, hateful, merciless. Eyes as black as pits bored into him, savouring his torment.

'Your suffering is only just beginning,' it promised, its voice matter-of-fact and even.

Needles plunged into his veins.

Then the prisoner heard a cry, the bestial roar of an animal in pain, and it took him a moment to realise that it originated from his own raw throat.

Blades slid from the tips of Death's long fingers and sliced through his skin, each deft incision drawing forth a wave of pain. Blood welled beneath each cut and was hungrily sucked up into tiny tubes attached to the grooved scalpel blades. The tubes ran along the back of Death's fingers and joined the protruding veins on the backs of his hands, feeding the filtered vitae into its bloodstream.

'Give in to the pain,' it said calmly. 'Beg for mercy.'

He gritted his teeth, and felt the metallic taste of blood on his lips. The vision of death leant closer.

'Fear me,' it whispered, and fresh agony jabbed through his body.

A needle appeared in front of his left eye, its barbed tip dripping with fluid. His muscles strained to turn away, but his head was held fast, and he could do nothing as the needle was pushed agonisingly slowly into the soft tissue of his eyeball. He hissed as it slid through his pupil and deep into his cornea.

The prisoner whispered something, and his tormentor turned, straining to hear.

'You will never break me,' the prisoner said again, this time with more force. 'Pain holds no fear for me.'

'Pain? You know nothing of it yet,' said his tormentor calmly.

Flaps of skin were teased back, exposing the vulnerable flesh beneath. Nerve endings were seared and his body jerked spasmodically as agonised muscles tensed involuntarily. His primary heart palpitated erratically and the needle in his eye twisted, grinding against the inside of the socket.

'You *will* come to fear me, in time,' mused the softly spoken image of death, plucking at his captive's exposed tendons, making the fingers of his left arm twitch. 'We are in no rush.'

Memories struggled to surface on the edge of the prisoner's mind. He tried to grasp them, but they were as elusive as shadow, taunting him, just out of reach.

Fresh agonies assailed the captive as dozens of barbed needles stabbed into his spinal column, sliding between his vertebrae and plunging into the tender flesh within.

Darkness rose to claim him, but he fought it with all his being, straining to possess the elusive memories that hovered just beyond his reach.

Abruptly, a name rose to his lips from the very depths of his being.

His name.

'Marduk,' he whispered. Fresh strength flowed through him as the dam holding his memories at bay broke. He smiled, his sharp teeth stained with blood.

'My faith is strong,' Marduk whispered hoarsely. 'You will not break me.'

'Every living thing can be broken,' said his tormentor, black eyes gleaming. 'Everything begs for death come the end. You and I, we will find that point together. You will beg come the end. They all do.'

'Not in this lifetime,' snarled Marduk. Then his eyes rolled back in his head and he succumbed to darkness, a bloody grin on his face.

BOOK ONE: PERDUS SKYLLA

'In true faith there is enough light for those who want to believe, and enough shadow to blind those fools that don't.'

– Apostate Evangelistae Paskaell

CHAPTER ONE

MACHION-DEX, PROCURATOR of the Adeptus Mechanicus archive facility of Kharion IV, strode across the grilled deck, his footsteps echoing loudly through the enclosed space. Ten expressionless skitarii warriors marched in a protective cordon around him, hellguns hard-wired into their brainstems held at the ready in black-gloved, augmetic hands.

The procurator came to a halt mid-deck, alongside an array of cogitator banks that rose from the floor. A blank data-screen reflected his image back at him. A servitor, nothing left of its original body other than a head and torso of morbidly pale flesh, was plugged directly with the logic-engines. Ribbed tubes connected its eye-sockets to the data-slate, and clusters of wires and cables ran from its severed torso into the machine's innards.

The skitarii warrior-units broke into two groups and stepped out to either side of Machion-Dex to form a corridor, their movements in perfect, robotic synchronicity. They moved to within a metre of a strip of yellow and black hazard stripes upon a plate bisecting the room. Their heavy boots stamped as they came to attention, awaiting their next command.

Machion-Dex folded his arms across his chest. He wore a vermillion tabard over a black bodysuit, its hems stitched with bronze wire, and his head was shaved to the scalp. Cables and clusters of wires sank into the flesh around the base of his skull, and a tattoo of a cogwheel, half black and half white, was emblazoned on his forehead.

'Initiate lock-down,' he said to the servitor, which twitched in response.

A series of red glow-globes began to strobe, and to the sound of wailing klaxons, heavy-duty plasteel blast doors, half a metre thick and containing a sandwiched core of interlaced adamantine, slammed down from the ceiling in front of the procurator and his entourage. Secondary layers of reinforced ceramite dropped down on either side of the main blast doors with a crash, and tertiary armoured plates of thirty-centimetre thermaplas slid from wall recesses, slamming together with titanic force.

Pistons wheezed as arcane locking mechanisms rotated and clinched shut, sealing off the sole entrance into the installation of Kharion IV. Not even half a kiloton of military grade explosive would be able to penetrate those doors without destroying half of the asteroid that the installation was embedded within.

The blaring klaxons stopped abruptly, along with the flashing red warning lights.

'Connect screen feed,' said Machion-Dex, and the servitor twitched again.

The blank data-screen before the procurator burst into life, covered in a snowstorm of static. Machion-Dex murmured a blessing to the Omnissiah and pressed a ritualistic sequence of buttons upon the data-slate's side panel. A green, pixellated image of the room beyond the blast doors appeared on the screen's surface.

The procurator folded his arms, and the fingers of his right hand began to tap a nervous rhythm on his bicep as he waited for his guest's arrival.

The walls of the room beyond the blast doors were scorched black, and half a dozen automated heavy flamers rotated in their mounts, aiming towards the circular bulkhead on the far wall. The pilot-flames of the weapons burnt hot white on the green data-slate screen.

There was a shuddering clang beyond the bulkhead as the access artery connecting to the docking facility clamped into position. There followed a burst of superheated steam that partially obscured Machion-Dex's view of the audience room, and a pair of lights located above the bulkhead began to rotate, sending shadows dancing across the fire-blackened walls.

The circular locking mechanism located in the centre of the bulkhead clicked outwards and rotated a full turn clockwise, before turning half a turn anticlockwise and sinking back into its recess. Then, with a shuddering groan, the bulkhead doors slid aside.

There was a hiss as atmospheric pressure equalised, and Machion-Dex leant forwards, squinting at the image on his data-screen. At first, nothing could be seen beyond the gaping aperture revealed by the parting bulkhead doors, and the darkness there was heavily pixellated and vague. Then a bulky robed and hooded shape appeared.

A single, unblinking light shone from beneath its hood, positioned where a left eye would have been. It limped down the fire-blackened steps to the metal grilled mechanical floor. Four massive individuals accompanied it; they too were heavily robed, their faces obscured by deep hoods. They turned their heads to regard the heavy flamers that rotated to fix upon them.

The lead figure limped across the room, unconcerned, and came to a halt before the blast doors.

'Blessings of the Omnissiah upon you,' it intoned , looking up at the armoured relay camera box positioned above it. Up close, Machion-Dex could see the cogged wheel symbol of the Adeptus Mechanicus upon its chest.

'And upon you, servant of the Machine God Incarnate,' replied the procurator, speaking into a grilled vox-unit.

'Knowledge is the supreme manifestation of divinity,' said Machion-Dex, invoking the sixth of the Mysteries, one of the sixteen Universal Laws memorised by all adepts of the Cult Mechanicus.

'Comprehension is the key to all things,' came the reply.

'The Omnissiah knows all,' said Machion-Dex.

'The Omnissiah comprehends all.'

Satisfied, Machion-Dex keyed a sequence of commands into the data-slate, and a control pillar rose from the floor beside the image of the hooded figure beyond the blast doors. The procurator saw a mechanical tentacle emerge from within the figure's robes. It lifted up before the camera, its mechanical claws snapping open and shut. A thirty-centimetre data spike slid from the centre of the snapping claw, and it was thrust into the control pillar.

A flood of data flowed over the data-screen in front of Machion-Dex, the apparently never-ending stream of scrolling information overlaying the motionless image of the hooded figure. The procurator's eyes flicked left and right, and his mouth moved soundlessly as the internal processors built into the left hemisphere of his brain-unit registered and recorded the flow of data.

The information was quickly processed and Machion-Dex blew out a slow intake of breath, impressed. With a click of a button he dismissed the stream of information from the screen.

'Deactivate weapon hardware,' he said, and the heavy flamer units went off-line, their pilot lights cutting out. They turned away from their targets and retracted back into their housings.

Machion-Dex cleared his throat and leant forward to speak once more into the vox-unit.

'Access granted, Tech-Magos Darioq. Welcome to Kharion IV.'

MAGOS DARIOQ STOOD stock still, his features hidden in the darkness beneath his hood as the blast doors were opened. Steam from the disengaging lock mechanisms vented around him.

'Revered magos,' said the procurator, bowing his head and touching his fingers to the symbol of the Adeptus Mechanicus, 'your visit is most unexpected.'

Darioq remained motionless as his four companions jerked into motion, marching suddenly forwards. Each of them stood almost two and a half metres in height, and their massive shoulders were twice as wide as the procurator's.

Machion-Dex's eyes flicked between the intimidating figures in alarm. He had thought them combat servitors, but he saw now that their movements were arrogant and self-assured, far from the ungainly, stilted gait of a servitor.

Robes were thrown aside and archaic bolters raised, and before the skitarii warriors' targeting arrays registered a threat, the first of the weapons began to roar.

Fire burst from the barrels of the ancient weapons. The sound was deafening, filling the enclosed space and echoing painfully off the walls. Fully half the skitarii were destroyed in an instant as high explosive shells tore through their bodies, ripping them apart in bloody explosions of armour and flesh.

Machion-Dex stumbled backwards, falling to the ground, his face a mask of horror as he gazed upon the massive, augmented beings. Their armour, inscribed with heretical symbols and litanies, was the deep red of congealed blood, and they fired with controlled discipline, eliminating each target with practiced efficiency.

The remaining skitarii brought their hellguns to bear, energy capacitors humming as the weapons surged into life. Electric-blue las-beams stabbed from the barrels of their guns, knocking one of the towering warriors back a step, searing holes through his robe and leaving smoking black impacts on his armour.

Two more of the skitarii were cut down, one of them spinning as a bolt slammed into his shoulder and exploded, severing its arm and leaving a gory head-sized hole in its torso. A bolt round detonated in the brainpan of the other and its head exploded, spraying blood, brain matter and splinters of skull in all directions.

A las-blast struck one of the warriors in the helmet, jolting his head backwards. With a snarl of anger, he ripped the skitarii apart with his return fire.

The firefight was over in seconds. The acrid smell of gunfire rose from smoking, silent barrels, and two of the giant warriors moved in to inspect the kills. One of the skitarii, who had been cut in half by a burst of gunfire, was still twitching. His movements were halted as a heavy armoured boot slammed down on its head, crushing its skull like a nut beneath a hammer.

Machion-Dex lay on his back, his breath coming in short gasps as he stared up at the terrifying figures. Each was massive, their every movement filled with power, and their inscrutable, Heresy-era Astartes helmets extensively modified to make them all the more fearsome in appearance. One had been fashioned in the likeness of a snarling daemon, and others had fierce sets of curving horns and tusks that gave them a brutal, barbaric look.

One wore no helmet at all, but its true face was far more terrifying than any of the helmets. The left side was a mess of scar tissue and augmetics, and its skin was so pale as to be translucent; blue veins could be seen within its flesh. A lidless, baleful red orb had replaced its left eye, and an infernal glyph of the ruinous powers was emblazoned prominently in the centre of its forehead. The figure snarled down at him, lips pulling back to expose sharpened teeth.

'Area secure,' growled one of the warriors, and the one standing over Machion-Dex nodded, not taking his eyes from the procurator.

'The location of the target will be found here, Enslaved?' he said over his shoulder, his voice filled with power and authority.

'That is correct, Marduk, First Acolyte of the Word Bearers Legion of Astartes, genetic descendant of the traitor Primarch Lorgar,' replied Magos Darioq in his monotone voice.

'Then let's get this done,' replied Marduk. He stepped towards the cowering form of Procurator Machion-Dex, and looked down at the terrified man.

'Do you need this one?' he asked over his shoulder.

'His continued existence is not required in order to retrieve the information held within the logic-centres of this installation,' replied the magos.

Procurator Machion-Dex gasped and began to scramble backwards, desperate to get away from the image of death looming over him.

Marduk's bolt pistol was levelled at the procurator's head and he froze.

'No,' begged the man. 'Omnissiah, protect your servant.'

Marduk smirked.

'Your profane god does not heed your cry, heathen,' said Marduk. 'You have devoted your entire, pathetic, worthless life to the worship of a false deity, a silent, profane image of the unbelievers. I will show you the path to the true gods. In death, you will bear witness to the glory of the true gods. They will feed upon your soul, and you will cry out in your torment. Embrace it, little man. Embrace your damnation.'

He shot the procurator in the head, and blood and gore splashed across the grilled floor.

'Glory be to the true gods,' declared Marduk.

MARDUK STOOD WITH his arms folded, deep in the bowels of Kharion IV. He stood upon a grilled gantry within the hollowed core of the asteroid, a massive pillar of machinery rising from the roughly hewn floor before him, glittering with lights and dials.

The magos stood before the humming pillar, fluid leaking from the severed input-jacks in his spine. He was connected to the pillar by the one mechadendrite tentacle that had been re-grafted to his body, and his pallid, dead lips twitched as he extracted information from the heart of the installation's data-library.

At last, the flexible tendril was retracted, and Magos Darioq jerked spasmodically as the connection was severed.

'Well?' growled Marduk.

'I have disabled the automated defence system that protects the installation,' said Magos Darioq, 'and initiated the self-destruct mechanism, so that our presence will not be transmitted to the god-cogitators of Mars.'

'Good,' said Marduk. He grabbed the waving mechadendrite tentacle with a violent motion and gave it a solid wrench. It was ripped from the magos's spinal column, writhing in his hand like a serpent. Darioq twitched, and milky liquid seeped from his mouth.

'You have the information we need?' asked Marduk, ignoring the mixture of blood, oil and protein-fluid that dripped from the thrashing mechadendrite onto his boots.

'That is correct, Marduk, First Acolyte of the Word Bearers Legion of Astartes, genetic descendant of the traitor Primarch Lorgar,' replied the magos. 'I have identified the location of the one in whom the forbidden knowledge of xenos tech devices is installed. With this knowledge obtained, Darioq will be able to unlock the xenos tech device.'

It was an odd quirk of the daemonic essence growing within the magos that he had begun to refer to himself in the third person. Marduk found this amusing, but at this moment he was concentrating fully on the words of the corrupted magos.

That the magos had not been able to unlock the device himself was infuriating, but it seemed that he could do little other than find the one of whom it spoke.

'Where?' snapped Marduk in impatience.

BENEATH THE SURFACE of Perdus Skylla, tens of thousands of people surged down access tunnel 25XI, a never-ending stream of humanity, desperate and fearful.

They were crushed together like animals being led to the slaughter, and the air, stale and hot, was filled with shouts and curses.

Mothers clutched wailing children to their chests, and men barked at each other, pushing and shoving. Some stumbled and were trampled underfoot, while others were pressed against the rockcrete walls, crushed by the relentlessly driving push of humanity. Others fainted, overcome by the heat and the lack of oxygen. The crowd was so tightly packed that, unable to fall, their limp bodies were carried along in the suffocating press.

The stink of sweat and oil was heavy, the turbines of the labouring air recycling units unable to cope with the demands required of them. The rockcrete ceiling, above which was half a kilometre of solid ice, pressed down oppressively.

The access tunnel was some forty metres wide and bisected by barriers and rockcrete pillars. Beyond these barriers, traversing down the centre of the corridor, was a sunken area of open space in which wide-gauged tracks were embedded. People pushed, shoved and cried out as they were carried along the platforms on either side of the rail tracks.

With a blast of solid displaced air, a high-speed auto-mated carriage sped by, gushing superheated steam and making the access corridor reverberate as it screamed along the slick, steel tracks. Knocked back a step by the force of the conveyance, people covered their eyes and gazed ruefully at the mirrored sides of the carriage as it passed. Only the wealthy guild masters and their staff had the funds and access privileges to use the high-speed conveyances.

It was a two hundred kilometre journey to Phorcys, the sole starport off Perdus Skylla within five thousand kilometres. Access tunnel 25XI was the only link between Antithon Guild and Phorcys, unless one wished to traverse across the frozen surface of the moon. Few ventured up to the inhospitable surface of Perdus Skylla other than outcasts; those unlucky enough not to be born into any of the great guild-houses, or who had been exiled from them for serious infractions.

Twelve other mining guilds were connected to Phor-cys, each of the proud guilds situated around the starport like the points of a compass and connected by artery tunnels like the spokes of a great wheel.

Most of the people of Antithon Guild had never left the hab-blisters deep in the ice other than to commute to the mining facilities some five thousand kilometres below. Fewer still had been to Phorcys, and few amongst the tide of humanity had any real understanding of the distance involved. To them, Antithon Guild and its environs was their world and universe, harsh and uncompromising, but familiar and safe, and they had no need to know of anything beyond its boundaries.

Or at least it had been safe until the first of the sirens had begun to wail and the pict broadcasts had declared that Perdus Skylla was being evacuated.

No reason for the evacuation had been issued from the guildmaster general's office, and the twenty-three million strong population of the moon had been in shock. Shock had quickly descended into panic as rumours spread of an imminent xenos invasion, rumours that were not in any way refuted by the Administratum.

Groups of the Skyllan Interdiction Force pushed through the crowds, attempting to maintain order. They wore their customary white body armour over sky-blue uniforms, and held high-powered laslocks across their chests. Snarling, shaggy-coated mastiffs with gleaming mechanical eye-augments strained at their leashes, sensing the tension in their masters.

An armoured Catalan-class squad vehicle moved slowly along one of the platforms, its white, high-compound plasteel chassis gleaming beneath the humming strip-lights overhead. Its flashing lights and blaring siren urged people out of its path, but its progress was slow, for there was no room to allow the vehicle through.

The winged emblem of the mercenary force was resplendent across the broad grill on the front of the heavy vehicle, and a pair of armoured soldiers stood in its dual turret at the rear, swinging the massive twin-linked heavy bolters left and right. Their faces were all but obscured by their white helmets, and black visors hid their eyes from view.

For twenty-five generations, Perdus Skylla had employed the Skyllan Interdiction, an outside mercenary agency funded by the wealthy mining guild conglomerates. They served as the military force protecting the guilds' assets in lieu of a Planetary Defence Force, while simultaneously acting as local law enforcement. Better trained and equipped than most Imperial Guard regiments, the hiring of the Skyllan Interdiction Forces had allowed the mining guilds to concentrate on their endeavours without having to draw away any of its skilled workforce to form a PDF.

Still, even with the mercenaries present within the tunnel to help restore order, the flow of humanity was little short of a rout.

One of the long-furred mastiffs let out a long growl, eyes locked on the ceiling. Seeing nothing, its master jerked its chain hard, silencing the beast.

A creature of shadow clung to the ceiling of the corridor, virtually undetectable to the naked eye or the sophisticated targeting matrices built into the helmets of the Skyllan Interdiction Force. It moved like a spider, making its way across the ceiling with slow, purposeful movements. Its lean, black armoured body disappeared for a second, its menacing form turning as insubstantial as smoke, only to reappear within the shadow of a grilled turbine further along the roof.

The creature's skin was inky black, and elegant runes of alien design were cut into its flesh. The runes glowed with a cold, inner light.

Turning its gaze downwards, it peered malevolently over the sea of humans with eyes that were milky white. It paid particular attention to the armed forces of the Skyllan Interdiction, and its limbs quivered with barely contained bloodlust. The blades running up its forearms hummed in anticipation.

The mastiffs below went into a frenzy of barking as the creature's scent carried to them, and their handlers struggled to control the powerful beasts. The creature disappeared into shadow once more as eyes scanned the ceilings, straining to pick out what had disturbed the dogs.

The air recycling turbines cut out, abruptly. The few who registered the sudden change in air pressure gazed up at the slowing fans in concern. Without the recycling units, the air in the tunnel would turn to poison within hours, as all the oxygen was used up and replaced with the toxic carbon dioxide exhaled by the masses.

Skyllan Interdiction Forces tapped their helmets as their communications went down, as if jammed by interference.

Then the first of the lights went out.

First, one of the lights faded to darkness, then another. The strip lights began to fail, one after another, in both directions, like a wave. People screamed as darkness engulfed them. The lights were going dark faster than a man could run, and within less than a minute every light in sight was dead.

The darkness was complete, all consuming and as black as the abyssal depths of the oceans below. People clutched at one another in panic, unable even to see a hand waving in front their face, and the crowd surged. Spotlights on the Skyllan armoured vehicle clicked on, and they wove back and forth, piercing the darkness like beacons.

People pushed towards the light sources, like moths being drawn to an open flame, and their panicked faces shone like ghosts in the cold light. They pressed against the armoured vehicle as if it was a talisman, those at the front crushed against its armoured sides by those pushing from behind.

Overhead, the nigh-on invisible figure had reappeared, and the runes carved into its flesh glowed with power. Still hugging the ceiling in defiance of gravity, it slid a curved, double-bladed punch dagger from its sheath. Other blades slid from the back of its hands, jutting forward over its fists like the talons of a great cat, and a low hiss of anticipation passed its lips as it waited for its dark kin to arrive in response to its summons.

It did not have to wait long.

A ball of lightning appeared, hanging in mid-air for a fraction of a second before it exploded outwards, blinding those nearby with the sudden burst of energy and throwing them to the ground. The crackling energy was gone in an instant, and an impenetrable void was left in its wake. It was like an inky black pool of water, though it was vertical and hung in mid-air, a plane of absolute darkness no thicker than a single molecule.

Ripples appeared across its surface, as if a pebble had been tossed into its centre, and whining shapes sped from the rent in real space, hurtling up the access corridor at tremendous speed. They screamed overhead, slicing like knives through the darkness. Blades cut through flesh, and hot blood splattered into the faces of hundreds of people, who screamed in terror. Many threw themselves to the ground in fear and were trampled to death by their brothers, sisters and wives in their panic to escape. However, with no lights, and with the tunnel packed from wall to wall with terrified people, there was nowhere to run.

The spotlights atop the armoured Skyllan Interdiction vehicle turned frantically, trying to lock onto the enemies that screamed past them, but they could only hold the speeding shapes in the light for a fraction of a second. A shape dropped from the ceiling, landing lightly atop the vehicle, and the troopers saw a shadowy blur in the rough outline of a humanoid figure perched on the roof of the armoured car before the spotlights were shattered.

The panicked troopers manning the turret-mounted heavy bolters opened fire into the darkness, and muzzle flare lit the area.

A sleek black shape hurtled past, and the mercenaries chased it with high-explosive rounds. They hit nothing but the walls and pillars of the tunnel, ripping away head-sized chunks of rockcrete.

The troopers' mastiffs had erupted into frantic barking and were fighting at their chains. Their masters turned around on the spot, laslocks held to shoulders as they struggled to sight the enemy. Dark shapes were zooming through the tunnel, but the troopers' targeting systems were unable to lock onto the targets.

There was a blur of movement and one of the troopers was sliced open from groin to throat. He squeezed the trigger of his weapon as he fell, blasting into the crowd of surging people, cutting several of them down.

People screamed and ran as the sounds of gunfire echoed deafeningly, fighting each other in their desperation to get to safety. The other troopers turned left and right, trying desperately to hold their targets in sight. A shape screamed overhead, and a trooper's head was severed from its body. The shape was a hundred metres further up the tunnel before the head hit the ground.

Streams of tiny bladed splinters spat out of the darkness towards the mercenaries manning the turret of the armoured vehicle. The razor-sharp shards sliced through their armour and flesh, and blood sprayed out across their pristine white armour.

Their gun silenced, the darkness was once more complete. Screams of terror and pain accompanied the speeding shapes, invisible in the darkness, as they cut through the air. There was a sudden gust of displaced air as another high-speed carriage screamed along the tracks in the middle of the tunnel, the lights from within the automated, servitor-controlled conveyance shining brightly, sending shadows dancing.

Tall-helmeted figures were visible in the flash of light, dragging people kicking and screaming back into the darkness.

A beam of pure darkness stabbed into the high-speed transport, rocking it. The beam tore through the fore-carriage, cutting through the engine block, seats and half a dozen occupants before passing through the roof, leaving a scorched black ring on the ceiling of the tunnel.

Two more searing beams struck it, and the front carriage was knocked off the rails. With the squealing of protesting metal, it slammed into the side-barriers, tearing through them in a shower of sparks. Striking the raised platform at speed, the conveyance tilted up on its nose, and the second and third carriages buckled behind it and rolled onto their sides.

The whole machine flipped onto its side and smashed over the platform's edge, tearing the barrier fully away and smashing through the surging masses. Hundreds were crushed as the carriages flipped across the platform to the sickening sound of metal being wrenched out of shape and scraping across the hard platform surface. It slammed into the tunnel wall, crushing more people between its bulk and the rockcrete walls, and finally came to rest. Electricity discharged across ruined metal wheels and sparked from the rails that had been half-ripped from the floor.

In the wake of the mayhem and silhouetted against the sparks, more black figures advanced through the press of bodies, smashing people to the ground with sharp blows before dragging their semi-conscious bodies back into the darkness.

Mastiffs yelped as they were torn to shreds by concentrated bursts of deadly fire. A blurred shape, little more than a vague, hazy outline, moved like quicksilver through the press of humanity, slicing and cutting, and the last of the Skyllan Indictment Forces were slaughtered without holding any of the enemy in their sights long enough to fire upon them.

A trio of shapes, in tight formation and moving impossibly fast, veered around the wreckage of the ruined rail conveyance, banking over the heads of the terrified masses as they screamed towards the rear of the Catalan-class armoured vehicle. It was peppered with spitting gunfire and detonated as its fuel tanks ruptured, exploding in a blinding fireball that hurled the vehicle across the seething platform.

The three sleek shapes sped through the inferno unscathed and gunned their engines, hurtling once more up the tunnel into the darkness, travelling hundreds of metres in seconds.

THE BLADES OF the turbine fans began to spin once more, and the strip lights flickered falteringly before humming back into life. The carnage unleashed in the last twenty minutes was revealed under the cold light of the glow-strips.

Hundreds of bodies were strewn across the floor, blood pooling beneath them where they had fallen. The blackened shell of the Catalan-class vehicle was upside down against a wall, pinning half a dozen charred corpses beneath it. Sparks burst intermittently from the rails, which had buckled and been torn from their housings.

The ruin of the conveyance's carriages was testament to its speed when it had crashed, for they were wrenched out of shape, and their plasglass windows were shattered ruins. Its curved roof had been half ripped off, and the shattered barrier it had crashed through was twisted beneath it. Bodies, their heads smashed and limbs severed, were spread around the wreck, either crushed when the conveyance rolled off the tracks, or thrown from their seats inside. Blackened holes the size of fists showed where the vehicle had been struck by dark-matter weapons.

There was no sign of any living thing within the tunnel, and not one of the corpses twitched or groaned. Where earlier the tunnel had seethed with life, now it was utterly bereft, and the only sounds were the humming of the strip lights, the reverberations of the recycle units and the odd spark from the ruined tracks.

Of the thousands of people not slain, there was no sign. Nor was there any sign of their attackers. Only the carnage left in their wake was evidence of their having existed at all.

CHAPTER TWO

STARING THROUGH THE twenty-metre wide observation portal of the bridge, Admiral Rutger Augustine looked out over the vast length of his flagship vessel, the mighty Retribution-class battleship *Hammer of Righteousness*.

She looked like an immense, armoured Imperial cathedral, majestic and of such a scale as to be almost incomprehensible. Six kilometres from stern to prow, hundreds of spires ran along her length, joined together by flying buttresses and archways, and she bristled with the finest weapon systems that the Imperial Navy could boast.

Hundreds of close-range turrets were set across her armoured hull, each the size of four super-heavy battle tanks, and a dozen torpedo tubes, each gaping almost forty metres wide, were inset into her sweeping, massively armoured prow. It was in her broadside batteries, however, that the *Hammer of Righteousness's* true power lay.

Running almost the complete length of the battleship, the starboard and port batteries were capable of unleashing an incredible amount of firepower, easily enough to cripple even the largest warship with a single barrage, or lay waste to entire continents if she entered the upper atmosphere of a rebellious planet. Indeed, the resistance of entire planets had crumpled merely at her appearance in their sub-system, fearful of the wrath that she could unleash.

Tens of thousands of indentured workers and servitors slaved within the confined gun decks to load and ready the batteries for firing, and Admiral Augustine was proud to know that his gunnery crew, under the stern guidance of his master gunner and master of ordnance, were amongst the most efficient in all of Battlefleet Tempestus.

He never grew weary of looking out across the *Hammer of Righteousness*, and he knew in his heart that he never would. Even after all these years of service, the power and scale of the battleship filled him with awe. Set against the sheer scale of space with its untold millions of solar systems, she was tiny and insignificant, but it was her duty to protect Imperial space from all threats, xenos or otherwise.

Constructed in the Adeptus Mechanicus shipyard moons of Gryphonne IV over a period of a thousand years, *Hammer of Righteousness* had been in commission, defending Imperial space for nigh-on eight thousand years. Admiral Augustine had served on her for almost one hundred and fifteen years, first as a junior officer before moving steadily up through the ranks. He had served on two other ships after fulfilling his commissioned appointments on the *Hammer of Righteousness*, first as a flag-lieutenant on the Lunar-class cruiser *Dauntless*. After a tenure of fifteen years he had been promoted to flag-captain of the recommissioned *Emperor's Wrath*, which had recently been reassigned to Segmentum Tempestus. Augustine served aboard this Overlord-class battle cruiser – a famed veteran of the Gothic wars – for ten years, before he was reassigned back to the *Hammer of Righteousness*, the ship where he had began his naval career.

He had held the rank of admiral for forty-two years, and at the age of one hundred and sixty-two, he was one of the most experienced officers in the fleet. No one knew the nuances and quirks of the ancient battleship like he did, save perhaps for the ship's long-serving flag-lieutenant, Gideon Cortez. Only two other ships assigned to Battlefleet Tempestus were of comparable size, and they were facing off against the xenos menace in distant sectors of the segmentum. The eastern expanses were his responsibility, and it was here that he had formed his blockade.

He could not see the enemy with the naked eye, for they were still millions of kilometres away, but he knew that they were out there and closing on them inexorably. He could see flashes in the distance. From here, they looked almost incongruous, but he knew that more of the enemy bio-ships were being subjected to concentrated barrages of ordnance.

His fleet was making a good account of itself in this engagement, the most recent of dozens over the last months, having destroyed two dozen hive-ships for no losses. Still, the xenos fleet continued to plough relentlessly on into Imperial space. The losses they had suffered made no discernible impact on the vast tyranid hive-fleet.

Vile bio-organisms that consumed everything in their path, like the locusts of Augustine's home world but on a galactic scale, the tyranid menace was a very real threat to the Imperium as a whole.

Four years previously a new hive-fleet had been identified, dubbed Hive Fleet Leviathan. It was a fitting name. Already billions had lost their lives to its insatiable hunger.

Admiral Augustine stared balefully out into the darkness. For all his years of service he had proudly defended the reliant worlds of the Imperium from its enemies. Now he was tasked with destroying those same worlds that he had dedicated his life to protect.

By Lord Inquisitor Kryptman's order a galactic cordon stretching before the encroaching xenos fleet was formed. The band of worlds directly in front of the cordon were evacuated, and many of them utterly destroyed, in order to deny the hive fleet raw organic matter. Any world already under tyranid invasion was to suffer Exterminatus – the theory being that the xenos would expend much energy in claiming a world, only to have all living things on the world exterminated. The inquisitor believed that by stalling the hive fleet's advance, it would eventually turn aside, towards more lucrative killing grounds, and thus save the Imperium from devastation. However, it was a cruel and callous strategy, and not one that sat well with Admiral Augustine, even if it was humanity's only hope of stalling the hive fleet. Billions of Imperial citizens had already been evacuated, their home worlds destroyed, and hundreds of millions had perished, killed by orbital barrages and virus bombs launched by those sworn to protect them.

He turned away from the observation portal, his movements, like his appearance, crisp and precise. He strode back along the command deck, his expression unreadable. His staff upon the bridge went about their work with practiced efficiency and calm, talking in low voices. Several of them looked up as their admiral passed them by and were greeted with curt nods. Banks of logisticians, hard-wired into the battleship's logic engines and monitoring a constant flow of technical data, murmured as stylus-fingers traced the mnemo-papers feeding from skull-faced machines. A pair of enginseers were reporting to the flag-lieutenant, Gideon Cortez, and humming cogitator arrays flickered with updates from the fleet, the eyelids of servitors flickering as information was relayed.

Augustine moved to the holo-table positioned within a sunken recess in the floor, stepping down to look upon the position of his fleet. The table was criss-crossed with a grid of glowing green lines, indicating spatial parameters, and scale models of the entire fleet were positioned across its smooth expanse.

He took a moment to study the formations. Most of the fleet, seventy-two vessels of escort class and higher, had formed a bulwark spreading across the system with the *Hammer of Righteousness* at its centre. The cruiser *Valkyrie*, accompanied by three squadrons of smaller frigates and destroyers, was out in front, slowing the vanguard of the tyranid fleet to enable the pleasure world of Circe to fully evacuate, formless black spheres being placed on the table to represent the known enemy forces. More of them were being put on the table all the time, placed there by lobotomised servitors hanging like twisted marionettes amid the gently hiss-ing mechanics above the table.

The bio-mechanical amalgamations had no lower torso or legs. Their upper bodies, replete with wires and cables protruding from their pallid flesh, were attached to multi-jointed mechanical armatures that whirred and hissed as they extended and retracted, accurately mov-ing and placing the fleets, accordingly, as fresh data was transmitted into them. Augustine was so used to their movements that he barely registered their presence;

they were merely part of the ship; one more tool to help him with his strategy.

Two other cruisers with squadrons of smaller escorts clustered in front of other populated worlds, the agri-world Perse, and the mining moons of Perdus Skylla and Perdus Kharybdis, rotating slowly around the uninhabitable gas giant, Calyptus.

Small, featureless scale models, representing a host of transports and carriers engaged in the evacuation efforts, were positioned touching the inhabited worlds. Several other models representing similar transports were positioned en route to the blockade. Almost two hundred million people were being evacuated from this system alone. Already, there had been problems with some of the mass transports associated with the fleet, as riots had broken out within the civilian populations already evacuated. He pushed these thoughts out of his mind; it was his job to enact the strategy laid down to him and see the worlds evacuated safely, not to police those populations once they were safely onboard the mass transport ships.

As he watched, an Imperial light cruiser was placed on the table on the lee-side of Perdus Skylla, and then removed. The arm of the servitor jerked spasmodically, and it placed the light cruiser back down upon the table.

'What's that?' asked Admiral Augustine, pointing towards the ship, which was once again removed from the table.

One of his aides, a junior lieutenant, shrugged.

'It's been doing that for the past hour, admiral,' he said, 'interference from the hive fleet, or a radiation field, perhaps. The flag-lieutenant thinks it may be nothing more than a technical glitch in the servitor unit. He is speaking to the enginseers about it.'

Admiral Augustine raised an eyebrow and regarded the peculiar behaviour of the servitor with a frown. Once again it put the ship back on the table, and then removed it.

'Useless bastards,' said Cortez, shaking his head as he extricated himself from the enginseers and walked to Augustine's side. 'They say the unit was serviced last week.'

The servitor-unit seemed to be operating as normal, again, and the phantom ship was nowhere to be seen on the table.

'Give me an update on the evacuations, Cortez,' said Augustine.

'Circe is almost completed, admiral,' said Cortez. 'The *Valkyrie* will be disengaging and pulling back within the hour.'

The flag-lieutenant was a stocky man of indeterminable age. A livid scar tracked across his chin, and a gleaming, bronze-rimmed lens stared from the hollow socket of his left eye. He was a natural officer and Augustine's closest confidant, the one and only man that he would class as his friend.

'And the evacuations of Galatea? And the Perdus moons?' asked the admiral.

'Galatea goes well; the moons of Calyptus less so. There are not enough transports. It's going to take those transports that are available three trips to complete the evacuation of Perdus Skylla and Perdus Kharybdis.'

'Three trips,' mused Admiral Augustine. He hissed through his teeth, gauging the position of the moons and the advancing enemy hive fleet. 'It's going to be tight.'

'If the evacuation is not completed before a ground invasion commences, anybody still on the moons must be forgotten,' said Cortez, moving to the opposite side of the table to the admiral.

'We shall buy the moons as much time as we can,' Admiral Augustine said, 'but you are correct, I cannot risk the fleet for the benefit of two moons. Our orders are clear.'

His orders *were* clear, as much as they rankled with him. They were the same orders that all of the fleets engaging Hive Fleet Leviathan had been issued, and he knew that they were being enforced all across the war-front.

The tyranids were a deadly menace, there was no disputing that, but it sat badly with the admiral that they were giving way before the xenos forces rather than making them fight for every bit of Imperial space. Of course, he would not allow his personal feelings to colour his judgement, and he would never go so far as to voice his feelings in front of his officers. Their orders were clear. He had sent an astrotelepathic message to the lord admiral on receiving the dictate, but once confirmation of the order had been returned, his path was set.

The new tyranid advance was potentially more catastrophic than any ever seen before, and the strategy that had been decreed to be used against it was similarly extreme.

It was genocide. Those worlds that were already suffering under the first waves of ground assault were effectively condemned to death, along with their Planetary Defence Force and any force of the Imperial Guard that could not be extricated.

Admiral Augustine knew that the political ramifications and backlash from this modus operandi would be devastating, but he also knew that no fleet captain would fail in his duty. They would carry out their orders, and leave the politicking to the bickering bureaucrats of the Administratum.

Cortez cursed, and Augustine shook his head slightly as the malfunctioning servitor unit once again placed the phantom Imperial light cruiser back on the table.

'Have a destroyer do a sweep around the moon, just to be sure,' said Augustine, and Cortez nodded his assent, even as he was shouting for the enginseers to be returned to the bridge.

Augustine's gaze focused on the spherical representations of the twin moons of Perdus Skylla and Perdus Kharybdis.

The evacuation of the moons would continue, and he would hold the fleet in position for as long as possible. However, looking again at their position, and the advance of the tyranid fleet, he knew instinctively that it would not be long enough.

Before the week was out, he would be ordering their Exterminatus.

THE CHAMBER WAS a shrine to death. Part of Marduk's personal quarters within the labyrinthine *Infidus Diabolus*, its high, domed ceiling was formed from the ribs of sacrifices, and eight pillars, each constructed from thousands of bones, rose into the gloom. Oily candles had been set into the hollow craniums of the skulls set into the pillars, and an infernal glow exuded from fire blackened, hollow sockets.

Braziers of black iron burnt low, and black, acrid smoke rose from the smouldering coals. Hunched figures, their abhorrent faces hidden from view beneath deep cowls, stalked the darkness outside the circle of pillars, swinging heavy censors from which thick, heady incense spilled.

Inside the pillars, the floor was rough granite, carved into the image of a holy eight-pointed star, the symbol of Chaos in all its guises. A massive figure stood at its centre, his augmented arms raised out to either side as he was prepared for the forthcoming ceremony.

Marduk was silently fuming, still angry at Magos Dārioq's inability to unlock the secrets of the Nexus Arrangement. Silently incanting the Nine Levels of Enlightenment, he forced himself to calm. From the archive facility of Kharion IV, the magos had identified the location – a backwater Imperial moon called Perdus Skylla – of the one whose knowledge would release the artefact's power, and Marduk forced himself to breathe evenly. Be patient, he reminded himself.

More than a dozen hooded figures, stunted creatures that stood not even to the mighty warrior's chest, clustered around their master, making him ready for the ceremony. Their eyes had been ritually sutured closed with thick staples, for it was regarded as a sin for them to look upon such a revered warrior. They brushed his blessed armour with sacred unguents, and fixed icons and holy charms to his armour.

Marduk, First Acolyte of the Word Bearers Legion, acting Dark Apostle of the Host, stood over two metres tall, his limbs encased in thick reinforced plate the colour of congealed blood. His holy power armour had been worked upon by the artisans of the Host in recent months, the plates rimmed with dark meteoric iron, and battle damage repaired.

Marduk had meticulously scrimshawed hundreds of thousands of words across them in tiny script, scriptures and sacred litanies of Lorgar that he knew by heart. The entire third book of the Tenets of Hate was inscribed around the armoured vambrace encasing his left forearm, and the titles of the Six Hundred and Sixty-Six Enumerations of Erebus were carved across the curved mass of his left shoulder pad.

The left shoulder pad had been dutifully painted black, as had those of the entire Host, in mourning for the loss of their revered leader, the Dark Apostle Jarulek. That Marduk had been integral to Jarulek's death made the symbolic act particularly ironic, and he smirked.

Over his painstakingly worked armour, Marduk wore a bone-coloured robe, tied at his waist with chains hung with icons of dedication to the dark gods of the ether. A book of hymnals and battle-prayers from the Epistles of Lorgar hung at his side, its dusty pages bound in human leather.

His head was bare. A bolt round fired by his former master, the Dark Apostle Jarulek, at point-blank range had rent the helmet beyond repair, and Marduk's features bore testament to the damage that shot had wrought. The entire left half of his face had been blasted away, and it had taken all the skill of the Host's chirurgeons and chirumeks to rebuild his facial structure.

Adamantium had been fused to his skull, and he had grinned as the procedure had taken place. Pain, it was taught, was a blessed gift that fortified the spirit and brought one closer to the gods. As such, it was a sensation to be welcomed. No proud warrior of the Legion would ever consider allowing a chirurgeon to distance him from the blessed pain of his battle wounds with narcotic opiates or psychotropic injections, for such a thing was regarded as blasphemy.

His shattered left cheek was rebuilt, and the muscles and tendons of his face re-grown or replaced with bionic implants. Marduk's skin had yet to grow across this new facial structure, and the ceramic gleam of his sharpened teeth could be seen through the strands of muscle tissue that linked his upper and lower jaws.

His left eye socket had been blasted to splinters, and the eye turned to molten jelly by the concussive force of

the bolt round. Once the socket had been recon-
structed, a replacement eye grown in a culture of
amniotic-fluid infused with warp energy was surgically
attached to his brain stem. The daemonic flesh hybrid
replacement stared out from his adamantium eye
socket, an angry, red, lidless orb. The pupil was little
more than a sliver, like that of a serpent's eye, reflecting
all that it saw.

For all his reconstructive surgery, Marduk's face bore
the patrician features that spoke of his genetic ancestry.
Every warrior in the Legion bore the genetic makeup of
his lord, the blessed daemon primarch Lorgar, and the
similarity between them was marked, characterised by
their pale skin, their noble profile, their proud bearing
and their hair, which was as black as pitch.

Marduk's long black hair had been combed and oiled
by his robed attendants, before being tied into a long
braid and secured behind his head, atop the cluster of
cables that entered his flesh at the base of his skull. A
cloak of matted fur, skinned from a blood-beast that
Marduk had slain on the death world of Anghkar Dor,
was draped over his shoulders and fixed to leering, daemonic bronze faces on his breastplate. The inside of the
fur was lined with velvet, and symbols of Chaos
resplendent had been scorched into the fabric.

Holy scriptures of Kor Phaeron, cut into the flayed
flesh of innocents, were driven onto the spikes rimming
his shoulder pads, and fresh blood, drawn from the
bodies of mewling sacrifices artificially bred in vats on
the lower decks of the *Infidus Diabolus* for that sole purpose, was daubed reverentially onto his gauntlets.

One of the attendants lined his right eye with coal,
and smoke rose from the holy mark of Lorgar on Marduk's brow as the servant's withered hand brushed it.
The stink of scorched flesh rose from the attendant's

hand, and it pulled it back sharply as smoke rose from the mark. Marduk growled in annoyance, and the attendant was dragged away into the darkness by two of its kin. Its flesh would be consigned to the cleansing fires, its body fed to its kin and its soul, if it had one, subject to eternal torment for displeasing its master.

Marduk's eyes lit up as his weapons were brought forth, led by a procession of censer-bearing attendants. They were the tools with which the Dark Faith was delivered to the heathen masses of the galaxy and as such, they were borne with reverential care. They lay upon black cushions, and were carried upon the backs of creatures whose flesh was completely swathed in black cloth to hide their obscene forms.

Marduk picked up his customised bolt pistol, its squat barrel protruding from the carved maw of a daemon. It felt natural and light in his hand, though a mere mortal would struggle to bear its weight, and he rammed a sickle-shaped clip into place before holstering it at his hip.

Even in times of relative peace the brothers of the Host bore live weapons, for though they were disciples and custodians of the Dark Creed, they were holy warriors first and foremost, and it was part of their tenets to be always reminded of the Long War against the cursed Imperium, to be ever in readiness for holy battle. Bitterness fuelled their beliefs and passion, and the holy bolter and chainsword were the tools with which the proper order of the galaxy would be instated. No warrior could forget the betrayals of the Corpse Emperor, or the fallacy of his church, while they held their sacred weapons.

Next, he lifted his archaic chainsword from its cushion. His grip closed around the hilt of the weapon, and he felt the familiar rush as it bonded with him, barbs piercing the flesh of his palm. The power and rage of Borhg'ash, the daemon eternally bound within the chainsword, surged through him, and he restrained the urge to lash out, to feed the beast's hunger. The blood of thousands had been shed beneath its biting teeth, and it was with some reluctance that he sheathed it, allowing the locking clamps to secure it at his waist.

'Soon you shall feed, dear one,' said Marduk to appease the daemon, and he felt a twinge of unease as his bond with the daemon weapon was severed, as if a part of his body had been cut from him.

Marduk dismissed his servants with a wave of his gauntleted hand. They retreated into the dark recess-hollows in the chamber walls, disappearing from mortal sight.

Whispering a prayer, he turned and walked across the chamber. The great doors reared up before him, intricately carved into a representation of the maelstrom, replete with daemonic forms and the souls of mortals writhing in agony. The amorphous carving shifted maddeningly, souls screaming out in silent torment as flames consumed them and devils cavorted.

Pressing his palms against the doors, Marduk pushed them open, and they swung aside soundlessly.

An entourage of twelve chosen warriors knelt upon the flagstones beyond the doors, their heads bowed low. At their fore was the icon bearer, Burias, his head lowered to the ground before his master.

'Arise, my brothers,' said Marduk.

THE DEVOTIONAL CEREMONY lasted for twelve hours, and the mournful voices of the Host rose and fell as they intoned their hymnal responses. The morbid peal of bells echoed out across the cavernous expanse of the cavaedium, signalling the end of the communal worship of the gods. Marduk's throat was raw from his elocutions and recitals from the books of Lorgar, but he felt refreshed and invigorated by the communion with the great powers of the ether. It was always this way for him.

For three months it had been this way, with prayers, sermons and services dominating the lives of the Word Bearers as their ship, the *Infidus Diabolus*, ploughed its way through the roiling sea that was the warp. The Host was eager for battle, for the fields of war were the truest halls of worship to the gods, but these hymnal services served their needs, while not engaged against the enemy, and they fuelled the hatred and stoked the fires of vengeance that burnt within the breast of every warrior brother.

Warp travel allowed the *Infidus Diabolus* to travel vast distances in months or years rather than decades or more, but Marduk would allow none of his battle-brothers to enter stasis while on these journeys, for these times were important lulls during which affirmations could be renewed and dedications and oaths of servitude to the great gods blooded anew.

As the Host filed away, returning to their cells for individual, silent communion, reading of scripture, the blessings and refitting of holy bolters and other daily rituals, Marduk found himself gazing upon the blessed crozius arcanum, lying dormant upon a plinth at the front of the alter overlooking the nave where the Host had gathered.

The crozius arcanum was the hallowed staff of office of the Dark Apostles, the bearers of the true faith. Once it had symbolised belief in the Great Crusade, in the Imperium of Man and the optimism of the Crusade bringing enlightenment to the galaxy, but the Emperor's lies had long been revealed.

The Emperor had claimed that gods did not exist, that they were merely the creations of weak minds.

Hypocritically, it was this same Emperor, though his body was now a mere rotting corpse, that the Imperium prayed to as their patron deity. The fallacy of the lie and its hypocrisy filled Marduk with bitterness and rage. In truth, that anger had not waned with time, but rather had grown stronger and deeper.

In ignorance, blindness or perhaps fear, the Emperor had proclaimed that there were no great godly powers in the universe, but he had been wrong. He had *lied*. There *were* deities in the depths of the warp, tangible and very real, and they were more powerful than anyone could have imagined. It was to these ancient gods that the Word Bearers had pledged their allegiance, and it was the faith in them that they sought to bring to the universe.

Once the Great Truth had been revealed, the Legion had thrown off the repressive, enslaving beliefs of the Imperium and dedicated themselves fully to their holy cause.

The crozius arcanum had been sanctified to the true gods, and it was a potent symbol of the Dark Creed and faith. It had been purified in the blood of millions, and countless unbelievers had been smitten beneath it.

Its haft was as black as ebony and studded with spikes. Marduk longingly traced the blood-red veins that ran up its length with a finger, marvelling at the workmanship. The hilt of the crozius was bound in the tanned skin of a cursed unbeliever, the Chaplain Atreus of the cursed Ultramarines Legion, who had been flayed alive on Calth by Lord Kor Phaeron. The head of the holy weapon was like a flanged mace or power maul, eight raised, spiked wedges forming its shape. When activated, the spiked head was wreathed in energy, and it would sunder the foes of Lorgar with the selfsame potency of a power talon.

Marduk longed to lift the weapon up in both hands. Only two Dark Apostles had wielded this mighty weapon: the ancient Warmonger, long since interred in the sarcophagus of his mighty dreadnought, whose sanity was only barely kept in check; and Jarulek: Jarulek the Blessed, Jarulek the Glorified, beloved of the gods.

Not anymore, thought Marduk with savage relish. This was *his* time. His star was in the ascendant, and once he had faced the Council of Sicarus, he would be allowed to wield this potent artefact himself. As it was, he had held it in his hands once, when he had rescued it from oblivion within the xenos pyramid, but even he was loathe to break the taboos and traditions of his order by bearing the holy weapon into battle before he had been fully embraced into the fold by the council.

He felt the approach of his underlings behind him, and his eyes narrowed. Running his hands lingeringly over the crozius, he left them waiting for a moment, to reinforce their place, and his.

At last, he turned towards them. They stood at the foot of the raised platform, and with a gesture, he beckoned them closer.

They ascended the steps side-by-side, and though they both bore the hallmarks of Lord Lorgar's gene-seed, they were as different in appearance as night and day.

Kol Badar was ancient, having been a captain of one of the great battle companies of the XVII Legion long before the great Warmaster Horus had aligned himself with the true powers of the universe. His face was broad and bullish, though his flesh was wasted almost to the point of emaciation, and creases so deep they looked as if they had been carved with knives lined his face. His head was bald, and pipes and cables sank into his cranium, connecting him to his immense battle suit. He wore archaic, age-old Terminator armour and towered over Marduk by half a metre. He walked with heavy steps, his every movement filled with power and weight.

Kol Badar was the Host's Coryphaus: strategos, war leader, and the voice of the battle-brothers. It was his role to lead the chorus of hymnal responses in prayer, and to act as the link between the Host's Dark Apostle and his warriors. At his side, dwarfed by his sheer bulk, swaggered the Host's icon bearer, Burias.

Where Kol Badar was all brute power and smouldering anger, Burias walked with a warrior's subtle grace, his movements relaxed and fluid. He was wolf-lean and darkly handsome, his full head of pitch black, waist-length hair oiled and scented. His pale face encapsulated all the noble bearing of his heritage, and it was said that he resembled Lorgar, before he had ascended to daemonhood.

Burias was the epitome of the warrior ideal: a consummate, balanced warrior. His body was as proud and strong as his faith, and though he was young in comparison to Kol Badar, he had been blooded in battle across a thousand worlds. He was quick to smile, though there was a lingering, dangerous intensity in his wide eyes, just a hint of the power lurking within, straining to be released. Burias was one of the possessed, and though he kept the daemon Drak'shal at bay with sheer force of will, he willingly gave way to the beast once the fires of battle were met, and the results were invariably bloody.

Burias bowed low, dipping his tall, eight-pointed icon before him, and Marduk acknowledged him with an incline of his chin. Kol Badar bowed his head, carefully measuring the movement to be at once mildly insulting, yet not overtly disrespectful.

'The Enslaved one is requesting that he be allowed to reconstruct his armature arrays, that he may continue his work upon the Nexus Arrangement, lord,' said Burias, his voice neutral.

'It is foolishness to allow it such privileges,' said Kol Badar.

'Walk with me,' ordered Marduk, turning on his heel and striding away. He did not speak as they exited the cavaedium by a side portal within the sacristy, walking up corridors lined with skulls.

One of the kathartes, skinless daemonic furies that inhabited the *Infidus Diabolus*, perched upon the shoulders of a winged angel of death statue above them, baring its teeth at their passing. Marduk flicked his gaze up towards the daemon, and it lowered its head, whimpering like a dog beneath the switch. Blood glistened across its exposed musculature, and it shimmered like a distorted pict image before disappearing once more into the sea of souls that was the warp. Immersed in the tides of the ether buffeting the *Infidus Diabolus*, the katharte would take on its truer form, that of an angelic maiden, as dangerous as it was alluring, propelling itself through the formless other world upon feathered wings, its siren call signalling the death of those of weak mind that heard it.

They passed dozens of dark arches, each leading off into different areas of the labyrinthine ship. Warrior brothers stood aside, their heads lowered, as they passed. Black-cloaked slave-creatures scurried out of their path, while others prostrated themselves pathetically, faces pressed to the floor. Moans and tortured cries came from darkness beneath the walkways, and wasted, skeletal fingers extended through the metal grids in appeal. Thousands of wretched slaves were kept aboard the *Infidus Diabolus*, existing in the darkness and squalid conditions below deck in order to perform all the horrific and mundane jobs required to keep the ship running. They were condemned to a lifetime of servitude, and they cried out for death.

'The priest-magos of the Machine-God is necessary,' said Marduk finally, as the trio walked the musty halls of the strike cruiser. 'The Nexus Arrangement will never be unlocked without him; he is the Key-master,' he said, referring to a prophecy that told of one, the Enslaved, who would unlock the potent device that the Host had uncovered from a xenos pyramid upon the shattered Imperial world of Tanakreg. It would be a powerful weapon in the arsenal of the Word Bearers, and much favour would be granted to he who controlled it.

'The Key-master?' scoffed Kol Badar. 'The wretch has proven useless in unlocking the device thus far. He cannot be trusted.'

'The magos is mine,' said Marduk. 'He is my puppet, and will do exactly what I want.'

MAGOS DARIOQ WAS changing. At first, the effects on his body had been subtle, barely noticeable, but, as the daemon took further control of his purged system, the change was coming on with alarming, exponential swiftness.

Stripped of his robes and chained to the wall of his cell, he shuddered in torment as the carefully cultured daemon essence writhed within him. He opened his mouth soundlessly, exposing a secondary set of teeth, thick and sharp, pushing up through his bleeding gums behind his own.

His flesh was wasted and pallid, though most of his body had long been replaced with mechanical augmentations. His entire lower body had been replaced with heavy-duty bionic replacements, immensely powerful leg-units with inbuilt gyro-stabilisers that enabled the magos to bear almost two metric tonnes of weight upon his frame. This was necessary, for with a fully activated servo-harness, the magos weighed as much as a small tank. Black tendrils crawled and pulsed beneath his skin, and his flesh rippled from within as the daemon made its claim on him.

Augmetic telescopic braces were fused to his spine for stability and strength, but the distinction between mechanical augmentation and flesh was blurring. Blood dripped from rents in the metal.

The heavy bulk of Darioq's servo-harness was clamped between his hips and his shoulders, and again, the hybrid amalgamation of fusing metal and flesh could be seen. Fleshy muscles had grown over several of the pistons, enhancing their mechanical strength with that of the daemon and giving the corrupted magos an even more hunched appearance. The four servo-arms of his harness had been sheared away, along with half a dozen mechadendrites that plugged into the nerve endings of his spinal column, and they wept blood and ichor as their stubby remnants twitched and jerked spasmodically. Two of the severed mechadendrites had already re-sprouted, fleshy tentacles of glistening muscle growing from his spine. Plugs and sockets covered his wasted skin, and from some of these leaked a milky ichor that hissed as it hit the floor.

With his hood and robes stripped away, Darioq's head was laid bare. Only a fraction of his original face remained, the rest encased in mechanics. A grilled voice box was implanted in his throat, and his left eye was an impressive display of sensors and optical arrays.

The distinction between the mechanical and the human was blurring all over the corrupted magos's body. Even as the trio of Word Bearers watched, the metal cranium of the magos swelled and rippled like water, and a curving horn pushed up from the right-hand side of Darioq's skull. Its tip was hard and bony, but clearly organic.

His right eye, which had been milky and blind when the Word Bearers had first captured him, was now solid black. His brain units, held in protective bell-jar casings that protruded from behind his hunched shoulders, were filled with dark, writhing clots, and black, oily tentacles burrowed through them, like a mess of bloodworms.

'Magos Darioq is no more. This,' said Marduk with a wave of his arm, 'is Darioq-Grendh'al.'

CHAPTER THREE

GUILDMASTER POLLO SCANNED the latest despatches, blinking his augmented silver eyes intermittently to record their contents. After several minutes of reading and recording, he dropped them onto his desk and leant forward to pour himself another drink from the half empty crystal decanter in front of him.

He raised his glass up to his eyes, gazing at the play of light upon the ruby liquid as he sloshed it around the ice. Then he knocked the drink back, savouring its bite. He placed the glass down on its coaster, and rubbed at his temples with both hands, his eyes closed.

'Bad news, guildmaster?' ventured a voice.

Pollo turned to face his young adjutant, Leto. He was little more than a boy, barely having the need to shave yet, and his eyes flicked around nervously as he waited for his answer. He was young, but he was a good officer and had a mind like a sponge. He knew that in time he would have made a suitable guildmaster, but such a thing was not to be.

'You should have gone with the others, Leto,' he said, his voice tired.

'I will leave when you leave,' replied his adjutant.

When the first astrotelepathic despatches had come, warning of the xenos hive fleet's approach, Pollo's distaff had been aghast. That had quickly descended into panic when the extreme dictate to combat this threat had been transmitted, and that panic had not been aided by the sudden departure of the Administratum's advocate of Perdus Skylla.

'This world has been condemned to death,' the administrator had whined as he frantically gathered up his possessions. 'You are a fool to stay behind,'

'I will not leave until the guilds are fully evacuated,' Pollo had replied, his voice unwavering. '*I* will not abandon my post and leave those who depend upon me to their fate.'

'Do not judge me, guildmaster,' the administrator had snapped. 'I am a servant of the Administratum, and with the mining facilities abandoned I see no purpose in my remaining here. If you have any sense at all, you will leave Perdus Skylla immediately. Coordinate the evacuation from space if your conscience demands such a thing.'

Guildmaster Pollo had wanted to strike the man, but he had held his anger in check. He had turned his back on the administrator, and had watched as his shuttle left the moon for the safety of the Imperial blockade. He had ordered his distaff to vacate Perdus Skylla, and he had seen the relief in their faces at his order. He did not think badly of them as they saluted him and boarded the first chartered evacuation ships.

'Why will you not go?' Leto had asked him.

'I swore an oath of service to the guilds of Perdus Skylla. My leadership will be needed in the evacuation effort. It sends a message to the guilds, and the populace, if I remain.'

'Then I shall remain with you, sir,' said the boy.

Pollo had promoted him to be his adjutant, and had been pleasantly surprised to find that the young man adapted to his role admirably.

Pollo sighed, picked up the reports and flicked them to Leto. The young man caught them awkwardly, and scanned their contents. The guildmaster poured himself another drink as his adjutant looked at the first of the reports. Leto looked up in shock, his face pale.

'Keep reading,' said Guildmaster Pollo.

The reports contained disturbing information: evidence of slaughter in three of the main mid-ice access highways that linked the Phorcys starport to the guilds. The attacks had occurred just hours earlier, and there had been no survivors nor any eyewitnesses. It was impossible to gauge the number of casualties, but there was something in the realm of twelve thousand citizens reported missing. Thousands more had been killed in the stampede to get out of the tunnels, and the Skyllan Interdiction Forces had shut the access tunnels down, pending an armoured investigation.

Three guilds, two of them major houses, had no direct access to the evacuation freighters. That translated as almost four million people, trapped on Perdus Skylla until the tunnels were opened, for it would be almost impossible for them to make the journey on foot.

Three days had been the estimate before the xenos fleet made planet-fall. It had been a logistical impossibility to evacuate all of Perdus Skylla in that time, but now with access tunnels locked down?

Guildmaster Pollo was a realist. He did not delude himself into thinking that he ever had even half a chance of getting more than perhaps twenty per cent of the population of Perdus Skylla off-world; there were just not enough ships to facilitate the evacuation. He cursed the bureaucracy of the Administratum that had given his world such callously short notice of its doom.

He had finished his glass of amasec by the time his adjutant had read through all the despatches.

'What does it mean, master?' asked Leto, his face pale.

'It means,' said Pollo, cradling his empty glass, 'that there are enemy forces already on Perdus Skylla.'

'The... the tyranids?'

'I don't think so, no,' said Leto. 'Something entirely else.'

WITH A SOUND akin to the birth-scream of a fledgling god, the *Infidus Diabolus* ripped through the skin of the warp and entered real-space. Flickering arcs of energy danced across its hull, coalescing over the towering spires and cathedrals devoted to the dark gods of the ether. The full awesome majesty of the strike cruiser slipped from the protective womb of the immaterium, and the rift was sealed behind it.

Within the bridge of the colossal vessel, Marduk and Kol Badar leaned over the flickering data-screens before them, studying the stream of information being relayed. They saw an image of the sub-system, spinning slowly, and flashes of light began to appear, marking the positions of planets, ships and radiation fields.

Remnants of the warp remained within the ship, and scenes of depravity and bloodshed flashed up over the screens, momentarily disrupting the feed of information. For a fraction of a second, the screens showed a skinless face, its eyes on fire and its cheeks pierced by blades, before they returned to normal. A moment later, the screens flashed again, and an image of a writhing, blood-soaked figure appeared on the pict screens for less than a tenth of a second, accompanied by the blare of static, overlaid with unholy roars and screams.

The pair of Word Bearers ignored the distractions, peering through the ghost-images of daemons ripping apart flesh and bubbling blood that appeared on the screens, focusing on the wealth of sub-system information being picked up by the daemonic sensor-arrays protruding from the prow of the *Infidus Diabolus*. They saw the conglomeration of Imperial vessels forming an unbroken line across the system and the flickering waves of warp-energy that marked jump-points, and located the position of the target: the moon the Imperials called Perdus Skylla.

The sounds of Chaos croaked from grilled vox-speakers and discords throughout the ship, a blaring cacophony of madness and rage. Bellows and screams were overlaid with inhuman screeches and hateful whispers, and the painful squeal of scraping metal blurred with the relentless pounding of hammers and gears, the sound of flesh being rent by steel, the roar of the fires of hell and the plaintive weeping of children. It was a beautiful din, one that calmed Marduk's mind, though to listen too deeply was to give yourself over to insanity.

A face appeared on the central pict screen, its eyes black as pitch and its cheeks carved with bloody sigils, and it opened its mouth wide, exposing a mass of writhing serpents, spiders and worms.

'Enough,' barked Marduk, banishing the daemon with a wave of his hand. Instantly, the snarling image disappeared.

More flashing lights and runic symbols appeared on the representation of the surrounding galactic plane, and both Marduk and Kol Badar leant forward to peer upon them. Kol Badar snorted and leant back. A bitter laugh burst from Marduk's lips, the sound making the image on the pict viewers shimmer with static.

'It would seem, Coryphaus, that the Imperium is engaged in a war in this little solar system,' said Marduk, 'and they are losing.'

'ADMIRAL,' SOMEONE SHOUTED.

Rutger Augustine pulled his gaze away from the scale model representations of the fleet and turned to see one of his petty officers moving towards him.

'Go ahead,' he said.

The petty officer was flushed and he carried a transmission card, its waxy surface punched with a series of holes. He thrust it towards the admiral.

'Sir, Battle Group *Orion* has picked up a warp-echo emanating from jump-point XIV. It has been verified by our own Navigatorii.'

Augustine frowned at the transmission card, and then turned and fed it into the chest-slot of the servitor unit wired into his command console. The servitor jerked, and its needle finger began to punch away at a set of keys in front of it. Ignoring the drooling servitor, Augustine looked at the transmission data as it was relayed onto the screen.

'What is it?' he asked. 'A rogue hive ship? Don't say the bastards have got behind us.'

'No sir. Initial sweeps indicate a vessel of cruiser mass, but it is not an organic entity.'

'No? Probably another trade vessel come to aid the evacuations. Why are you bothering me with this?'

asked Admiral Augustine. 'The fleet is engaging the xenos threat, petty officer!'

'I'm sorry, sir, and it may be nothing, but the long-range scan that Battle Group *Orion* performed seemed to indicate that the vessel may be an Astartes strike cruiser or battle-barge.'

Augustine frowned.

'I was notified of no Space Marine presence inbound, though we could do with their aid.' He rubbed a hand across his freshly shaved chin. 'Have *Orion* send a frigate squadron on an intercept course with the vessel, and keep me informed of any updates.'

With that, the admiral turned away from the petty officer.

'Yes, admiral.'

THE INFIDUS DIABOLUS ploughed through the vacuum of space, its plasma-core engines burning blue-white as it closed towards the vast red giant sun around which the solar system rotated. Solar flares a million kilometres in height burst from the daemonic red corona, leaping up from around dark sunspots that blemished its unstable surface.

The sun was dying. Five billion years earlier it was less than one hundredth of its current size, though it had burnt over ten times as hot. Having exhausted its gaseous core, it had expanded exponentially, engulfing its nearest planets. Even as it grew in size, it was diminished in mass, and the outer planets circling it began to pull further away, its gravitational hold over them weakening. Now it burnt the colour of hell itself, but in another billion years it would be no more.

The *Infidus Diabolus* dropped closer to the hellish, glowing corona, buffeted by solar winds. There, with intense spikes of radiation spilling around her hull, she drew anchor.

'I WOULD HEAR your council, revered Warmonger,' said Marduk. He ran the fingers of his hand thoughtfully along the surface of a stone column. A cold wind gusted through the darkness, tugging at Marduk's cloak, and a mechanical scream of insane rage echoed from deeper within the crypt.

Marduk and Kol Badar stood beneath the shadow of a wide archway, facing into a cavernous alcove set into the side of the expansive passageway. They were deep within the depths of the *Infidus Diabolus*, in the under-croft that housed those warriors of the Host that had long ago fallen in holy battle, but had not been allowed to pass on into blessed oblivion.

The damned warriors lived on in the deepest labyrinthine catacombs of the strike cruiser, con-demned to a tortured limbo, neither living nor dead, the shattered remnants of their earthly forms interred in great sarcophagi that they might serve the Host even after their time had long passed.

A delicate mural decorated the back wall of the alcove, detailing the great moments of the Warmonger's life before he had been condemned to an eternity of servitude within the towering mechanical form of a Dreadnought.

Once he had been amongst Lorgar's most favoured and devout chaplains, the first Dark Apostle of the 34th Company Host that Marduk now led. He had fought alongside the god primarchs, and counted such exalted heroes as Erebus, Kor Phaeron and Abaddon as his battle-brothers. Marduk had listened in awe to the scratchy vox-recordings of his passionate sermons, and had pored over a thousand volumes of his thoughtful scripture, and his fiery rhetoric and hate-filled sermons never failed to inspire.

Though the other warriors interred within the Dreadnoughts of the Host had long ago lost any semblance of sanity, cursed as they were and unable to attain oblivion yet denied the physical sensations of holy war, the warmonger retained a coherent self-awareness, and was a source of great wisdom and council.

It was his unshakeable faith that kept him lucid, Holy Erebus had once said, the power and conviction of his rapturous belief that kept him from toppling off the precipice into madness.

A thousand blood-candles ringed the mighty warmonger, tended day and night by a pair of slave-proselytes to ensure that the flames never died, and their light cast a divine glow over the Dreadnought's sarcophagus.

It towered over Marduk, even Kol Badar, standing over five metres tall with the armoured sarcophagus that held the Dark Apostle's shattered remains at its heart. The Dreadnought stood on squat, powerful legs, and immense arms bearing ancient heavy weapons systems were held immobile at its side.

For hundreds of years at a time the Warmonger stood motionless within its own death shrine, lost in contemplation, waiting for holy battle to be joined once more.

'It is pleasing to my soul to see you once more, First Acolyte Marduk,' boomed the Warmonger, its voice a deep reverberating baritone, the words spoken slowly and deliberately, 'and you, Kol Badar, finest of my captains.'

The two warriors bowed their heads in deference.

'The loss of Jarulek pains me,' continued the warmonger. 'Though in you I see a worthy successor, young disciple Marduk.'

'Jarulek's death cuts me deeply as well, revered warmonger,' said Marduk. A slight smile curled his lips as he felt Kol Badar's anger at his words. 'I am honoured to fill the role of religious leader of the Host, though I feel... unworthy of such a hallowed duty.'

'It is only right that you step into the breach and guide the flock,' said the warmonger. 'Your star is in the ascendant. Feel not unworthy of the duty; be humbled by it, but never doubt your right to serve. The gods have ordained it.'

Marduk turned his head to Kol Badar and smiled.

'I fear that some amongst the Host feel I am not ready for such an exalted position, my lord,' he said.

'Tolerate no insubordination, First Acolyte,' boomed the Warmonger. 'Crucify any who seed dissent, for theirs are the voices of poison and doubt.'

'I shall heed your council in this matter, revered one,' said Marduk.

'You are walking the black path, Marduk,' said the Warmonger. 'You are the dark disciple, moving towards the light of truth, and you shall, in time, be granted enlightenment. You did not, however, come here for my acceptance, for you already know that you have it. What is it you would ask of me?'

'I had wished to descend on the Imperial world of Perdus Skylla with the full force of the Host, laying waste to the world and claiming that which is needed. While it pleases me to see the Imperium weakened in their battles with the xenos, for it will make our eventual victory in the Long War come all the sooner, the size of the battlefleet here in this sector forces me to change my intentions. Mighty as she is, the *Infidus Diabolus* would not survive long enough to get us to the Imperial moon.'

'I say we abandon this fool's errand here and now,' growled Kol Badar. 'Let us return to Sicarus and leave the Imperials to wage their war against the xenos hive-creatures. We will recoup our strength in the Eye while the Imperium suffers.'

'Kol Badar speaks, as always, with wisdom,' said the Warmonger, and for a moment Marduk thought he had horribly misjudged the way this conversation would go. He felt a flicker of unease at having instigated it in the presence of the Coryphaus as Kol Badar flashed him a look of triumph.

'And yet,' continued the Warmonger, 'Jarulek saw in the xenos device something of great import. He was always a gifted zealot and the power of his gods-gifted dream visions were stronger than my own. If he saw that the item was worth waging war for, then it is an artefact of great importance, and is destined to further the spread of the holy Word of Truth.'

'We already have the device in our possession,' said Kol Badar. 'We need not tarry here and risk it further.'

'We have the device, that is true,' admitted Marduk, 'but as it is, it is worthless to us; its secrets are locked within it. It is nothing more than a xenos curio, an inert and useless sphere of metal.'

'The chirumeks of the Legion will unlock its secrets, whatever they may be,' said Kol Badar.

I will not return to Sicarus in anything but glory, thought Marduk fiercely, glaring at the Coryphaus. Were he to return empty-handed, he feared that the council would not endorse his rise to Dark Apostle. With the secrets of the Nexus Arrangement unlocked and his to command, they would be forced to heap honour upon him.

'You know that the knowledge that will unlock the device will be attained upon this Imperial world?' asked the Warmonger.

'I do,' said Marduk. 'It is held within the mind of a servant of the false Machine-God.'

'You base that belief only on the word of another servant of the Machine-God,' snarled Kol Badar. 'The Enslaved's loyalty does not lie with the Legion. For all you know, he may be leading us into a trap, to deliver the device unto his Mechanicus brethren.'

'The Enslaved is mine,' growled Marduk. 'It has no will of its own any more. It is not capable of such duplicity.'

'Speak with respect to your First Acolyte, Kol Badar,' chided the Warmonger. 'Marduk, if you trust the knowledge you have, then the path is clear.'

'The *Infidus Diabolus* cannot approach Perdus Skylla,' said Kol Badar, changing tack. 'If anything, we should return to the Eye and gather the Hosts to our cause. Then we can return, and take the moon by force.'

'The xenos threat will have obliterated it by then,' snapped Marduk. 'We have both seen worlds ravaged by their kind; nothing is left behind. The secrets will be lost forever.'

'You do not need my council, then, disciple Marduk. Kol Badar, if brute force will not suffice, explore more subtle ways of gaining victory for your First Acolyte.'

Marduk smiled as he saw Kol Badar's jaw twitch in anger.

'As always, Warmonger, you are the voice of wisdom,' said Marduk, bowing. 'My purpose is clear; you have allayed my fears and stripped away the shadow of doubt. I am confident that my *loyal* Coryphaus will find a way forward.'

'One last thing, Marduk. I am disturbed that there are those within the Legion who doubt your holy right to lead them. I would have it known that I fully endorse your appointment.'

The Warmonger shifted its immense weight, servos and gyro-compensators hissing. It turned on the spot, each step making the floor shudder, and reached out with its immense power-claw, scooping something up in its grasp. Then it turned back towards Marduk, and the First Acolyte strained to see what the Warmonger held.

The sickle-bladed talons of the Dreadnought's power claw opened, and Marduk saw a gleaming helmet, its porcelain features moulded into the form of a grimacing skull. An eight-pointed star of Chaos was carved into its forehead, and its sharpened fangs were fixed in a grinning rictus. A crack, not battle damage, but rather a carved affectation, ran across the left brow and continued below the glimmering eye-piece onto the cheek.

It was a revered, ancient artefact of the Legion, and had been crafted by the finest artisans of Mars in the years before the commencement of the Great War for the Warmonger himself.

Marduk stared at the sacred helmet with covetous eyes.

'I ordered my helmet removed from its stasis field within the bone-ossuary,' said the Warmonger, 'though at the time I did not understand what it was that urged me to do so. I see clearly now that it was the will of the gods for you to have it, young Marduk.'

The First Acolyte stepped forwards and lifted the helmet from the Warmonger's outstretched claw, marvelling at the mastery with which it had been rendered. The morbid visage, a dark reflection of the helmets worn by the chaplains of those blinded Legions that had not joined with the Warmaster, was a potent symbol of death, the face of damnation for all those who refused to cow to Lorgar's word.

Marduk placed the helmet over his head, and he heard a mechanical whine as it adjusted to fit his cranium. It fitted firmly in place, and there was a hiss as coupling links connected. Then all sound was blanketed out, before the integrated auto-senses powered up and his hearing returned. He breathed deeply, sucking in a lungful of recycled air, and registered the flickering array of sensory information and integrity checks being relayed onto the front of his irises. Servos whined as he stretched his neck from side to side, and an enticing targeting matrix appeared before him, locking onto Kol Badar as he turned to look upon the Coryphaus. The towering war leader was scowling, and Marduk grinned. He dismissed the targeting matrices, somewhat reluctantly, with a blink, and dropped to one knee before the warmonger.

'I have not the words to express the honour you do me, Warmonger,' he said, his voice growling from the vox-grills cunningly concealed behind the fangs of the death mask.

'Leave me now, my captains,' said the Warmonger. 'The preparations for the final push against Terra must be made. Join your brothers, and rejoice in prayer and exaltation for within the month, we shall assail the walls of the Emperor's Palace.'

'Rest well, Warmonger,' said Marduk, and he and Kol Badar backed away from the towering Dreadnought, recognising that the ancient one's lucidity was slipping. Often it was this way, as the Dreadnought relived battles of days past.

The pair left the crypt, leaving the Warmonger to relive his memories. Marduk strode out in front, a triumphant strut to his walk. Kol Badar stalked behind, a deep scowl on his face as he glared at the First Acolyte's back.

COWLED SLAVES PUSHED the skull-inlaid doors wide, and Marduk stalked out into one of the expansive docking bays of the *Infidus Diabolus*. The entire Host was gathered there, and, as one, the warrior brothers dropped to their knees as the First Acolyte strode through their serried ranks, heading towards the stub-nosed transport ship, the *Idolator*.

Indentured workers, their bodies augmented with ensorcelled mechanics and their eyes and mouths ritualistically sutured shut, hurried to ready the ship, pumping fuel into its gullet through bulging intestine-hoses and daubing its armoured hull with sacred oils and unguents. Four Land Raiders, massively armoured tanks that had borne the warriors of the Host into battle on a thousand worlds, were moved into position beneath the stubby wings of the *Idolator*, and reinforced clamps locked around them from above, securing them for transport.

Marduk was wearing the deaths-head helmet gifted to him by the warmonger for the first time in front of the Host, and he felt awe and reverence ripple out across the gathered warriors. Passages freshly scribed upon the flayed flesh of slaves hung from devotional seals fixed to his armour, and he felt savage pride as he looked upon the warriors of the Legion.

He stalked to the front of the assembly, where a group of thirty warrior brothers knelt facing the rest of the Host. These warriors uniformly bowed their heads as Marduk came to a halt in front of them, his gaze, hidden behind the inscrutable red lenses of his helmet, sweeping over them.

With a nod to Burias, the icon bearer stood to attention and slammed the butt of his heavy icon into the floor. The sound echoed loudly, and with an imperious gesture, Marduk motioned for the thirty warriors to stand. Kol Badar stepped out of their ranks and began to prowl along the lines, inspecting them with a grim expression on his broad face.

The thirty warriors were gathered into four coteries and Marduk's gaze travelled over the waiting warrior brothers, reading their eagerness for the forthcoming descent towards the Imperial planet in their faces and their stances.

Each holy Astartes warrior stood armed for war, his helmet held under his left arm, and weapons readied. They stood motionless and attentive as they awaited Marduk's word, their heads held high. Each was fiercely proud to have been selected to accompany the First Acolyte.

Including Marduk, Burias and the enslaved daemon-symbiote Darioq, they would number thirty-two. It was an auspicious number that equalled the number of the sacred books penned by Lorgar. It augured well. Marduk had read the sacred number in the entrails of the squealing slave-neophyte he had butchered in the blooding chamber not an hour earlier, and he knew that the gods had blessed his endeavour.

'Brothers of Lorgar,' said Marduk, addressing the thirty, though his voice was raised, so that it carried to every member of the Host, 'you are blessed, for amongst all the glorious Host you have been chosen to be my hon-our guard, to accompany me in doing what must be done to ensure that victory is ours, for the glory of blessed Lorgar.'

Marduk strode along the line of warriors, seeing the fire of religious fervour and devotion on their faces. They stared at him passionately, fanaticism in their eyes.

Each member of the four coteries was a veteran of a thousand wars fought across a thousand battlefields, and each had been tested and found worthy time and again in the forge of battle. These were the most vicious, fanat-ical and devoted of all the vicious, fanatical and devoted warriors of the Host. Each was a holy warrior, who would follow his word without question, for his was the voice of the gods, and through him their infernal will would be enacted without question and without remorse. Devout, holy warriors, they would not flinch in their duty, and their fervour lent them great strength.

Each of the four coteries was led by a favoured warrior champion of the Host.

Kol Badar stood before four of his anointed brethren, each of them enormous in their heavy Terminator armour. The other coteries consisted of eight warriors each. Towering Khalaxis, his cheeks covered in ritual scars, stood before his 17th coterie, brutal warriors all. Namar-sin, shorter than his brothers, though he made up for this deficiency with sheer bulk, stood before his warriors of the 217th coterie, Havoc heavy weapon specialists. Last of the champions was Sabtec, who led the highly decorated 13th coterie. Neither as tall as Khalaxis, nor as broad as Namar-sin, Sabtec was a lean warrior whose tactical nuances had won countless glorious victories for the Host. A row of horns protruded from the skin across his brow, a clear mark of the god's favour upon him, and his hand rested upon the hilt of his power sword, gifted to him by Erebus.

'Kneel,' commanded Marduk, and the gathered warriors dropped to their knees instantly. He placed his fingertips upon the forehead of each champion in turn, murmuring a benediction. He felt heat radiate beneath his fingers, and the smell of burning flesh rose. The imprint of his fingertips remained on each champion's brow, five searing points where the skin had blistered away to the bone.

Having completed the ritual, Marduk turned towards the remainder of the Host, gathered in silence as they witnessed the blessing. He saw yearning and jealousy in the eyes of the warrior brothers who had not been chosen to accompany him. Their champions would castigate the coteries not chosen, and when next they entered the field of war, they would fight with redoubled ferocity.

'Look upon your chosen brothers and feel pride, my brethren,' roared Marduk, spreading his arms out to each side. 'Glory in their successes as if they were your own, for they fight as representatives of you all. Pray for them, that your strength may buoy them in the days to come, for they will return victorious or not at all. In the true gods we place our trust.'

Burias slammed the butt of his icon onto the floor once more, and the Host as one hammered their fists against their chests in response, the sound echoing through the docking bay.

Turning back towards the chosen thirty, Marduk dropped to one knee and drew forth his serrated *khantanka* knife. Thirty other blades were drawn instantly. Each warrior of the Host carried a sacred blade, and it was with his own *khantanka* knife that each warrior brother had been blooded when first inducted into the Legion. Each khantanka blade was individual, fashioned by the warrior it belonged to, and it was said that the true essence of the warrior could be read in its design.

Marduk's blade was curved and serrated, while Kol Badar's was broad and heavy, bereft of ornamentation. Burias's blade was masterfully fashioned and elegantly curved, and its hilt was fashioned in the shape of a snarling serpent.

'Gods of the ether, we offer up our blood as sacrifice to your glory,' growled Marduk, cutting a deep vertical slash down his right cheek. The gathered warriors echoed his words, mirroring the First Acolyte's action. Blood ran from the wounds, running down the faces of the warriors before the powerful anti-coagulants in their bloodstreams sealed the wounds.

A pair of murderous kathartes flickered into being high above, the skinless daemons circling down over the congregation, borne upon bleeding, leathery wings, and settled upon the *Idolator* to witness the ritual.

With his sacred blood dripping from his jaw and onto his armour, Marduk carved a horizontal line across his cheek, bisecting the other cut to form a cross.

'Garner us with strength, and let your dark light flow through our earthly bodies,' intoned Marduk as he made the incision. Again, his words and actions were replicated by the chosen thirty, and more of the kathartes flickered into being, breaching the skin between the real and the warp.

'We give of ourselves unto you, oh great gods of damnation, and open ourselves as vessels to your immortal will,' said Marduk, making a third cut that bisected the other two diagonally.

'With the letting of this blood, we renew our pledge of faith to the Legion, to Lorgar, and to the glory of Chaos everlasting,' said Marduk, completing the ritual and making the final cut upon his face, forming the eight-pointed star of Chaos upon his cheek.

A flock of thirty-two kathartes had gathered atop the *Idolator*, silent witnesses to the conclusion of the ritual. They kicked off from their roost, and circled low over the heads of the Host, blood dripping from their skinless muscles, and their hideous faces contorted as they screamed. Then they scattered, filling the air with their raucous cries, and one by one they flickered and disappeared, rejoining the blessed immaterium.

Again Marduk raised his arms up high, and his vox-assisted voice boomed out across the docking bay.

'The portents bode well, my brothers, and the true gods have blessed this venture; let us go forth, and kill in the name of Lorgar.'

'For Lorgar,' echoed the Host, their voices raised, and Marduk smiled.

'Let's get this done,' snapped Kol Badar, and the thirty warriors boarded the *Idolator*. Darioq was brought forth from a side-door, having been rightly excluded from bearing witness to the khantanka blooding ritual, and was marched towards the waiting transport ship. Marduk had allowed him to reconstruct his servo-harness armatures, though he had ensured that the weapons systems of the unit had been stripped, and had personally branded an eight-pointed star upon his hooded forehead.

The First Acolyte was the last to enter the transport ship, and the engines roared as the boarding ramp slammed shut behind him.

'Gods of the ether, guide us,' he whispered to himself.

THE THREE FIRESTORM-class frigates of Battle Group *Orion* sent their sweeps out in front of them, searching in vain for the suspected Astartes vessel. Every scan came back negative, and attempts to locate the ship through astrotelepathic means proved equally fruitless. It was as if the ship had never existed.

'It could be a ghost-image from a jump a thousand years ago,' remarked the captain of the *Dauntless*, the lead ship of the patrol. 'There is nothing out here.'

With reports of the escalating engagement with the tyranid hive-ships coming in and eager not to miss out on the hunting, the captain ordered the frigates to come around and rejoin the rest of the battle group.

Unseen and invisible in the radiation field of the red giant, an Imperial-class transport vessel blasted from the hangar decks of the *Infidus Diabolus* and began to make its way across the gulf of space, heading towards the Imperial blockade and the moon of Perdus Skylla beyond.

CHAPTER FOUR

MARDUK FELT HIS anger rising as he stared out at the Imperial armada. He could see dozens of ships, ranging in size from immense battleships bristling with weapons to small civilian transports. The warships were long, inelegant vessels with thick armoured prows, like the ironclad ships that he had once seen ploughing the oceans of the Imperial world of Katemendor, before that world had been put to the sword. Cathedral spires rose behind the giants' command stations, immense structures that housed thousands. Marduk clenched his fists in hatred as he looked upon the giant twin-headed eagle effigies at the tops of the spires, and snarled a benediction to the gods of Chaos.

They glided by the vast and silent Imperial ships, and Marduk stared at the immense cannon batteries, torpedo tubes and lance arrays. If the enemy suspected them, they would blast them to pieces in an instant, and nothing could be done to stop them. The shields of the transport vessel were enough to protect it from showers of small meteors and other space-born debris, but a single broadside from even the smaller battle cruisers would easily overpower them, and the ship would be ripped apart.

'This is insanity,' said Kol Badar.

'Have faith, Coryphaus,' said Marduk mildly, masking his own unease.

At the dawning of the Great Crusade, before the War-master Horus had led his divine crusade against the Emperor of Mankind, the Legion had been outfitted with hundreds of Stormbird gunships, impressively armed and armoured transport ships that doubled as attack craft. Borne within the Stormbirds, the Word Bearers had sallied forth from the docking bays of their strike cruisers, bringing the word of the Emperor to the outlying planets on the fringe of the empire. As the crusade ground on, many of the Stormbirds were replaced with the newer Thunderhawk gunships, which were less heavily armed and had a smaller transport capacity, but had the benefit of being quicker and cheaper for the forge-worlds to manufacture.

With the advent of the crusade against the Emperor, the Adeptus Mechanicus forge-worlds that had thrown their weight behind the warmaster produced more of the Thunderhawks for his Legions, and the Stormbirds were all but fazed out within the XVII Legion. However, with the shocking defeat of Horus, and the subsequent retreat to the Eye of Terror, the majority of the forge-worlds that supplied the Legions of Horus were virus bombed, and thus the Word Bearers Legion had no way of replacing its lost attack craft.

Few original Stormbirds remained in service within the 34th Company Host. Those that remained had had their hulls patched and repaired a hundred times. Many of the original Thunderhawks were still serviceable, though they had been altered and modified over the millennia to fit the needs of the Host and as a response to limited manufactory facilities.

The flotilla had also been increased with vessels stolen from enemies. One Thunderhawk gunship, a new model fresh from the forge-worlds of Mars, had been claimed from the loyalist White Consuls Chapter, out on the fringe of the Cadian Gate, and an ancient, near fatally damaged Stormbird that had been claimed from the cursed Alpha Legion in a raid upon one of their cult worlds was currently being refitted for use.

As well as these original Astartes-pattern attack craft, there were dozens of recommissioned civilian transports, assault boats, refitted cargo ships and auxiliary vessels that had been captured by the Host, rearmed and armoured for use as makeshift assault craft. These had all been modified and refitted by the chirumeks of the Host, and some of them barely resembled their original model.

Marduk and his hand-picked entourage of Word Bearers were aboard one of these salvaged and refitted vessels as they made their way towards the Imperial moon of Perdus Skylla.

It was an ugly brute of a ship, a squat, stub-nosed vessel that the Host had crippled and boarded centuries earlier. Dubbed *Idolator* by its new owners, it had been part of a small convoy used by smugglers running the blockades of Imperial space, rogue traders that had been circumventing Administratum taxes on the outskirts of the Maelstrom. The *Infidus Diabolus* had scattered the convoy, emerging from the darkness behind a shattered planet and ripping two of the ships apart with full broadsides. The *Idolator* had been crippled with lance strikes, and a single dreadclaw had been launched from the *Infidus Diabolus*. The boarding pod latched onto the hull of the *Idolator* like a limpet, cutting through its armour with ease, and a boarding party of Word Bearers, led by Kol Badar, had stormed aboard. The crew were slaughtered, and the reeling vessel claimed by the Host.

Marduk stood with Kol Badar looking out through the curved blister portal of the bridge of the *Idolator*. Behind them, serfs of the Host were guiding the ship to its destination, directing it in towards the Imperial moon. They had once been men, but their humanity had all but abandoned them. Their flesh was stretched and covered in vile, cancerous blemishes and the hands of the pilots had become fused to their controls. Tears of blood ran down their cheeks.

The bridge was dim, the only light coming from the crimson-tinged sensor screens, bathing the room in a hellish red aura.

The Coryphaus glared balefully out at the Imperial vessels, and he clenched and unclenched the bladed fingers of his power talon unconsciously.

'If they realise what we are, all the faith in the warp will not save us,' he snarled.

'They will not,' said Marduk calmly. 'We are but another transport vessel, aiding the evacuation efforts.'

'Such deception is beneath us,' said Kol Badar. 'It belittles the Legion. We are the sons of Lorgar; we should not need to conceal ourselves from the enemy.'

'Were we to have an armada of our own, I would joyfully engage them,' said Marduk, 'but we do not. Have patience, Coryphaus; we will take the fight to the cursed Imperium soon enough.'

One of the Imperial cruisers, not one of the larger vessels by any stretch, though it dwarfed the *Idolator*, rotated on its axis and moved above them, throwing them into deep shadow as it blotted out the system's dying sun. Its port weapons batteries came level with them, and Kol Badar hissed.

The cruiser continued to turn, and its weapon arrays slid away from the *Idolator*. They passed beneath its mass, and though hundreds of kilometres of empty space separated the two ships, it seemed that every intricate detail of the cruiser could be made out. It felt close enough that Marduk had but to reach out his hand to touch it, and he wondered if people aboard it looked even now upon the *Idolator*. Did any of them realise that their mortal enemy was passing beneath them so close?

The shadow of the cruiser passed, and Marduk nodded his head to the Coryphaus. Kol Badar barked an order, and the *Idolator* turned onto a new bearing. The engines were fed more power, and the ship pushed through the blockade of the Imperial cordon and began to power towards Perdus Skylla.

It looked so insignificant from here: a tiny white moon circling in the orbit of a green gas giant.

'Five hours until planetfall,' said Kol Badar, consulting a glowing data-slate built into the command array of the bridge.

'See that the warrior brothers are ready. I want to move out as soon as the landing is made,' said Marduk, not looking at the Coryphaus.

Kol Badar's lips curled back, and his ancient eyes burrowed into Marduk's face.

'What?' asked Marduk, turning to face the larger warrior brother. 'I am your master now, Kol Badar. Be a good dog and do as you are told.'

Kol Badar struck with a speed that belied the bulk of his Terminator armour, wrapping his power talons around Marduk's throat, his eyes blazing in fury.

Marduk laughed in his face.

'Do it,' he barked. 'Do it, and be cursed by Lorgar.'

Kol Badar released Marduk with a shove.

'Know your place, Kol Badar. Jarulek is dead. This Host is mine now, mine alone,' said Marduk. 'Just as *you* are mine.'

'The Council of Sicarus will repudiate your claim over the Host,' growled Kol Badar. 'They will strip you of your brotherhood, flay the flesh from your bones and have your eyes burnt from your sockets. Bloody and blind, you will be cast out into the corpse-plains, where the souls of the condemned will torment you, and the kathartes will strip the muscles from your limbs. You will wander in agony for ten thousand years, unable to die, your mortal body a wretched shell, your soul stripped and gnawed upon by the denizens of the darkness. All this awaits you, Marduk. Such is the punishment for one who plots against his Dark Apostle.'

'Jarulek groomed me as a sacrifice,' said Marduk, 'and I know that you were party to his schemes, but I do not hold a grudge against you for that; you were following your Dark Apostle's orders. The gods of Chaos chose for Jarulek to fall, however, and for me to flourish. They abandoned him in favour of me.'

'You fear to return there, and that is why we have not gone back,' said Kol Badar.

Marduk laughed, genuinely surprised.

'I fear to return there? I think not, my Coryphaus. I *yearn* to return, but I will not return without the secrets of the Nexus unlocked. I thought that you merely wanted me to return a failure, with a lifeless hunk of xenos metal, with no knowledge of what it did or how it is activated. I had no idea that you thought that the council would punish me. Punish me?' Marduk laughed. 'The council will *honour* me.'

'You are a dreamer and a fool, then,' said Kol Badar, turning away.

Marduk moved in front of the Coryphaus, standing in his way. He stared up at the older warrior, the light of fanaticism in his eyes.

'Look into my eyes, Kol Badar, and tell me that the gods do not favour me. Ever since we left Tanakreg, I have felt their favour upon me. My skin is crawling with their power. I can feel it writhing within me.'

Something moved beneath the skin of Marduk's face.

'I am the favoured of Lorgar, and the council *will* embrace me. Tell me that you do not see the gods' favour upon me. Even you, who can barely feel the touch of the warp or the gods, must surely sense my growing favour. Tell me that you cannot.'

Kol Badar clenched his jaw, his eyes blazing with fury, but he did not speak. Marduk laughed softly.

'You *do* sense it then,' he said, as the Coryphaus stalked past him. Kol Badar barged his shoulder into Marduk as he passed, knocking the smaller man aside, but Marduk merely laughed again.

The Coryphaus turned at the doorway.

'Maybe you could trick the council,' he said, 'but you have to make it there alive first.'

THE ARMOURED NOSE of the *Idolator* glowed red hot as the ship screamed down towards the surface of Perdus Skylla.

'Unto those who in ignorance and stubbornness refuse the Word, bring the fires of hell. Sunder their flesh, and burn them of their impurity. Take vengeance upon them for their failings, and teach them the weakness of their false idols,' roared Marduk, the vox-amplifiers built into his skull-faced helmet booming his words through the enclosed space of the transport. 'Thus spoke Lorgar, and so it shall be done. Open their veins that the truth might enter them. Cut upon them and let their blood flow. With holy bolter and chainsword we shall slaughter the unbelievers, and usher the word of truth into the world!'

Strapped into their harness restraints, the warriors of the Host roared their approval as the G-forces assailed them, the words of their holy leader fuelling their hatred and religious fervour.

'No mercy, no remorse,' barked Marduk. 'Such things are for weaklings. We are the faithful, Lorgar's chosen! None shall stand against us. Give praise to the gods of Chaos as you kill. Death will be our herald, and all who look upon us will know fear.'

The *Idolator* broke through the upper atmosphere of Perdus Skylla, streaking down through the darkness like a fiery comet from the heavens.

'Let us pray, brothers of the Host, and let the gods bear witness to our eulogies and bless us with their holy strength,' bellowed Marduk. 'Great powers of the warp, guide the arms of your servants that they might let the blood of your enemies in your honour. Gird us with the strength and fortitude to do your bidding, and let our faith protect us from the blows of the faithless. Let your dark light shine upon us, filling us with purpose and belief. With thanks, we give ourselves unto you, pledging body and soul to your glory, for now and for time immaterial. Glory be.'

'Glory be,' came the response from the warriors of the Host, led by Kol Badar.

'And unto those who would do harm to your faithful servants,' said Marduk, locking eyes with Kol Badar, 'bring an eternity of torment and pain.'

The *Idolator* continued its descent until, after several minutes, the relentless g-forces began to ease and the transport started to level out. Flying low, it screamed across the frozen wasteland, kicking up a great turbulence of snow and ice in its wake. Powerful winds rocked the transport, jolting its occupants from side to side, as it roared into the face of a fierce ice storm. Sudden drops in pressure and blasts of wind made the *Idolator* rise and fall by ten metres at a time, threatening to slam the ship into the ice crust at any moment.

Marduk grinned fiercely, exposing sharpened teeth. Adrenaline pumped through his system.

Kol Badar had plotted the approach course that the *Idolator* was now following with keen tactical acumen. They had entered the atmosphere along the equatorial belt of the moon, four thousand kilometres from the closest Imperial listening post, and they were now approaching the northern polar cap on the lee side of the moon, under the cover of darkness. The Imperials were based solely at the extreme northern and southern tips of the moon, where they had mining colonies, starports and fortress bastions. Immense defence lasers protected these settlements, each of which Kol Badar had estimated consisted of between eight and twelve million people, living beneath the ice.

Virtually nothing lived on the surface, its conditions too severe to maintain life or even any permanent structures other than the bastions. Even the starports were carved into the ice. Reinforced titanium roof structures covered the circular starports, protecting them and the vessels within from the harshest of weather conditions, and those roofs would open like the petals of a flower to allow transport vessels and freighters to dock.

From the information garnered from the Adeptus Mechanicus archive on Kharion IV, the most recent location of the explorator who held the secrets of the device had been ascertained, and it was towards this bastion station that the *Idolator* was bound.

They would get as close as they were able to the Imperial bastion, flying low across the windswept landscape and using the sweep-jamming ice storms to conceal their approach. Kol Badar had factored in the swirling eddies of low pressure, continent sized cyclones that wracked the empty wasteland, in order to further conceal their approach, though he had loudly voiced his displeasure at such subterfuge.

Regardless of the Coryphaus's misgivings, Marduk could not fault Kol Badar's execution. They would be upon the bastion long before their presence was known, and it would be a simple matter of breaching its defences and locating the custodian. The portents had boded well, and Marduk felt assured that it would be a simple undertaking.

He freed the restraints that locked him to his seat, and stood up, easily compensating for the roll of the transport as it was buffeted by howling winds. Stretching out his shoulders, his gaze wandered up the rows of seated Word Bearers, assessing them each in turn.

Khalaxis's teeth were bared, his aggressive nature mirrored in the expressions of his members of the 17th coterie. He jerked his head to the side, flicking his braided hair out of his eyes, concentrating on his knife as it carved into his flesh. He and his warriors had removed their left vambraces and were cutting ritualistic slashes across their forearms. Always the first into any breach, and the last to be extracted, his warriors were lethal combatants all.

Namar-sin, in stark comparison to Khalaxis, was composed and silent, though his one eye gleamed with a fervour no less passionate than Khalaxis's. His Havocs were dutifully tending their weapons, apparently oblivious to the shuddering transport and the roar of the engines. They went about their duties with utter focus, silently incanting benedictions of the dark gods upon their revered heavy weapons.

Brother Sabtec's face was serious, his stoic demeanour familiar and unwavering, and he led the hallowed 13th coterie in a low chant as they checked over their life-systems, and ensured that grenades, spare ammunition clips and devotional chapbooks were secured at their sides.

The final coterie, Kol Badar's veteran Anointed, glared ahead blankly, their expressions grim. Their faces were covered in ritual tattoos and each in turn lowered his head in deference as Marduk looked upon them.

Burias was looking at his hand as the fingers fused and elongated into talons, before he forced the daemon Drak'shal back and his hand took on its natural form once more. Marduk realised that his control over the daemon was growing. Often the possessed would become little more than screaming wretches, their will enslaved to one of the myriad entities that inhabited the warp, but Burias's mastery over Drak'shal was almost complete. Again, Burias let Drak'shal begin to rear within him, and his hand blurred into daemonic talons, before he reasserted his dominance and pushed the daemon back within him. Feeling Marduk's gaze upon him, Burias's eyes flicked up, and he winked at the First Acolyte.

Darioq stood apart from the brothers of the Legion. The corrupted magos could not sit even had he wished too; his mechanical body was not constructed to accommodate such luxury, and the bulk of his servo-harness would have made it impossible. The activated electro-magnets within his heavy, augmented boots kept him locked to the floor, and his four mechanical servo-arms were braced between two bulkheads. Weighing well over a metric tonne, nothing was going to move the techno-magos.

'You have a wish to converse, Marduk, First Acolyte of the Word Bearers Legion of Astartes, genetic descendent of the traitor Primarch Lorgar?' said the magos. The timbre of his voice was different, a growling, daemonic presence underlying his usual robotic monotone.

'Speak the word "traitor" once more when referring to the blessed daemon-lord of our Legion, Darioq-Grendh'al,' said Marduk, 'and I shall allow Kol Badar to rip your limbs off one by one, and no, I have no wish to converse with you.'

The *Idolator* made its way through the darkness across the featureless surface of the moon for two hours, and as they drew near the target, Marduk intoned a final benediction, and the warriors of the Host made ready to disembark. With his skull-faced helmet in place, Marduk ritualistically ran through his final diagnostics, checking his life-systems and those of his revered power armour.

At last, throbbing blister-lights warned of the final approach, and Marduk rammed a fresh sickle-clip into his bolt-pistol. Retro-blasters fired, slowing the *Idolator*, and the nose of the transport craft lifted as its momentum dropped.

Kol Badar relayed his debarkation orders with curt commands, ensuring that each of the four coteries knew their position.

Restraint harnesses were thrown off as the rear landing legs touched down, and the vacuum seals of the rear embarkation ramp were released with a hiss. Before the *Idolator* had even settled, the ramp was thrown outwards, and snow and ice blasted into the interior, swirling around in blinding eddies.

'Get him moving,' shouted Kol Badar over the screaming of engines and the howling of wind, pointing towards Darioq, and two members of Namarsin's coterie urged the corrupted magos towards the lowering ramp.

The first warriors were already pounding down the ramp, moving towards their allotted positions, filing off left and right. Marduk stomped down the assault ramp and stepped onto the frozen surface of Perdus Skylla. The enhanced auto-sensors in his helmet allowed his sight to pierce the raging blizzard, though mere mortal eyes would have seen nothing but a blinding sheet of white.

Marduk filed off to the right just as the Land Raiders, two tucked beneath each stubbed wing, were lowered onto the ice. They growled like angry war-beasts as they were released from their locking clamps. Their engines revved, and smoke billowed from their daemon-headed exhaust stacks. Marduk ducked his head as he entered the armoured hull of the closest Land Raider and locked himself into a seat. Burias slammed into the seat opposite, a feral grin upon his features. As usual, he did not deign to wear his helmet; his witch-sight easily the match of any automated sensors. Long strands of oiled black hair that had escaped their binding whipped around his head like a gorgon's serpents.

Brother Sabtec and his esteemed 13th joined them, piling into the Land Raider and taking their seats, and the assault ramp was slammed shut. The frenzied wind died away instantly, and the shower of snow and ice settled on shoulder pads and greaves.

The Land Raider's massive tracks spun on the ice for a second before catching, and the heavy assault tank lurched into motion. Less than thirty seconds after the *Idolator* had landed, the four Land Raiders, each filled with blessed warriors of Lorgar, were speeding across the surface of Perdus Skylla.

Marduk was shaken as the assault tank hit a bank of snow, and there was a moment of weightlessness as the front of the vehicle lifted up before crashing down again with titanic force.

'Twenty minutes to target,' growled Kol Badar over the vox.

Burias's features shimmered like a faulty pict viewer, and the face of the daemon Drak'shal was momentarily superimposed over his features. Tall, uneven horns rose from his brow, and deeply slanted, hate-filled eyes blinked. Then Burias shook his head, pushing the daemon back within, and the image was gone.

'Not long, Drak'shal,' said Marduk in the guttural tongue of the daemons. Burias grinned at him once more.

CHAPTER FIVE

HUNDRED-KILOMETRE WINDS whipped across the ice flow, and the roar of the storm was such that no human ear would have heard any shout or the staccato reverberations of gunfire. The darkness would have concealed anything from the naked eye, and the blinding swirl of ice, snow and fog was such that all but the most sophisticated sensor arrays were rendered useless. Still, Marduk was taking no chances as he elbowed his way cautiously forwards, edging nearer to the Imperial bastion.

He could see the dark shadow of the structure rising before him, though even his advanced auto-sensors and magnifier auspexes had difficulty piercing the blinding gale. It was built into a massive pinnacle of rock that pierced the thick ice, the first geological landmark that the Word Bearers had thus far seen on Perdus Skylla. Marduk snarled up at the hateful silhouette of the fortress. It had been constructed in the form of an immense aquila, the two-headed eagle that was the symbol of the Imperium and the Emperor's rule.

It rose some three hundred and fifty metres above the ice plains, the highest point on all of Perdus Skylla. If the weather had been clearer, it could have been seen for kilometres all around, an immense structure that dominated the landscape. Doubtless it had been built to remind the populace of Perdus Skylla of the Emperor's authority, to cow the people it loomed over and never let them forget who it was that ruled their lives.

To the ignorant people of Perdus Skylla it might have been a symbol of reverence, but to Marduk it represented all that he hated about the Imperium, all that he desired to see toppled.

What sort of empire would allow a lifeless corpse to be venerated as a god, and let pompous fools and bureaucrats dictate how a galaxy was to be run? For the millionth time, he cursed the holy warmaster for being laid low by the trickery of the enemy. Had Horus overthrown the Emperor, the galaxy would never have fallen into stagnation and torpor. The Great Crusade would still be underway, wiping all xenos and non-believers from the universe. Humanity would be united in faith.

Marduk froze, pushing himself flat to the ground as his keen auto-senses flashed a warning before his eyes. The massive gates of the bastion began to open, folding in upon themselves and sliding into a hidden recess within the rock. Four armoured vehicles emerged, the sound of their engines lost in the howling wind.

They were non-standard template vehicles protected by thick plates of white-painted armour. Marduk's targeting arrays locked onto the foremost vehicle, and a flood of data streamed in front of his eyes. A heavy weapons sponson unfolded from behind the main engine block, sliding forward and locking into place, and the weapon panned left and right. They were light vehicles, roughly the size of Rhino APCs, and they were clearly built for traversing the ice flows, with heavy, thick tracks at the rear and a single upwards flaring ski as broad as the tank at the front.

If it came to it, they would easily be neutralised by his Land Raiders, but he had no wish for the enemy to know, prematurely, that they were under attack.

The vehicles moved up the steep ramp of ice and snow that led from within the bastion, heavy weapons turrets rotating with precise, mechanical movements.

They turned to the north-west, and soon disappeared into the storm.

'Do not engage,' said Marduk.

'Acknowledged,' came Kol Badar's response, his voice blurred by static.

Resuming his advance, Marduk elbowed his way closer to the enemy fortification.

The aquila fortress reared up above him, its twin heads glaring out into the darkness. Despite his anger, disdain and disgust as he thought of what could have been, *should* have been, it gave him perverse pleasure to see how far the Imperium had fallen. This world was evidence of its failings. It was being abandoned, as was the entire sub-system, in the face of a xenos threat. He shook his head in mockery at such weakness.

The long, insulated barrels of defence lasers rose up behind the aquila structure, angled towards the heavens. He knew that the vast power source for the formidable weapons would be located deep within the rock below. They were weapons of awesome potency, though useless against an enemy that had already landed.

Marduk advanced a further two hundred metres, assailed by the relentless wind and biting ice. The brutal environmental conditions did not concern him. His archaic power armour, a bastard hybrid of marks IV, V and VI, was capable of withstanding far more demanding situations.

Within fifty metres of the enemy structure, Marduk hunkered down to assess the defences of the bastion. Snow began to settle on his power armour, so that he was almost completely concealed. Indeed, a human could have stood five metres away and not have seen him, blinded by the gale and the fog.

His gleaming, black, reflective eyepieces panned upwards, targeters locking onto autocannon turrets and demolisher cannons built into the sides of the rock face. Had the weather been less severe, the static defences would have taken a heavy toll on the Host as it approached. Such a thing was unacceptable, for Marduk had brought less than thirty warrior brothers with him on the mission to Perdus Skylla.

In ideal circumstances, he would have descended upon the moon with the entire Host, and the taking of the bastion would have been a simple thing. However, with the size of the Imperial blockade in the sub-system such an endeavour would have been folly, for the *Infidus Diabolus* would have been annihilated long before it reached the moon's atmosphere. As such, he had chosen to lead just a small strike force onto the surface of the moon, and slipped unseen through the Imperial cordon.

It was not the way that he would have liked to have achieved victory, for Marduk, like Kol Badar, would have been more pleased to have laid waste the Imperial world, to unleash the full force of the Host and leave nothing but corpses and edifices to the great gods behind. Victory here was important, however, and the manner in which it was achieved, less so.

Pushing his extraneous thoughts aside, Marduk turned his attention to the task at hand.

Two twin-linked autocannon turrets guarded the approach to the bastion gates, and they panned back and forth across the open ground before them. Each was restricted to a ninety-degree firing arc, though the arcs of the two turrets, and the others nearby, were overlapping, ensuring that no enemy could approach the bastion from any angle without coming under fire. Heavier siege cannons protruded from the rock face above the gates, but they were of less interest to Marduk, for he was below their arc of trajectory. They were designed to fire upon enemy two hundred metres and further out, not at a foe already at the base of the bastion. Still, he opened up a visual feed with Kol Badar, allowing the Coryphaus to see what he did, so that the war leader was aware of what he would be riding into once the gates were breached.

'Brother Namar-sin,' said Kol Badar in a growled response to the visual feed. 'Move your coterie into position and target the turrets. Fire on the First Acolyte's command.'

'So it shall be, Coryphaus,' came the response. Somewhere behind Marduk, invisible even to his augmented sight, the Havoc Space Marines of Namar-sin's coterie would be targeting the autocannons with their ancient heavy weapons.

Marduk again looked up, peering through the blinding ice storm.

'Come on, Burias,' he hissed in impatience.

TWO HUNDRED AND fifty metres up, Burias scaled the vertical rock face, hauling himself up hand over hand.

Kol Badar had identified one last possible escape route from the bastion, and it was the icon bearer's duty to close it off.

He had allowed the change to come over him, bringing the daemon Drak'shal to the fore, and great horns rose from his head. Hellfire burnt within his eyes, and his teeth were bared, exposing a double row of serrated shark-like teeth. Impossibly, his darkly handsome, immaculate features could still be seen beneath the image of the daemon, as if both beings were coexisting in the same space.

Bunching his leg muscles, Burias pushed off from rock face, leaping upwards. He grabbed a rocky overhang with one hand, and for a second he hung there over the vertical drop. The ground could not be seen below, lost in the swirling storm, though the glow of lascannons could be dimly discerned. Hauling himself over the edge, the heat of his breath clouded the air around him, and feral eyes locked onto the hateful shape of the giant aquila that reared above him. He dug his taloned hands into stone carved in the form of feathers and continued his ascent.

Up above, roughly a hundred metres away, the twin eagle heads of the colossal stone aquila glared out across the landscape, one facing east, and the other west. A bright light shone like a lighthouse from the eye of the right eagle head, while the eye of the left head was dark and blind.

Burias ascended towards the shining eye, his talons easily finding handholds between the massive carved feathers. He ascended the sheer exterior of the immense statue, swiftly, barely pausing as he climbed, like a dark stain upon the noble eagle's body. The wind howled around him, buffeting him and threatening to rip him loose, and ice and snow drove into him at gale force.

Climbing swiftly and surely, he scurried up the curving neck like a spider until he was directly below the head. With a snarl he sprang out, twisting in mid-air, and one hand locked around a feathered grip three metres higher. Without pause, he continued up beneath the immense head, crawling upside down along the underside of the monolith. He paused as he reached the beak, for the stone was as smooth as glass and there were no handholds. He changed the angle of his climb, and scrambled up the vertical eagle head, being careful to stay out of sight of the shining eye, and pulled himself atop the massive structure.

Oblivious to the danger the winds presented as they assailed him, Burias threw his head back and roared into the gale.

Dropping to a crouch, Burias made his way on all fours towards the eagle's shining eye. Cautiously, he peered inside.

He saw a man sitting at a desk, an almost completely empty decanter of dark liquid in front of him. By his manner of dress, he was clearly a high-ranking official, and another man, young and awkward, stood at his side. The two appeared to be engrossed in conversation, and they did not notice the daemonic vision of the possessed warrior glaring in at them. There were two exits from the room: an elevator lift that would descend into the body of the aquila, and a heavy blast door.

Climbing backwards, Burias-Drak'shal reached the top once more, looking down. On the back of the eagle head, fifteen metres lower, was a protected platform where a small shuttle was docked, and where the blast door led.

Burias-Drak'shal perched some ten metres above the blast door, and settled down to wait. If any eye had been able to pierce the darkness and the howling gale he would have looked like a malicious gargoyle, crouching motionless as he awaited his prey.

'In position,' he growled, his fang-filled mouth forming the words awkwardly.

'Received, Burias-Drak'shal,' replied Marduk. The snow settled over him, so that only his baleful skull-faced visage peered from beneath the white blanket, his black eyes staring hatefully at the enemy structure.

'217th Havoc coterie, split,' Kol Badar ordered. 'Heavy weapons, hold position. Namar-sin, move the rest of your squad forward to support the First Acolyte, and ready melta-bombs. Move on the First Acolyte's word.'

'Forwards on me,' motioned Marduk as Namar-sin and three of his coterie emerged from the blanketing gale behind him, crawling stealthily forwards, their horned helmets covered in a thick layer of snow.

Marduk resumed his advance, inching his way forwards. Imperial sweeps arced across the ice three times, and the Word Bearers froze each time, instantly cutting relay feeds and vox-transmissions to make themselves all but invisible.

The distance to the closest turret was no more than twenty metres, and the bastion gate was less than forty. Metre by metre, Marduk and his chosen brethren crept forwards. The wind suddenly dropped, and warning sensors flashed in Marduk's helmet. Without the interference of the billowing ice-crystals in the air, the turrets swung towards the Word Bearers and opened fire.

A fraction of a second before the autocannons unleashed their fury, Marduk rolled to the side and high-calibre rounds ripped up the ground where he had lain. One of the Havoc Space Marines was hit by the opening salvo, his helmet smashing apart beneath the heavy weapons fire, staining the snow with his blood.

'Now,' barked Marduk into his vox-relay, and a beam of light stabbed out of the storm as one of the heavy weapon-armed Havocs of the 217th coterie fired his lascannon, and one of the turrets fell silent. A stream of white-hot plasma engulfed another turret, and plasteel and rockcrete ran like liquid as it was destroyed.

Marduk was up and running, roaring a catechism of devotion as he unslung his chainsword. Autocannon rounds screamed past him, and one of them clipped his shoulder, jerking him to the side, but not halting his progress. Another lascannon beam stabbed from the gale, and a third turret was destroyed, detonating from within as its ammunition cache was hit. The resulting explosion threw chunks of rock in all directions. Marduk swayed his head to the side as a piece of red-hot rockcrete the size of a man hurtled past him.

Marduk was five metres from the last remaining turret, and he threw himself forwards into a roll as its barrels swung towards him, spitting a torrent of high-velocity rounds. He came up to his feet beneath it, and grabbed one of the barrels. Servo-muscles straining, he pushed upwards with all his might, overextending the automated turret housing, exposing cabling and ammo feeds. Sparks spattered off Marduk's skull-faced helmet, and he slashed his chainsword across the turret's internals. The whirring chain links tore through the cables, and oil gushed like blood. Releasing his grip on the barrel of the weapon, the turret flopped lifelessly to the side.

More turrets, higher up on the bastion's face, were opening fire, raining down a hail of gunfire, which was answered by the heavy weapons fire of those warrior brothers further back. One of Namar-sin's coterie was caught in a fusillade from two directions, and fell to one knee as his body was pierced a dozen times. Still, he refused to fall, and pushing himself back to his feet, he ran on towards the bastion gates.

Bullets glanced off Marduk's shoulder plates, and a round caught him in the chest, knocking him back a step, though it did not penetrate his thick ceramite armour. With a hiss of anger, he lurched forwards, running down the incline towards the bastion gates. Beneath the overhanging lip, he was protected from the worst of the fire, and Marduk pulled a melta-bomb loose from a chain around his waist. He whispered a prayer to the Great Changer as he primed the potent grenade and slammed it onto the thick door, placing it over one of the locking mechanisms. Electromagnets held it firmly in place, and a red light on the melta-bomb began to flash.

'On approach,' said Kol Badar, his voice overlaid with static and interference.

As another melta-bomb was slammed into place by a warrior of the 217th coterie, the champion Namar-sin staggered into the protection beneath the gateway, smoking bullet craters across his armour. His left arm was gone, blown clear by autocannon fire, and his armour was awash with blood.

'You took your time,' growled Marduk.

'I apologise, my lord,' he said. The powerful anti-coagulants in the warrior's blood had already stemmed the flow, and formed a thick crust around the shocking wound.

'I can still do my job,' said Namar-sin defensively, feeling Marduk's gaze on his injuries. Gritting his teeth, the champion primed his melta-bomb somewhat awkwardly with one hand, before slamming the bulky grenade into position.

More lascannon beams stabbed from the ice storm towards the bastion's defences as the Land Raiders approached. In response, the first of the battle cannons spoke, firing blindly into the gale, the ensuing reverberations shaking the ground.

The melta-bombs detonated, and the metre-thick gates buckled inwards. The force of the super-heated explosions was directed inwards, searing through the reinforced metal barrier. It was not fully breached, but as he lowered the arm that shielded his face, Marduk recognised instantly that its integrity was compromised.

'Twenty seconds,' said Kol Badar's voice in Marduk's helmet.

Lascannons fired from the blinding gale, and then the dark shadow of the first Land Raider could be seen, driving at speed for the gatehouse. An explosion slammed into the ice beside the behemoth, knocking it to the side, and for a second its left-hand tracks lifted, spinning wildly before it slammed back on the ground and corrected its angle of approach.

Marduk moved to the side, his back to a rockcrete support buttress, as the immense Land Raider gunned its engines. Its ancient hide was inscribed with passages from the books of Chaos, and symbols of devotion and allegiance marred its clotted-blood coloured armour plates. Autocannon rounds ricocheted off the Land Raider, unable to penetrate, and heavy bolter rounds were deflected off its angled plates. Its side sponsons lit up the darkness as they stabbed into the gates, further weakening them, and Marduk pressed himself backwards so as not to be struck by the monstrous battle tank as it dropped down the incline towards the entrance to the bastion.

It slammed into the weakened gates with the force of a battering ram, and they collapsed inwards. Another Land Raider bedecked with chains from which severed heads and limbs hung followed the first, its daemon-headed exhausts spewing black smoke as it roared down the incline and into the belly of the bastion, followed by the third. The last of the Land Raiders would hold position, scanning for any sign of the enemy out on the plain. With the enemy bastion breached, the heavy weapons toting Havocs of the 217th coterie pulled back towards the Land Raider, as per Kol Badar's orders, though their champion Namar-sin was to enter the bastion alongside the First Acolyte.

As the third Land Raider roared past, Marduk broke into a run behind it, using it as moving cover. He drew his chainsword as he ran, and felt the impatience of the daemon Borhg'ash within the daemon weapon.

Already he could hear the sounds of gunfire, the hiss of lasguns and the whine as they re-powered, and the deep percussive boom of heavy bolter fire.

The ramp descended into the interior of the bastion, which had been carved into the solid rock. The interior was not unlike the hangar deck of the *Infidus Diabolus*, with high ceilings and various levels and gantries running around its walls. Around thirty APCs, light scout vehicles and a couple of heavier tanks, all armoured in the same uniform white plates, were lined up in serried ranks, and white-armoured soldiers were running forwards. Officers were shouting, and men were running in from portals in the north and south. Others were taking up positions upon the gantries lining the walls, firing down at the Word Bearers.

The two Land Raiders had ground to a halt, heavy-bolters built into their hulls pumping explosive rounds into the enemy, ripping men apart in bloody detonations. The frontal assault ramps slammed down onto the rockcrete floor, and the bulky forms of the warriors of the Host appeared from the red-lit interiors, smoke billowing around them.

Kol Badar strode from the lead Land Raider, his face hidden beneath his quad-tusked helmet and fire spitting from the barrels of his archaic combi-bolter. The Coryphaus roared, the daemonic sound resounding from vox-grills as he cut a white-armoured man in half with bolter fire. Behind him, the four warriors of the Anointed, the warrior elite of the Host, stalked forwards heavily. The servos of their ancient Terminator armour hissed and vented steam as the Anointed advanced from the interior of the battle tank, their weapons roaring.

Sabtec and Khalaxis emerged from the other Land Raiders, leading their respective coteries. The 13th instantly took cover, bolters spitting death as they coolly split into two teams and manoeuvred into good firing positions. As Sabtec's warriors laid down their hail of suppressing fire, Khalaxis and his 17th coterie disdained any attempt to seek cover, and raced headlong towards the enemy, revving the motors of their chainblades and snapping off shots with their pistols.

A portal lifted beside Marduk, and he swung his bolt pistol around and fired. A troop of white-armoured soldiers ran at him, and his first rounds took one of them in the chest. He fell with a strangled cry as his ribcage was shattered. A second enemy dropped as his head exploded, and Marduk pumped another pair of shots into the body of a third warrior.

The soldiers halted, those in front dropping to one knee as they raised their lasguns. Others sought cover against the pipes protruding into the corridor, and they fired as their sergeant shouted an order.

Las-rounds impacted with Marduk's chest and shoulder pads, knocking him back half a step. They left blackened scorch marks on his armoured plates, and Marduk snarled in fury as he leapt forwards, his chainsword roaring.

More las-rounds pinged off his armour as he closed the distance, and he began to recite the Litanies of Hate and Vengeance, barking the words like a mantra. Several of the enemy soldiers baulked and stumbled back from his charge as his vox-enhanced voice made their eardrums bleed. Marduk blew the arm off one of them with his bolt pistol fired at close range, and then he was amongst them.

His chainsword hacked into the neck of the first, teeth biting through armour, flesh and bone, and hot blood splashed across Marduk's tabard. Blood ran down the feeder grooves carved into the sides of the chainsword and was sucked into the internals of the weapon, and Marduk felt fresh power and strength flow through him as the daemon Borhg'ash fed. Veins pulsed along the length of the ancient weapon, and the daemon urged Marduk on to feed it further.

He dropped to one knee, and a las-bolt seared above him where his head had been a fraction of a second earlier. He hacked out again, cutting through another soldier's leg, the bone ripped apart by Borhg'ash's eager teeth. He fired his bolt pistol, and another enemy was slammed backwards into its comrades as the back of its head exploded outwards.

Brother Namar-sin was at Marduk's side, and he buried his axe in the chest of another of the soldiers, the pain of his severed arm lending him additional strength and fervour. He planted his boot on the chest of the man and ripped his axe free, kicking the soldier to the ground. He hacked his axe into another man, severing his arm and cutting half way through his torso.

Another warrior of Namar-sin's 217th fired his bolter at point blank range, blasting the soldiers back, chunks of flesh and blood spraying in all directions. One man, his lifeblood running from his wounds, was on his knees before the warrior brother, and his skull was pulverised by the butt of a bolter.

Marduk continued reciting from the Litanies of Hate and Vengeance and rammed his chainsword into the gut of another enemy. The whirring, barbed links of the weapon ripped the soldier in two, cutting off his pitiful cries of agony.

Borhg'ash was gorged with blood, and it leaked from the internals of the chainsword like a syrup, but the daemon still hungered for more. Marduk felt the sentience within the chainsword urging him to kill again, and he gladly indulged its will.

Having emptied his bolt pistol clip, he holstered the weapon as he hacked a lasgun being levelled at him in two with a backhand sweep of his chainsword. The sparking halves of the lasgun were ripped from the terrified soldier's hands, and as he staggered backwards in shock, Marduk cleaved him from shoulder to hip with a powerful two-handed blow with his chainsword.

There were no more living threats, and Borhg'ash revved its engine, expressing its desire for more blood. Seeing one soldier on the ground still living, though he was dying fast as his blood pumped from his severed leg, Marduk reversed his grip on his chainsword and drove it downwards into the man. The soldier shuddered as the sharp teeth of the weapon ripped apart his flesh, and Borhg'ash greedily sucked up the gore.

Marduk loaded a fresh sickle-clip into his bolt pistol as he marched back out onto the main concourse. A frantic gun battle was still underway, with enemy soldiers high up on gantries sniping down at the Word Bearers below. Scores of white-armoured men were lying dead or dying throughout the area, some crawling vainly for the futile safety of cover.

Sabtec's 13th coterie was taking cover behind the bulk of the Land Raiders, positioned at corners and snapping off beams at the enemy soldiers. Lasgun shots impacted uselessly against the armoured hulls of the massive vehicles, and those few Word Bearers that were struck shrugged off the las-fire as if they were irritating mosquito bites.

One of the 13th dropped to one knee, aiming his stubby, daemon-headed missile launcher up high, and smoke billowed out the back of the missile tube as he fired. The missile screamed upwards and struck the underside of one of the gantries where a cluster of snipers was positioned, exploding in a billowing cloud of flame. The flesh of the soldiers was sliced apart as super-heated fragments of metal lacerated them, and the metal grid gave way. Those not killed by the explosion dropped ten metres to the next level of gantries, and were crushed as metal bracings were wrenched out of shape and pulled down in their wake.

Khalaxis and his warriors stormed across the gantries, unstoppable juggernauts of muscle and power armour that smashed through the enemy, throwing them over railings to fall fifteen metres to the ground, hacking limbs from bodies with sweeps of chainswords and killing everything in their path.

Three of the light armoured vehicles of the enemy were thrown upwards as a lascannon ignited fuel cells, and a mushroom of fierce orange flame billowed upwards, black, oily smoke licking at its edges. One of the vehicles spun end over end and slammed into a wall, while the other two came crushing down onto other unmanned vehicles behind which more enemy soldiers were hunkered down. They staggered back away from the inferno, and were dutifully gunned down by concentrated bolter fire.

Kol Badar strode through the firefight snapping off shots with his combi-bolter, his entourage of Anointed warriors walking steadily alongside him. They eschewed any attempt to take cover, the ancient, ceramite and adamantium plates of their Terminator armour offering them more protection than rockcrete or steel.

One of the Anointed swung the heavy twin barrels of his reaper autocannon before him like a scythe, laying down a withering hail of high-calibre fire that ripped everything apart indiscriminately: armour, men, vehicles and rockcrete.

A body landed in front of Marduk, having been hurled from a gantry above. The soldier's helmet was smashed, and his eyes stared blankly up at the First Acolyte. Marduk kicked the man in the head, splashing blood and brain matter across the floor.

More enemy soldiers were appearing, assailing the Word Bearers from all directions. They were caught in the middle of a crossfire, but were cutting the enemy down ruthlessly. Marduk saw that two Word Bearers had fallen, though their injuries were not mortal and they continued to fight on. At least fifty enemy soldiers had been slain, and the casualties were mounting.

Under Kol Badar's direction, Sabtec's 13th began advancing up through the hail of fire towards the gantries, while the Anointed laid down a hail of fire that kept the enemy's heads down. The Land Raiders pivoted on the spot, their lascannons destroying everything they targeted, and their heavy bolters ripping paths across the rock walls as they chased the enemy soldiers.

Marduk raced up a steel staircase, taking the steps four at a time. A las-blast struck him in the head, scorching his pristine alabaster skull helmet, and he snapped off a shot with his pistol in response, sending a man flying five metres backwards, a crater exploding from his back.

The enemy officers were shouting their commands, frantically attempting to rally their men and reposition them in the face of the relentless advance of the Word Bearers, but they were panicking, and their orders were not followed. Men crawled backwards, attempting to find any place to hide from the unholy fallen angels of death stalking towards them, firing off hasty shots with lasguns.

Marduk stomped onto one of the gantries and shot down two men, their blood misting the air. With a kick, he smashed aside a stand of barrels behind which three men were taking cover, and gunned the first two down. The other was torn apart by a concentrated burst of bolter fire from below, and Marduk moved on, his pistol raised before him as he fired more shots into the enemy arranged along the gantry.

One of the white-armoured soldiers raised a melta-gun, and Marduk threw himself against the wall as the weapon fired. It scorched across his left shoulder pad, and warning symbols appeared within his helmet display. Namar-sin, coming up behind Marduk, hurled his axe, the weapon spinning end over end and slamming into the soldier, cleaving into his face and embedding itself deep in his skull.

Men screamed in agony as they were engulfed in flame, as Khalaxis's 17th coterie advanced opposite Marduk, trapping a score of soldiers on the gantry between them. The flamer roared again, and fire consumed half a dozen men, their flesh blistering as it burned. Several fell over the railing, plummeting to the floor where they smouldered and lay still. The survivors were hacked apart as Khalaxis led the charge into their midst, his chainaxe screaming as it tore through bone and tendon. Marduk waded into the terrified soldiers from the other side, clubbing men to the ground and executing them without mercy.

Less than five minutes after the bastion gates had been breached, the echo of gunfire ceased. The Word Bearers moved among the enemy soldiers, dispatching any who still breathed with swift blows to the head.

Marduk came across one of the officers, his face awash with blood and his breath coming in short, sharp gasps. He looked up at Marduk's inscrutable skull-faced visage in terror.

'Emperor preserve me,' he gasped.

Marduk bent down and gripped the man, his massive hand closing around the soldier's face.

'The False Emperor as a deity is a lie,' he growled, squeezing, feeling the soldier's skull straining. 'No one will answer your prayers. Where is the commander of this facility?'

'The... the lift,' gasped the man. 'Top floor. Emperor save my soul.'

'The Corpse Emperor is not divine, and he does not care about the sanctity of your soul. You will see.'

Marduk crushed the man's skull effortlessly, blood bursting from the soldier's eyes, nose and mouth as he died. Standing up, he wiped his hand clean upon his tabard, and turned to face Kol Badar, down below in the main concourse.

'I grow tired of this world. It is time we ended this,' said Marduk, his voice booming across the open expanse. 'Bring forth the Enslaved One, and let us get what we came for.'

As THE FIRST alarms sounded, Guildmaster Pollo was taking a drink of his seventy-five year old vintage amasec. He almost choked on the fiery draught, and his adjutant, Leto, visibly paled. Pollo slammed his glass down onto his table and was up and moving instantly.

The portal slid open as he approached it, and he stormed out into the adjoining room.

'What in the name of Holy Terra is going on?' he barked at his personal guard, a group of five soldiers of the mercenary Skyllan Interdiction Force. 'Captain? This better not be another perimeter glitch.'

The captain of his guard, a tall, broad-shouldered soldier with a serious face, had his hand to his earpiece, his brow furrowed in concentration.

'No, sir,' he replied. 'The automated turrets have identified hostile targets on approach.'

'Hostile targets?' breathed Leto from behind the guildmaster.

'Have they been identified?' asked the guildmaster.

'No, sir, not as yet. Wait,' he said, raising his hand to forestall any response as he listened to incoming communications. The soldier's face turned grim. 'What?' he asked. 'Are you sure?'

'What is going on?' asked Guildmaster Pollo forcefully.

'Sir,' began the captain, 'the bastion has been breached.'

'Emperor preserve us,' said Leto.

'There must be some mistake,' said Pollo.

'No mistake, sir. A heavy firefight is underway on the garage concourse level.'

The captain swore, tapping at his earpiece as it went dead. The other soldiers of the guildmaster's guard looked uneasily at each other.

'We must get you out of here, sir,' the captain said, his face dark. 'The bastion is compromised.'

He strode towards the guildmaster and his adjutant, barking orders to his men. They responded instantly, and their lasguns hummed as they powered into life.

'I will not go,' said the guildmaster hotly. 'How many men do you have here?'

'Only three demi-legions, sir. The others are all out keeping the peace at the Phorcys starport, or aiding the evacuation efforts.'

'That is still, what, three hundred men?' asked Pollo.

'It will not be enough, sir,' said the captain softly.

Guildmaster Pollo glared at the captain. 'The Skyllan Interdiction Force is paid damn well to protect this fortress and hold the peace. You are not filling me with the confidence that the guild money is well-spent, captain.'

'My lord,' said the captain, his expression stoic in the face of the guildmaster's simmering anger, 'the enemy below are Astartes.'

'Space Marines?' breathed Leto. 'But we… we are loyal subjects of the Emperor. Aren't we?'

'Of course we are, Leto,' said Pollo.

'They are rebel Astartes, my lord, and I have lost all contact with the demi-legions. We leave, now,' he said, brooking no argument.

Pollo felt a sense of panic stab at him, though he was careful to maintain a calm exterior. He felt the flush of amasec clouding his mind, and he cursed himself for drinking so much. He licked his lips, and nodded to the captain.

With clipped commands, the soldiers fell in around the guildmaster, and the group marched back into the senior official's office. The captain was steering Pollo forcefully by the elbow, moving him quickly towards the reinforced door that led to his personal shuttle.

'My records,' protested the guildmaster.

'I'll get them, my lord,' said Leto.

'No,' snapped the Skyllan guard captain, 'we leave now.'

'My data-slate, Leto,' hissed the guildmaster, and his adjutant swept the book-sized piece of arcane technology up off his master's desk as he was hurried past.

The captain whispered the requisite prayer to the machine god as he entered the code sequence into the door, and the circular locks slid anticlockwise with a hiss. The soldiers lowered their visors to cover their faces at a nod from their superior. Then the captain leant his weight against the door. It opened with a groan and snow billowed into the office, driven through the portal by the deafening gale outside.

Guildmaster Pollo covered his face with his arm as the biting chill struck him, and he took an involuntary step backwards.

Three soldiers moved out onto the landing platform, their lasguns panning left and right. Pointless, thought Pollo. No enemy could be up here.

His personal Aquila-class lander was perched some twenty metres away, covered in a thick layer of snow. The guard captain pulled an exquisite pistol of ornate design from his holster, and began guiding Pollo out onto the landing platform.

The cold was almost unbearable, and ice crystals formed instantly on his eyebrows and lips. His eyes stung from the cold, and even breathing was painful.

One of his guards, out in front, reached the shuttle and slammed his fist into an activation panel. Instantly, the embarkation ramp began to lower.

With his head down, Guildmaster Pollo allowed himself to be hurried towards the waiting shuttle, his boots slipping on the ice-slick landing pad. The captain supporting him shouted something, but he couldn't make it out over the roar of the wind.

* * *

BURIAS-DRAK'SHAL GRINNED in feral anticipation as he stared down at the men ten metres below him, battling against the gale as they made their way towards the shuttle.

He dropped down amongst them and landed in a crouch, rockcrete cracking beneath the impact. A soldier was a step behind and to his left, and he swung around, taking the man in the head with one of his massive, fused talons. The force of the blow slammed the soldier into the rockcrete wall, his skull pulverised, Burias-Drak'shal's buried talon thirty centimetres into the rock.

Ripping the talon free, letting the soldier slump to the ground, he spun and lashed out with a backhanded blow that ripped across the throat of another soldier as he turned towards the possessed warrior, lasgun raised.

The man's throat was ripped open to the spine, and he spun, blood fountaining from the mortal wound.

SOMETHING HOT SPLASHED the back of Guildmaster Pollo's head, and he stumbled and fell to one knee. As the captain hauled him back to his feet, he reached up and touched a hand to his head. He stared blankly for a second at the fresh blood on his hands, before turning to look back the way he had come.

A daemonic beast from the deepest pits of hell had dropped down behind them.

Its bulk was immense, more than three times that of a normal man, and its lips curled back to expose the barbed teeth of the ultimate predator. Two men lay dead at its feet.

The captain saw the beast just as the guildmaster did, and he shouted a warning, pushing Pollo roughly towards the shuttle as he raised his pistol.

Another man died before the pistol fired, as the daemon punched a claw up through the soldier's sternum.

The blow lifted the soldier off his feet, and the dae-mon's talons emerged from his back. With a dismissive sweep of its arm, the daemon hurled the man off the landing pad, disappearing in the gale to fall the three hundred metres to the base of the bastion.

The captain's pistol boomed, but Pollo did not wait to see if he had felled the beast. Terror coursing through him, he half-ran, half-stumbled towards the lowering ramp leading into his shuttle, his heart beat-ing wildly.

The guard standing by the shuttle had his lagsun raised to his shoulder, and he fired past Pollo twice before running up the ramp to initiate the launch. Pollo heard several more shots as the other remaining guards brought their weapons to bear, and he paused at the foot of the embarkation ramp to look back. He saw his adjutant crawling towards him on all fours, blood splattered across his terrified face.

Without thinking of his own safety he ran to the young man. As he helped him up to his feet, Pollo looked back through the swirling snow.

Another man was down, his head ripped from his shoulders, and the captain was backing away from the daemonic beast stalking towards him. His pistol boomed, but the beast swayed its head to the side with preternatural speed, and the shot hissed past its face.

The captain risked a glance behind him, and his eyes locked onto the guildmaster's.

'Go!' shouted the captain, though his voice was lost in the roaring wind.

'Watch out!' roared Pollo at the same time, for the beast had sprung forwards as soon as the captain had taken his eyes off it.

Leto scrambled past his master, clambering up the ramp into the interior of the shuttle, but Pollo was locked in place, staring in horror at the daemon as it leapt at the captain of his guard.

The soldier staggered backwards and pumped three shots into the daemon as it bore down on him. The first shots hit the monster in the chest and the gorget, ricocheting uselessly off its blood-red armour, but the third shot struck it in the cheek, shattering bone.

It fell with a roar of anger before the captain, and the soldier levelled his pistol at the back of its horned head. Before he could squeeze the trigger, the beast was up and moving, and one of its immense clawed hands closed around the captain's arm. The pistol boomed, but its aim had been skewed, and the bullet glanced off the beast's skull.

The captain screamed in pain and fell to his knees as the bones in his arm were shattered, and the beast loomed over him, its visage twisted in fury. Blood dripped from its wounds, bubbling and hissing as it struck the snow.

Opening its mouth impossibly wide, it lunged down, its jaws clamping around either side of the captain's head.

His eyes wide with terror, Pollo staggered backwards. His movements attracted the attention of the beast, and it swung its burning gaze towards him, the captain's head still locked in its jaws. It clamped its mouth shut, and the soldier's head cracked like a nut in vice.

It dropped its lifeless prey to the ground and leapt towards Pollo, closing the distance with shocking swiftness, bounding towards him on all fours like an ape. Turning, Pollo ran.

The engines of the Aquila lander were roaring, and for a moment he thought he would make it. He saw Leto at the top of the ramp, frantically urging him on with beckoning waves of his hands, and he scrambled up the ramp into the shuttle.

A stink akin to rotting meat and the acrid stench of electricity reached his nostrils, and a hand close around the back of his head. With a jerk, he was hurled backwards, skidding down the ramp to fall in a crumpled heap at its base.

One of his arms was broken, and he cried out as splinters of bone grated against each other. He saw Leto at the top of the ramp quaking before the immense daemon just before the adjutant was ripped in two by the beast.

Pollo tried to rise to his feet, the muscles and tendons of his back protesting, but he fell in a crumpled heap once more in the blood-splattered snow.

The daemon turned back towards him and stalked down the ramp, and Pollo scrambled back away from the monster, the heels of his boots slipping in the ice and snow.

BURIAS-DRAK'SHAL FELT the terror of the Imperial official wash over him like an intoxicating wave, and he relished the sensation. He wanted to kill the man, slowly and excruciatingly, but the rational side of his mind knew that such a thing would anger Marduk, for his order had been clear.

He grinned as the man scrambled back away from him, a pathetic and futile attempt to escape. With sheer force of will, he pushed Drak'shal back, and his features were once again his own, pristine and unmarred, the bullet wound on his cheek already healed. Blood caked his mouth and chin, and he smiled at the man as he stepped towards him.

The engines of the shuttle roared behind him and the ramp began to close, and Burias swung his head around, Drak'shal instantly rearing within him once more.

'Let none escape,' Marduk had ordered.

Burias-Drak'shal turned and leapt onto the shuttle, his talons biting deep into the reinforced hull. He hauled himself hand over hand onto its top, and bounded across its fuselage until he was positioned above the cockpit.

The shuttle began to lift just as the pilot registered the shadow looming above him, and Burias-Drak'shal punched his fist through the glass, grabbing the man around his throat. With one swift motion he ripped the man's throat away.

The shuttle tilted suddenly to the side, its landing gear scraping against rock as the dying pilot fell across the controls. Burias-Drak'shal bounded across the top of the shuttle as it slid over the edge of the landing pad, its engines sending it into a death spin.

He hurled himself across the growing gap and landed in a crouch as the shuttle slammed into the body of the aquila eagle-structure thirty metres below, and erupted into a ball of fire.

He shook his head as he saw the wounded Imperial commander frantically punching a code into the reinforced door that led back into the building, and bounded after the man.

The commander was slamming the door when Burias-Drak'shal reached it, and he smashed it open with the palm of his hand.

The man, all hope of escape lost, collapsed on the floor of the office, staring up fearfully at him.

'Emperor curse you,' breathed the terrified man.

'Too late for that,' remarked Burias, slamming the door closed behind him.

CHAPTER SIX

LIKE A SLOWLY rolling fortress of steel, the ice crawler moved across the ice flow, unaffected by the gale force winds ripping across the desolate landscape. Temperature gauges read that it was minus forty standard, though with wind chill it was closer to minus seventy. Banks of spotlights lit up the ice directly in front of the colossal vehicle. Fog rose from the moon's surface and the wind sent eddies of snow and ice particles ripping across the flows, rendering visibility almost non-existent.

The crawler was immense, over fifty metres long and almost twenty metres high. Its wedge-shaped hull sat upon eight sets of tracks, each more than five metres wide and powered by massive engines.

High up within the control booth of the crawler, Foreman Primaris Solon Marcabus reclined on his well-worn padded seat, his heavy boots up on the dash. He sucked in a long drag on his lho stick and closed his eyes.

'I've decided I don't much like people,' Cholos said, from the steering rig. 'Too much damn trouble. I'll take transporting ore yields over people any day.'

Solon grunted in response, exhaling a cloud of smoke. The expansive cargo holds below were filled to the brim with desperate evacuees. Perdus Skylla was being abandoned in the face of imminent xenos invasion, and it had fallen to the crews of the ice crawlers to aid in the evacuation. In return, they would receive double pay for this run. Small comfort, thought Solon, if they didn't manage to secure a berth off-world.

The cabin was small and stuffy, and the stink of Solon's ashtray, brimming with lho stubs, was strong. He was jolted back and forth as the crawler continued to make its way through the darkness, but he was well used to that. Rosary beads hung above Cholos, and they swung back and forth wildly as the crawler drove slowly over an embankment.

'Guilders,' spat Cholos with a shake of his head, 'think they are so much better than us. Treat us like shit all these years, but who is it that comes to bail them out? Us. And do we get a word of thanks? Nope. Just complaints. "It's too cold, it's too hot, there's not enough room, the water tastes funny". You'd think the bastards would be thankful. Makes me sick.'

Solon grunted again.

'That sergeant, Folches, is the worst of 'em,' said Cholos. 'Left those people back there to die. That is one cold son of a bitch.'

'Nice to hear I made an impression,' said a voice.

Cholos visibly jumped. Solon sighed and slowly opened his eyes. He dropped his feet from the console dash and spun his chair around towards the door to the cabin, though he remained slouched. He blew out a puff of smoke.

Sergeant Folches stood in the doorway, big and imposing in his black and white Interdiction body plate. He had removed his helmet, and his thick-featured face glared down at Solon.

'This is a restricted area, sergeant. Rig personnel only,' said Solon. 'Be so kind as to get the hell out.'

'How long till we get to the Phorcys spaceport?' asked Folches.

'In this storm? Two and a half days, minimum,' said Solon.

The sergeant swore.

'The storm won't lift before then?' he asked.

'You haven't spent much time on the surface, have you?' asked Solon, taking another drag on his lho stick.

'What the hell does that have to do with anything?'

'Once a storm like this has set in, it might not clear for a month, maybe two,' said Solon, stubbing out his lho stick.

'You can't make this heap of crap go any faster?'

'No, sergeant, I can't.'

Folches swore and rubbed a hand across his head.

'Why don't you and your boys just settle down and enjoy the ride,' he said, 'and try to stop the guilders killing each other. They're only women and children, right?'

'Boss,' said Cholos. Solon felt the crawler begin to slow, but he didn't take his eyes of the sergeant.

'You ought to watch your tongue, you whoreson bastard,' said Folches, putting one hand on the autopistol holstered prominently at his hip.

'Easy, big fella,' said Solon. 'All I'm saying is that we are moving as quick as we can, and you coming up here to throw your weight around ain't gonna make us go any faster.'

Folches let out a tense breath and took his hand off his gun.

'What's the problem, anyway?' asked Solon. 'Three days and we'll be off this moon.'

'Something hit the access tunnels leading from Antithon guild to the spaceport.'

Solon frowned.

'Four demi-legions were gone, like that,' said the sergeant, clicking his fingers. 'And Emperor knows how many guilders.'

'Four demi-legions?'

'Four hundred soldiers. The enemy is not on its way to Perdus Skylla,' said the sergeant. 'It is already here.'

Solon bit his lip.

'Boss,' said Cholos, breaking the silence.

'What?' asked Solon in exasperation, turning to face his second in command.

'You better take a look at this.'

Solon spun his chair around, turning his back on the sergeant, and peered out of the small, ice-encased cabin window.

The wind was whipping across the landscape at over a hundred kilometres an hour, and virtually nothing could be seen except the glare of the crawler's spotlight reflected back at them by the snow and ice in the air.

'I don't see a damned thing, Cholos.'

Sergeant Folches leant down at Solon's side, looking out into the storm, and Solon felt his irritation rise.

'Damn it Cholos, what am I looking at?'

'Wait for the wind to drop,' said Cholos.

He slowed the crawler further and the three men looked intently out into the storm. At last the wind fell momentarily and Solon could see a dark, shadowy shape up ahead. It was another crawler, motionless and dark. Then it was hidden as the winds picked up again with a vengeance.

'That's Markham's rig,' said Solon.

'Looks like it, boss,' said Cholos.

'Hail them,' said Solon.

'You recognise it?' asked Folches as Cholos tried to make voice contact with the stationary crawler with the short-ranged vox-caster built into the dash console.

'Yeah,' said Solon. 'It should be at the starport by now. What the hell is it doing out here?'

'There's no response, boss,' said Cholos. The sound of static was hissing from the vox-caster. 'Might be the storm's interference though.'

Solon swore.

'Right, take us alongside it. If it still doesn't respond, then it looks like we'll be getting cold.'

'My squad will come with you,' said Folches.

'That would be appreciated,' said Solon.

THE LIFT HALTED its ascent and drew to a shuddering halt.

'Restricted access. Band XK privilege required,' croaked the robotic voice of the servitor built into one of the interior walls of the lift.

Marduk sighed in impatience.

A panel on one wall bore the symbol of the Adeptus Mechanicus, and the First Acolyte ripped it clear, his gauntlet wrenching the metal out of shape as if it were paper. Wires and cables spilt behind the panel like intestines, sparking and buzzing.

'Open it,' he ordered impatiently.

A mechadendrite tentacle stabbed into the open panel, and Darioq twisted it left and right.

'Access granted,' croaked the servitor as the magos retracted his metallic tentacle, and the lift doors hissed open.

Kol Badar stepped out of the lift in front of Marduk, swinging his combi-bolter from side to side. The lift rose a few centimetres as the Coryphaus's immense weight was removed from the straining winch mechanics.

'Clear,' the towering Coryphaus growled, raising his combi-bolter into a vertical position. Kol Badar held the sacred icon of the Host in the power talons of his left hand, the snarling daemon face of the Latros Sacrum in its centre, slamming the butt of the staff into the ground as Marduk stepped from the lift.

The First Acolyte took a moment to get his bearings before marching into the guildmaster's office.

'Stay, *Darioq-Grendh'al,*' he said over his shoulder, exerting the force of his will into his intonation, forcibly commanding the daemon within the corrupted magos.

Burias was leaning casually against a wall, drinking from a bottle that had had its neck smashed off. His mouth and chin were covered in blood, and a man lay shivering on the floor before him.

The icon bearer drained the fiery liquid from the bottle and smiled at Marduk, wiping his mouth with the back of one hand.

'Stand to attention when your seniors are present, warrior,' barked Kol Badar, the vox-amplifiers built into his quad-tusked helmet making his voice even more of an animalistic growl than usual.

Making no attempt to hurry, Burias languidly rose from his slouch and tossed the empty bottle away. It shattered on the floor.

'Consumption of all but necessary sustenance is a sin that leads to weakness, icon bearer,' snapped Marduk. 'You will submit yourself to three months of fasting and flagellation once we return to the *Infidus Diabolus.*'

'I am duly castigated, my master,' said Burias, bowing his head in a show of obeisance and mock remorse. Marduk's eyes narrowed.

Burias held a hand out to Kol Badar.

'My icon?' he said.

The Coryphaus flicked the heavy icon at the smaller Astartes warrior with far more force than was needed, but Burias caught it deftly in his hand.

'Enough,' said Marduk. 'This is the commander?' He motioned with his chin towards the man shivering on the ground.

'It is, my master,' said Burias, running his hands lovingly over the spiked length of his icon, as if he had been separated from it for years and was savouring being reunited. 'Alive, as you wished.'

·Marduk knelt down before the man, who stared up at him fearfully, his face waxy and pale.

'You have something that I want, little man,' said Marduk, removing his skull-faced helmet and handing it to Burias, 'and you are going to tell me where it is.'

'Wha… wha… what is it you want?' managed the man, gritting his teeth in pain, gingerly cradling his left arm in his hand. He stared up at Marduk, a mixture of fear and defiance in his eyes.

'A person, if you could call it that,' said Marduk. 'Someone who was posted here, at this very facility: an adept of the weakling Machine-God.'

'What do you want with them?'

Marduk reached out towards the man, his movements slow and almost caring. The guildmaster recoiled from his grasp, but there was nowhere for him to run.

'You are injured, I see,' said Marduk, taking the man's arm carefully in his hands. 'This must hurt.'

With a slow twisting motion, Marduk turned the man's hand over, making the shattered bones grind against one another. The man screamed in agony and Marduk twisted it again. Then he stopped.

'Do not question me again, little man. This was punishment for doing so. Now, tell me, where is… What was its name?'

Marduk turned his head around, looking back towards the adjoining room and the lift.

'Darioq-Grendh'al,' he barked. 'Come.'

Like a hound coming to its master's call, Magos Darioq entered the room, his steps slow and mechanical. Having been allowed to reconstruct his servo-harness, four massive robotic arms emerged from his back, two coming around his sides, and two over his shoulders, like the stabbing tails of an insect. Black veins pulsed within the servo-arms as the lines between organic, mechanical and daemonic were increasingly blurred, and one of the arms twitched awkwardly as he walked.

The guildmaster's agonised eyes were locked on the magos, who wore a robe of black in place of his red Mechanicus garb. The red glow of Darioq's augmented left eye gleamed malignly from within his deep cowl.

'What is the name of the target?' Marduk asked.

'Explorator First Class Daenae,' said Magos Darioq in his monotone voice, 'originally of the Konor Adeptus Mechanicus research world of UL01.02, assigned to c14.8.87.i, Perdus Skylla, for recon/salvage of the Dvorak-class interstellar freighter *Flames of Perdition*, which reappeared within Segmentum Tempestus in 942.M41 and crashed onto the surface of c14.8.87.i, Perdus Skylla, in 944.M41 after being missing presumed lost in warp storm anomaly xi.024.396 in 432.M35.'

Marduk turned back towards the guildmaster with the hint of a smile on his face.

'How foolish of me to have forgotten its name,' he said. The smile dropped from his face. 'Where is this Explorator Daenae? Tell me now, or you shall be further punished. And I promise you, the pain you have already experienced will be but a fraction of what you will come to know should you displease me further.'

'I don't know who you mean,' hissed the man.

Marduk sighed.

'You are lying to me,' he said, and gave the man's arm a further twist. This time he did not relent quickly, and he ground the broken bones of the guildmaster's arm against each other with vigour.

Behind Marduk, Burias grinned at the man's pain.

'The explorator was assigned to this facility,' said Marduk over the guildmaster's screams of torment, 'therefore you know where it is. Tell me now, or your death will not be swift in coming to you.'

The guildmaster's eyes were shut tightly against the pain, and he passed out suddenly, going limp in Marduk's arms. The First Acolyte threw the man's arm down in disgust, the bones of the forearm bent almost at right angles.

'Permission to speak, Marduk, First Acolyte of the Word Bearers Legion of Astartes, genetic descendent of the glorified Primarch Lorgar,' said Darioq.

'*Glorified* Primarch Lorgar?' asked Marduk with a grin. 'You are learning, Enslaved. Permission to speak granted.'

'With the surgical removal of the inhibitor functions of my logic-engines, and the rearrangement of the frontal cortex of three of my brain-units, I find…' began Darioq-Grendh'al.

'Get to the point,' interrupted Marduk.

'Summary: it is not required that the location of Explorator First Class Daenae be obtained from the brain-unit of Guildmaster Pollo,' the magos intoned.

'What gibberish does it speak? Who is this Guildmaster Pollo?' growled Kol Badar.

'Guildmaster Pollo is the flesh unit whose radial and ulna bones of the left arm have been rendered inoperative and non-functioning by Marduk, First Acolyte of the Word Bearers Legion of Astartes, genetic descendent of the glorified Primarch Lorgar,' replied Darioq.

Burias snorted his amusement, though Kol Badar growled and took a step towards the black-robed magos, electricity coursing into life around his power talons. Marduk forestalled his advance with a raised hand, and looked at the magos intently.

'What do you mean, Darioq-Grendh'al? Speak simply,' he said.

'In order to garner the required information about the whereabouts of Explorator Daenae, all that is necessary is to gain access to the cortex hub of this bastion facility.'

Marduk turned to look at Burias. The icon bearer shrugged and Marduk turned back towards Darioq with a sigh.

'What do you need to find the location of the explorator?' asked Marduk, speaking in a slow and measured voice.

'In order to access the cortex hub of this bastion facility, a sub-retinal scan of the commanding officer must be made,' said Darioq.

A hint of a smile touched Marduk's lips, and he turned towards Burias.

'Fetch me his eyes, icon bearer.'

Burias grinned and flexed his fingers.

'As you wish, my master,' replied the icon bearer.

THE HEAVY CRAWLER doors slid aside with a sound like a mountain shifting, and snow and ice billowed into the cargo hold. The frightened refugees from Antithon

Guild were huddled as best they could against the far wall, protecting their faces from the biting wind.

'Let's do this quickly,' shouted Solon over the wind. At his side, Cholos gave him the thumbs up. Solon looked towards Sergeant Folches, who stood with his soldiers. The soldier nodded.

'Keep her running,' shouted Solon to Cholos. 'The last thing we want out here is the engines seizing up.'

Solon pulled his mask and respirator over his face, obscuring his features, and turned around awkwardly in his bulky exposure suit. He grabbed the sides of the ice-encased metal ladder on the exterior of the crawler and began to climb down to the ground.

His breathing sounding heavy in his ears and he felt a momentary stab of claustrophobia. He hated these suits. The pair of circular synth-glass goggle-panes obscured his peripheral vision and the suit made all movement heavy and laboured. Still, they kept the cold out, and without one he wouldn't last more than an hour in these conditions.

He climbed down the eight metres from the cargo hold to the ground and stepped onto the ice. The wind threatened to knock him down, and he steadied himself with a hand on a massive wheel.

He turned around to look up at the bulk of Markham's lifeless crawler as the others descended. It reared, black and imposing, like an ancient monolith, dark and dead.

With his mask in place, he had no means to communicate with the others except by hand signals, and he pointed towards the front of the crawler. Sergeant Folches nodded his head and signalled for him and his men to take the lead.

'Be my guest, you bastard,' said Solon, gesturing his ascent.

The soldiers had their weapons in hand as they approached the derelict crawler. It was clear to Solon that its engines had not been running for some time, for there was a thick layer of snow across the crawler, including over its engine stack. Normally, a crawler's engineer maintained enough heat in the boilers that no snow would settle. Snow was banked up high against one side of the massive crawler, and Solon guessed that it must have been sitting dormant for at least five hours for such an amount of snow to have settled against it.

The white-armoured Skyllan Interdiction soldiers began moving towards the front of the crawler, their guns raised to their shoulders. With swift hand signals, the sergeant sent two men ahead on point, and they covered each other's blind spots as they moved forward. Solon and Cholos stomped through the snow behind the soldiers.

'Doesn't look like anyone is home,' Solon said to himself.

One of the crawler's immense tracks had been ripped loose, and it lay twisted and broken beneath the behemoth. This was no accident; nothing could tear a crawler's track loose except an immense mining detonation, or concentrated fire by a well-armed enemy.

Solon saw one of the soldiers gesture up at the side of the crawler, and he followed the direction of his hand. A hole had been blasted through the side of the immense transport, roughly the size of a man's head, scorch marks surrounding the strike.

Solon walked closer to the side of the crawler, peering at a line of smaller marks up the side of one of its wheels. Splinters of barbed metal were embedded in the steel rim off the wheel.

He peered closely at one of the splinters. It was viciously barbed, and he winced at its cruel design. Had it been embedded in a living body, the flesh would be torn to shreds in attempting to pull it free.

Solon jerked as a heavy hand slapped him on the shoulder, and he looked up into the faceless visor of one of the soldiers, who motioned for him to move on. Solon nodded his head, and began slogging through the snow and ice once more.

He stumbled as his foot caught on something, and fell awkwardly onto his front. A soldier helped him back to his feet and he looked to see what he had tripped over.

A hand, blue and frozen, was protruding from the snow.

Solon swore and staggered back, pointing frantically at the frozen hand. The soldier nodded grimly and motioned for him to keep moving.

Tearing his eyes from the grisly display, Solon hurried to catch up with the rest of the group. His breathing was coming in short, sharp gasps, sounding too loud in the enclosed space of his mask.

The group moved around the front of the crawler, and Solon saw that the reflective plasglass of the cabin had been shattered. Several holes had been punched through the front chassis of the crawler, and Solon marvelled at the immense power of the blasts. The front of the crawlers were heavily armoured, allowing them to push through ice, rock and snow if necessary, and he had been led to believe that even a lascannon would be unable to pierce its reinforced layers. Whatever had struck this crawler though had made a mockery of his teaching.

The soldiers moved warily around the side of the crawler, and Solon froze as the sergeant raised his hand.

One of the soldiers dropped to one knee at the corner of the crawler and risked a quick glance around it before giving the all clear and moving on.

They were out of the worst of the wind behind the lee-side of the crawler, and Solon breathed a sigh of relief to be out of the relentless gale. The snow was not banked up so heavily here, and with a flurry of hand signals, the sergeant relayed his orders.

One of the cargo bay doors was wide open, and one of the soldiers warily climbed the icy ladder up to the cavernous opening. As he crouched below the lip of the cargo bay, he raised his lasgun and clicked on the powerful light under-slung below the barrel.

Rising up on the ladder, the soldier held his lasgun to his shoulder and swung the beam of his light around within the crawler's cargo hold. He signalled the all clear, and climbed up into the interior, disappearing from sight. The other soldiers moved towards the ladder, Solon being herded in the centre of the group.

Sergeant Folches and one of his men ascended quickly, while the other members of the squad covered them, and then Solon was signalled to climb up.

His bulky exposure suit made the climb difficult and he was breathing hard as he reached the top. Sergeant Folches grabbed him under one arm and hauled him over the edge, his pistol held at the ready in his other hand.

The sergeant held up a hand for Solon to stay put and his soldiers began advancing through the darkened cargo hold, the focused beams of their lights swinging left and right. They were swallowed by the darkness as they penetrated deeper into the stricken crawler, leaving Solon standing alone.

He turned around, the weak lights mounted on either shoulder of his exposure suit illuminating the area around him in their yellow glow. One of the lights flickered and buzzed, and Solon hit it with one hand. The flickering stopped, but then the light gave out all together, and he swore.

Feeling exposed and alone, he moved further into the cargo hold, trying to see the soldiers' lights. He couldn't see them, and the sound of his own breathing filled his ears. He also noticed evidence of fighting. Blackened scorch marks marred the sides of ore containers and severed cables hung limp from holes blasted in the walls.

The massive ore containers were loaded on top of each other and tightly packed, forming a maze of narrow corridors within the vast hold. The containers disappeared in the gloom above him, and Solon felt a rivulet of sweat run down his spine.

Turning a corner, he almost stepped on the corpse. It wore the uniform of a crawler orderly, and Solon recoiled in horror and disgust. The man looked as if he had died in absolute agony, his mouth wide in a scream, his eyes huge and staring, and his body frozen in a contorted death spasm. His hands were twisted like claws, and his legs were bent beneath him. It looked as though he had been writhing in agony as he had died. Solon saw a line of wicked splinters across his chest, embedded in his flesh.

Solon turned away, feeling his stomach heave. He ripped his mask away and vomited the contents of his stomach onto the floor. He pulled his canteen from one of the deep pockets of his exposure suit, and took a swig of the cold water, cleansing his mouth and spitting it out onto the floor.

He didn't look again at the corpse as he walked away, sucking in the cold air in deep breaths.

It felt like the soldiers had been gone for hours, though it was more likely just minutes, and Solon felt panic begin to rise within him. What had hit the crawler? What enemy was loose in the darkness? And was it still here?

The walls formed by the containers rearing up on either side of him seemed to close in, and Solon's breath was coming in shorter gasps.

'Stay here, he says. To hell with that,' said Solon, deciding to find Sergeant Folches and his soldiers. He might not like the man, but if there was still an enemy in the crawler, he would feel a lot more comfortable with the armed soldiers.

Thinking he heard a noise behind him, Solon spun around, his heart beating wildly. There was nothing there. The weak illumination given off by his sole functioning shoulder lamp made the shadows jump, and Solon's eyes darted around in fear.

'There's nothing here,' he said to himself.

He turned around to continue his search for the sergeant, and his lamp illuminated a pale face less than a metre behind him.

Solon staggered backwards, a strangled cry tearing from his throat and his heart lurching. His sudden movement made the light from his lamp swing wildly, making shadows dance in front of him, though his eyes were locked on the motionless figure.

He heard a shout, and boots pounded across the grilled flooring, coming closer, but still the face stared up at him.

It was a child, no more than ten years old by his reckoning, his face pale and gaunt. Solon stared at the boy in horror, as if the ghosts of his past had risen to haunt him; for a fraction of a second, the child was the spitting image of his son, dead these last eighteen years.

As the soldiers arrived, they shone their lights upon the child, and Solon saw that he was of flesh and blood, not some ethereal phantom come to haunt him, and his resemblance to his dead son faded. The boy's eyes were deeply ringed by shadow, and he recoiled from the bright lights, shielding his eyes.

The boy looked up in fright as Sergeant Folches and one of his soldiers appeared, their weapons levelled at the boy. In the cold light of the soldier's lights, his face took on a blue tinge. He must be half-frozen, thought Solon. He let out a long breath, and tried to force his pounding heart-rate to slow.

'Where in the hell did he come from?' barked Folches, sliding the visor of his helmet up.

'No idea,' said Solon, hardly able to take his eyes off the boy.

'You, boy,' said Folches. 'Are you the only one here?'

His face fearful, the boy merely stared up at the soldier.

'What happened here, boy?' asked Folches again, more forcefully. The boy backed away a step, looking as if he was going to bolt at any second.

'Ease up, sergeant,' said Solon, fumbling at one of his pockets. He pulled out a protein pack, and tore off its foil seal.

'You hungry?' he asked the boy, offering the food.

The boy merely stared back at him, and Solon took a small bite of the protein pack. It was bland and tasteless, but he nodded his head and made a show of enjoying it. He saw the boy lick his lips, and this time when Solon offered it to him he snatched it eagerly.

'You find any survivors?' Solon asked the sergeant in a low voice, though he kept his eyes on the boy.

'No,' said Folches. 'We found some... remains, but nowhere near as many as I would have expected.'

'Think they got away? Fled on foot, or something?' asked Solon.

'I don't think so,' said Folches. 'Whatever hit here, it hit hard and fast. I don't think anyone got away.'

'What then? They just disappeared? There must have been a couple of hundred folks onboard.'

'They were taken,' said the boy suddenly.

Solon and Folches exchanged a look.

'Who took them, son?' asked Solon.

'Ghosts,' said the boy, his eyes haunted.

BOOK TWO: GHOSTS

'Hate the xenos as you hate the infidel, as you hate the non-believer. Feel not mercy for them, for their very existence is profane. What right have they to live, those that are Other?'

– Kor Phaeron, Master of the Faith

CHAPTER SEVEN

THE FOUR LAND Raiders roared across the ice, passing the burnt-out shells of enemy vehicles. The bodies of men lay strewn around the smoking wrecks, their blood staining the snow beneath them.

'The last known location of the target is here,' said Kol Badar, indicating a position on the schematics that appeared in flickering green lines upon the data-slate. He was seated within the enclosed space of the second Land Raider, his hulking form filling the space around him, making the interior cramped. He had removed his tusked helmet, and the red lights of the interior of the tank gave his broad face a daemonic glow.

A passage from the Book of Lorgar was etched upon the skin of his right cheek, a gift cut from the face of Jarulek, back on the Imperial world of Tanakreg before the Dark Apostle fell.

Marduk too had borne a similar passage on his cheek, though it had been obliterated when the Dark Apostle had shot half his face off. He had removed his skull-faced helmet and stowed it in an arched niche above his head, alongside a pair of lit blood-candles, and the dark outline of the mark of Lorgar was clearly visible on his forehead.

Incense wafted from one of the daemon-headed braziers, filling the air with its cloying stench.

Marduk snatched the data-slate from the Coryphaus, and looked where Kol Badar had indicated.

'What is this structure?' he asked.

'A mining facility, a hundred and fifty kilometres to the east. But there is a problem.'

'Of course there is,' spat Marduk. 'Well?'

'The mining facility is located on the ocean floor. It is over ten thousand metres below the surface of the ice.'

'Lorgar's blood,' said Burias from the other side of the Land Raider. Blood still caked the icon bearer's lips and chin, and Marduk glared at him for a moment.

'On the ocean floor,' he said.

'That is correct, First Acolyte,' replied Kol Badar, 'if the information the magos extracted can be trusted.'

'It can,' said Marduk. He balled his right hand into a fist and slammed it down onto an armrest carved in the likeness of a spinal column.

He quickly recovered his composure, and quoted from the Epistles of Kor Phaeron, the revered Master of the Faith whom he had served under during the campaign on Calth fighting against the hated sons of Guilliman.

'*Through our travails we journey further down the blessed spiral,*' he quoted. '*Through pain and struggle and toil we prove ourselves before the true gods. Each new obstacle should be welcomed as a test of faith, for only the strong and true walk the Eightfold Path of Enlightenment.*'

'Indeed,' said Kol Badar dryly.

'You have formulated a battle order?' asked Marduk. They had been back within the Land Raiders for less than fifteen minutes, but he knew that Kol Badar's keen strategic mind would have already concocted a dozen plans to ensure victory for the Host, each one more complete than the last.

'There is an access tunnel beneath the ice here,' said the Coryphaus, indicating on the schematic map with one of his massive armoured fingers. 'It runs for two hundred kilometres, connecting this habitation base with a starport located to the west. Air recycling hubs connect the tunnel to the surface at intermittent positions,' he said, stabbing his finger into the data-slate at several points along the line of the access tunnel. 'This one is twenty-five kilometres from the habitation base. We proceed to that air-recycling hub by Land Raider, across these ice flows here, and here, and approach from the south. The wind will be behind us, and we should be able to approach without detection, or at least neutralise any resistance before a defence can be established.'

'The defences of this world are pitiful,' said Marduk. 'The majority of the standing defence force has already been vacated. Darioq-Grendh'al picked up an incoming transmission as he gathered the information. The xenos invasion is expected to make planet-fall within the next sixty-three hours. Sixty-two hours now,' he corrected.

'Sixty-two hours,' said Kol Badar. 'This foolish mission cannot be achieved in sixty-two hours.'

'Find a way,' retorted Marduk.

'It cannot be done,' said Kol Badar hotly. 'It could not be done even were we to encounter zero opposition. I suggest that we vacate this place. There is nothing of value to our Legion here.'

'I am not asking for your council, Kol Badar,' said Marduk. 'You are the Coryphaus. You enact *my* will. I am giving you an order; make it happen.'

'The xenos will have commenced their invasion before we are back on the surface,' said Kol Badar.

'Explain to me how that changes anything?' snapped Marduk, losing patience. 'If they get in our way, we kill them. It is not complicated.'

'You wish to be here in the midst of a full-scale invasion? With less than thirty warriors?'

'That is the voice of cowardice, Kol Badar,' said Marduk, his voice low and dangerous. 'You shame the Legion and the position of Coryphaus with your fear.'

Kol Badar's eyes flashed, and he ground his teeth, clenching his power talons. Burias, sitting opposite, grinned.

'You go too far, you whoreson whelp,' said Kol Badar, his eyes blazing with fury.

'Learn your place, Kol Badar,' growled Marduk, leaning in to the bigger warrior and snarling in his face. 'Jarulek is dead. *I* am the power of the Host. Me! The Host is mine, and mine alone. *You* are mine, and I will discard you if you prove of no use to me.'

Kol Badar bared his teeth, and Marduk could see him fighting to restrain himself from lashing out. With the fall of Jarulek, there was no question as to who was next in line. Marduk, as First Acolyte, was rightfully the leader of the Host, at least until such a time as the Council of Sicarus deemed otherwise.

Marduk knew Kol Badar well. They had fought alongside each other in a thousand wars since the fall of the Warmaster Horus, and over that time he had come to understand, and despise, what he was. The Coryphaus was a deeply regimented warrior, who clung to ordained command structures and protocols with an almost holy fervour. Marduk had always seen it as a weakness, and had goaded the Coryphaus regarding it, many times.

'You should have been born into Guilliman's Legion,' he had said on more than one occasion, drawing a parallel between Kol Badar's stifling adherence to command structures and official stratagems of the puritanical weaklings of the Ultramarines.

Doubtless, there was a certain strength in Kol Badar's dogmatism. The Coryphaus had commanded the Host in battle thousands of times, and his understanding of the ebb and flow of combat, when to push forward and when to pull back, was second to none. In truth, Marduk had come to value the keen, perhaps brilliant, strategic mind of the Coryphaus, though his refusal to adopt more unconventional tactics was infuriating at times.

For all that, Marduk felt assured that if he pushed home his unquestionable position in the hierarchy of the Host, then the Coryphaus would back down. After ten thousand years of adherence to strict military hierarchy, Kol Badar would be lost to madness and insanity were he to abandon it.

Respect can wait, thought Marduk. For now, it is enough that he does what I wish.

'I am the leader of the Host,' continued Marduk, still staring into Kol Badar's eyes, 'and you will obey my will.'

Marduk felt the power of Chaos build within him, as if the gods of the immaterium were pleased. Things writhed painfully beneath the skin of his skull, and he smiled as he saw Kol Badar's eyes widen.

'Never question me, Kol Badar,' said Marduk evenly. 'Continue.'

Kol Badar's thick jaw tensed, but he lowered his gaze from Marduk's, and stabbed a finger towards the schematic in his hands.

'We use that hub to gain entry to the tunnel, and proceed along the access way into the heart of the hab-station. We secure one of the lifts located here,' he growled, pointing, 'which will take us to the mining facility on the ocean floor. This here,' he said, zooming in on the data-slate, through dozens of floors and focusing on a specific part of the mining facility, 'is the last recorded location of the explorator. The hulk crashed to the ocean floor around twelve kilometres distant from the facility. Here, the explorator boarded a maintenance submersible to investigate the wreck. He never returned. I would surmise that the explorator fool is still within the hulk, or dead.'

Marduk nodded.

'Fine,' he said.

'I still say this is a fool's errand,' said Kol Badar.

'Your opinion has been duly noted, Coryphaus,' said Marduk. 'Now, pass the word. We move on that air recycling hub.'

APPROACHING THE AIR recycling station unobserved had been pathetically easy. The armed forces of the moon were virtually non-existent, most of them having already been evacuated, and the one patrol they had encountered on the ice flows had been destroyed with consummate ease.

It was insulting, Kol Badar thought as he had killed.

Clouds of steam rose from the turbine vents that cycled air into the tunnels deep in the ice below, and the hub station had been protected merely by thick rockcrete walls and a reinforced door, half buried in the snow. There were no guards posted on its walls.

There had been no sign of a living presence at all, cowering inside against the storm like frightened rodents, Kol Badar had correctly surmised.

He had ripped the door from its hinges and hurled it away, before stalking into the interior of the complex. The Land Raiders were situated half a kilometre away, hidden completely in the storm, where they would remain until this fool's errand of a task was completed.

He had been angry when the first shouts of warning from the Imperials within the complex had reached his ears, and he stormed into their midst, ripping them apart with concentrated bursts of his combi-bolter, tearing arms from sockets with his power talon.

It had taken only minutes to gain control of the facility.

It was strange, though; it appeared that the enemy had known they were coming, and prepared some hasty defences. No, that was not correct. They knew *something* was coming, but they had not barricaded the door out onto the ice, but rather, the entrance to the stairwell that led down to the access tunnel fifty metres below, as if they expected an attack from there.

'Don't try to understand them,' he reminded himself. 'They are heathen, blinded fools. Their ways are madness.'

Kol Badar levelled his combi-bolter at the last of the civilian workers. The man was breathing hard, staring up at the towering Terminator-armoured warrior in abject terror.

A waste of ammunition, the Coryphaus decided, and lifted the barrel of his weapon from the target. A flash of hope reared in the Imperial citizen's eyes, but that was extinguished quickly as Kol Badar stepped menacingly towards him.

'Please, no,' wailed the man, shaking his head as the Coryphaus loomed above him.

Kol Badar grabbed the man around one shoulder, power talons digging deep into flesh. Then he slammed the pistol-grip butt of his combi-bolter into his face, splintering his nose. The man's skull was caved inwards by the shocking blow, killing him instantly, but the Coryphaus continued to strike, until the man's face was an unrecognisable mash of blood and flesh.

He dropped the Imperial worker to the ground, feeling a small amount of satisfaction, though it did little to abate his simmering rage.

Why had Jarulek left him, allowing the whelp Marduk to assume control of the Host? For months, he had raged at Jarulek's failing. Long had he hated the First Acolyte, and long had he waited to kill him, just as Marduk had killed Kol Badar's blood brother so long ago.

He would have killed Marduk then and there had not Jarulek stayed his hand.

'Not now,' the Dark Apostle had said, though at that time he had been nothing more than a First Acolyte himself. 'He will be yours to kill, but not yet. He has a purpose yet to perform.'

It had been three hundred years into the Great Crusade, and Kol Badar had waited long and impatiently for his time to come, but waited he had, through all the long spanning millennia, until at last his time had come.

'If we both return, then you may kill Marduk, my Coryphaus. Your honour will be fulfilled,' Jarulek had said, just moments before he had descended into the heart of the xenos pyramid on Tanakreg. The pleasure of finally being given free rein to kill the whelp had been ecstatic. That had been shattered when only Marduk had returned.

'Damn you, Jarulek,' said Kol Badar to himself.

* * *

'You SHOULD DISPOSE of him,' said Burias in a voice low enough for none but Marduk to hear him. 'The insubordinate old bastard is long past his time. He is a weight hanging around the neck of the Host, and he will drag it down, slowly but surely.'

'You still hunger for power, Burias?' asked Marduk.

'Of course,' replied Burias sharply, his eyes flashing. 'Such is our teaching.'

'That is true, icon bearer,' said Marduk.

'He does not fear you,' said Burias.

'What?' asked Marduk.

'Kol Badar. He feared Jarulek, we all did, but he does not fear you.'

'Perhaps not yet,' agreed Marduk, 'but he will come to. I am changing, Burias. I feel the touch of the gods upon me.'

Burias sniffed, savouring the air. There was an electrical tang in the air that left an acrid taste upon his tongue, a sensation he had long come to embrace and recognise for what it was: Chaos.

Jarulek had exuded a potent aura so strong that it made those of lesser faith bleed from their ears, and this was the same, though admittedly less potent, force.

'If he does not learn his place,' said Marduk in a low voice, 'and soon, then I shall allow you to take him. I would enjoy watching you rend him limb from limb.'

Burias grinned savagely.

'But that time is not yet,' reminded Marduk.

'No LIFE SIGNS detected, Coryphaus,' said one of the members of the 13th, looking at the gleaming red flashes on the blister-screen of his corrupted auspex, 'though there are cooling heat signatures ahead. Possible weapons discharge.'

'Understood,' growled the war leader.

Burias placed one hand upon the cold metal surface of the door and closed his eyes.

'The air within is rich with fear,' he said.

'Good. That will work in our favour,' said Kol Badar. 'Burias, take point. Go.'

Without ceremony, Burias kicked the door off its hinges, wrenching the reinforced steel out of shape and sending it smashing inwards.

A steel landing extended beyond, and Burias moved forward warily, his bolt pistol in one hand, the holy icon of the Host in his other. The landing was narrow, and a steel stairway descended from it. Moving swiftly and silently, elegant and perfectly balanced despite his bulk, Burias stepped down the steel stairs that led into a corridor. The hallway extended ten metres ahead, before turning sharply to the right.

The walls, carved from solid ice, radiated cold, though he barely registered the sub-zero temperature. Moving swiftly forwards, his every daemonically enhanced sense alert, Burias rounded the corner and came up against a mesh-link fence that rose from floor to ceiling, barring the way forward. A chained gate was set into the fence, and a frozen corpse was slumped outside it.

Curious, Burias moved forwards. It was the body of a man, wearing the same white plas armour as the soldiers they had fought at the Imperial bastion. One hand was clutching at the locked gate. Clearly, the man had been shot down while attempting to flee, but the locked gate had barred his progress. Half a dozen dark splinters were embedded in his armoured back plate, and Burias frowned.

The icon bearer holstered his bolt pistol and grasped the heavy chain that secured the gate shut.

With a sharp jerk, he snapped the heavy chain and dropped it to the ground. He wrenched the gate open and the corpse of the enemy soldier was dragged across the floor as it swung wide; frozen, dead fingers locked around the mesh-links.

Stepping over the corpse, Burias continued along the corridor. After several twisting turns and intersections, it opened out into an access tunnel at least fifty metres wide. Down the centre of the tunnel was a sunken carriageway, and two wide platforms ran alongside it.

Moving warily into the tunnel, Burias stepped over wreckage and debris, amongst which were sprawled a number of corpses. Their bodies had been slashed by blades and ripped apart by unfamiliar projectile weapons. Several burnt out vehicles were scattered throughout the tunnel, like the discarded toys of a giant. Several were upturned and leaning against the walls, while others had fallen into the sunken carriageway.

Climbing atop one of the ruined armoured vehicles, Burias squinted into the distance in each direction. There was no living soul in sight, though the gently curving tunnel ensured that the icon bearer could see no more than half a kilometre ahead.

He dropped onto the bonnet of the white-armoured APC, which buckled inwards beneath his weight, and stepped lightly to the floor.

'All clear,' he said into his vox-relay. 'Looks like someone got here before us.'

As the remainder of the Host moved on his position, he dropped to his haunches to inspect one of the corpses.

It was another of the white-armoured soldiers, whose face was purple and had swollen like a balloon. Burias plucked a long, barbed splinter from the corpse's neck, and studied it with interest. It was half the length of a finger, and so thin that if he turned it sideways it was all but invisible. He lifted it carefully to his lips, and his tongue flashed out to sample the serrated tip.

The taste was acrid, and he registered unknown toxic agents upon the splinter. He tasted blood as the barbed shard sliced his tongue.

Xenos toxins entered his bloodstream, and his limbs began to shudder. A slight sweat broke out on his brow, and he lifted a shaking hand in front of his eyes, attempting to keep it steady, but failing.

He felt the unknown serum coursing its way towards his twin hearts, but remained unconcerned. Indeed, as soon as the venom had entered his bloodstream, his bio-engineered defences had activated, and were even now isolating and breaking down the xenos poison. His heart rate increased as his body combated the threat, pumping his blood swiftly through his oolitic kidney implant, cleansing it of the deadly serum.

After less than a minute, Burias's heart rate had returned to normal and the shaking sickness had left him.

'Intriguing,' he said to himself.

THE COTERIES HAD been moving through the tunnel system for about an hour. They had encountered no sign of life, though there was evidence of furious firefights. The tunnels were as silent as tombs, and cold light blazed down upon them from the rows of strip-lights overhead. Abruptly the lights flickered abruptly and died.

'FIVE UNKNOWNS, MOVING on our position,' barked Namar-sin, breaking the silence. 'Coming fast. Very fast.'

Marduk and the Stetavoc Space Marines of Namar-sin's coterie were instantly moving for cover. A faint whine could be heard, approaching rapidly.

'Ware the north,' Marduk bellowed, just as five blurred shapes roared out of the darkness of the side tunnel, moving with impossible speed. They scythed through the air, skimming two metres above the ground and banked sharply into the access tunnel. They were as sleek and deadly as knives, and shot forward as their engines were gunned.

Khalaxis and his coterie were caught in the open, and before they could even raise their weapons to fire, three of their number were cut down beneath a hail of barbed projectiles.

Another was dropped as the jetbikes streaked through the coterie, a curved blade slicing off one of the warrior brother's arms, severing it at the elbow.

Then the jetbikes were past, hurtling by the Word Bearers and jinking around the scattered debris.

Bolters coughed, lighting up the darkness, but they were too slow and the enemy too fast. One of the Anointed unleashed the fury of his reaper autocannon, and hundreds of high calibre rounds chased the jetbikes as they banked around in a wide circle, passing behind the wreckage of the derailed carriages of the rail conveyance. The autocannon tore through the carriages of the train and ripped out great chunks from the rockcrete walls, but even the enhanced targeting sensors built into the Anointed's Terminator armour could not match the speed of the enemy.

Empty shell casings fell like rain from the mighty weapon, but the jetbikes roared on through the darkness unscathed. A missile, launched by one of Namar-sin's Havoc Space Marines, streaked through the darkness towards one of the jetbikes as it rounded the debris. With preternatural reflexes, the jetbike's rider spun his vehicle around in a spiralling corkscrew roll, and the missile passed beneath it harmlessly, impacting in a fiery explosion against the wall.

Marduk fired his bolt pistol on semi-auto at the enemy silhouetted against the flames of the explosion, but even though he had compensated for their speed, still he was too slow.

Two more of Khalaxis's coterie were cut down as they scrambled for cover, and then the jetbikes were gone, disappearing up the tunnel that they had emerged from only seconds before.

Kol Badar was roaring orders, and the remains of Khalaxis's 17th coterie dragged their fallen brethren into cover.

The one-armed Namar-sin and his heavy weapon toting Havoc warriors rose from their position and ran forwards, half-dropping into cover behind a wrecked Imperial vehicle while others took up position behind rockcrete pillars. They readied their heavy weapons, hefting them to shoulders or bracing them in their arms, their stances wide as they sought targets.

'More hostiles inbound,' shouted Sabtec.

'Where?' snapped Kol Badar.

'Behind us,' replied Namar-sin, and Marduk swore.

'Sabtec, protect the rear. Enfilading fire,' ordered Kol Badar. The warriors of the 13th moved instantly into position, moving with practiced efficiency. All the warrior brothers were in cover, with one line facing north, one west.

'Khalaxis, report,' ordered Marduk.

'One dead, one as good as,' growled the towering champion of the 17th.

The Anointed split, two moving to join the 13th in the rear, the other two standing with Kol Badar at the entrance to the north tunnel.

'Burias,' hissed Marduk, as he dropped in alongside Sabtec, watching the rear. He couldn't see anything moving in the distance, but, respectful of the speed of the enemy, he judged that that did not mean much.

'Yes, my lord?' came the silken response on the vox-net. 'Guard Darioq-Grendh'al.'

Burias was slow to respond, and Marduk read the resistance to his orders in the silence.

'Protect him, icon bearer,' snapped Marduk. 'He dies, and you die.'

BURIAS CROUCHED ATOP the wreckage of one of the train's carriages, sniffing the air. He sensed something nearby, but could not locate its whereabouts.

Movement out of the corner of his eye attracted his attention, and he snapped his head towards it, emitting a low growl. Even with his daemon-enhanced witch-sight, he could see nothing.

'Burias,' said Marduk, and the icon bearer hissed in frustration.

'Fine,' he replied, giving the area where he had sensed movement a final glare.

As he dropped down from the carriage to the cracked plascrete platform below, a whip-thin figure crawled forward across the top of the carriage behind him, its form vague as if it dragged the surrounding darkness around it like a shroud.

The icon bearer flicked a glance over his shoulder, and the shape melted into the shadows. In an instant, it was once more invisible, and Burias turned away, jogging towards Magos Darioq.

The stink of Chaos was strong around the magos, who was standing immobile behind the twisted wreckage of what may once have been an Imperial vehicle, oblivious to the preparations going on around him.

'Move there,' snapped Burias, giving the magos a shove. Darioq-Grendh'al walked mechanically forward, each slow step accompanied by the hiss and wheeze of servos.

'Here they come again,' said Kol Badar in his warning growl.

'Kill them, in Lorgar's name!' roared Marduk.

'CONTACT FROM THE east,' said Sabtec, his voice calm and measured.

Marduk glanced around the twisted metal he was taking cover behind, and saw a number of lithe figures darting from cover to cover, heading towards them up the tunnel. Even with his advanced vision and the supplementary enhancements provided by his helmet, they were difficult to focus on, for they moved so quickly.

The First Acolyte narrowed his eyes, as he focused on one of the xenos humanoids. For a moment, it was clearly visible as it crouched, the long fingers of one hand splayed out on the floor.

Its slim body was encased in a form-fitting suit of reflective black armour that moulded to its movements: a far cry from the heavy, inflexible plate worn by the Word Bearers. Barbed ridges rose along its forearms and shoulders, and its head was completely encased within a sleek, backwards sweeping helmet. It carried a long, slim weapon of alien design, and elegantly curving blades protruded from the barrel and hand-grip.

Then the alien was moving once again, its movements sharp and precise as it darted into cover. Its speed was almost unnatural; one moment it was perfectly still, utterly balanced and focused, the next it was gone. There was a grace and fluidity to its movements that no human, however enhanced, could ever hope to match.

'Eldar,' spat Marduk.

CHAPTER EIGHT

SOLON SAT ALONE in the mess room. His tray vibrated slightly on the metal table from the reverberations of the crawler's engines, and the mugs hanging against the wall rattled. He still wore his bulky exposure suit, though he had slipped free of its upper half, which hung down behind him. He pushed away his half-eaten meal of bland synth-paste gruel as the door to the mess room was pushed open.

The foreman primaris tapped one of the nicotine sticks from his packet, and lit it with a deft flick of his butane lighter. He nodded to Cholos through the haze of blue-grey smoke as he sat down opposite.

The boy that they had found in the abandoned crawler unit moved forward from behind the door, his wide eyes wandering around the room.

'You gonna eat that?' asked Cholos, gesturing to the half-eaten meal.

Solon pushed the tray towards the orderly in response, blowing out another cloud of smoke.

Cholos coughed once and cleared his throat.

'Come on, kid. Get some food into you,' said Cholos, patting his hand on the seat of the vacant chair encouragingly. The boy moved forward warily, and his eyes locked on the food.

Solon stared at the boy, still seeing his son's dead face. The boy wore an exposure suit that was much too large for him, its hood drawn back away from his head. The sleeves hung well past his hands, and the cuffs of its legs were bunched up around his ankles. As he shuffled forward, trying not to trip, he would have made a comical sight were he not so clearly malnourished.

He'd spoken not a word since they had brought him aboard, except to say his name when questioned: Dios. The boy's words when they had found him still haunted Solon.

'They were taken,' the boy had said. There were some corpses aboard the crawler, but the vast majority of the people that had been onboard had apparently disappeared into thin air.

'By who?' Solon had asked.

'Ghosts,' the boy had replied, and the words had made Solon's skin crawl.

'There is no such thing as ghosts,' the Interdiction sergeant, Folches, had said, though there had been little conviction in his voice, and Solon wondered whether he had been trying to convince the boy, or himself.

Solon had to agree with Folches, though. He didn't believe in ghosts or spirits, but *something* had taken all those people. Fifteen hundred people do not just disappear.

Since bringing the boy onboard, the child had shadowed every step of Solon's second, Cholos. Solon was just glad that the boy had not latched onto him. For his part, Cholos seemed to be enjoying the attention, and had even suggested making the boy the crawler crew's mascot.

'That's the way,' said Cholos as the boy tucked into Solon's discarded food with gusto. 'Hungry, aren't you?'

'Find a woman amongst the refugees that has lost her son,' said Solon. 'Give the boy to her.'

'Oh, I don't mind lookin' after him,' said Cholos.

'We don't need a pet kid underfoot, Cholos,' said Solon. 'Foist him off on one of the refugees. There are plenty of women down below who would take him.'

Cholos glared at Solon for a moment.

'Don't listen to him, boy,' said Cholos. 'He's nothing but a mean old man.'

The boy, for his part, seemed oblivious to the conversation, focused on the meal before him. With a last lick of the standard issue spoon in his hands, he finished off the meal, smacking his lips loudly.

'Cholos,' began Solon, but his words were interrupted as the room shook violently. The crawler came to a shuddering halt, and warning lights began to flash. The wail of sirens blared from the hallway, and Solon was instantly up and moving.

'What the hell?' asked Cholos, knocking his chair over as he stood.

A second impact rocked the crawler, and mugs fell from their hooks to clatter on the floor. Solon clutched at the door-frame to steady himself.

'Ghosts,' murmured the boy, his eyes wide and fearful.

'Go, go, go!' shouted Folches as the crawler bay doors slid open.

The sergeant dropped to the ice and landed in a crouch, his laslock rifle humming as its charge powered up.

The storm had, if anything, become fiercer, and punishing winds lashed against the soldiers of the Skyllan Interdiction as they peered into the whitewash of billowing snow.

'Can't see a damn thing,' muttered one of Folches's men, the sound crackling through on the sergeant's micro-bead in his left ear.

'The crawler was hit from the north-east,' said Folches. 'Move out, dispersal formation.'

'How can we engage what we can't damn well see?' asked another of his team, his voice strained. Fear, Folches realised. He rounded on the man, and grabbed him by the shoulder, pulling him close.

'You done?' barked Folches into the man's face, and the soldier nodded curtly. With a shove, Folches pushed him away, and gestured for two of his men to move around the front of the crawler, and for the other two to proceed around its rear.

His men nodded their responses, and the sergeant began moving towards the rear of the hulking behemoth, loping along the length of the crawler with his body low and the butt of his laslock pressed into his shoulder. Behind him, the two soldiers loped through the snow and ice. The other two men, moving in the opposite direction, disappeared instantly into the storm.

Reaching the rear of the ice-crawler, Folches gestured for his men to halt, and risked a glance around the back of the immense vehicle. Smoke was billowing from the engine stacks, and hot oil was spilling out onto the ice. Steam rose from where the oil was pooling.

Crouched low, he signalled for his men to take cover.

One of the soldiers, Leon, dropped to his stomach and began crawling elbow over elbow through one of the deep depressions created by the crawler's track units, easing himself into position and sighting his long-barrelled lasgun out towards the north-east. The other ducked beneath the undercarriage of the crawler, and squirmed forward to take up a position looking out to the north-east.

Folches leant around the corner of the crawler, peering through the sight of his weapon. The scope rendered the landscape in shades of green, and though it lit up the darkness as if it were day, the fury of the storm was such that he could see no more than twenty metres ahead.

There was nothing to see, just a swirling blanket of snow and ice.

'Julius, you seeing anything out there?' he said into his micro-bead.

'Negative, sir,' came the response.

'Hold position,' he said.

The wind howled around Folches, and he remained motionless, waiting. Minutes dragged by, and the biting cold began to seep through his limbs.

He lifted his head away from his gun sight, and stared out into the blanketing white gale. A shadow of movement ghosted behind the veil of swirling ice.

He dropped his eye to his sight once more, straining to pick up the movement. He saw nothing, and swore under his breath.

'You see that, Leon?' he hissed into his micro-bead.

'Didn't see anything, sir,' said the soldier.

'Damn it. There's something out there. Julius, anything?'

There was no response from the other soldiers of his squad, just the relentless roaring of the wind.

'Julius, Marcab, come in,' said Folches, but again just silence answered him.

'Hell,' he swore.

The sergeant felt movement behind him, and he swung around, his heart thumping, bringing his laslock to bear on… nothing.

He was jumping at shadows, and he cursed himself. He forced his racing heart to slow, breathing in slowly.

'Calm yourself, man,' he said to himself as he resumed his position. He'd give anything for a blast of his stim-inhaler around about now, but he had left the black market narcotics back onboard the crawler.

Trying to push the cravings away, Folches took a deep breath, and tried to contact his other soldiers once more.

'Marcab. Julius. Come in,' he whispered hoarsely into his vox-bead. 'Where the hell are you?'

Again, nothing but silence.

He flashed a glance towards Leon, lying concealed in the crawler tracks. The motionless soldier was face down, and blood was splattered out around his shattered head.

Folches pulled back from the corner of the crawler, and a flurry of projectiles impacted with the metal, centimetres from his face.

Several of the rounds sliced past the corner of the crawler, whistling sharply as they sped through the air.

A strangled grunt carried to Folches's ear on the wind, and he knew that the last of his squad, Remus, was dead.

Swearing, Folches leant out around the corner of the crawler, presenting the smallest target possible.

Half a dozen figures in glossy black armour were darting through the snow, and he saw larger, shadowy shapes gliding forwards behind them, several metres off the ground.

The sergeant snapped off a quick shot towards the closest of the figures, and ducked back into cover as return fire spat towards him. One of the enemy rounds struck him, slicing a neat cut through his body armour and scoring a wound across his forearm.

The cut was impossibly thin, and at first there was no pain, but then blood began to well and he cried out, clutching a hand to the deep wound.

Leaving a trail of blood drips that hissed and steamed as they struck the snow, the Skyllan Interdiction sergeant staggered away, dragging his laslock with him. He slipped in the hot oil pooling from the damaged engine block, and fell to his knees. Scrabbling through the sinking mire, Folches pushed himself back to his feet, and ran blindly around the corner of the immense ice-crawler, looking fearfully over his shoulder.

A thin, wickedly barbed blade entered his guts, sliding easily through his armour and flesh and halting him in his footsteps. His laslock dropped from his hands, and he stared up into the face of his killer. Nothing could be seen behind the cruelly slanted eyes of the blank helmet, and all Folches saw was his own face reflected back at him.

The figure was a good head taller than him, though it was inhumanly thin, and it cocked its head to the side, leaning into him as it twisted the blade embedded in his stomach, as if savouring every moment of the kill. Blood gushed from the wound as it opened up, and steam rose from the heat of his innards.

A hand, fingers like the black legs of a spider, clamped around Folches's neck, and he was pushed up against the crawler. The blade slid from his gut and was held poised in front of the sergeant's eyes, blood dripping from its elegantly curving tip.

The figure pressed almost intimately close to the dying sergeant, as if it wanted to experience every last dying sensation of the soldier. Then it pushed the blade into Folches's side, sliding it slowly up between his ribs to pierce the lungs.

Blood foamed up in the soldier's mouth as his lungs began to fill, and he gasped for breath as he slowly drowned on his own blood. The black fingers remained clasped around his neck almost lovingly until his heartbeat fluttered and stopped.

Then the black figure released its grip, and the sergeant slid to the ground.

SOLON RAN TOWARDS the control cabin of the ice-crawler, barging workers out of his way. The sirens in the claustrophobically narrow hallways were deafening, and he winced and clamped his hands over his ears as he ran past one of the blaring klaxons.

A burly orderly, his overalls covered in oil, ran into Solon as he rounded a corner, knocking him back into the wall.

'Sorry, boss,' said the man, helping him back to his feet, and Solon pushed past him.

He vaulted a steel banister, landed on the gantry below and ran on, turning to the right towards the control cabin. His boots rang out sharply as he climbed a short flight of stairs, and slammed the door to the control cabin open.

'What in the hell–' he began, but his words of reproach to the relief driver died in his throat.

A fist-sized hole had burned through the side window of the cabin and driven through the drive-mechanics on the wall opposite, leaving a smoking hole that dripped with molten metal. The driver was slumped back in his seat, half his head missing, the devastating blast having clearly passed through him when it had struck.

Solon gagged at the stink of burnt flesh, but moved into the cabin, trying not to look at the corpse, and failing. There was no blood. Whatever had struck him had cauterised the wound completely, forming a blackened crust. The blast had hit him in the temple, and everything in front of the line drawn between his ears was missing, down to his mouth, which was drawn in an almost comical expression of shock.

Tearing his gaze away from the corpse, Solon moved to the control console. It was dead, no lights flickering along the length of its panel at all, and he swore. He flicked a few switches, muttering an entreaty to the Omnissiah, but nothing happened. He balled his hand into a fist and stuck the console.

'Come on, damn you,' he swore.

Red warning lights flickered, the needles of the dials wavering back and forth, and Solon let out a surprised laugh of success.

His small victory was short-lived. A beam of solid darkness punched through the side of the control cabin, destroying the console in a shower of sparks. Cables and wires were fused by the lance strike and flames exploded outwards with immense force, shattering the already ruptured plasglass windows of the cabin and hurling Solon backwards through the cabin door.

Thrown backwards down the stairs leading to the cabin, the flesh of his face and arms blistering from the heat, Solon hit the deck hard. Frantically, he fought to rip his thermal undershirt off, for the synthetic material was melting onto his skin. Shaking the smoking, skin-tight shirt loose, he hurled it away from him, and began to stagger back.

The crawler, the closest thing he had to a home since he had been expelled from Sholto guild eighteen years ago, was beyond redemption. It was dead, and the vultures were circling outside to descend on its carcass.

He had to get away.

Rounding a corner, he almost ran headlong into Cholos, with the frightened boy Dios in tow.

'Solon,' began his second, his face panicked.

'Not that way,' he shouted, turning the man around and pushing him before him. 'The crawler's done. We have to get the hell out of here.'

Screams and shouts echoed up through the corridors, and Solon and Cholos fought their way through panicked workers. The crew looked to Solon for guidance.

'Get your exposure suits on,' the overseer bellowed. 'We stay here and we are all dead.'

Or as good as, he thought, thinking of the distinct lack of bodies aboard the crippled crawler they had come across just hours earlier.

'Damn,' swore Cholos. 'My suit.'

'Where is it?' asked Solon.

'In my locker,' answered his second. 'But Solon, the refugees... there are not enough suits for them all. We can't leave them.'

'We stay here and we die.'

'But all those people?'

Solon swore and punched the wall, bruising his knuckles.

'What do you want me to do, Cholos? I can't save them, and with the generators down, they're going to freeze to death as surely in the cargo bays as out on the ice.'

'There must be something we can do,' said Cholos.

'Well, if you come up with something, I'm all ears. Maybe that bastard Folches can call in support from the Skyllan Interdiction, or something. I don't know.'

Cholos let out a long breath, and rubbed a hand across his face.

'Take Dios, Solon,' he said. 'I'll meet you down below. I'll be quick'

Solon looked down at the boy, who was staring up at him with wide eyes, and swore. Cholos dropped to his knees.

'Go with Solon,' he said slowly to the boy. 'He'll see you safe. You understand?'

Dios nodded solemnly.

'That's the way,' said Cholos, ruffling the boy's short-cropped hair as he stood once more. 'I won't be long.'

'I'll meet you on deck three,' said Solon.

'I'll be there, boss,' replied Cholos, giving Solon a tense smile.

'You'd better be,' said Solon, and slapped his second heavily on the shoulder, urging him to move. 'Go.'

Cholos ducked through a side hatch, and Solon glanced down at Dios once more.

'Come on, boy. Move,' he said, gruffly.

The boy gave him a salute, his face serious, and the two of them set off towards the cargo bays. It took them the better part of five minutes to move from the crew area to the cargo holds, passing through twisting corridors and past dozens of panicked crewmen.

Punching the locking plate of cargo bay three, the door hissed open and swirling wind struck him. Screams were lost in the gale roaring through the cargo hold, and Solon saw that one of the cargo bay hold doors was wide open.

Through the blinding snow and ice, Solon saw a dark shape hanging in the air outside, hovering four metres above the ground. It was sleek and black, with wicked blades and spikes protruding along its sides, and it rocked slightly as the winds buffeted it, like a ship rolling on the open sea.

Black figures, taller and slimmer than a man were dragging people kicking and screaming towards the skiff hanging in the air outside. As he stood frozen on the spot, transfixed by the horror of what he was seeing, a struggling woman was knocked to the ground by a backhanded slap, and hauled towards the gaping cargo bay door by her hair.

A score of people were already trussed up on the mid-deck of the skiff, lying in a moaning pile, their hands bound behind their backs.

One of the black figures turned its faceless helmet towards Solon, and he felt a fear that he had never before experienced as the reflective eye lenses bore into him.

The figure barked a word in a language that Solon could not understand, spun on its heels like a dancer and swung something up from its side. With a flick of its arm it hurled the object towards him, spinning it end over end.

Even as the dark figure cast its weapon, Solon was backing away, and he tripped over the boy, Dios, who was clinging to one of his legs. Solon fell, swearing, and the spinning weapon scythed above him to strike one of his crewmen who had come up behind him.

The man fell, gagging, his hands clutching at the weighted wires wrapped around his neck. A flicker of energy coursed along those constricting wires and the man fell, convulsing violently, to the ground.

Scooping the boy up in his arms, Solon punched the door panel, bringing the hatch slamming back down, and turned and ran, leaping over the twitching figure on the ground.

The other cargo bays were to the left, the engines to the right, and Solon paused for a second, not knowing where to go. The boy wrapped his arms around Solon's neck, burying his face against his chest, and a pair of Solon's crew came running down the stairs towards him, their faces fearful.

'Run,' shouted Solon, and as he heard the hatch behind him slide open he made his decision, turning and bolting to the right.

The pair of crewmen stood staring behind Solon, firstly in incomprehension, then in dawning horror. There was a rapid sound like air being expelled, and one of the men collapsed, his left leg peppered with tiny splinters that tore through his overalls and the flesh beneath. The other man turned to run, but he was too slow and splinters shredded his legs from under him. His agonised scream followed Solon as he ran into the engine room, slamming his shoulder against the wall as he rounded a sharp corner.

The massive twin-engines were silent, and he raced between them, his heavy boots echoing loudly. Steam billowed up from beneath the walkway grid, where the massive drive shafts and gears of the crawler lay dormant and motionless. He swung around to the right, and grabbed the metal rungs of a narrow ladder that climbed one of the inner-hull walls.

'Hold on, boy,' he said, and the child tightened his grip, clinging to Solon like a limpet. With his arms free, Solon pulled himself up the ladder, expecting at any moment to be cut to shreds by the enemy.

Half way up, he leant out from the ladder and tried to loosen the access hatch that led out to the exhaust stacks. The circular wheel-lock wouldn't budge.

'Come on, damn you,' Solon hissed, casting a quick glance towards the entrance to the engine room as another strangled cry echoed down the hall. His hands were slipping on the wheel, and he strained with all his might to turn it. His face was red with exertion, and he had almost given up hope when he felt the hatch lock give a little. With renewed strength, he yanked the wheel into the unlocked position, and pushed it outwards.

Snow billowed in through the hatch, blinding him for a second, before Solon urged the boy through the hole.

'Go, boy. Now! I'll be right behind you,' he said in a hoarse whisper, casting a quick glance behind him. A shadow was stalking into the engine room, a bladed pistol of alien design in its hand.

Solon pushed the boy through the hatch, receiving a kick in his face for his troubles, almost making him lose his grip on the ladder. With a shove, he pushed the boy clear, and scrambled his way through the hatch. His hands slipped on the ice-encased metal exterior of the crawler, and he could not get any purchase. He kicked his legs awkwardly, half in the hatch and half out, expecting a hand to grab him at any moment and drag him back inside. The boy tugged at his arm ineffectually.

Awkwardly, he managed to squirm through the hatch onto the small balcony outside from where running repairs could be made to the exhausts. He cast a glance back through the open hatch to see a lithe figure looking up at him. In an instant, it raised its pistol, and Solon threw himself to the side, dragging the boy with him.

Splinters of rapidly propelled metal hissed through the open hatch and sliced through the steel exhausts as if they were made of synth-paper. Lifting the boy, Solon threw him over the edge of the crawler, and vaulted the balcony railing, praying he wouldn't crush the boy.

He hit the ground hard, and winced as shooting pain lanced up his left leg. He could hear screams on the wind, and he dragged the boy with him as he ducked beneath the crawler, squeezing himself between its massive tracked units.

He was already shivering uncontrollably, having discarded his thermal undershirt. There was little room in the cramped space beneath the crawler, but he managed to struggle his exposure suit up over his body, and he pulled its hood down low, securing it over his face. The boy too had pulled his exposure suit hood over his head, and he stared back at Solon through its two circular goggle-lenses.

Together, they crawled beneath the massive undercarriage of the tracked hauler. Solon saw the slumped form of one of the Skyllan Interdiction soldiers and his hopes were raised for a moment before he saw the blood.

Drawing the boy away from the grisly sight, Solon squirmed further beneath the hulking vehicle, moving towards the darkest recesses, the boy crawling silently behind him.

They froze as a weight crunched down into the snow nearby, and Solon looked into Cholos's terrified face. The crewman had landed on his hands and knees, and his exposure suit hung half off down his back. Solon gestured swiftly for him to crawl under. Clearly not having seen them in the darkness beneath the crawler, Cholos scrambled to his feet, and began running blindly into the storm.

Solon almost shouted out to him, but a pair of slender shapes dropped down into the snow, silent and deadly. They landed lightly, and took a few unhurried steps towards the fleeing man. Their glossy black legs were all that was visible, but Solon stared at them in horrified fascination. The spiked, overlaying plates of armour flexed as easily as synth-fabric, moulding to the contours and muscles of the figure's legs.

Cholos continued his mad flight into the storm, but Solon knew that he would not escape, and his heart wrenched as he heard the cruel laughter of the black-clad raiders as they watched his plight. They will gun him down any second, Solon thought.

They didn't.

Instead, a sleek shape hurtled out of the darkness, its form blurred by speed and the howling gale. A missile, was Solon's first thought, but then he saw that there was a figure hunched upon the rapidly moving object, and he realised that it was a bike propelled by anti-grav technology.

The rider leant down and slashed with a blade as the jetbike streaked past.

Cholos was spun by the impact, blood spraying out onto the snow. Still, the wound was not fatal, and he leapt back to his feet, a hand clutching at his shoulder. His assailant was nowhere to be seen, lost in the darkness and the storm, and Cholos turned around on the spot, eyes wide. Solon felt sick as the raiders laughed once more, the sound making his skin crawl with its cruelty.

The bike roared out of the darkness behind Cholos, streaking past him, knocking him down before being once again swallowed up in the storm.

Cholos was slower to rise this time, and blood gushed from his arm. Solon didn't want to watch any more, for the raiders were toying with the man, but he found that he couldn't look away.

Again, the bike came out of nowhere, and Cholos fell with a scream as one of his hamstrings was slashed. He couldn't rise from that blow, but still he tried to escape, crawling forward desperately, leaving a trail of blood in the snow.

Once more, the bike appeared, but this time it slowed as it approached him, dropping its speed with remarkable swiftness. It hovered in the air alongside Cholos as he tried vainly to stand. The rider of the anti-grav vehicle was garbed in a skin-tight glossy black suit with bladed plates of armour over its chest and shoulders, and a long topknot of blood-red hair streamed from the back of its elongated helmet.

The gleaming, blade-like bike sank towards the ground, and the rider reached out and grabbed Cholos by the scruff of his undershirt. Then the bike accelerated sharply, and Cholos was dragged behind it, his legs smacking into the ground every ten metres. He was dropped unceremoniously in front of the waiting pair of reavers, and the bike zoomed off into the storm once more.

The pair of reavers laughed again, and dragged Cholos away. It was the last time that Solon would ever see him, and he knew that the image of the terrified man, covered in blood and with both legs twisted horribly beneath him would be ingrained in his mind until his dying day.

Horrified and sick to his stomach, Solon slunk backwards into the concealing darkness, dragging the boy Dios with him. They cowered in the darkness behind the shadow of one of the main drive-wheels of the tracked crawler. Solon didn't know how long they hid there, but for the first time since he was a child he prayed.

MARDUK GRUNTED AS a line of splinters struck his left shoulder plate, embedding deep into the ceramite-plasteel alloy, but not penetrating. He replied with three quick shots of his bolt pistol before ducking back into cover as more fire was directed towards him. With a practiced flick, he discarded the spent sickle-clip, and rammed another into place.

'Jetbikes,' warned Kol Badar, and again the rapidly moving vehicles screamed out of the darkness of the north passage. The heavy weapons of Namar-sin's Havocs roared, and two of the accelerating bikes were taken down, one as a gout of hot plasma turned its elongated faring molten, and another as heavy bolter rounds ripped through its drive mechanics. The bike struck by the heavy plasma gun struck the floor, nose first, and flipped end over end, sending its rider flying. The other bike veered sharply to the left, spinning uncontrollably and impacted with the tunnel wall, disintegrating in a shower of sparks and flame.

Then the other bikes were screaming through the main access tunnel, banking sharply as they roared overhead. A shower of splinter-fire raced along the floor and peppered one of the Anointed, but the Terminator-armoured warrior brother stood against the fire pelting him like a man bracing himself against the wind. His twin-linked bolters roared, ripping head-sized chunks from the front of one of the bikes, but it did not fall, and continued to slice through the air in tight formation with its peers.

Marduk and the warrior brothers of the 13th were caught with their backs vulnerable to attack from the bikes, and they spun around and unleashed the fury of their bolters.

One of Sabtec's warriors was caught in the fire of two bikes, and though the splinters could not fully penetrate his thick armour, dozens of the cruel barbs sank through the gaps between the plates of his Mark IV armour, and he fell without a sound. Splinters had pierced the small gap between his breastplate and his helmet, filling his throat with slivers of metal, and two other splinters shattered his left eye lens, driving into his brain.

Another bike was brought crashing down by the combined fire of the 13th, and Marduk blew the head off another rider with a carefully aimed shot of his bolt pistol. The headless rider was ripped from the saddle of his bike and hurled backwards, and Marduk threw himself into a roll as the rider-less bike speared towards him, skimming across the surface of the floor like a stone hurled across still water.

The bike smashed into the remnants of the ruined Imperial armoured vehicle that Marduk had been crouching behind, the force of the impact spinning it sideways. The last bike was gone, screaming away into the distance as its rider accelerated.

A flurry of splinters struck him in the back, and Marduk was knocked forwards as he rose. He cursed, and pushed himself to his feet, swinging around and firing in one motion. With satisfaction, he saw the frail chest of one of the advancing black armoured eldar explode as the mass-reactive tip of the bolt-round detonated.

'Thirteenth, advance on me,' roared Marduk, having had enough of cowering in cover.

BURIAS HISSED IN hatred as the last remaining jetbike banked around once more, chased by bolter rounds that pinged off the debris scattered around the access tunnel. It moved so fast that it was little more than a shadowy blur, and he narrowed his eyes and allowed the daemon Drak'shal to rear up within him.

The eldar vehicle speared through the air like a dart, jinking around the burnt-out hulls of Imperial vehicles, dodging the blanket of incoming fire.

It straightened and gunned its engines, accelerating directly towards Burias-Drak'shal and Magos Darioq, who stood immobile behind him, apparently unconcerned by the carnage.

The cannons, under-slung beneath the chassis of the jetbike, roared, spitting a stream of splinters towards the possessed warrior, but he was already

moving, springing into the air, the heavy icon of the
Host held in one hand as if it weighed nothing at all.

The fire of the jetbike's cannons flashed towards Darioq, but a glowing sphere of light surrounded him, and
they rebounded off the energy barrier to leave him
unscathed.

Burias-Drak'shal leapt over the elegantly tapering
faring of the jetbike, his taloned hand locking around
the eldar rider's throat and ripping him from his saddle. The rider-less bike veered sharply and flipped,
exploding against the tunnel wall as Burias-Drak'shal
landed in a crouch, the eldar warrior helpless in his
grasp.

Lifting the eldar as if he was a child, Burias-Drak'shal
slammed its head into a corner of scrap metal, once
part of an Imperial vehicle. Its head splattered, the frail
skull splintering like porcelain.

'Weakling thing,' commented Burias-Drak'shal, flicking the corpse away from him.

A blade rammed into his back, and Burias-Drak'shal
roared in anger and pain. The blade was wrenched agonisingly against his spine and he twisted, swinging the
icon around in a lethal arc.

The blow didn't hit anything, indeed, there did not
seem to *be* anything behind him. With his witch-sight,
he registered a shadowy shape in the corner of his
vision, and then twisted away as a blade stabbed
towards him once again, putting some space between
him and his nigh-on invisible assailant.

His eyes narrowed as they locked on a lean, ghostlike
figure. It became visible for a second, taunting him,
and he saw a slim figure, its skin as black as pitch, with
arcane sigils cut into its flesh. Its eyes were milky white,
with no pupils, and it snarled at him, exposing a maw
filled with tiny, barbed teeth.

Then the figure was nothing more than a shadow again, a vague ghostly shape that surged towards him in a blur of motion. Burias-Drak'shal swung his icon like a hammer, the spiked tip humming as it arced through the air. The shadow-creature ducked beneath the blow and came up inside his guard, and Burias-Drak'shal hissed in pain as a blade rammed into his side.

Burias-Drak'shal connected with a heavy backhand blow that sent the shadow-creature tumbling backwards. It came to rest on all fours, and its form once more became visible as it snarled up at him in hatred. Then it was gone, disappearing into thin air as if a veil had been drawn over it.

Burias-Drak'shal experienced an unfamiliar emotion: unease.

The creature had seemed at once familiar and alien. He thought he had scented the power of the warp within its being, but the creature had been no daemon, nor truly one of the possessed.

His slit eyes flicked from side to side, wary for another sudden attack, but none came. He slammed the butt of his icon into the floor, cracking the plascrete platform, and roared his defiance.

MARDUK HEARD THE roar, but pushed it out of his mind as he drew his chainsword, feeling the ecstatic bond as the daemon weapon melded with him. Thorns in the hilt burrowed into the flesh of his palm through the plugs in his gauntlet, and he surged towards the eldar warriors.

The disciplined warriors of the 13th coterie responded instantly to his rallying cry, rising from cover with bolters thumping. They began to advance on the enemy, bearing down on them, moving in two unstoppable phalanxes, the zones of their fire-arcs overlapping.

Each of the coteries had been joined by one of the Anointed, and these behemoths of muscle and metal stomped forwards, shaking off the fire directed against them and snapping off bursts from their twin-linked bolters.

The closest enemy was less than twenty metres away, and still, foolishly Marduk thought, advancing towards the Word Bearers.

'Slaughter the unbelievers!' roared Marduk, breaking into a run, his bolt pistol bucking in his hands as he fired.

The warriors of the 13th moved up in support, snapping off shots as they bore down on the enemy.

Marduk saw two of the enemy ripped apart by bolt fire. One bolt round detonated in the shoulder of one of the eldar figures, ripping its arm clear in a spray of blood, and another was torn in two as a burst of fire caught it in its slender midsection.

A spray of splinters embedded themselves in Marduk's chest plate, but he did not slow his charge, and pumped another burst of shots towards a pair of eldar raiders. Displaying inhuman speed, they darted to the side and his shots went wide, ripping chunks out of the wall.

He roared his hatred as he closed on one of the eldar, and swung his chainsword in a murderous arc that would have cleaved the frail warrior in two had it connected. The eldar swayed under the blow with a speed that, for all his Astartes genetic coding and training, made Marduk feel slow and awkward, and slashed a groove across Marduk's thigh with the curving bayonet blade beneath the barrel of its rifle.

The blade bit into his flesh, and Marduk hissed in anger. He threw a backhanded slash towards the eldar's midsection, the hungry teeth of his chainsword whirring madly. The black-armoured figure dodged backwards, the very tip of the chainsword scant centimetres from its belly, and stabbed with the tip of its blade towards Marduk's throat.

The First Acolyte twisted his body as the blade darted towards him, and its length sank into his shoulder plate. Punching with his right hand, which held his bolt pistol, Marduk snapped the blade off, leaving the tip embedded in his armour. Dropping his shoulder, he threw himself forward, slamming into the frail xenos warrior even as it tried to sidestep.

The force of the blow shattered the eldar's chest, and Marduk bore it to the ground. He smashed the pommel of his chainsword into the raider's face, driving it downwards like a blunt dagger, smashing the faceplate of its helmet into splinters and pulverising its skull.

Rising, his chest heaving, Marduk grunted as a blade stabbed into his side, sliding between his armour plates and burying itself deep in his flesh. Dropping his bolt pistol, he grabbed the arm of his attacker, crushing the slender bones of its forearm. It struggled to get away from him, but his grip was like iron, keeping it pinned in place, and he hacked his chainsword into its neck.

Whirring teeth shredded through black armour and blood began to spray as Marduk forced the weapon into the alien's body. It ripped through tightly bound muscle and sinew, and tore apart the delicate vertebrae of the eldar's neck. With a heavy kick, Marduk sent the dead eldar flying away from him, and dropped to one knee to retrieve his bolt pistol.

Hefting the pistol, Marduk found no new target to unleash his wrath upon. The eldar slipped away into the shadows with ungodly speed, moving like shadows being dispelled by the appearance of a lantern. They were gone in an instant, and Marduk stood breathing heavily as he surveyed the carnage of the frantic battle.

The fight had lasted less than a minute, all told, but the savagery, swiftness and effectiveness of the attack was staggering.

Three members of the 13th were down, one of them not moving as blood poured from a wound to his head, too severe for the potent larraman cells of his Astartes make-up to seal. Two members of Khalaxis's 17th coterie were dead, two more injured. Nine eldar had been slain, and three more had been injured and callously abandoned by their brethren.

Marduk strode towards one of the injured lean warriors. Its left leg had been blown off at the knee, and it was trying to crawl away, leaving a bloody smear on the floor beneath it.

Marduk placed his foot on the lower back of the wounded eldar, pinning it in place as Kol Badar stalked to his side. The black armour was curiously soft and pliable beneath his foot, but as he exerted more pressure he felt it strengthen and grow rigid, resisting him. He kicked the eldar over onto its back, and it stared up at him through elongated eye lenses. Its hatred of him was palpable, and its hand flashed down to its thigh, reaching for a jagged blade strapped around its lean limb.

Its movement was crisp and precise, and the blade was flashing towards Marduk's throat. He caught the eldar's wrist and gave it a wrench, breaking its slender bones with a snap, and it dropped the blade to the ground, hissing.

'I've never seen their faces,' said Marduk, pinning the eldar's broken arm beneath his knee and reaching for its helmet, ignoring the feeble attempts by the xenos humanoid to fight him off as he tried to work out the best way to remove it. Growing quickly frustrated, he simply hooked the fingers of both hands under the lip of the helmet around the eldar's scrawny neck and pulled. With a wrench, he ripped the helmet in two, almost breaking the alien's neck in the process.

The First Acolyte tossed the ruptured helmet aside as he stared down at the revealed face.

It was unnaturally long and thin, ethereal and other-worldly. High cheekbones and a pointed chin gave it a severe, angular shape that was at once delicate and darkly handsome, yet utterly alien. Its head was bereft of hair, and sharp, jagged runes or glyphs of xenos origin, similar in shape to the elegant blades of the eldar, were tattooed across the left half of its face. Its lips were thin and sneering, and its eyes were shaped like almonds, elegant, alien and filled with hate.

'It's a frail as a woman,' said Marduk. 'Reminds me of Fulgrim's Legionaries.'

Kol Badar snorted.

Although the III Legion, the Emperor's Children, were mighty warriors and had wisely thrown their weight in behind the Warmaster and embraced Chaos, there was no love lost between the Word Bearers and the Emperor's Children.

Where the Word Bearers were severe, their lives dominated by ritual, prayer and penance, the Emperor's Children were renowned for their flamboyant decadence, embracing excess in all its guises. Where the Word Bearers worshipped Chaos in all its varied manifestations, the Emperor's Children dedicated themselves solely to the darkling prince of Chaos: Slaanesh.

The eldar glared up at Marduk hatefully.

'I agree, yet they are a worthy foe,' said Kol Badar.

'Worthy? They are xenos. They deserve nothing more than extermination,' replied Marduk.

'I do not disagree,' said Kol Badar, 'but it does my soul good to fight against an enemy that can at least test us.'

'Their tainted, alien weaponry is potent,' agreed Marduk, reluctantly, gripping the eldar roughly behind its neck with one hand. He raised his fist.

'And they are certainly quick,' said Marduk. slamming his fist down, punching through the eldar's face, 'but they break easily enough once you get a hold of them.' Marduk shook blood, brain matter and shards of skull across the floor.

CHAPTER NINE

IKORUS BARANOV WAS an optimist. When he first heard of the plight of the worlds being evacuated in the face of the tyranid menace, he had smiled.

Hundreds of inhabited worlds were being abandoned. Countless millions had already perished, either consumed to feed the insatiable hunger of the xenos hive fleet, or utterly destroyed by the zealous policy of Exterminatus employed by the Imperium. Any world not fully evacuated before the tyranid ground invasion began was stricken from the Imperial records and bombarded from high orbit. Already a score of colonised planets had been put to the sword, every living thing – tyranid, human, animal, vegetable – utterly consumed in purifying flame.

Baranov cared nothing for the millions of destroyed lives. He saw the positive flip-side of every ill turn, and while others regarded this time as one of terror and darkness, he saw it as a time to make himself filthy rich.

His ship, the *Rapture*, was docked at landing zone CXVI, a privately-owned docking pad of the Phorcys starport. Only those wealthy few with the required access privileges were allowed entrance onto this private dock.

Baranov had heard that the regular docks were over-run with tens of thousands of frantic guild workers and their families, desperate to secure passage off-world. In contrast to that mayhem, landing zone CXVI was a veritable utopia of peace and tranquillity.

The private lounge adjacent to the dock was opu-lently decorated with extravagant off-world flora, for it had been designed to mimic a fecund, semi-tropical rainforest. Paths of fine gravel wove through the undergrowth, and ferns and broad-leafed plants grew up overhead, hiding the strip lights in the high domed ceiling. A waterfall crashed down over rocks imported from a distant feral world, creating a mist of warm water vapour in the air, and butterflies, with wingspans as wide as a man's forearm is long, bobbed lazily through the air.

Baranov shook his head in amazement and envy. Perdus Skylla was a desolate wasteland of frozen, wind-swept plains, the crude worker class living beneath the ice, and yet there were those with enough wealth to create an oasis of life like this in its midst.

The pursuit of wealth had dominated Ikorus Bara-nov's life, and he liked to think that he had achieved much from his humble beginnings, but it was at times like these that he was reminded that his wealth was not so great. *This* was the wealth that he desired. He wanted to be able to build a sub-tropical rainforest in the mid-dle of an ice-locked ocean world just because he could. Of course he didn't literally want to build a rainforest – he found this place with its high humidity and crawling things quite unsettling – but he wanted the wealth to be able to do so at a whim had he desired it.

These were the people to lift him to that stage of wealth.

There were thirty-two men here, most with young, surgically enhanced women clinging to their arms like leeches. Some were accompanied by older women, fierce beasts that clearly dominated their husbands or lovers, but they were few in comparison to the glittering array of nubile young women, bedecked in fine jewels and headdresses.

Baranov smirked. Clearly many of these high-ranking guild officials had chosen to bring their courtesans along with them rather than their wives. If he had not been a callous man he might have been offended by how easily these men cast off their wives, abandoning them to their fate while they fled for safety. A few had brought both wife and courtesan with them, but that was rare. The price that Baranov was charging for a berth on his ship was nothing short of extortionate, even for this upper echelon of the truly elite.

'Lords and ladies,' began Baranov, his voice silken, 'may I please have your attention.'

The group was gathered upon a decked clearing in the middle of the rainforest façade, seated on cane high-backed chairs. The hum of conversation died as the gathered social elite turned to regard Baranov. Baranov saw fear in their eyes, which was understandable for their world was being abandoned in the face of an alien menace that would destroy and kill everything in its path. But even so, they regarded him with considerable distaste, as if he were common vermin that had some-how infiltrated into their elite company.

Baranov suppressed a grin. In truth he *was* vermin, but he was vermin that was about to get seriously wealthy.

He gave a mock bow, waving his hand in a flourish. He was a short man of middling build, and he wore a long-tailed coat of regal blue with overly prominent gold buttons. His hair was pulled back in a ponytail that hung down his back, and his fingers were bedecked with rings. He knew that to these rich guilders who were born to their wealth, he looked like a rogue or a pirate, an individual who had some wealth but not the class to know what to do with it, but he didn't give a damn what they thought of him. Right now, he was their only ticket off this cursed world, and he fully intended to milk that for all it was worth.

'Thank you for your patience, my esteemed friends,' said Baranov. 'My ship, the *Rapture*, is refuelled and provisioned, and is now ready for embarkation.'

'About time,' stated one of the guilders, a scowling, porcine individual pawing at a girl who looked little more than a child, though she was clearly his mistress. Other men muttered and huffed impatiently. These people were not used to having to wait for anything.

'I regret to have kept you waiting, noble lords, but I assure you that the *Rapture* is now ready to receive your esteemed selves. She is a humble craft, but I trust that you will find her suitable for your use.'

'Get on with it, man,' snapped another man, an imposingly tall individual with a hooked nose.

'I shall forestall you no longer, my lords,' said Baranov, holding up a hand. 'However,' he added with a rakish grin, 'there is just the small matter of my compensation.'

With a snap of his fingers, four of Baranov's crewmen stepped out of the shadows of the foliage to join him. Two of them guided a container forward, which hovered just above the ground, held aloft by anti-grav technology. They were rough sorts, and Baranov saw the noses of the lords and ladies crinkle as they stared disdainfully at them. He grinned again.

One of the crew, sat down at a desk facing the nobles, a data-slate and stylus in his hands. An immense brute with a shaved head took his place behind him, standing with his thick arms folded across his chest.

'If you would be so kind as to make your monies ready, my associates will collect your dues,' he said. 'Step forward if you will, and make a line behind Lord Palantus. This will be as quick and painless as possible, and we shall all be on our way shortly.'

The nobles shuffled into line, huffing and muttering, angry at being treated like commoners. The first in line, Lord Palantus, Prime Magnate of Antithon Guild, stepped forward and slid a slim hand-case onto the desk.

'Name?' said the seated crewman, tapping at the data-slate.

'Oh, for the love of the Emperor,' said Lord Palantus, outraged at having to commune with such a lowborn cur. The seated man looked up at him, eyebrows raised.

'Get on with it, Antithon,' muttered one of the other nobles.

'Palantus,' the lord spat, glaring down at the man before him as if he were a bug that he had just found in his food.

'Open it,' said the seated man, indicating the hand-case with the tip of his stylus.

'You are going to check it's all there, Baranov?' asked the noble imperiously. 'I am a noble of Antithon Guild, and my word is my honour. It is all there, as agreed.'

'My dear lord, of course I trust your esteemed word,' said Baranov smoothly, 'but please, indulge my men. They are unused to dealing with such luminaries. Please, open it.'

The prime magnate huffed and folded his arms, looking away. He nodded to his mistress at his side. She clicked the release nodules of the case with her thumbs and it opened with a hiss.

With a nod, the seated man made a mark on his dataslate. The heavily muscled crewman standing behind the desk sealed the case, and it was placed inside the hovering container.

'Now, my dear Lord Palantus,' said Baranov, guiding the man to the side with his hand on his elbow, 'if you would please go with my associates, they will see you safely onboard.'

The lord looked outraged that Baranov dared lay a hand on him, but allowed himself to be guided away.

'Next,' said the seated man, tapping with his stylus.

WITH ALL PAYING customers aboard the *Rapture*, Baranov smiled and let out a slow breath. He had made an absolute killing today, and he couldn't keep the smile from his face. The engines of his ship roared, and he gave a last look around the starport before climbing the embarkation steps.

'A good day's work,' he said. Keying a sequence of buttons, he sealed the hatch behind him.

Minutes later, the *Rapture* was cleared for take-off. The wedged segments of the dome far overhead peeled back like the petals of an immense flower, opening up the landing pad to the fury of the elements outside. Wind swirled furiously, ice and snow spiralling in mad eddies as the *Rapture's* engines roared into life, flames gushing from the powerful downward-angled thrusters. The ship lifted, rising vertically out of the landing dock, and as the petal segments of the dome began to close once more, the *Rapture's* thrusters rotated backwards, and it screamed up towards the heavens, leaving the doomed ice-world of Perdus Skylla behind it.

MARDUK SHOT AN Imperial soldier in the face, and the back of the man's head exploded outwards, spraying blood and brain matter across the wall.

'That the last of them?' he growled, kicking the corpse out of his way.

'There are a few survivors,' said Kol Badar. 'They are being executed as we speak.'

'Move in, secure the area,' ordered Marduk.

The Coryphaus barked his orders, and the warriors of the Host closed in.

For three hours they had proceeded along the access tunnel, homing in on the location pinpointed by Magos Darioq-Grendh'al as the access lift that would take them down to the mining facility below, to the last known whereabouts of the Adeptus Mechanicus explorator.

They had encountered little resistance en route.

One Imperial patrol of soldiers had been encountered, escorting some two thousand civilians, and they had engaged and neutralised the foe for no losses. Not all of the civilians had been killed in the resultant slaughter, for it would have been a waste of ammunition to gun them down. Almost three hundred had been killed, caught in the middle of the firefight or hacked down in close combat, but the remainder had been allowed to flee, running wildly back the way they had come, though there was evidence to suggest that most of them had been subsequently taken by the dark eldar.

Of the eldar themselves, the Word Bearers had seen no sign since their first, frantic encounter. On several occasions, the whine of their jetbikes had been heard in the distance, accompanied by the echoing screams of Imperial citizens from further along the tunnels, but no bodies had been discovered that spoke of battle.

'They are a piratical race,' Kol Badar had said to Burias, who had never encountered the eldar before and seemed, Marduk noted curiously, to have been somewhat unnerved by his first encounter.

'What are they doing here? What purpose could they possibly have on this gods-forsaken Imperial moon?' asked Burias.

'Certain eldar sects have been observed taking captives, though for what purpose has not been ascertained,' growled Kol Badar. 'I assume that the eldar on this world are such a sect, taking advantage of the confusion of the evacuations to reap a tally of slaves.'

'It doesn't matter why they are here,' said Marduk. 'The only thing that need be understood is that they are xenos, and therefore the enemy.'

'Had the Great Crusade been allowed to fulfil its purpose,' Kol Badar added bitterly, 'with the Warmaster at its head, then the foul race of witches and sorcerers would have been eradicated from the galaxy long ago. But they remain a cunning foe, swift and deadly. They are not to be underestimated.'

'Overestimation of the foe reeks of fear and weakness,' snapped Marduk. 'The eldar are nothing more than the last fragmented strands of a dying race. We are the chosen bearers of the great truth, the favoured sons of Chaos. We are the greatest warriors the universe has ever seen, and will ever see. We need not be concerned with the appearance of a handful of xenos pirates.'

Marduk felt pride surge through the warriors of the Host in response to his words, and he knew that they would fight even harder against the eldar if they appeared again. He doubted that they would, in truth, for he believed that Kol Badar was correct in his assumptions: that they had encountered a dark eldar sect engaged in slave raids upon this doomed world, and that they expected little resistance. Certainly, they had not expected to encounter members of an Astartes Legion. Marduk knew that the eldar were a long-lived race, and one that was on the brink of dying out altogether. He was certain that the eldar would rue the day that they had attacked the revered XVII Legion. They would move on, avoiding the warriors of the Host, to find easier pickings elsewhere.

Nevertheless, the progress of the Word Bearers was slowed, for it would be foolishness not to show caution after the lightning attack of the dark eldar. Though it defied logic for the eldar to attack them again, he knew that they were xenos, and so could not be understood. He had studied reports of engagements against the eldar, and everything that he had read spoke of their unpredictability.

The priority target was an access lift that linked one of the dozens of sub-ice hab-cities with its mining facility on the ocean floor far below, and it was towards this location that they were moving. On the approach to one of the many entrances to this guilder hab-city, they had come upon a blockade of enemy soldiers, accompanied by sentry guns with servitors hard-wired into their targeting systems and lightly armoured vehicles similar to those they had encountered on the ice above, though modified for use on man-made surfaces rather than the nebulous ice-flows. The soldiers had been ready for them, either having received warning of the Word Bearers approach or merely prepared for a dark eldar attack, but it mattered little.

The Anointed had led the attack, marching resolutely through the weight of fire while Namar-sin moved the

Havocs of the 217th coterie up in support, targeting and neutralising the enemy sentry guns. With the Anointed still weathering the brunt of the enemy fusillade, Sabtec's veteran squad took up position on the left flank, laying down a blanket of fire that allowed Khalaxis and his warriors to charge up the middle, with Marduk at their forefront roaring catechisms of vengeance and hate.

Every carefully targeted burst of fire from the Anointed had ripped another of the enemy soldiers apart, but it was Marduk's charge that signalled the commencement of the real slaughter. Up close, the enemy had no hope of survival. Hastily fired point blank lasgun shots had seared burning furrows across power armour plates as Marduk and Khalaxis entered the fray, chainsword and axe cutting and ripping. Bolt pistols created gory craters of flesh in chests, and limbs were ripped from their sockets as Khalaxis's warriors tore through the heart of the enemy defence.

Those cowards that had turned to run were hacked down without mercy, chainswords and heavy axes severing spines and cutting arms away at the shoulder. Kol Badar and his Anointed moved through the mayhem, ripping apart the remnants of the Imperial defenders, gunning them down with combi-bolters and heavy reaper autocannon fire. The Coryphaus smashed the scorpion-legged rapier sentry-guns aside with backhand blows of his power talons, sending them crashing into cowering defenders, crushing limbs and breaking bones.

As the last enemies were brutally butchered, and as Sabtec's squad moved forward to secure the area, Darioq-Grendh'al stamped mechanically forward, each heavy step accompanied by a whine of servos.

The magos, Marduk noted with a smile of satisfaction, was now truly a being of Chaos. The four powerful arms of his servo-harness were as much organic as metal, and bony protuberances, serrated thorns and hooked spines ridged the once pristine metal limbs. Fleshy lumps of muscle had grown around the servo-bundles and coupling links that joined the servo-limbs to his body, and a large curving horn emerged from the left side of the magos's head, bursting through the blood-stained fabric of the low cowl that hid his face in shadow.

Waving mechadendrite tentacles sprouted from his spine, and where before they were tipped with mechanical claws, sensory apparatus and data-spikes, now several of them ended in gaping lamprey mouths, filled with rings of barbed teeth, from which ropes of oily saliva dripped. The surface of many of the tentacles too had changed, their metal bands morphing into smooth, black skin, wet and slick like the body of an eel.

The insignia of the Adeptus Mechanicus had been altered and corrupted, for such a reminder of the false machine faith was offensive to the fundamentalist Word Bearers. The cogged wheel of the Mechanicus had been overlaid with the holy eight-pointed star of Chaos, and the black and white skull motif of the machine cult had been corrupted, now bearing daemonic horns and wreathed in flames so that it mirrored the sacred Latros Sacrum borne upon the left shoulder of every warrior brother of the XVII Legion.

As if to emphasise the corrupted nature of the magos, Darioq-Grendh'al paused besides a dying Imperial soldier, who stared up at him in horror, face awash in blood. The magos peered down at the man, his unfathomable red glowing right eye boring into the soldier. Four of the lamprey mouths of the semi-organic mechadendrites waved towards the fallen man, who recoiled away from them in horror. The tentacles were drawn to him as if they tasted his blood in the air, and latched onto him, attaching to his neck, his chest and his face.

The man screamed in horror and pain as the tentacles twisted back and forth, burrowing into his flesh and began sucking away his vital fluids. The man died in torment, and as the feeder mouths pulled away from the corpse with a wet sucking sound, blood dripping from their gaping apertures, the magos tilted his head to one side and, with an almost tender, tentative movement, lifted one of the man's limp arms with one of his own mechanical power lifters. Releasing the man's arm, it flopped back to the ground, and Darioq-Grendh'al stared down at it in incomprehension.

Amused, Marduk watched as the magos tried to raise the man to his feet, lifting him up gently in his mechanical claws, careful not to crush him in his powerful grip, but the body collapsed to the ground as soon as it was released.

'The life-systems of this flesh-unit have failed,' said the magos. 'Already its body temperature has dropped 1.045 degrees, and its cellular make-up is entering corporal decay.'

'He's dead, magos,' said Marduk softly. 'You killed him.'

The magos looked at Marduk, and then back down at the corpse. Then, slowly, he raised his head once more to meet Marduk's gaze.

'Feels good, doesn't it?' said Marduk.

The magos paused, looking down at the corpse at its feet in incomprehension. Then the corrupted once-priest of the Machine-God straightened.

'I wish to do that again,' he said.

'Oh you will, Darioq-Grendh'al,' promised Marduk.

* * *

HAVING BREACHED THE defences of the guild hab-city, the Word Bearers made swift progress through the tunnelled streets and boulevards, encountering no resistance and sighting few living beings. The citizens that still remained in the city fled before the advance of the enclave, scurrying like vermin into the darkness of side-tunnels and alleys.

Marduk gave them no mind. He cared not for the fate that awaited them once the tyranids had descended on the planet. They would all be slaughtered, their bodies consumed to feed the growth of the hive fleet.

They descended deeper into the guild city, guided inexorably onward by schematic maps that flickered across auspex screens, uploaded from the data banks of the guild bastion. They marched through what must have been the mercantile district of the sub-surface city, which was rife with detritus and evidence of looting. Doors were smashed from hinges, and goods and foodstuffs lay scattered across the tunnel floor, along with the occasional corpse.

'Trampled to death in the exodus,' said Sabtec evenly as he knelt by one of the bodies.

'The cowards won't even stand to fight for their own world,' said Khalaxis, a fresh array of scalps and death-skulls hanging from his belt, 'and they kill each other in their panic to escape. These are not worthy foes.'

'Rejoice at the weakness of the Imperium,' said Marduk. 'Namar-sin, which direction?'

'East, two kilometres,' said the champion of the Havoc squad, consulting the throbbing blister display of his auspex. 'There, we must rise four levels towards the surface, and proceed a further kilometre to the north-east before we get to the ore docks. That is where the lift rises from the ocean floor.'

'Burias, take point,' rumbled Kol Badar. 'Khalaxis, move in support of the icon bearer. Let's move.'

DRACON ALITH DRAZJAER raised one thin eyebrow a fraction, his almond-shaped eyes glinting dangerously. That one small movement would have been all but unseen by a human, but to the keen eyes of the eldar, the subtle nuance spoke volumes.

The dracon reclined languidly on his command throne, his thin chin supported by the slender fingers of one hand as he stared down at the supplicant kneeling before him. He was bedecked from neck to toe in tight fitting segmented armour, like the scaled skin of a serpent, glossy and black. A mask covered the left half of his face, its barbed blades, like the legs of spiders, pressing against his flesh. A pair of blood-red tattoos extended down his pale cheeks from his eyelids, like bloody tears.

'How many?' Dracon Alith Drazjaer said, his voice a soft purr.

The sybarite supplicant, Keelan, paled and licked his thin lips. Unable to hold his master's gaze, his eyes moved to the figures behind the throne. A pair of the dracon's incubi guards stood there, but there was no hope of support from them. They were as still as statues, their faces hidden beneath tall helmets, and they held curving halberds in their gauntleted hands. Keelan's eyes flicked to the other two figures standing by the dracon's side.

On the left stood the firebrand, Atherak, her tautly muscled body covered in swirling tattoos and wych cult markings. The sides of her head were shaved to the scalp and tattooed, and a ridge of back-swept hair ran along her crown like a crest, falling down her back past her slim waist. A myriad of weapons were strapped to her limbs, and she sneered at Keelan.

On the right was the haemonculus, Rhakaeth, unnaturally tall and thin even by eldar standards, his cheeks sunken. He looked like nothing more than a walking corpse, and his eyes burnt feverishly hot with the soul-hunger. Keelan quickly averted his gaze, looking at the floor.

'How many?' Drazjaer asked again, a subtle change in his inflection registering his displeasure, and the sybarite knew that he would not escape without punishment. Dracon Alith Drazjaer of the Black Heart Kabal was not a forgiving master. Doubtless he would experience torment beyond imagining at the hands of the haemonculus, Rhakaeth, but not death. No, he would not be allowed death.

'We lost twelve of our number, my lord,' Keelan said finally.

'Twelve,' repeated his master, his voice expressionless.

'It was not the regular mon-keigh forces that we faced, my lord,' said the sybarite, desperation in his voice. 'The… augmented ones were there.'

A line furrowed the dracon's brow for a second, and the haemonculus, Rhakaeth, leant forwards hungrily.

'You are sure?' asked the dracon.

'Yes, my lord,' said Keelan. 'It was not my fault; it was Ja'harael. He is to blame. He drew us in, and we had no warning that we faced anything but the regular mon-keigh forces.'

'We should not have sought the service of the half-breed and its kin in the first place,' spat Atherak, her cruel features sharpening. Her muscles tightened, her hands clenching and unclenching into fists, and beads of sweat ran down her long limbs.

'The mandrake half-breeds serve us well,' said Drazjaer evenly, dismissing the wych's words. 'How many slaves did you take, sybarite?'

Keelan licked his lips again. The dracon doubtless already knew the answer to his question. He looked up, feeling eyes upon him. The haemonculus, Rhakaeth, was staring at him hungrily, a slight smile upon his lips. He looked like a grinning corpse, and Keelan swallowed thickly.

'None, my lord,' he said, his voice little more than a whisper.

'None,' said Drazjaer flatly, 'for the loss of twelve of my warriors.'

'Ja'harael is to blame, my lord,' protested Keelan. 'If anyone is to be punished, it should be him.'

'What have you to say on the matter, mandrake?' asked the dracon, and Keelan stiffened. Ja'harael materialised out of the shadows next to him, darkness clinging to him like a shroud. His milky eyes stared into Keelan's for a moment, and the sybarite recoiled at the half-breed's presence. He was an abomination, a thing that should not be, and his mouth went dry.

The mandrake's skin was as black as pitch, and sigils were cut into his flesh, marking his damnation. The mandrakes were shadow-creatures. Once, they had been eldar, but they had long ago given themselves up to darkness, inviting the foul presence of *others* into their souls. Now they were something altogether different, living apart from the eldar race, preying on their own in the darkness of Commoragh and the webway. They existed in three planes – the real, the webway, and the warp – and were able to slip between the realms at will.

'I did not realise that I was employed to safeguard your warriors from harm, Drazjaer,' hissed Ja'harael.

'You are not,' said the dracon. If he was offended by the casual use of his name, he gave no indication.

'Their failure shames you, Drazjaer,' hissed the mandrake. 'They make you look weak.'

The dracon smiled coldly.

'Do not seek to goad me, half-breed,' said the dracon stroking his chin thoughtfully. The haemonculus leant over the dracon, whispering. Drazjaer nodded, and leant back in his throne, stretching his back languidly.

'The presence of the mon-keigh elite intrigues me,' he said finally. 'Their souls are much sought after in Commoragh, and will garner much favour.'

'And perhaps offset a certain amount of your Lord Vect's displeasure,' hissed Ja'harael.

Drazjaer's eyes flashed angrily, but the mandrake continued regardless.

'Perhaps you see your time running out, Drazjaer, and your quota not yet achieved.'

A blade appeared to materialise in Atherak's left hand so fast did she draw it, and in her right she flicked her long whip, its barbed tips writhing like serpents across the floor at her feet. Her muscles quivered with anticipation, and Ja'harael smiled at her, exposing his array of teeth, flexing his fingers. The wych cracked her whip and took a step towards the mandrake, but was halted by a sharp word from the dracon. Drazjaer's anger was gone, and he smiled coldly.

'It seems you know much, half-breed,' he said, 'but be careful, knowledge can be dangerous, and my patience can be stretched only so far.'

The mandrake spread his arms wide and gave a mocking bow.

'The souls of the enhanced ones will offset any shortfall in the quota, it is true, and Rhakaeth desires to work upon one of the enhanced mon-keigh creatures,' said the dracon, indicating the haemonculus with one languid gesture, 'though why he would wish to perform his art upon their brutish forms is beyond my understanding. However, he has pleased me of late, and I shall indulge his whim. Bring him some specimens, Ja'harael.'

'You would honour the half-breed abomination with this hunt?' sneered Atherak. 'Let me lead my wyches in. You owe me that honour.'

'You would make demands of me now, wych?' asked the dracon. He did not look at Atherak, and the words were said casually, but Keelan could feel the underlying threat in his voice.

'I make no demands, lord,' said Atherak, 'merely a request.'

'Ah, a request,' said Drazjaer. 'I refuse, then. Ja'harael will go. He and his kin are being well compensated for their service, and it is high time that they began earning it. We shall see how well he fares, since my warriors have failed me so. Go, half-breed. Get out of my sight, for your presence is beginning to offend me.'

The mandrake grinned and then was gone, as if he had never been there in the first place.

'I'd like to gut the filthy creature,' hissed Atherak, and the dracon smiled.

'All in good time,' he said, stroking his chin. Then his gaze dropped once more to Keelan, who was trying to remain inconspicuous on his knees, praying that his lord and master might have forgotten about him.

'Take him,' said the dracon, banishing any hope that Keelan had of escaping punishment. 'Rhakaeth, see that he is suitably chastised for his failure. I leave the level of his punishment to your discretion.'

Keelan felt his heart sink as he saw the hungry light in the haemonculus's dead eyes.

'Thank you, my lord,' said the haemonculus, and Keelan was dragged away.

* * *

MARDUK STOOD GAZING down into the gaping hexagonal shaft that descended into darkness below. Yellow and black hazard stripes lined the edge of the impossibly deep drop-off, and a steel barrier stood along its rim to protect the unwary or the clumsy from falling.

It had been time-consuming but not difficult to breach the guild city, nor to penetrate to its heart.

Warning lights were flashing, and the immense cable that descended down the centre of the shaft vibrated as the lift rose from the stygian darkness. The cable was over five metres in diameter, and was formed of thousands of tightly bound ropes of metal. It connected the guild city to the mining facility on the bottom of the ocean far below, and it shuddered as the lift ascended.

The surrounding loading area was vast, easily the size of one of the embarkation decks of the *Infidus Diabolus*. Scores of loading vehicles lay dormant in neat rows, as if in readiness to unload the next shipment of the ore transported up from the mining facility below. Over a hundred servitor units stood immobile within the arched alcoves lining the loading dock walls, their arms replaced with immense power lifters. Massive hooks and clamp-mouthed lifters hung from thick chains linked to heavy machines overhead that would come to life to lift the heavy containers of mining ore onto waiting transport pallets when a fully laden lift ascended from below.

The lift rose from the shaft, water streaming from its sloping sides. It was shaped like a diamond, with powerful engines positioned in either tip that hauled it up the thick cable. It came to a grinding rest, and steam and smoke spewed from the engines as they powered down. The sides of the pressurised, octagonal lift hissed as they slid upwards, exposing the expansive interior.

The lift was spartan, consisting of a single grilled, open floor-space where cargo could be loaded, with a barricaded area around the thick cable that spooled through its centre. In effect, the lift was like a massive bead through which the thick cable was threaded, and its interior, though the ceiling was low, was large enough to house half a tank company. Its sides were thickly armoured to withstand the intense pressure of deep sea

'Sabtec, Namar-sin,' said Marduk. The two named champions snapped to attention. 'You and your squads are to stay behind, to hold this position. Khalaxis, you and your brethren will join me, Burias and the Anointed for the descent.'

'You heard the First Acolyte,' barked Kol Badar. 'Let's get this done. Move out.'

The chosen warriors stamped forward into the expansive interior of the lift. Buzzing strips of glow lights hung from the roof of the lift. More than half of them were dark, but the flickering remainder lit the space with a dim, unnatural light.

'Darioq-Grendh'al,' said Marduk, his voice commanding, 'come.'

Impelled by the power in the First Acolyte's voice, the magos stepped forward obediently.

Marduk slammed his fist down onto a large button on the lift's command console, and the sides of the lift began to close, venting steam.

'May the gods be with you,' said Sabtec, bowing his head as the doors slid shut.

'Oh, but they are,' said Marduk.

Burias tensed, sniffing the air as an unusual scent reached his nostrils. It was the same odd scent that he had registered just before the dark eldar attack in the tunnels. His every sense alert for danger, he registered a flicker of movement outside the lift.

He roared a warning, but his cry was lost as the lift doors sealed shut.

CHAPTER TEN

SABTEC AND NAMAR-SIN watched as the lift descended into darkness down the abyssal shaft in the floor. Neither of them had heard Burias's cry of warning, and neither of them noticed the shadowy figure crawling head-first down one of the hanging chains ten metres above their heads.

The black figure dropped soundlessly from above, twisting in the air like a gymnast and landing in a crouch, with one foot on each of Namar-sin's shoulders and one hand steadying itself on the top of his helmet. Before the sergeant-champion could react, the shadowy creature punched a blade through the back of his neck, severing the vertebrae. Its serrated tip emerged from the front of his throat, the monomolecular blade sliding through his gorget as if it were made of paper.

The Word Bearer champion fell soundlessly, blood spurting from the fatal wound as the blade was retracted. Sabtec bellowed a warning as he lifted his bolter. The shadowy creature, its skin as black as pitch and with glowing runes cut into its flesh, sprung from the dying Word Bearers champion's shoulders, throwing itself into a back flip even as Sabtec began to fire.

The explosive-tipped bolt-rounds passed straight through the creature as it became as ethereal as smoke, even as Namar-sin fell face-first to the floor, dead.

Sabtec lost sight of the murderous eldar and threw himself into a roll as he felt a second presence materialise behind him. A blade slashed the air where he had been standing a fraction of a second earlier, and he came up firing. Again, his bolt rounds found no target.

Shouts and screams echoed through the lift bay, accompanied by the percussive barking of bolt weapons as more of the ghostly attackers materialised, dropping from overhead and emerging from shadows that had been empty moments before.

Moving faster than he could track, one of the insubstantial attackers darted around Sabtec, a fraction of a second in front of his coughing bolter, and the Word Bearer backed up a step, attempting to put some extra space between him and his ethereal attacker.

The creature darted forwards, dissipating into mist as Sabtec fired upon it. It re-formed just to his left, and he swung his bolter towards it. A blade slashed down in a diagonal arc, slicing the holy weapon in two, and a second blade stabbed towards Sabtec's throat. He swayed aside from the attack, but such was its speed that it still gouged a line across the faceplate of his helmet. Dropping his useless bolter, he grabbed his attacker's slim arm. Feeling solid armour and flesh beneath his grasp, he hurled his attacker away from him, sending it spinning through the air, and drew his sword from his scabbard.

'Thirteen!' he roared, bellowing the rallying cry that would bring the warriors of his coterie together.

Thumbing its activation glyph, Sabtec brought his sword humming to life. The metre-and-a-half blade gleamed as a sudden wave of energy raced up its length, and he swung it around in a glittering arc to deflect a dark blade that sang towards his groin. The blade severed the attacker's hand at the wrist, and the eldar warrior gave out a hiss of pain before becoming one with the shadows once more.

'Thirteen!' roared Sabtec again, breaking into a run towards the bulk of his coterie, which was fighting its way towards him through the confusing blur of darting shadows.

'Twenty-third, form up on me,' he roared, seeing Namar-sin's warriors becoming isolated and surrounded.

Even as he closed with his warriors of the 13th coterie, he saw one of them hamstrung by a slashing blade from behind and fall. Instantly, a trio of shadows materialised around the fallen warrior, looming like shades of death over him, and they dragged him backwards.

One of the black-skinned eldar warriors made a slashing motion with its hand that parted the substance of the air, cutting aside the veil between real space and beyond. In an instant, the fallen warrior was bundled through the rent in reality, which sealed up behind him as if it had never been.

Sabtec slashed with his blade, keeping the darting shadows around him at bay. He focused on one of the creatures as it materialised behind another of his squad brothers, its slanted, milky white eyes focused on its prey.

Sabtec roared as he launched himself forwards and impaled the shadow eldar on his power sword, plunging the weapon into its throat. Its blood danced upon the energised blade, spitting and jumping. Sabtec freed his weapon, slicing it out through the side of the eldar's neck. Its head flopped to the side, and it dropped to the ground. The glowing runes across its body blazed with sudden light, and then faded, smoking slightly, leaving just a shattered eldar corpse lying on the floor.

Having formed up, the 13th coterie fought back to back, protecting each other's vulnerable flanks. The enemy was coming at them from all directions, yet the warrior brothers had fought alongside each other for countless centuries, and each could predict his brothers' movements with the understanding that came from a lifetime of shared battle.

Heavy bolter-rounds from one of the Havoc Space Marines of the 217th ripped a swathe through the shadows, tearing two of the eldar apart. A pair of blades punched into his back and he was dragged into another dark rift that swallowed him, closing off behind him.

Sabtec's 13th blazed away at the shadows, most of their shots missing their targets, but a few striking their attackers, blasting bloody chunks out of armour and flesh.

The attack ceased as quickly as it had started as first one of the mandrakes stepped into shadow and was gone, and then another and another, until the Word Bearers were alone, smoke rising from the barrels of their boltguns, and steam venting from the cooling chambers of plasma weapons. The sudden silence was eerie, and Sabtec's breathing sounded loud in the confines of his helmet. The warriors of the 13th took the moment's respite to load their bolters, dropping empty clips to the floor.

Sabtec turned his head left and right, seeking the enemy, but it seemed they had truly gone. Still wary, he broke from the circle of his squad, and moved cautiously forward.

'Report,' he snapped.

Of 13th coterie, two members were dead and one was missing, taken by the dark eldar. Three of the surviving members were wounded, but not seriously. The 217th Havoc coterie had fared even worse, with three members dead, Namar-sin included, and two of their squad missing, leaving only three members remaining.

Sabtec swore.

'You three,' he said, stabbing a finger towards the remaining warriors of Namar-sin's coterie, 'you are 13th now. 217th is dead.'

The brother warriors bowed their heads in assent. It was a great honour to be taken into the hallowed 13th coterie, but they had fought as part of the 217th under Namar-sin for centuries.

Ammunition was running low, and the Word Bearers moved amongst their deceased kin, stripping them of weapons, grenades and clips. Sabtec knelt alongside each of the fallen warriors, speaking the oath of the departed over each in turn. With his combat knife, he carved an eight-pointed star into the forehead of each warrior, solemnly intoning the ritualised words, and daubed their eyelids with blood.

Kneeling over the corpse of Namar-sin, Sabtec removed his helmet, and placed it on the floor alongside his fallen brother. Then, he reverently lifted one of the champion's hands up, and stripped it of its gauntlet. Cradling the warrior's meaty fist in one hand, he reached again for his knife, and began to saw through the champion's fingers, using the serrated edge of his blade.

After hacking through each of the digits in turn, he tossed a severed finger to each of the members of Namar-sin's coterie. He kept one for himself, for Namar-sin had been his battle-brother since the Great

Crusade, and he had respected the warrior greatly, and valued his comradeship.

He began to strip his battle-brother's body, removing his shoulder plates and placing them carefully at his side, before moving onto his gorget and outer chest plates, removing each piece carefully and reverently. The other members of his squad stood by solemnly.

He pulled the breastplate away with a sucking sound, taking with it the outer layer of skin that had long fused with the armour.

The flesh of Namar-sin's broad torso was heavily muscled, and the tissue of that muscle glistened wetly. With a deft movement, Sabtec sliced a deep cut from the breastbone to the navel. Inserting his hand into the cut, he searched around in the chest cavity, groping behind the thick, fused ribcage. Grasping Namar-sin's motionless primary heart, he pulled it free, cutting it loose with his knife.

Sabtec stood and lifted the heart up in his bloody hands.

'Namar-sin was a mighty warrior and devoted brother of the true word,' said Sabtec. 'We mourn his passing, yet rejoice, for his soul has become as one with Chaos. In honour of his service in the name of Lorgar, we eat of his flesh, that he may live on with us as we continue the Long War without him, and that we may carry his strength with us, always.'

Lifting the heart to his mouth, Sabtec took a bite, ripping the flesh away with his teeth. Blood covered his chin, and he chewed the lump of flesh briefly before swallowing it. Then he stepped in front of the first of the three remaining warriors that had belonged to Namar-sin's coterie, offering the heart.

* * *

MARDUK STARED THROUGH the thirty-centimetre thick porthole into the inky blackness beyond as the lift continued to power its way down into the stygian depths of the ocean. Little could be seen apart from occasional bubbles of expanding gas, and the visage of his skull helmet was reflected back at him, distorted in the curved therma-glass.

'There is no going back now; we have not the time. I feel the threads of fate weaving together. The time of the completion of this… necessary task, draws close,' said Marduk with a hint of impatience and irritation. 'Sabtec and Namar-sin are veterans. They can look after themselves.'

The lift strained and creaked alarmingly as the building pressure of the water outside pressed in. The thick metal plates of the hull, supported by countless brackets and thick bolted girders, flexed inwards, groaning like a beast in torment.

The lift had descended at a steady rate, down the shaft carved from solid ice. The rate of descent slowed as they reached the lower crust of the ice and plunged into the sea, before increasing in speed once more as they sank further into the icy depths. They were some four thousand metres below the surface, nearing halfway to the ocean floor.

Burias was pacing back and forth like a caged animal, glaring hatefully at the bulging hull as if daring it to give way.

'Be calm, icon bearer,' snapped Marduk, turning away from the porthole. 'Your restlessness is distracting.'

Marduk could feel Burias's impatience like a living thing, intruding on his spirit.

'What is the matter with you?' asked Marduk in irritation.

'I am envious,' said Burias, pausing in his pacing for a moment, flashing Marduk a dark glance. 'I had wished to fight the eldar again. I wish to test my speed against them.'

'You sound like a spoilt child,' spat Marduk. 'Recite the Lacrimosa. Begin at verse eighty-nine. It will calm your nerves.'

Burias glowered at Marduk.

'Eighty-nine?' he said, furrowing his brow.

'*And when the accused are confounded and confined to flames of woe, rejoice and call upon Me, your saviour,*' he quoted.

'The Lacrimosa has always been a favourite of yours, hasn't it, brother?' asked Burias.

Marduk smiled. Alone amongst all the warriors of the Host, he tolerated Burias referring to him as brother, in honour of the blood-oaths that the pair had sworn aeons past, when they were both idealistic young pups, freshly blooded in battle. Nevertheless, Marduk allowed the icon bearer the honour only when they were alone, or out of earshot of the other warrior brothers of the Host, for such familiarity was unfavourable, especially now that he was certain that his ambitions of becoming Dark Apostle were fated to be, at last, fulfilled.

A Dark Apostle must be aloof from his flock, a symbol of the undying faith of the holy word. He had learnt that from Jarulek, and it was, his arrogant master had taught him, part of the reason why the role of the Coryphaus was important. The Dark Apostle must be more than a warrior; he must be an inspiration, a saint, the holiest of disciples. He must be raised above the warriors of the Host, for the gods spoke through him. A Dark Apostle had no brothers except others of his rank, for it was deemed that familial relations within the Host humanised him too much, weakening the awe he was held in by his warriors. Such a thing led to a weakening of the strength of the Host, and a lessening of the faith.

'A Dark Apostle,' Jarulek had lectured him condescendingly, 'must be above reproach, above question. He cannot have close ties with the warriors of his flock. Your Coryphaus is your closest confidant, and your will is enacted through him. He is the bridge that spans the gap between the Dark Apostle and the Host.'

Marduk pushed the distracting, errant thoughts back, his mood darkening.

'The Lacrimosa brings me great calm,' said Marduk. 'It at once soothes my soul and rekindles my hatred.'

'I shall do as you suggest, brother,' said Burias. 'So long as Sabtec leaves a few for me, I guess I can wait.'

Another loud groan shuddered the lift, and Burias scowled.

Kol Badar stamped towards them, and the cordial companionship between Marduk and Burias evaporated. At once, they were no longer long-time friends and blood brothers; now they were once again First Acolyte and icon bearer.

'This lift is a relic,' remarked Kol Badar. 'If a fault in the hull appears, we will all be crushed to death. This is a foolish endeavour, an unnecessary risk.'

'Are you going senile in your dotage Coryphaus?' snapped Marduk. Burias sniggered. 'You are repeating yourself. Your protestations have been heard before, and duly noted. I don't care what you think. I am your leader now, and you will do as I wish.'

The Coryphaus's brow creased in anger.

'If a fault appears, then we are dead,' Marduk said, more calmly. 'Such would be the will of the gods, but I do not believe it will be so.'

'How can you be so sure?' asked Kol Badar.

'Have faith, Coryphaus,' said Marduk. 'Each of us is in our allotted place, as per the will of the gods. If it is our time to die, then so be it, but I do not think that it is. The gods have much more in store for me, of that I am certain.'

'And for me?' asked Burias.

Marduk shrugged.

'You speak as if all our actions are already predetermined,' growled Kol Badar.

'Are you so sure they are not?' countered Marduk. 'I have seen things in dream visions that have come to pass. Many amongst the Host have. Does such a thing not suggest that every decision that we think we make has not already been determined beforehand? A path set in front of us that we, try as we might to avoid our fate, are condemned to walk?'

'By that rationale, why should we strive for anything? Why should we seek to destroy our enemies, if the outcome has already been decided?' asked Burias.

'Don't be a fool, Burias,' said Marduk sharply. 'The gods help those that help themselves. If you were not going to try to defeat your enemies, then you were already fated to lose.'

'If what you suggest is correct, then this,' said Kol Badar, levelling his combi-bolter at Marduk's head, 'is the will of the gods?'

The Coryphaus's weapon system whined and clicked as fresh bolts were loaded into the firing chambers. Burias licked his lips, glancing between the First Acolyte and Kol Badar.

Behind them, kneeling in a tight circle with his squad, Khalaxis half-rose to his feet, but the heavy hand of one of the Anointed held him in place.

The sergeant-champion glowered up at the Terminator-armoured warrior, his rage building, but he relented and remained kneeling, watching the outcome of the confrontation.

Marduk took a step forward so that the twin barrels of the Coryphaus's weapon pressed against his forehead.

'Pull the trigger and find out,' said Marduk.

After a tense moment, Kol Badar bent his arm, removing the weapon from his superior's head, and stalked away angrily.

'What if he had pulled the trigger?' asked Burias quietly.

'Then I'd be dead,' said Marduk.

SINKING EVER DEEPER, the lift continued descending through the inky-black water. This was more of an abyss than the depths of deep space, thought Burias. At least there pin-pricks of light could be glimpsed, distant stars and coronas a hundred million light years distant. Here, the darkness was complete and all-consuming.

Still they descended. It felt like they had been descending for days, though it had been less than an hour, and Burias continued his restless pacing, stalking back and forth, clenching and unclenching his fists.

Khalaxis's squad knelt in a close circle around Marduk, who was in a half-trance, intoning from the unholy scriptures. The warriors of the Anointed stood in a second circle around the kneeling figures, the Coryphaus leading a morose counter-chant.

Of the warrior brethren, only Burias stood apart, for he could not calm his mind enough to be part of the communion.

Impatience knotted his stomach, and he snarled in frustration.

Burias stamped around the interior of the lift, slamming the butt of his icon into the grilled flooring with each step. The flickering lights above were irritating him with their incessant buzzing and for a moment he toyed with the notion of smashing them.

While other Astartes warriors within the Host took pleasure in creation, painstakingly copying the illuminated volumes of the Books of Lorgar into new volumes, labouring for weeks on end over each page, Burias had not the patience for such pursuits. He took pleasure in destruction, whether it was ripping apart a living creature and watching its life fade, or smashing apart the profane statues of the Imperium.

What worth was a hundred years of toil if a man could destroy it in seconds?

Thankfully, the Host was almost constantly at war. It was at times like these, however, when the enemy was so close, yet the thrill of battle was denied him, that his fury rose, clouding his mind and shattering his concentration.

He paced around the extent of the lift, until finally he saw a soft glow permeating up from below through the porthole windows.

In the distance below, the lights from the mining station were radiating up from the ocean floor.

It looked like some outpost station on a desolate asteroid or moon, with the blackness of space all around it. A broad, domed central hub, roughly the size of the largest galactic battleship, was rooted in the rock bed, surrounded by dozens of bulbous satellite outbuildings. Cylindrical, transparent corridors connected all the sub-structures to the main hub. Light, harsh and unnatural, spilled from the arterial tubes, and peering closely, Burias thought he could see vehicles and people moving through them, like tiny insects within an artificial environ-farm.

Burias rolled his shoulders and stretched the muscles of his neck.

'Finally,' he muttered.

* * *

PRESSURE GAUGES VENTED, equalising the compressed air within the lift with that of the mining facility. The sides of the lift slid aside with a clatter and water gushed down from above, slipping off the angled surfaces of the lift's hull, and draining away through the grates set in the floor. Darkness greeted them inside the mining facility, though an infrequent strobe of light sparked from severed cables hanging loose from the low ceiling.

The Word Bearers walked cautiously forward, stepping through the dripping water, weapons seeking targets. There were none.

Kol Badar's Anointed led the way, combi-bolters and repeater autocannon tracking from side to side.

The air was hot and humid, a far cry from the dry, gelid atmosphere on the planet's frozen surface.

'There is no one down here,' growled Kol Badar.

'There *are* people here,' said Burias. 'I saw them on the descent.'

The warriors drew towards the main entrance into the mining facility, an immense arched processional that led from the lift base to the main hub of the structure.

Marduk's eyes were drawn up above the archway. A massive figure had been roughly painted onto the plascrete wall, like a mural, though its workmanship was crude to say the least. A low hiss escaped his lips.

'What is it?' asked Burias, his eyes wide. 'A daemon? Are these miners cult worshippers?'

'No, it's not a daemon,' said Marduk, not taking his eyes from the primitive mural.

'You are sure?' asked Kol Badar, glowering upwards.

'I feel no touch of the warp here,' said Marduk. 'Worship of the great gods of the immaterium would leave a palpable trace, a lingering presence, but there is none. No, this is no daemon. I could command a daemon. There is no commanding *that*.'

The warriors of the Host shuffled uneasily.

A four-armed figure was daubed on the wall above the archway, painted in garish blues and purples. Two of its arms ended in claws, while the others ended in human-like hands. Its eyes were yellow and its mouth was wide, exposing a caricature of sharp teeth, painted as simple triangles and dripping with garish red paint representing blood. A long, stabbing tongue protruded from the toothy maw.

'I think your battle-lust will soon be sated, Burias,' said Marduk in a soft voice.

CHAPTER ELEVEN

'You want us to go in there?' asked Kol Badar flatly, looking in disdain at the maintenance submersibles bobbing slightly on the surface of the dark pool of water.

'This is the way that the explorator came; we must follow in his footsteps,' said Marduk evenly.

'That statement is categorically false, Marduk, First Acolyte of the Word Bearers Legion of Astartes, genetic descendant of the glorified Primarch Lorgar,' intoned Darioq-Grendh'al.

Marduk turned slowly towards the daemonically infused magos, glowering within his skull-faced helmet.

'What?' he said in a low, dangerous voice.

'Repeat: "This is the way that the explorator came; we must follow in his footsteps" is categorically false,' said the magos.

Marduk licked his lips. If he did not feel like he had such control over the daemon inhabiting Darioq's body, he would think that the magos was being wilfully obtuse.

'What is incorrect about that statement?' asked Marduk slowly.

'Explorator First Class Daenae,' said Magos Darioq in his monotone voice, 'originally of the Konor Adeptus Mechanicus research world of UL01.02, assigned to c14.8.87.i, Perdus Skylla, for recon/salvage of the Dvorak-class interstellar freighter *Flames of Perdition*, which reappeared within Segmentum Tempestus in 942.M41 and crashed onto the surface of c14.8.87.i, Perdus Skylla, in 944.M41 after being missing presumed lost in warp storm anomaly xi.024.396 in 432.M35, is of the female gender.'

Marduk blinked.

'Well I am certainly glad that we got that cleared up,' he said in a deadpan voice.

'I am pleased to have caused you gratification, Marduk, First–' began the magos, but Marduk held up a hand to stop him.

'Enough,' he impelled, the word laced with the power of the warp, and the magos fell silent mid-sentence.

'Why don't we rip out his tongue?' suggested Burias. 'Or his speaker box, or whatever.'

'The thought had crossed my mind,' said Marduk, before turning back towards the line of docked submersibles.

'We are going in those,' he said to Kol Badar. 'No discussion.'

Though wary of possible attack and on edge having witnessed the profane mural upon entering the mining facility, they had encountered no resistance as they penetrated deeper into the complex. They had come across several shrines that appeared to venerate the four-armed creature that Marduk recognised as xenos in origin, with crudely scrawled images of the beast in alcoves surrounded by offerings of tokens, charms and coins. He ordered these fanes destroyed, and the walls cleansed with bursts of promethium from flamer units.

Though they faced no resistance, a growing crowd of humans, miners it would seem, were shadowing their progress. At first, just a few figures were seen ghosting their steps, ducking into the shadows whenever warrior brothers looked in their direction. As they continued onward they attracted more of a following, until hundreds of miners were following in their footsteps, though they still maintained a wary distance. Marduk felt their anger as the shrines were obliterated but, wisely, they did not dare to attempt to stop the actions of the Word Bearers.

Not wishing to be slowed, Marduk ordered the warrior brothers to ignore the growing crowd that shadowed their progress, pressing on with an increasing sense of urgency.

The interstellar freighter *Flames of Perdition* had settled on the ocean bed some eight kilometres from the mining complex, and the last recorded location of the explorator he sought had been a docking station of submersible maintenance vehicles. Presumably, the explorator and her team had commandeered a flotilla of the craft to investigate the submerged ship, and so Marduk's progress had led here, to the very same dock.

Half a dozen submersibles were docked here, held in place by massive locking clamps that looked like giant, mechanical crab claws. Each of the submersibles was the size of a Land Raider and roughly spherical in shape, with an array of sensors protruding from forward hulls like the antennae of insects. A pair of mechanical arms were under-slung beneath their bulbous chassis, just visible in the dark water, and the monstrous insectoid limbs ended in powerful claws, industrial-sized welding tools and drills the length of two men.

Hundreds of onlookers watched from the shadows, crowding in around the gantries overlooking the holding pool of the dock. Marduk glimpsed hooded faces, eyes gleaming with feverish light and their skin an unhealthy, blue-tinged pallor. The tension in the crowd was palpable, and the warriors of the Host kept their weapons ready, yet the miners made no move to obstruct them.

Four-armed stick figures had been scratched into the circular boarding hatches in the sides of the submersibles, as well as phrases scrawled in what must have been the local Low Gothic dialect. It made little sense to Marduk, though he was schooled in dozens of Imperial dialects, but the general message could be understood. The scratching seemed to indicate that the submersibles were the 'carriages of the earthly gods', and that to enter them would bring enlightenment.

Marduk was repulsed by the idolatrous pseudo-religious sentiments, but he had not the time nor the inclination to 'educate' these wretches of their misguided beliefs. They would all be dead soon enough anyway.

'You still maintain these people are not daemon worshippers?' asked Kol Badar, tracing his finger along the deep gouges that formed the stick figure of a four-armed monster. It certainly did look daemonic, but Marduk was certain.

'I believe these people are held in the sway of xenos creatures,' he stated. 'A tyranid vanguard species, perhaps. I feel that there is some form of psychic control over these miners that draws the hive fleet like a lure. These deluded fools are worshipping a xenos creature, or a host of them, that will be the death of them.'

'Worshipping xenos as gods?' asked Khalaxis, his voice expressing his disgust.

Marduk nodded.

'A powerful foe, then,' said Burias with relish.

'Oh yes,' agreed Marduk. 'A powerful foe.'

MARDUK PEERED AT the small view-screen. The submersible had no viewing portal; it was built to traverse the deepest abyssal channels of the ocean floor, and at extreme depths even the most heavily reinforced window would crumple beneath the tremendous pressure. In its stead, the grainy, black and white pict screen fed visual information from the sensor arrays on the exterior of the deep-sea vessel.

The interior of the submersible was cramped and hot, and the Word Bearers had needed to commandeer four of them to fit all of the warriors accompanying Marduk. The secondary locking gate on the underside of the sub-docks slid aside, and the four mining craft descended into the open water, powerful impeller motors whirring.

Burias sat at the controls of the craft, looking ludicrously large hunched over the dials and levers that controlled the pitch, speed, depth, direction and roll of the submersible. It was a simple control system akin to that of a shuttle, and he had little trouble becoming familiar with it. He grinned like a madman as he discovered the controls of the exterior robotic arms, and in the view-screen Marduk could see the massive power-claw snapping, and the huge drill spinning, creating a small whirlpool of turbulence.

'Burias, it is not a toy,' said Marduk.

The submersible struck one of the underside legs of the mining facility, and Burias looked around at Marduk guiltily.

'Sorry,' he said, and stopped fooling around with the robotic arms to concentrate on piloting the craft. It wanted to turn to the left all the time, and he struggled with the controls to keep it steady.

It levelled out abruptly and swung around smoothly to port, its impeller motors whining as the submersible powered forwards. Burias swore.

'You seem to have got the hang of it,' said Marduk.

Burias held his hands up, removing them from the controls.

'I'm not controlling it,' he said. 'It is following an automated piloting route.'

He consulted the stream of data on a side-screen.

'It's taking us to the downed ship.'

They could do little but watch the grainy pict screens as the submersible carried them away from the mining facility, following its pre-determined route.

The ocean floor was jagged and uneven, and jutting spears of rock reared up before them, but the submersible traversed the terrain carefully, rising above the smaller outcrops, and accelerating beneath vast bridges of rock.

The undersea landscape was breathtaking, with vast cathedral-like spires of rock rising thousands of metres up into the dark water. Their vision slowly diminished the further they got away from the glow of the mining facility, until they could see only what was lit by the powerful spotlights on the prow of the submersible.

The lights of the other craft blinked, as all four of the submersibles travelled along the same line. As they passed beneath yet another towering arched causeway, they came upon a sheer drop-off, an undersea cliff that plunged down into blackness. It was down this vertical wall that the submersibles dropped, leaving trails of bubbles in their wake.

The sheer drop seemed to have no bottom. The chasm must have been over two kilometres in width, and it dropped away into utter darkness.

At last, something came into view, something immense.

'Gods of the ether,' swore Burias as they came upon the wreckage of the *Flame of Perdition*.

The Dvorak-class freighter was wedged between the walls of the chasm, its prow and stern ground into the sheer walls of the drop-off, bridging the bottomless gap.

As the submersibles ploughed on through the clear water, impeller engines whirring, the sheer size of the ship became apparent. It was one thing to see battle cruisers hanging in space where there were few reference points to give an indication of their sheer scale, but seeing this ship wedged firmly between the two distant sides of the chasm was breathtaking.

A portion of the lower stern looked as though it had been sheared away. It might have suffered the damage as it struck the mouth of the chasm, or it might have occurred thousands of years before the ship entered this sub-system, long before it had smashed through the ice crust of Perdus Skylla. According to Darioq-Grendh'al, the ship had been lost in a warp storm anomaly for some six and a half thousand years. Anything could have happened to it in that time.

Warp storms were notoriously unpredictable, and time and distance became blurred within their bounds. The *Flame of Perdition* might have been drifting through the nebulous warp storms for fifteen thousand years, twenty thousand years, thrown like a leaf on the wind through the ether. Or, equally as likely, it might have seemed to its crew to have been gone only a fraction of a second before it struck the surface of the frozen moon, and plunged into the oceanic depths.

During its time in the warp, and wherever else it may have emerged, the ship may have encountered any number of daemonic and xenos entities, and it was highly possible that some of the creatures remained onboard.

Apart from the shattered stern, the ship appeared to be in a remarkably complete state, and though Marduk feared that its interior had been flooded, there was every likelihood that at least the upper decks might still contain breathable air.

At such depth, and with its integrity compromised, what air did remain within the ship would have shrunk to a tiny fraction of its previous volume, but if any man-made structure could withstand the immense pressure as deep as this, it was a space-faring cruiser.

The submersibles ploughed inexorably towards the ship that grew ever larger in the small pict screen. As they drew closer, Marduk could see that the sides of the ship were scarred. Entire sections of its thick armour had bubbled, and other portions looked unnaturally smooth, like the skin of a burn victim, or as if they had been splashed with corrosive, high-grade acid.

The four submersibles drew towards the immense freighter, dipping down towards one of its gaping, water-filled hangar bays, still following an automated route.

'At least they seem to know where they are going,' said Marduk.

'Or they are leading us into a trap,' said Burias, angrily flicking switches and yanking on the controls.

The four deep-sea craft, dwarfed to insignificance by the sheer size of the *Flame of Perdition*, entered the cavernous hangar bay. It was a surreal experience to drift through the submerged bay, to pass by upturned shuttles that had clearly been tossed around the expansive hangar bay by the force of the impact with the ice, or the chasm sides. The four submersibles ghosted through the massive open space, leaving a swirling wake of turbulence behind them that blurred the water.

They began to ascend vertically, climbing up through the flooded levels of the ship, the automated controls carefully navigating them safely through the tangle of shattered girders and twisted metal.

The corpse of a man dressed in naval fatigues reared up in front of the submersible, filling the pict screen with its cadaverous rictus grin. The flesh was almost completely rotted from its bones and as the submersible bumped the corpse out of the way, one of its arms came loose. A host of wriggling eel-creatures squirmed from the cavity, thrashing madly, and then the corpse drifted out of sight.

As they continued to ascend, passing through flooded cargo bays and freight holds, they passed more corpses, all being slowly devoured. They powered along a wide corridor, the tilt that the ship had come to rest at forcing the submersible to travel at an obtuse angle.

They entered another area of the ship, and the submersibles bobbed to the surface of the water like corks. Automated pressurisation systems kicked into gear, slowly equalising with the outside pressure, and once the dials began to flash green, the access hatch began to release. It swung wide with a slight vacuum hiss, and Marduk stepped out into knee-deep water. The submersible had brought itself up to a raised gantry twenty metres above what appeared to be a holding area. Evidently, the upper portion of the ship was still structurally sound, and air had been trapped within it.

Marduk's helmet readouts gave him a flood of information and he saw that the air was unsafe for an unprotected human to breathe. Astartes warriors, with their superior, genhanced physiology, would probably last around an hour before they expired.

Marduk saw that the submersible he had emerged from was drawn up alongside half a dozen others.

'The explorator and her team's vessels, presumably,' said Kol Badar, stamping through the water to Marduk's side.

A massive doorway yawned behind them, leading further into the Imperial freighter. With no other obvious way of proceeding, Marduk led the warriors through its arched expanse.

They came upon a series of bulkheads, part of the latticework that subdivided the ship into distinct sections, adding strength to the whole and allowing areas of the ship to be isolated from each other in the event of hull breach.

Though there was no power within the ship – its plasma core reactors were clearly dead, or at least dormant – the bulkheads could be accessed manually. Kol Badar ripped one of them open with a wrench, half-expecting to be washed away by a flood of water. Once all the warriors had passed the bulkhead it was sealed behind them once more, and the next bulkhead opened. The ship beyond was dark, but the air was breathable without danger, and Marduk felt certain that this was the way that the explorator had taken.

He grinned within his helmet. He could almost feel the presence of the wretched devotee of the Machine-God. He had but to reach out to possess her.

'She is here, somewhere,' said Marduk. 'I know it.'

'She'd better be,' growled Kol Badar.

Warily, the warriors of the Host began to move further into the wrecked hulk that was the *Flame of Perdition*, weapons at the ready.

* * *

THEY HAD ADVANCED for over three hours, though in that time that had been forced to retrace their steps a dozen times as their way was blocked by shattered sections of the ship, or by bulkheads that led back into the flooded lower sections.

Burias's mood, previously buoyed by Marduk's optimism, had slowly soured as the sheer improbability of finding the explorator within this confusing maze was driven home. Kol Badar was right. The cursed worshipper of the profane Machine-God could be anywhere within the ship, *if* she were here at all. The ship was over two kilometres in length and consisted of almost fifty deck levels, depending on where within the ship one was located. In addition, a myriad of air ducts, sub-floor tunnels and inter-deck stowage vaults made the *Flame of Perdition* a veritable labyrinth, and despite the fact that perhaps seventy per cent of it was flooded and impassable, it would take a Herculean effort and incredible luck to locate a single individual within its confines.

'There is no such thing as luck,' Marduk snapped angrily, picking up the vagaries of the icon bearer's unfocused thoughts. This was a test of his faith, the First Acolyte reminded himself, ridding his thoughts of any shadow of doubt. The explorator would be delivered to him; it was the will of the gods. He had only to open himself up to the powers of the ether, and allow his earthly flesh to be guided.

'Keep moving,' said Marduk.

Kol Badar and two of his Anointed warriors were leading the advance, walking in single file, their massive shoulders sometimes scraping along the walls of the narrow, dark corridors.

Terminator armour had been originally constructed with brutal ship-to-ship boarding actions in mind, where the immense protection its heavy plates provided far outweighed its lack of speed and manoeuvrability. Within the flooded hulk, they were the obvious choice to lead the advance.

Khalaxis walked a pace behind them, a blinking auspex held before him, scanning for movement. The amount of interference from the ship was playing havoc with its accuracy, limiting its range to less than fifty metres. Anything moving within the range of its sweeps would appear as a blinking icon, but thus far only the other members of the Host had appeared on its blister screen.

Marduk walked with Burias in the centre of the group, along with the hulking form of Darioq-Grendh'al. Members of Khalaxis's coterie surrounded them, and the other two members of the Anointed brought up the rear.

They moved with well-practiced discipline. Despite no movement or heat signatures being picked up by the auspex, individual warriors peeled off to lay fields of over-watch down side corridors and into darkened rooms. Those behind moved past the sentinels, which filed back into line towards the rear. At the very back of the formation, the Anointed ensured that no enemy was able to approach unannounced. The formation was in constant movement, each warrior providing cover for his brethren before moving on, and though their progress was slow, they moved inexorably deeper into the hulk. It was standard practice in unknown, tight confines such as these, and centuries of drilled combat doctrine ensured that everyone knew his place.

The air within the ship was perfectly still, like the inside of a mausoleum, and the silence was oppressive. The darkness was all consuming, and with the utter absence of any form of light, even the enhanced vision of the Word Bearers was impaired. Their footsteps echoed painfully loudly along the empty corridors, and Marduk ground his sharp teeth in frustration, drawing blood. In the desolate silence of the hulk, sound travelled easily, and their quarry may already have heard their advance and moved deeper into the freighter.

The line of warriors emerged from a branching corridor into a room that might once have been a thriving workshop. Piles of mechanics and engine parts were strewn across the grilled, uneven flooring, and heavy machinery that would have taken a dozen power-lifter equipped servitors to shift lay overturned, like the discarded toys of an infant.

Half a dozen dark, uninviting corridors led from the room, as well as at least four closed, powered doors. Warriors had taken up position at each entrance, autosensors straining to locate any threat.

'Which way?' asked Kol Badar.

The Coryphaus's tone conveyed the warlord's thoughts clearly, without need for words, that this was a hopeless venture, but Marduk ignored his inference and paused, calming his breathing and closing his eyes.

He had entered this half-trance a dozen times already within the ship, searching for any residual warp-trace that might suggest the explorator had come this way, but so far had found nothing. The soul of every living creature in the universe was a flaring beacon within the warp – those individuals who manifested latent psychic powers burning the most fiercely – and to those schooled in the occult teachings of the Word Bearer's priesthood, it was possible to perceive this soul glow in the material realm, sensing it even at distance.

Marduk strained to pick up anything, and had almost resigned himself to failure once more when he felt...

something. It was very faint, like the fading heat image that surrounded a body an hour dead, but it was definitely there.

His eyes snapped open.

'There,' he said, pointing towards one of the corridors.

Without a word, the Word Bearers continued deeper into the *Flame of Perdition*.

Somewhere in the distance there was an echoing clang. It was impossible to gauge the distance of the sound, but to Marduk he felt it was confirmation of the whereabouts of the explorator.

'Quickly,' he urged.

THE ANOINTED WERE leading the way, their combi-bolters tracking for movement. Khalaxis's auspex throbbed with its steady light.

The remainder of the warriors followed single-file, weapons held at the ready.

They had been moving within the *Flame of Perdition* for over an hour, time enough to have walked its length twice over had their path not been so circuitous and slow. No further sound had been heard other than that one, distant echo, but Marduk was confident that his quarry was near.

The First Acolyte was lost in his thoughts when it happened.

A sheet metal wall panel punched inwards, crumpling like synth-board, and a blurred, dark shape leapt from the gaping hole in the wall. A clawed limb smashed into a warrior brother's helmet, crumpling it like paper, and hot blood spurted, splashing across the wall.

Marduk saw a blur of limbs, an exoskeleton of dark chitin, and another warrior brother was dead, claws tearing an arm from its socket and punching through a breastplate.

In the tight confines of the corridor, all was suddenly chaos, with warriors shouting and bolters barking.

The warrior in front of Marduk staggered backwards as the xenos creature turned its attention towards him, claws flashing. In an instant, his hand was severed at the wrist by the flashing claws, the bolt pistol in his hand still firing as it hit the ground, and Marduk stared into the venomous eyes of the deadly killer.

The creature was bipedal and hunched, its four arms hanging low from its armoured carapace, and its hypnotic eyes, glinting yellow slashes, set deep into a wide, pallid face. Marduk found himself ensnared by the power in those golden orbs, and for a second he was frozen in place, staring dumbly at the alien.

It pulled the disarmed warrior into a tight embrace, and its jaws closed around the Word Bearer's helmet.

Bolter fire struck the xenos creature from behind and a high-pitched, inhuman scream was ripped from its throat as chunks of chitin were blasted from its body, splattering Marduk with its vile, xenos blood.

The splatter of blood upon the skull-face of his helmet broke his hypnotic reverie, and Marduk lifted his bolt pistol. Even as his finger was squeezing the trigger, the xenos creature spun towards its assailant.

Marduk's shots took the creature in the back of the head, and its forehead exploded like a ruptured egg, spraying brain matter, blood and shards of skull, and it fell to the ground, dead, a tangle of alien limbs.

Khalaxis gave a warning shout as his auspex suddenly lit up with movement.

'Contact,' he shouted.

'Where?' bellowed Kol Badar.

'Everywhere!' came the frantic response.

Marduk swore, and stared down in disgusted fascination at the lifeless corpse of the xenos creature on the ground.

The exposed flesh of its head and hands was pallid, tinged slightly purple-blue, and its chitinous shell, like that of an insect's, was the colour of the night sky. It had been monstrously fast and strong, and the fact that one creature had managed to kill two veteran Astartes and injure another in mere seconds meant that this corridor was not a place Marduk wanted to be when more of them appeared.

'Move!' he hollered.

With a nod from the Coryphaus, the Anointed at the forefront of the group began advancing.

The Anointed in the rear began firing, their combi-bolters barking loudly as they fired at the wave of creatures surging at them from behind. Passing a side passage, Marduk looked to the left and began firing, seeing another of the creatures scuttling up the corridor towards him with sickening speed. He dropped it with a controlled burst from his bolt pistol.

The warriors at the front of the group halted, opening up with their weapon systems as more of the xenos creatures appeared.

'A powerful foe,' growled Burias-Drak'shal with relish, forming the words with some difficulty now that his mouth was filled with daemonic tusks and teeth.

Marduk shook his head, and swung to his right, blasting another of the xenos creatures.

A sheet of metal in the shadowy ceiling overhead smashed down in front of him, and another of the creature's leapt towards him, murderous claws flashing for his face.

Burias-Drak'shal leapt past Marduk and hit the creature in mid-air, driving it into the reinforced steel wall, which buckled inwards at the force of the blow. The possessed warrior and the deadly xenos creature were locked together as they slid to the floor, thrashing frantically, limbs entangled.

After a few frantic seconds of combat, the fight ended, Burias-Drak'shal pinning the creature's head to the wall with one of his thick talons. Pulling his talon free, the creature slumped to the ground. Burias looked up at Marduk, a feral grin plastered across his daemonic visage. His armour was hanging loose from his body in half a dozen places, and strips of flesh had been torn from him, but his pleasure was palpable.

'Good fight,' he said with some difficulty.

'Good fight,' said Marduk, with somewhat less enthusiasm.

The Anointed had picked up their pace again, blasting with their combi-bolters as they stamped forwards. Marduk heard the roar of a reaper autocannon firing on full auto, and the alien screams of dying xenos.

To Marduk's right, one of the 17th coterie was standing braced in an open doorway. A dozen xenos creatures were hurtling up the side-corridor towards him, their claws clicking like the legs of an insect scuttling along a metal table. The warrior's flamer roared, and they screamed and thrashed as they were engulfed in flaming promethium.

One of the creatures, its body wreathed in flame, leapt through the inferno, and ripped the warrior's head from his shoulders with one sweep of its claws. Marduk hacked his chainsword into the alien's neck, the teeth of the weapon whirring madly as they ripped through chitin and flesh, spraying blood in all directions, and the creature fell twitching to the ground, tongues of fire still burning across its body.

The corridor was a charnel house, promethium burning fiercely across the walls and floor, and the blackened corpses of the aliens were smoking ruins. Still, more of the creatures were leaping forwards, throwing themselves towards Marduk along the blackened hallway.

Snatching up the flamer from the lifeless hands of the headless warrior at his feet, Marduk squeezed the trigger, sending a wall of flame roaring down the corridor, lighting up the darkness and engulfing the wave of xenos creatures. They screamed as they died, chitin melting and eyes dripping down their blackened faces. Still, several of the creatures continued to claw their way towards him, and he sent another burst of flame shooting down the corridor.

The warriors of the Legion continued their advance for five minutes, being attacked by wave after wave of xenos assailants that hurtled headlong into their gunfire. They must have killed somewhere in the realms of thirty of the deadly creatures, ripping them apart with concentrated bursts of bolter fire and flame, though it was clear that they could not endure such a furious assault indefinitely.

It was impossible to gauge the number of the enemy in the shadowy confines, but the Word Bearers were already running low on ammunition. Firing a final burst of flame behind them, Marduk discarded the flamer unit, dropping it to the ground, its promethium canister expended.

'Keep moving,' he barked as he drew his bolt pistol once more.

KOL BADAR HISSED as the claws of a xenos creatures sheared through one of his immense shoulder plates, gouging a deep wound in his flesh. Firing his combi-bolter at point blank range, explosive rounds tore through the thorax of the creature, ripping it in two. He smashed another alien predator away with a backhand sweep of his fist, the blow crushing bone and sending it reeling into the wall. Another creature leapt upon him, claws scraping deep furrows through his Terminator armour, and its jaws opened wide as its thick, muscular tongue darted towards his throat.

The Coryphaus closed his power talons around his xenos attacker's head, coruscating energy rippling up the long blades. With a twist, he ripped the alien's head from its shoulders, half a metre of its spinal column still attached, and flung it away from him before unloading with his combi-bolter once more, tearing another two aliens apart with concentrated bursts of fire. Warning icons flickered before his eyes as the chambers of his weapon emptied.

'Swap,' ordered the hulking Coryphaus, and he stepped to the side to allow the Anointed warrior behind him to pass.

The massive warrior stamped forwards to take up the position at the front of the formation, and his freshly loaded weapon roared.

'Keep moving,' ordered Kol Badar as he reloaded, feeding a fresh pair of ammunition belts into his weapon system and locking them into position. His weapon whined and pulled the first bolts into the firing chambers, and the warning icon within his helmet flashed green and disappeared.

The formation approached a cross-junction, the side-passages hidden from view by the dull metal corners.

'Khalaxis,' said Kol Badar. 'Grenades.'

The column paused briefly as the sergeant-champion of the 17th primed a pair of frag grenades.

'Fire in the hole!' he shouted, tossing the grenades forward. Kol Badar's optic stabilisers compensated for the sudden flash as the grenades exploded, dimming his vision so that the sudden flash did not blind him, and instantly the column was moving once more, the lead warriors stepping around the blind corners.

Lumps of flesh and severed xenos limbs had been scattered by the explosions, and Kol Badar began to fire as he picked up movement. The creatures had been lying in ambush for them, and he gunned a pair of them down as his auto-sensors flashed up targeting cross-hairs before his eyes.

Too late, he registered a flash of movement to his flank, and tried to bring his weapon to bear on the alien leaping towards him from the side, but the bulk of his Terminator armour slowed his movements.

A chainaxe slammed the creature into the ground, whirring teeth ripping it almost in two, its hot blood steaming as it poured over the floor panels, dripping down between the metal grid. Khalaxis kicked the corpse off the blade of his axe, his bolt pistol making another alien's head disappear in a red mist, and Kol Badar nodded his thanks to the veteran berserker.

'Advance to the east,' said Marduk through the vox network. 'Our quarry is near.'

Kol Badar took up the lead once more, stamping forward down the long corridor leading to the east, wary of attacks, but sighting no enemies. The corridor was a hundred metres long, and he felt a growing unease as he led the advance.

Behind him, the rest of the formation was following in his footsteps, the Anointed warrior in the rear walking backwards steadily, his combi-bolter firing almost constantly.

Stepping over ribbed pipes and cables that made his footing uneven, Kol Badar came upon a closed room, its walls thick with a tangle of pipes and insulated wiring. His combi-bolter tracked around the enclosed space, registering no threats, but he saw that there was no exit from the room bar a heavy blast-door on the far side.

Cursing, he moved swiftly towards the blast-door, but it was sealed shut. It had been welded fast, and deep gouges in its thick surface attested to its strength. Clearly, the xenos creatures had attempted to gain access through the door, but even their deadly claws, which had torn through power armour and even the vaunted suits of Terminator armour with contemptible ease seemed incapable of penetrating this thick bulkhead.

A chainfist would make short work of the bulkhead, but of his Anointed warriors, only Elimkhar was equipped with one of the weapons, and he was bringing up the rear.

Swinging his heavy, quad-tusked helmet around, the Coryphaus saw that the bulk of the warriors had already entered the room. Only two of Khalaxis's 17th coterie still stood, and he cursed again.

'You have led us into a dead end, First Acolyte,' barked Kol Badar.

'She is there,' said Marduk, staring resolutely towards the sealed bulkhead door.

Only Elimkhar was still moving down the long corridor, walking steadily backwards, his combi-bolter firing almost constantly. The corridor was filling with the xenos dead, but still more of the creatures were surging forwards, throwing themselves uncaring into the deadly fire.

'Brother Elimkhar, keep moving, we need your chainfist,' ordered Kol Badar, urging the Anointed warrior to hurry. 'Brother Akkar, be ready to clear the corridor.'

Brother Akkar nodded his acknowledgement of the order, and stepped towards the corridor, the heavy barrels of his reaper autocannon extending forwards beneath his arm.

Abruptly, Brother Elimkhar's weapon jammed, and he stared down at the suddenly silent, overheated bolter.

'Move!' roared Kol Badar, but the strength and speed of the xenos creatures was staggering, and the Anointed disappeared as a wave of enemies smashed over him, claws stabbing and rending. He was dead in an instant, and Kol Badar swore again.

The reaper autocannnon of the Anointed warrior brother, Akkar, roared into life, the flame of the mighty weapon's muzzle flash lighting up the dark room as if it were daylight. Hundreds of shell casings poured from the heavy weapon as it unleashed its full power, and a constant stream of high calibre rounds ripped up the length of the corridor, shredding everything that they struck.

Scores of the aliens were ripped apart as the shells tore through them, the high-pitched screams of the dying aliens all but lost beneath the roaring of the autocannon's twin barrels.

'We must go back,' shouted Kol Badar over the roar of the heavy weapon. 'There is no way through here.'

'She is in there, I know it,' said Marduk hotly. 'There is no going back.'

'How do you propose to get through that?' snapped Kol Badar, gesturing with one of his powered talons towards the bulkhead.

Marduk stared at the door for a moment.

'Darioq-Grendh'al,' he ordered. 'Open it.'

'As you wish, Marduk, First Acolyte of the Word Bearers Legion of Astartes, genetic descendant of the glorified Primarch Lorgar,' said the hulking figure of the magos, stepping forwards, his four mechanical servo arms unfolding from his back.

CHAPTER TWELVE

SOLON MARCABUS TRUDGED through the blinding snow-storm, leaning into the relentless winds that threatened to knock him to the ground with every gust. He stumbled as he stepped into a small drift, sinking up to his knees. It took all his effort to haul himself out, and he lay on his back for a moment, catching his breath.

His eyelids flickered and closed as his breathing steadied. It would be so easy just to drift away, to give in to exhaustion. He knew that to fall asleep out here unprotected was to die, but he almost didn't care anymore. He would just close his eyes for a few minutes.

It had been almost a full day since they had left the dead husk of the crawler behind. It had not been an easy decision to try to make the starport on foot, for their chance of success was minimal, but it was better than waiting for what the boy called *ghosts* return. He was jolted from his micro-sleep as he felt a hand on his shoulder, shaking him, and he looked up at the boy, Dios, who was kneeling over him. Through the circular goggles set into the boy's oversized exposure suit hood, he saw the concern in Dios's eyes.

The boy's face was an unhealthy blue, and his eyes gleamed feverishly. Solon was impressed with the boy's stamina, and he realised that if he succumbed to the lure of sleep, he would not only be condemning himself to death; out here, lost in the wilderness of swirling snow, the boy would not last a day.

Nodding to the boy, Solon pushed himself painfully to his feet and continued to trudge on. Dios followed in his wake, walking through the furrow that Solon's feet made, one hand holding onto Solon's belt.

The boy's determination was driving Solon on, and he drew strength from Dios's indefatigable will to live. He gritted his teeth and cursed his momentary weakness. He knew that if the boy had not been with him, he would not have woken. He would have died out here but for the strength of a boy no more than ten years of age. Perhaps his body would have been buried beneath the snow, entombed within the ice of Perdus Skylla. Perhaps in a thousand years, erosion and wind may have exposed his preserved corpse, and someone would have wondered what had become of him. Why had this man been wandering the wastes, they might have asked.

Pushing such morbid thoughts from his mind, Solon concentrated on keeping moving, each painful step a challenge, but also a minor victory. *Just keep moving*, he told himself, and he repeated the phrase under his breath, like a mantra. *Just keep moving. One step at a time.*

Solon had no idea how long he had been walking when he realised that there was no longer a small hand grasping his belt. He turned around as quickly as the bulky exposure suit allowed him. Dios was no longer walking in his footsteps. The boy was nowhere in sight.

Cursing himself, Solon turned around in every direction, eyes straining to pierce the whitewash of billowing snow and fog all around him, desperately trying to sight the boy. He saw nothing.

Throwing his fatigue off, Solon began to backtrack, following the path he had cleared through the snow. It was not hard to follow, though the falling snow was already beginning to fill in his footsteps. In an hour, they would be gone.

He hurried back along his path, jogging heavily through the snow, stumbling several times, but pushing himself back to his feet, his fear for the boy's safety allowing him to plumb reserves of strength that he didn't know he had.

He had failed the boy, just as he had failed his son.

Despair lent him strength, and he pushed on, slogging through the mire of snow and ice, desperately squinting through the blinding blizzard.

At last, he saw a small, dark shape slumped in the snow, and he broke into a run as he drew towards it. It was covered in a light dusting of snow, and Solon prayed that he was not too late.

'You can't be dead,' said Solon desperately, and drawing near, he dropped to his knees before the figure of the boy. Rolling Dios over onto his front, he looked down into eyes that were half open and unfocused. Dark circles surrounded the boy's eyes, and his flesh was a sickly blue colour.

'No, no, no, no, no,' said Solon, feeling panicked and desperate.

He quickly erected his survival tent, pulling it loose from his thigh-pocket and unravelling it before turning it into the wind, which expanded it like a balloon. He dragged Dios's lifeless body into the cramped interior and ran a finger down the tent-flap, sealing it, before ripping loose the seals of the boy's hood, pulling it down away from his face.

Tearing his own suit away from his upper body, Solon pressed his fingers to the boy's throat. There was a pulse there, though it was weak and irregular, and he groaned in relief. Solon pulled off the insulating inner gloves from Dios's hands, and pulled off his own gloves with his teeth.

Ignoring the throbbing pain as feeling began to return to his fingers, Solon began rubbing warmth into Dios's hands. Blood was not circulating properly and the boy's fingertips were icy to the touch.

For an hour, Solon rubbed life back into the boy's hands and feet, until colour had returned to the digits, and his breathing had become steady. The temperature in the tent had risen sharply from their body-heat, and condensation had formed on its translucent walls.

Solon had set up his water distiller, and the trickle of purified water was now constant. He had filled both his water flasks, and the taste of the cold, fresh water on his tongue was like divine nectar. He had dribbled water into Dios's mouth, and had felt his spirits soar as the boy swallowed greedily.

At last, the boy had woken, and smiled weakly at Solon. Finally satisfied that the boy was out of immediate danger, Solon had allowed himself to fall into an exhausted slumber, as the wind battered the fragile tent outside.

Dios appeared as strong as ever when Solon woke, and the pair shared a small portion of the emergency ration bar that every exposure suit was equipped with. The dry protein ration was stale and old, but it tasted as fine as any meal Solon had ever eaten, though he was stringent in how much he allowed them to eat.

Water was not a problem. With his water distiller, and the amount of ice and snow around, they had an abundant supply. Food was another matter, however. This one ration bar was all they had, and though he portioned it out only sparingly, he knew that it would not last more than two days. Without food, they would become increasingly tired and sluggish, and they needed all the energy they had to make the long walk to the Phorcys starport.

In his heart, Solon knew that it was impossible, but as he saw Dios smile, the first smile he had seen on the boy, he felt rejuvenated and refreshed.

They had to dig themselves out of the tent, which was buried beneath five feet of snow, and Solon was exhausted as they clambered out onto the moon's icy surface, but his spirits were strangely high. He felt almost euphoric, and though he assumed it was a side effect of exhaustion and lack of nourishment, he didn't care at that moment.

Lifting the smiling Dios onto his shoulders, determined not to let the child out of sight, Solon began a new day of walking.

He would be damned if he allowed himself to succumb to fatigue before he saw the boy to safety.

'AMMUNITION THIRTY PER cent,' growled the Anointed warrior Akkar, registering the blinking icon that flashed before his eyes. Smoke rose from the twin barrels of the weapon, and he swung them before him, seeking a target.

Another wave of enemy creatures surged down the corridor, leaping the shattered remains of their kind, and Akkar depressed the thumb trigger of his heavy reaper autocannon once more, sending hundreds of high-calibre rounds into their line, ripping them apart without remorse.

'Weapon temperature peaking,' said Akkar.

'Understood,' said Kol Badar. Indicating with one of his glowing power talons, he organised the remaining warriors into a semicircle facing the corridor, and with a curt command ordered Akkar back from the corridor entrance.

The Anointed warrior stepped slowly backwards, still firing, the barrels of his high-velocity weapon glowing hot.

'Hold,' said Kol Badar, as Akkar's reaper fell silent. The hissing of the aliens was clearly audible in the sudden silence and clawed limbs clicked loudly on the corridor floor and walls.

'Hold,' repeated Kol Badar. The reaper autocannon's killing range was far in excess of the bolters and combi-bolters wielded by the other warriors, and conserving ammunition was becoming a serious issue.

'Now!' roared the Coryphaus as the first xenos creatures spilled from the corridor into the room, bounding forwards with inhuman speed. At his order, the warriors began firing, ripping the aliens apart. Within twenty seconds a score of the aliens were dead, and gore and blood splashed across the walls.

Marduk risked a glance behind him, seeing the hulking form of Darioq-Grendh'al working on the bulkhead. The lascutter on the tip of one of his servo-arms burned white hot as it seared through the reinforced, thirty-centimetre structure, but the magos was only half way around the bulkhead's circumference, and he growled in frustration before turning away and burying a bolt in another alien's brainpan.

The xenos attacked their position furiously, racing headlong towards the Word Bearers only to be shredded by the concentrated weight of fire. Still more of them poured into the room, and the pile of dead at the corridor entrance was growing.

'Have your Mechanicus lapdog hurry it up,' rumbled Kol Badar to Marduk. 'Our ammunition will not last forever.'

Marduk did not answer. No words would have hurried the methodical work of the magos, but he knew that the Coryphaus was right; if the enemy maintained this intensity in attack, they could not hold.

Even as the thought formed, one of the aliens reached the semicircular line of the Legion warriors, despite the weight of fire. Two of its arms were blown clear of its body by percussive blasts, but it did not drop, and it leapt forwards and drove its claws through the faceplate of a brother Space Marine's helmet, popping his skull like an overripe fruit.

The alien was cut from shoulder to hip by Khalaxis's roaring chainaxe, and then in half by the veteran's chainsword, retrieved from one of his fallen warriors, which he wielded in his other hand.

'Hold the line,' roared Kol Badar, but Marduk had seen Khalaxis's bloodlust dozens of times, and knew that the words would probably not penetrate the red haze that had descended over the warrior.

Alien blood splattered across his armour, Khalaxis roared as he leapt forwards into the no-man's land, spinning the pair of chain weapons around in a brutal arc that tore through the body of another alien as it was forced backwards by explosive bolt rounds.

Not wishing to be outdone by the blood-frenzied champion, Burias-Drak'shal leapt into the fray, slamming another of the aliens into the wall with a swing of his icon, his talons shearing the face from another.

The killing ground was gone, and firing into the melee risked hitting Khalaxis and the Icon Bearer, and so Marduk roared a deafening cry and hurled himself into the fray, his daemonic, heavy-bladed chainsword roaring.

The other warriors reacted instantly, throwing themselves forwards without thought for their own safety, firing their bolt pistols at point blank range into the melee and swinging their chainblades in murderous arcs.

Kol Badar stalked forwards, gunning down one of the creatures before swatting the head of another from its shoulders with a backhand sweep of his power talons. The Anointed advanced alongside the Coryphaus, power weapons humming with energy. One of them sent a white-hot gout of plasma shooting from his combi-weapon into the face of one genestealer, liquefying its flesh and rendering its bones to powder.

Still, the xenos creatures were fast beyond belief, and their strength was inhuman. Marduk fought with controlled rage, all the anger and tension of the last months fuelling every murderous stroke of his chainsword.

This is not my time!' he roared. His bolt pistol clicked impotently as his last bolts were expended, and he threw it to the floor in disgust. Claws slashed across his chest plate, gouging deep rents through the ceramite armour, and tearing through his flesh. He grasped the daemon chainsword with two hands, allowing the daemon's hunger for blood to flow through him, and hacked the blade into the widespread maw of the alien as it lunged towards him.

Marduk carved the daemon weapon through alien teeth, muscle and flesh, spraying blood and fang-shards in all directions, and the creature's lower jaw was torn away as he wrenched the chainblade clear. Inhuman, gargling screams burst from its throat, and it thrashed around madly, spraying blood left and right, slashing and tearing at Marduk's armour.

His left shoulder plate was ripped away, shorn almost in two, and a tri-clawed talon dug into his neck, punching through his armour and flesh, grinding against his hyper-strengthened vertebrae. Blood pumped from the wound, and he reeled backwards from the pain-fuelled, frenzied attack of the alien. It came after him, but was driven into the ground by a hammer-blow from Kol Badar's power talons. The Coryphaus silenced its screams, crushing its skull with a heavy stamp of his foot.

Khalaxis booted another in the face with the flat of his foot, cracking its skull before shearing a pair of its arms away with a downward sweep of his chainaxe. The claws of its remaining arms ripped across his chest, crumpling his breastplate like paper and gouging a deep wound through his fused breastplate, but his blood frenzy drove him on, and he rammed his chainsword into its midsection, disembowelling it. Sickly purple and pinkish steaming organs flopped from the wound.

Brother Akkar swung his reaper autocannon like a club, smashing an alien away from him as it hurled itself at him, sending it crashing into a wall. As it struggled to right itself, sinuous limbs thrashing, the Anointed warrior tore it to shreds with a burst of fire from his heavy weapon, the high calibre rounds ripping through its body and puncturing the pipes and cables behind, which spewed steam into the blood-soaked room.

A genestealer hit the Anointed brother from behind, driving claws into either side of his helmet, and his skull was crushed to pulp.

Burias-Drak'shal gripped the writhing alien in his arms, pulling it away from Akkar, who was already dead and falling to his knees, and bit down on its elongated cranium, his fangs piercing its skull. Black blood squirted into his mouth as the creature died, and the possessed warrior hurled it away, his forked daemon-tongue lapping at the blood covering his lips and chin.

The attack was repulsed abruptly, though the throbbing auspex showed that another wave of the aliens was gathering further along the corridor. The remaining Word Bearers hastily reloaded their weapons and began to fire once more.

Pulling his hand away from his neck, Marduk stared at the bright red blood on his fingers and palm, and his anger surged. The blood began to bubble and spit on his gauntlet, and inside his helmet, Marduk's eyes turned black as the power of the warp surged through him, fuelled by the bloodshed and the fury of the warriors around him, and jolting his body with its suddenness and its power.

Feeling the building power, Burias-Drak'shal was driven to his knees, clasping his icon in both clawed hands, his head lowered. Blood ran from his ears, and his hands shook as infernal power coursed through the icon, which began to vibrate and smoke, giving off an acrid, sulphurous stench.

The sounds of weapons firing and Kol Badar bellowing orders faded from Marduk's consciousness as the fury of the Lord of Skulls entered him, and he struggled to contain the unrelenting waves of insane anger coursing through his body.

His muscles tensed to the point of bursting, veins bulging in his neck and arms, and he struggled to maintain control over the bloodthirsty urges that assailed him, urging him to lash out, unmindful of who he killed so long as the blood flowed. Blood pumped loudly through his veins, drowning out all sounds, and his vision was red and hazy. Slowly, he gained mastery over the surge of diabolic power, forcing it to submit to his will.

'Darr'kazar, Khor'Rhakath, Borr'mordhlal, Forgh'gazz'ar,' intoned Marduk, speaking the true names as they formed in his mind's eye. Daemonic voices roared in rage and hatred at his command over them, but Marduk cared not, and continued to recite the names as they came to him.

'Borgh'a'teth, Rhazazel, Skaman'dhor, Katharr'bosch,' said Marduk, completing the eight names that burnt red-hot within his mind's eye. He dropped to his knees and spread his arms out wide, throwing his head back as he spoke the words of summoning and binding.

Akkar's body, lying on the floor with its skull a bloody ruin, began to bloat, as if his innards were expanding exponentially, like a balloon filling with gas. His hermetically sealed Terminator armour groaned and strained, threatening to rupture like a canister of promethium hurled into hot coals. A tiny hairline fracture appeared in the centre of the breastplate and it quickly expanded outwards, until, with the sickening sound of cracking bone and tendon, the armour ripped apart, like the shell being peeled from a crustacean.

A shapeless blood-bag swelled from the fissure, flopping down onto the floor alongside the ruptured corpse. The veined skin of the amorphous mass pulsed and heaved as something struggled to be released from within, and the whole mass swelled as it increased in volume, growing larger with every passing moment.

A blade pierced the birth-sac, its surface blackened as if by fire and with glowing, infernal runes carved upon its surface. A daemon rose to its clawed feet as the skin of the blood-bag sloughed from its body.

The daemon was one of Khorne's minions, a foot soldier of the Lord of the Brazen Skull Throne, and its flesh was the colour of congealed blood. It uncurled from its hunched, foetal position as the last vestiges of its birth-sac dropped away, and it sucked in a deep breath, its first in the material realm.

Its limbs were long and scaled, and they rippled with sinuous muscle. Its head was elongated and bestial, and the fires of hell burned in its hate-filled serpent eyes. It hefted its immense blade in one hand as it staggered drunkenly for a moment, getting a feel for its new, physical incarnation. The runes upon the hellblade's blackened surface glowed with the heat of an inferno, and as the daemon steadied itself, becoming instantly accustomed to its new-found body and the rules of the material plane, it exhaled, breathing out a blast of sulphurous black smoke.

Then it roared, throwing its horned head back, the infernal sound ripping forth from deep within its tautly muscled chest with all the fury of its patron deity. It clenched its tall hellblade tightly, quivering in anticipation of the slaughter, and took in its surroundings with malevolent eyes.

It snarled, eyes narrowing as it looked upon the red-armoured figures of the Word Bearers. Its gaze met Burias-Drak'shal's, and its muscles tensed as it prepared to hurl itself at the possessed warrior, the runes upon its brazen hellblade glowing like lava.

Marduk's carefully weighted words stabbed at the daemon like intangible blades and it recoiled, swinging its heavy head towards the First Acolyte in hatred. It bared its teeth at its summoner, but Marduk's mastery over it was complete, his will binding it more effectively than chains, and though it fought against him with every fibre of its being, muscles straining, it was powerless against him.

There was always an element of risk involved in summoning the infernal denizens of the ether, and Marduk would normally only beseech the warp for aid when he had the time to prepare the correct rituals. The tiniest mispronunciation, a slip of concentration, could have catastrophic and eternally damning results, and yet, the rewards were often worth the risk.

Eight of these bloodletters stood over the shattered corpses that had borne them. Eight was the sacred number of the blood god Khorne, and the muscles of the daemons in echo of their patson twitched with barely restrained rage as they waited for a command.

'Well?' asked Marduk, his voice infused with power. 'Go.'

As one, the eight lesser-daemons of Khorne threw themselves into the corridor, like rabid pack-dogs unleashed from their tethers. They roared their daemonic fury as they charged into the massing genestealers, their hellblades carving burning arcs through the air.

The aliens leapt to meet the daemons head on, talons ripping and tearing at bodies formed of the stuff of Chaos, alien speed and strength pitted against the diabolical fury of the god of battle and murder.

His limbs quivering with the residual power of the summoning, Marduk swung around and stalked towards Darioq-Grendh'al, who had almost completed cutting his way through the bulkhead.

With a barked order, infused with the essence of the immaterium, Marduk forced the defiled magos aside and slammed the flat of his boot into the bulkhead. It buckled under the blow, and another kick sent it smashing inwards.

Marduk's blood was up, and he stepped through the portal, brandishing his daemon blade, ready for anything.

A robed figure sat cross-legged on the floor, and it looked up as the First Acolyte stormed into the enclosed, darkened room.

Marduk crossed the distance in three steps, and grabbed the figure by the neck, lifting it a metre off the ground and slamming it back against the far wall.

'Tell me you are the one I seek, and you shall live to draw another breath,' said Marduk.

The figure's legs kicked uselessly in the air, and Marduk peered closely into its round, hairless face. Neural implants bedecked its bald head like feral ornamentation, and a fist-sized, cog-shaped badge of the Adeptus Mechanicus was fused to its forehead, puckering the skin.

The figure struggled to draw breath.

'Speak,' commanded Marduk. 'What is your name, dog?'

'Daenae,' came the gasped reply.

Marduk grinned within his skull-faced helmet. The figure's kohl rimmed eyes bulged, and feminine lips grimaced beneath his torturous grip. Marduk released his crushing hold, and the explorator crumpled to the floor at his feet.

'I do not know who you seek,' gasped the woman, her voice hoarse, 'but my name is Daenae, Explorator First Class Daenae of the Adeptus Mechanicus, and you are a traitor of the Imperium.'

'You have no idea how pleased I am to have found you, woman,' said Marduk.

EXPLORATOR DAENAE WAS of stocky build and considerable girth. Her waist was thick and strong, and her bosom heavy. Even had Marduk been more familiar with mortals, or cared, he would have been unable to gauge her age, for she had been extensively altered by juvenat surgery, one of the only vanities in which she indulged.

Her body was not augmented to nearly the degree of Darioq's, and what augmentation she had was relatively subtle. Both arms had been enhanced with mechanical bionics, though they had been fashioned such that their mechanised nature was not initially obvious, and she bore a slim-line power-source on her back that was a fraction of the size and weight of the immense generator that Darioq required to power his servo-harness and largely mechanised frame.

Power couplings linked her backpack to her bulky forearm bracers, within which were stored her tools. Neural implants allowed her to access these tools with a thought, extending lascutters, data-spikes or power drills behind her fist as required.

Her eyes opened wide as the bulky form of Darioq-Grendh'al entered the room.

'Darioq?' she whispered hoarsely. 'By the blessings of the Omnissiah, is that you?'

'Darioq is still here,' said the magos, and Marduk smiled to see the explorator recoil from the voice, interlaced with the voice of the daemon Grendh'al.

'He is pleased to see you, Explorator First Class Daenae,' continued Darioq-Grendh'al, 'originally of the Konor Adeptus Mechanicus research world of UL01.02, assigned to c14.8.87.i, Perdus Skylla, for recon/salvage of the Dvorak-class interstellar freighter *Flames of Perdition*, which reappeared within Segmentum Tempestus in 942.M41 and crashed onto the surface of c14.8.87.i, Perdus Skylla, in 944.M41 after being missing presumed lost in warp storm anomaly xi.024.396 in 432.M35.'

'What have they done to you?' asked the explorator in revulsion.

'Enough,' interjected Marduk. 'I have it on the authority of the magos that you are in possession of knowledge that I would own.'

'What?' asked the explorator. 'Me? You think I have knowledge that great Darioq, my *master*, does not possess? Surely you are mistaken.'

Her voice fairly dripped with scorn.

'The knowledge I seek is in regard to a xenos artefact, an artefact taken from the necrontyr.'

'I know nothing about any xenos tech,' said the explorator emphatically. *'Nothing.'*

Marduk glowered at her, and then looked up at Darioq-Grendh'al.

'A direct answer, magos,' said the First Acolyte, empowering his voice with command. 'Does she have the key to unlock the device?

'She does,' said Darioq-Grendh'al.

'What?' asked the explorator. 'I don't know anything! He lies!'

'He cannot lie, not to me,' said Marduk. 'You are coming with us. Your secrets will be revealed. My chirurgeons can be *very* convincing when I need them to be.'

'I do not lie! I know nothing!' said the explorator fiercely as Marduk yanked her to her feet.

'We have to move,' said Kol Badar from the doorway.

'You are certain that she has what we need?' hissed Marduk to Darioq, shaking the explorator like a rag doll. 'I sense no lie in her words.'

'I am not lying,' said the explorator emphatically.

'Quiet,' said Marduk, twisting her arm sharply, snapping the bone.

'I am certain,' said Darioq-Grendh'al, 'but she speaks the truth.'

'You dare speak in riddles to me, magos?' growled Marduk.

'Explorator Daenae speaks the truth because she does not *know* that the knowledge is locked within her brain unit. Magos Darioq implanted it within her sub-dermal cortex without her knowledge, for safe-keeping, before he ejected her from his service, and we do not need to take her with us to extract it.'

Marduk's scowl changed to a smile.

'Ah, Darioq-Grendh'al,' he said, 'I think I might be starting to like you.'

CHAPTER THIRTEEN

THE BODY OF Explorator Daenae lay face down on the floor, in a pool of tepid blood. The top half of her head had been removed and cast aside and her skull cavity was empty.

'You are done?' asked Marduk impatiently.

Darioq-Grendh'al sealed the bell jar, which now held the explorator's brain, joining the others that emerged from the back of his hunched, perverted body. Viscous, purple-hued liquid filled the receptacle, and dozens of needle-like proboscis connectors pierced the brain.

'One moment, while the neural pathways connect,' said Darioq-Grendh'al. The gently waving mechadendrite tentacles attached to the corrupted magos's spine quivered, and the magos's head twitched to one side. Darioq-Grendh'al uttered a low, mechanical groan, and a shiver ran along what flesh remained of his once-human body as the explorator's brain connected.

A veritable tidal wave of information flooded through Darioq's consciousness as the neural connections fired.

Memories, emotions and thoughts that were not his own flickered through his consciousness.

Neural pathways in the explorator's brain that had been dead for almost forty seconds during the transplant reconnected, and Darioq-Grendh'al plumbed their depths, driving towards the secrets that he had locked there decades earlier. Daemonic tendrils burrowed through the brain, re-forging the severed brainstem, and the knowledge was released in a wave of data.

Eight hundred years of knowledge deemed unfit for study by the High-Magi of the Cult Mechanicus: necrontyr, hrudd, eldar, borrlean. Knowledge of xenos tech that had been lost for eight hundred years was recovered in an instant.

Unannounced, a yearning dredged from the locked away depths of his brain-core resurfaced, dragged from beyond self-imposed restraints: a yearning, a thirst, a *need* for knowledge, a yearning that had long been restrained, castigated and repressed within the constrictive bounds of the Adeptus Mechanicus.

The quest for knowledge and understanding would begin afresh, this time with willing, supportive patrons that would not tether him/them with rules, regulations, outdated morals and archaic beliefs.

'It is done,' said Darioq-Grendh'al.

'Good. You have what you need to continue your study of the Nexus Arrangement?' asked Marduk hungrily.

'It has all become clear to us,' agreed Darioq-Grendh'al. 'We have what is needed to unlock the xenos tech device.'

'Then let us get the hell off this damnable moon,' said Marduk.

* * *

KOL BADAR TOOK point, leading the bloodied warriors through the labyrinthine corridors of the *Flames of Perdition* towards their submersibles. The Word Bearers moved swiftly, not wishing to linger within the xenos-haunted wreck any longer than necessary.

Distant daemonic roars filtered through the darkened hallways as the bloodletters continued their frenzied rampage. Such summoned daemons had only a finite existence in the material plane. If their physical bodies were not killed, they might last a day before their substance unravelled. They were tools for the First Acolyte to use and discard as he saw fit, and they had served their purpose.

Twice, the Word Bearers were ambushed en route, genestealers launching blinding attacks that saw two more warriors injured, one sustaining a deep wound in his side that would have killed a mortal man, and the other, one of the last members of Khalaxis's coterie, had half his face ripped off. He stoically continued on, hurling aside his sundered helmet and gritting his teeth, refusing to succumb to the pain in front of such vaunted warriors as his champion, the Coryphaus and the First Acolyte. Marduk had nodded his respect to the warrior, who had puffed out his chest and struggled on, pushing through the pain, at the unexpected acknowledgement.

They had not encountered any enemy for more than fifteen minutes, and they picked up the pace as they closed on the location of the submersibles, keeping a wary eye on the throbbing blister screen of their tainted auspex.

The *Flames of Perdition* shifted suddenly, the prow of the massive ship dropping as it tore loose from the submerged cliff. The entire ship tilted, and Marduk lost his footing as the floor tipped beneath him.

The Word Bearers were thrown to their left, smashing into the side wall of the passage as the immense freighter lurched. One of them tumbled down a side-corridor that was more like a vertical shaft, fingers scrabbling vainly for purchase. Marduk flailed for a handhold amidst the piping on the left wall, but found none, and began to slide down the corridor-shaft behind the power-armoured brother Space Marine.

Burias-Drak'shal held out his icon, his other hand grasping onto a side-rail as other Word Bearers tumbled past. Marduk reached and grabbed the proffered icon, fingers locking around its barbed haft, and Burias-Drak'shal hauled him to safety. With a nod of thanks, Marduk pulled his body over the lip of the shaft, dragging himself forward on his belly.

The ship rolled onto its side, its nose still tipping, before it finally came to rest, settling into its new position.

Outside, rocks dislodged from the chasm walls by the immense weight of the freighter dropped down into the abyss, tumbling down into the darkness.

'Who have we lost?' growled Kol Badar, picking himself up from the ground, ripping his power talons from the wall, which had been the ceiling.

'Darioq-Grendh'al?' said Marduk in concern.

'He's here,' said Burias, pushing the daemon back within him as he picked himself up.

The corrupted magos's mechadendrites had shot outwards, clamping to walls like the legs of a spider, halting his fall.

'Rhamel is gone,' growled Khalaxis.

'Is he the only one?' asked Marduk.

'Yes,' said Kol Badar, looking around, 'but the ship could fall at any moment. We have to get out of here.'

'Where is he?' asked Marduk, looking down over the lip of the corridor-shaft. It extended some fifty metres before disappearing into the gloom that even his augmented sight could not penetrate.

Khalaxis cursed. 'The auspex is gone,' he said.

'Brother Rhamel?' asked Kol Badar through the intervox.

A static-filled voice came back, though it was distorted and patchy.

'...amel... broken arm... faulty...' came the response.

'His vox is damaged,' said Marduk.

'He is not getting up there with a broken arm,' said Burias, assessing the climb. 'You want me to go get him?'

'We don't have the time,' snapped Kol Badar.

Burias looked over at Marduk, who reluctantly nodded his head in agreement. Khalaxis stared down the vertical corridor, his hands clenched around the hilt of his chainaxe. Rhamel was Khalaxis's blood-brother, having come from the same cult-gang on Colchis before the hated Ultramarines' cyclonic torpedoes had destroyed the Word Bearers' home world ten thousand years earlier. Together, they had been amongst the last batch of aspirants taken from the obliterated world.

'Brother Rhamel,' said Kol Badar, 'proceed to the rendezvous point. We will meet you there. Repeat, proceed to the rendezvous point.'

'...cknowledged... phaus,' came the stilted reply.

'Come,' said Kol Badar to the rest of the dwindling group of warrior brothers. 'If he makes it, he makes it. If not, then it is the will of the gods,' he said mockingly, with a nod towards Marduk.

Khalaxis stood stone still, looking down into the darkness.

'May the gods be with you, my brother,' said Khalaxis, before turning away.

The Word Bearers renewed their advance. With the ship on its side, the way they had come was foreign. What had been familiar was now strange, and where before they had advanced easily, they were now forced to half-climb through doorways that were horizontal, and half-leap across vertical corridors shafts that fell away below them.

The power-armoured warrior brothers leapt these expanses with ease, but the progress was not so easy for the bulky Terminator-armoured Anointed warriors, and Marduk ground his sharp teeth in frustration at their slow progress, drawing blood.

Burias ripped a pair of thick support girders from the walls, and dropped them over one of the expanses, and Kol Badar and his Anointed shuffled across them, though the girders strained beneath their weight.

Last to come was Darioq-Grendh'al, and Marduk swore.

'They will not take his weight,' hissed Kol Badar.

The corrupted magos, with his full servo-harness and plasma-core generator attached to his back, weighed almost twice as much as one of the Terminator-armoured Anointed warriors, and Marduk swore again, knowing that the Coryphaus was correct.

'We'll have to find another way round,' said Marduk, his voice terse with frustration.

'Wait,' said Burias, a smile playing on his lean face.

Marduk looked up to see the magos traversing the gap, his mechanical legs hanging beneath him in mid-air. Half-mechanical, half-fleshy mechadendrite tentacles punched through the panels in the ceiling, gripping tight as the corrupted magos's four immense servo-arms extended out to either side at full stretch, gripping the girders there. With a surprised barking laugh, Marduk watched as two of the servo-arms released their grips and reached forwards to grasp the girders further along, before releasing its other arms, and repeating the manoeuvre. Mechadendrites pulled free overhead before punching through the ceiling panels further along.

It was like watching some multi-armed, mechanical ape making its way through the treetops, and even Kol Badar was taken aback by the bizarre spectacle. The magos lowered himself safely to the floor once more, his daemon-eye glinting.

'Full of surprises,' said Marduk.

In the distance, they heard the percussive echoes of boltgun fire, and knew that the enemy had found Brother Rhamel. Khalaxis was tense and brooding, and the other warriors kept a respectful distance from the champion.

Marduk patted Khalaxis on the shoulder, and the Word Bearers pressed on in silence.

BROTHER RHAMEL PUMPED shot after shot into the never-ending swarm of genestealers coming at him. He had five confirmed kills, the bodies of the xenos creatures lying motionless on the ground, but they were coming at him from two directions, and he knew that it was just a matter of time before they overwhelmed him. The red icon warning him of low ammunition had been flashing before his eyes for some time, and he watched with grim finality as the icons displaying his last rounds were slowly depleted.

His left arm hung useless at his side, broken in three places. Turning to the left, he shot another genestealer in the head, before swinging back to the right and taking another one high in the chest, the percussive blast hurling it backwards.

Squeezing the trigger once more, he fired the last of his bolts, and dropped his useless weapon to the ground. He tossed the last of his frag grenades down one of the corridors, turning his back to the resultant blast and unslinging his heavy blade from his waist.

The blast of the grenade knocked him forwards a step as flame rolled up the corridor at his back. Steadying himself, he passed the wide blade before him, knowing that the end was near.

A handful of genestealers were stalking towards him, their backs hunched and their eyes glittering hatefully. They moved slowly, readying to pounce, as if knowing that their prey was all but defenceless.

'Come on, you whoresons!' Rhamel roared as a fresh batch of combat drugs was injected into his body.

One of the xenos creatures hissed in response, ropes of saliva dripping from its fangs. Feeling movement behind him, Rhamel flicked a glance around, and saw another half a dozen of the genestealers creeping forwards at his flank.

'Come on! Finish me!' Rhamel bellowed, keeping both groups of aliens in his field of vision.

At some unspoken command, both groups leapt forwards, covering the distance with horrifying speed.

Rhamel swung in towards the first creature, his blade biting deep into its snarling face, cracking its skull. The genestealer wrenched its head to the side, almost dragging the blade from Rhamel's hand, but the Word Bearer ripped his sword clear and stabbed it into the open mouth of another genestealer as it lunged towards him.

He buried the blade deep in the creature's throat, and hot xenos blood bubbled from the wound. He had no time to drag his sword clear, however, before he was overwhelmed. He was smashed to the ground, losing his grip on his weapon, and he bellowed at the pain that shot through his broken arm.

Gritting his teeth, murmuring a final prayer to the gods of the ether, he waited for the killing blow to fall.

It never came.

One of the creatures was crouching over him, pinning him to the floor. Rhamel strained within its grasp, powerless against its strength. Its hot breath fogged the eye lenses of his helmet.

'Do it,' he roared in the genestealer's face. 'Kill me!'

The alien leant forward and a thick rope of drool dripped from its maw onto Rhamel's helmet. With a darting movement, the xenos creature stabbed its tongue towards his neck. The powerful proboscis punched through his armour and sank into his neck. It stung painfully, and Rhamel roared.

Then the creature pushed off him, scuttling backwards.

Rhamel staggered to his feet, scrabbling for his blade. He stood in a fighting crouch, ready for the creatures to revert back to their murderous nature and come at him once more, to rend him limb from limb, but they continued to back away from him, slipping into the darkness.

In an instant, they were gone, and Rhamel was left alone.

His vision swam, and the throbbing pain of his neck wound made him wince. He presumed that his body's enhanced metabolism was working hard to overcome whatever foul poison had been injected into him, and he fought the sudden lethargy that assailed him.

Whatever had been done to him, he felt certain that his enhanced metabolism would combat it. No poison could kill one of the Legion, and he was confident that the discomfort he was feeling would pass with time.

Giving no more thought to the genestealer's bizarre behaviour, Rhamel set off, loping down the eerily silent corridors at a kilometre-eating pace, working his way towards the rendezvous point.

MARDUK HEARD THE distant gunfire cease abruptly.

'He has become one with Chaos,' he said to Khalaxis, whose anger was palpable. 'He was a fine warrior. Honour his memory.'

Khalaxis nodded his head, though his anger still seethed within him like a living thing.

It took them the better part of an hour to reach the submersibles, for they were forced to take a different path than they had travelled before, clambering up steep inclines, sliding down others, and navigating vertical shafts.

The holding deck where they had left the submersibles had been tipped onto its side when the ship had slipped, and the interior was only vaguely familiar. Only the bobbing shapes of the submersibles confirmed that they had reached their goal, though the aquatic vessels had been tossed around when the ship had shifted. One of them was stranded out of the water, like a beached deep-sea mammal, lying on its side on a gantry that had buckled beneath its weight.

With a clipped order, Kol Badar sent Burias clambering over the wreckage, and he leapt into the air to grab a ladder that was positioned horizontally above them. The icon bearer climbed hand over hand across the expanse of dark water before dropping down onto the top of one of the submersibles. He landed in a steady crouch, and grinned across the open water towards the others before unscrewing its top hatch and dropping down into its interior.

Within moments, Burias had powered the vessel to life, its twin spotlights piercing the dark water like a pair of glowing eyes, and manoeuvred it towards the waiting warriors of the Host, its impeller engines creating a whirlpool of turbulence.

One by one, the warriors stepped onto the submersible, clambering into its belly, until just Marduk, Khalaxis and Darioq-Grendh'al remained.

'You next,' said Marduk, nodding towards the corrupted magos.

'A biological entity approaches,' said Darioq-Grendh'al, and both Marduk and Khalaxis were instantly alert, weapons raised as they sought a target.

'I see nothing,' hissed Khalaxis.

'There,' said Marduk, nodding towards a darkened side-passage. His finger tensed on the trigger of his bolt pistol, before he relaxed and holstered the weapon.

A shape solidified out of the darkness, staggering towards them.

'Rhamel,' laughed Khalaxis, 'you whoreson! You had me worried for a moment there.'

'Fine, brother,' replied Rhamel, his voice strained. 'I don't die easily.'

Khalaxis laughed and slapped his blood-brother on the shoulder, knocking him forward a step.

'Are you well, warrior brother?' asked Marduk, eyes narrowing.

'I will be fine, First Acolyte,' Rhamel replied fiercely.

'Remove your helmet, warrior of Lorgar,' commanded Marduk.

Rhamel pulled his helmet clear, standing to attention before the First Acolyte. The flesh of his broad, ritually scarred face was pale and waxy, and deep rings circled eyes that glinted with a feverish light. A scabbed wound was located on his neck , and the skin around the puncture was tinged vaguely blue.

'You are… unwell?' asked Marduk. 'Poison?'

'Ovipositor impregnation,' intoned Darioq-Grendh'al.

'What is the machine speaking of?' asked Khalaxis.

'I don't know,' replied Marduk.

'Source: Magos Biologis Atticus Fane, Lectures of Xenos Bioligae, 872.M40, Consultation of Nicae, Tenebria, Q.389.V.IX. Ref.MBim274.ch.impttck. The xenos subject species, genus *Corporaptor*, observed implanting gene-template into body of host,' said Darioq-Grendh'al. 'Override of genetic coding documented. Bio-gene-splicing observed. Conclusion: *Corporaptor Hominis* overrides genetic makeup of host species, dominating upper cerebral cortex functions. Speculation: *Corporaptor Hominis* a vanguard species, locating and suppressing indigenous populations. Genetic corruption of local species suspected as a method of drawing Hive Fleet to suitable prey-worlds.'

The three Word Bearers looked blankly at the corrupted magos.

'Potential reversal of implanted host species' gene-corruption: nil,' concluded Darioq-Grendh'al.

'Gene-corruption,' murmured Marduk.

'The machine babbles nonsense,' growled Khalaxis.

'Speak more clearly, Darioq-Drak'shal,' said Marduk, 'perhaps in words that we might understand.'

'It is believed that the genestealers infiltrate potential prey-worlds for the tyranid xenos species to feed upon,' intoned the magos. 'They infect the populace, and some believe that the collective control they exert over those bearing their genetic coding acts as a psychic beacon, drawing the organic Hive Fleets to those worlds where the beacon burns strongest.'

'And you say this... implant attack that Rhamel has suffered is altering his genetic coding?' asked Marduk.

'That is correct, master.'

'The bodies of the warriors of Lorgar are sacred temples, for in them we bear the mark of Lorgar. From his genome were we created,' said Marduk, 'and such a... corruption is an abomination.'

The First Acolyte looked at Rhamel, who grimaced as another wave of pain shot through him.

'You understand what must be done, Brother Rhamel,' said Marduk. It was a statement, not a question.

'I understand, my lord,' said Rhamel through gritted teeth, and the warrior dropped to his knees before the First Acolyte.

'What if the machine is wrong?' asked Khalaxis. 'Could not the chirurgeons on the *Infidus Diabolus* reverse this corruption?'

'The machine is not wrong, brother,' said Rhamel. 'I can feel it working within me, changing me. Let me pass with honour, my brother.'

The warrior closed his eyes tightly against the pain.

'I would ask that you do it, Khalaxis,' he hissed, pleadingly. 'Do this for me, my brother. Please.'

Khalaxis looked at Marduk, and the First Acolyte nodded his head grimly.

'It is only fitting,' said the First Acolyte.

'As you wish, my brother,' said Khalaxis, moving in front of the kneeling warrior.

Marduk passed the champion of the almost obliterated 17th coterie his bolt pistol, and the taller warrior took it in his hands with great reverence. Then he raised the bolt pistol and placed it against Rhamel's forehead.

'Into the darkness he strode,' quoted Marduk, from the Trials of the Covenant, 'into the flames of hell, with his head held high, and he smiled.'

'Be at peace,' said Khalaxis.

Rhamel smiled, looking up at Khalaxis with eyes shining with belief.

'I'll see you on the other side, my brother,' he said.

Then the bolt pistol bucked in Khalaxis's hand, and the back of Rhamel's head was obliterated, exploding outwards in a shower of gore.

Marduk dipped a finger in the blood and drew an eight-pointed star on Rhamel's forehead, the hole of the entry wound at its centre.

'What was that all about?' Burias asked in a low voice as they climbed into the submersible, eyeing the brooding Khalaxis.

'Nothing,' said Marduk. 'A brave warrior is dead. He will be mourned.'

CHAPTER FOURTEEN

A CROWD OF hooded cultists was waiting for them as the
submersible entered the docking pool within the mining station, pushing in as Burias climbed out onto the
wharf. Nevertheless, they kept their distance, wary of
the immense red-armoured warrior and the potent aura
of savagery around him.

The icon bearer snarled as he looked upon the press
of humanity, and dropped onto the docking wharf, eyeing the crowd darkly. He allowed the change to come
over him and took a menacing step forwards, enjoying
the fear that made the people recoil. They did not run,
however, and there were shouts and jeers from the
masses. It was curious behaviour for mortals, and Burias
could not understand it. Lesser beings always reacted to
his presence with abject terror, so why did these ones
not flee?

As the other Word Bearers emerged from the deep-sea
scout/maintenance vehicle, one man pushed to the

front of the crowd. His pale face was cowled and thin, and a servo-skull hovered near his shoulder. His eyes gleamed with feverish light.

This man studied the Word Bearers as they disembarked, an expression of outrage upon his face. The anger twisted his features so that he looked barely human at all.

'They have spilt the blood of our brood-fathers!' he bellowed, holding his arms up high. The billowing sleeves of his robe fell back at the movement, exposing pale arms pitted with plugs. Spiralling tattoos covered his flesh, oddly alien embryonic shapes that wrapped around his forearms. An angry roar rose from the gathered crowd that stepped forwards, faces twisting into visages of hatred.

'Someone shut him up,' said Marduk.

Kol Badar stepped towards the man, who stood defiant before him even though the people around him shrunk back from the Coryphaus's titanic frame.

'You have befouled the inner sanctum of the brood-fathers,' howled the man at Kol Badar as he approached. He came up barely to the Coryphaus's chest, but held his ground defiantly. 'And for that grave insult, you will be punished.'

'Who is going to punish me, little man?' asked Kol Badar. 'You?'

The man quivered in rage, and with a scream of hatred hurled himself at Kol Badar's immense figure, hands outstretched like claws.

Kol Badar wrapped his power talons around the man's head, and lifted him off his feet, which kicked uselessly a metre off the ground.

The crowd surged forwards, many drawing laspistols and cudgels from their robes, screaming in outrage.

Bemused, Kol Badar clenched his fist and there was an audible wet crunch as the man's skull was crushed. He hurled the body into the crowd.

There were hundreds of the frenzied cultists, but they were as nothing next to the warriors of the XVII Legion. None of the Word Bearers deigned to expend any of their precious ammunition upon the crowd, and they weighed in with chainswords and fists as the crowd surged in to surround them.

It was as if the crowd was in the grip of some kind of group hysteria, thought Marduk, eliminating all fear, and replacing it with this frenzied hatred. That was exactly what this was, he realised these people were the dupes of the xenos hive mind.

The butchery was over in minutes. Bodies lay sprawled across the floor, many of them maimed and brutalised almost beyond recognition, life fluids smearing the metal flooring with a thick gruel.

Pulling his blood-smeared helmet from his head, Marduk sucked in a deep breath, inhaling the hot, heady scent of death.

'Glory be,' he said, a rapturous smile upon his face.

GEARS GROANED AS the giant lift rose from the shaft, powerful engines hauling it up the immense chain connected to the mining station eight kilometres below. It came to a clanking rest, and steam vented from its engines. The sides of the diamond-shaped lift crashed open, and Sabtec bowed his head as the First Acolyte stepped from within, his armour caked in blood.

The champion lifted his gaze once more, eyes flicking over the blood-drenched warriors marching from within the lift. He raised an eyebrow as he saw that only half of the warriors that had accompanied Marduk returned.

The First Acolyte's gaze wandered, coming to rest on the corpse of a Legion warrior, lying on its back and with its arms crossed over his chest.

'Namar-sin?' asked Marduk.

Sabtec nodded his head.

'Report,' said Kol Badar as he stalked out of the lift.

'Dark eldar,' said Sabtec, 'though ones we have not fought before. They were shadow-creatures, here and yet not here. Two brother warriors fell along with Namar-sin.'

'I do not see their bodies,' said Marduk.

'They were… taken, my lord,' said Sabtec.

'They were taken,' said Marduk flatly.

Sabtec stood with his head held high, looking resolutely forward.

'Yes, my lord,' he said.

'You allowed two warrior brothers of Lorgar to be taken by eldar slavers?' snarled Kol Badar.

'They were taken while under my command, my lord, yes,' said Sabtec, 'and I will accept any punishment that my shame requires.'

'You offer no excuses, Sabtec?' asked Kol Badar.

'None, my lord,' said Sabtec. His voice betrayed no fear. He moved his gaze towards Marduk. 'If it would please you, First Acolyte, I shall take my own life for the shame I have brought upon the Host.'

'That will not be necessary, Sabtec,' said Marduk smoothly, 'though I am pleased at your devotion to the great cause. I shall have need of loyal warriors in the days to come.'

'The tyranid invasion could begin at any moment,' said Kol Badar. 'It might already be under way. We move out, now.'

Marduk was left alone with Kol Badar as the warriors of the Legion made ready to move out once more, their movements crisp and full of purpose.

'This world has claimed many warrior's lives,' said Kol Badar. 'Six Havocs of the 217th, including their champion, Namar-sin; two warriors of the 13th; six of

Khalaxis's 17th, and two of my Anointed, all dead to secure the mind of a single mortal. I hope that it was worth it.'

'It will be,' said the First Acolyte.

'For the glory of Marduk?' sneered Kol Badar.

'For the glory of Lorgar. For the glory of the XVII Legion,' said Marduk, keeping his anger in check, though he felt the powers of Chaos stirring within him, feeding his desire to strike down the insubordinate Coryphaus.

Thoughts of blood filled his mind, and Marduk reached involuntarily for his blade. He saw Kol Badar's power talons twitch. With all his strength, Marduk pushed the hatred deep inside, where it would fester and grow strong, but where he could control it.

'Lead forth, oh mighty Kol Badar,' said Marduk, his voice thick with sarcasm.

THE WORD BEARERS moved out onto the ice, leaving the guild city, with its subterranean tunnels and claustrophobic chambers behind. They had not seen any further sign of the enemy, either Imperial or eldar. The storms wracking the landscape had not abated. If anything, it seemed that they had increased in intensity, furiously whipping ice and snow across the flows.

'How long?' asked Marduk. He spoke using his inter-vox rather than attempting to roar over the howling winds.

'Ten minutes,' said Kol Badar. 'Thirteenth, form a perimeter.'

Under Sabtec's crisp orders, the warriors of the 13th coterie, both old and new members, moved into position, weapons at the ready. It was probably an unnecessary precaution, for the chance of attack within the next ten minutes was unlikely, but having heard the reports of the dark eldar attacks from Sabtec, Kol Badar was taking no chances. Marduk also knew that it did the warriors good to have a duty, something to occupy them.

'The only certainty in a warrior's life is death,' was an old adage, though Marduk knew that such a statement was inherently false. For mortals, yes, death came for every soul eventually, but for one of the blessed warriors of Chaos, death was no certainty. Likely, but not certain. One could always be raised to daemonhood, and then one might live for all eternity, a demi-god worshipped in one's own right.

Something stirred within Marduk, and he felt the presence of Chaos writing within him. He had long become used to the bizarre sensation, and it gave him comfort to know that he was not alone.

'Incoming!' roared Sabtec suddenly, his crusade-era helmet angled skywards.

There came a whistling sound overhead, and the warriors scattered as something large came hurtling down through the gale.

Marduk threw himself to the side as it came smashing down and struck the moon's surface just metres away, sending snow and chunks of ice flying into the air, and sending warriors of the Legion sprawling. The First Acolyte rolled smoothly, coming up to one knee with his bolt pistol in his hand.

Had it been an explosive shell, he would be dead, but the thing that had struck the ice was no shell, nor was it an orbital strike… at least not one of Imperial origins.

At first, Marduk thought it was an asteroid, but now he saw it was something fleshy, something organic.

It was like the giant seed-pod of some fleshy fruit, and it had smashed a crater four metres deep and eight metres in diameter. Steam rose from it, and even as he watched, the tip of the roughly spherical shape peeled back, flopping down onto the ice, revealing a shapeless, quivering skin-sac the size of a Dreadnought.

Veins branched across this lump of living flesh, and shapes within strained to be released.

'What in the name of the true gods is that?' asked Burias curiously, stepping carefully towards the pulsating shape.

'Careful, icon bearer,' said Kol Badar.

The skin of the shape bulged and Marduk could make out the shape of a xenos head straining to escape.

'Tyranid,' he hissed, just as the first of the hive creatures burst from its embryonic birth sack. The death of the world has arrived, he thought.

Claws ripped through the film of skin and foul waters erupted from within, bio-fluids gushing out. Clouds of fog rose as the warm liquid melted through ice and snow.

Bolters began to fire, tearing gaping rents in the sac that gushed hot liquid. These amniotic fluids were pinkish and thick, like glutinous syrup. Inhuman screams burst from the spore as the bolts ripped through it.

Then the first of the creatures leapt from within, launching itself directly at Burias, four slender, bladed limbs poised to impale him. The blades of its two forelimbs were the length of swords, and though the creature was smaller than the genestealers they had encountered in the hulk on the ocean floor, the similarities were marked.

Burias swatted the creature aside with the holy icon of the Host, breaking its back, and it slid through the ice and snow, carving a furrow, until it came to a halt at Kol Badar's feet. It snarled up at the Coryphaus, struggling to stand on its powerful hind legs, which would not respond. It hissed, and tried to stab at Kol Badar, but the

Coryphaus planted a bolt in its head that ended its struggles.

Marduk fired, his round screaming less than half a metre past Burias's head to detonate in the chest of another of the creatures as it scrambled from the crater. The rest of the Host opened fire as more of the creatures leapt from the spore, their weapons ripping the creatures apart, spraying sickly ichor across the snow.

Another mycetic spore screamed from the heavens and smashed into the ground ten metres away, and then another.

'How long?' asked Marduk, his bolt pistol bucking in his hands as he killed another of the leaping tyranid creatures.

'Five minutes,' said Kol Badar.

More of the creatures ripped free from birth-sac as the sides of the spores flopped open, and they launched themselves at the Word Bearers, covering the distance over the snow in powerful leaps.

'Close ranks,' roared Kol Badar, and the Word Bearers formed a tight circle facing outwards, with Darioq-Grendh'al in the centre. Weapons barking, ripping the first of the leaping tyranids out of the air, smashing them backwards as their flesh and chitin was torn apart.

Another spore crashed down nearby, its impact spraying Marduk with snow and ice. One of the warrior brothers sent a missile screaming from the launcher braced against his shoulder into the fleshy pod as its sides flopped heavily to the snow. The missile detonated inside the convulsing birth-sac, lighting it up from within for a moment, and the mass of creatures inside could be seen clearly through the skin of the sac enclosing them. Then the sides of the pod were ripped apart, and the high-pitched screams of the dying tyranids echoed through the gale as they were consumed in flame and shrapnel.

The missile launcher was tossed aside, its ammunition spent, and the warrior drew his bolt pistol and combat knife.

Marduk blasted the head of another creature into pulp and tracked his pistol skywards as one of the xenos creatures leapt high into the air. It descended towards him, sword-bladed arms lancing at him, and he fired. The bolt took the creature in the chest, passing through its chitinous exoskeleton before detonating, creating a head-sized crater of ruined flesh. Still it fell towards him, its brain not yet registering that it was dead, its every instinct willing it on to kill.

Marduk swiped it out of the air with his chainsword, ripping the toothed blade through the creature from neck to sternum, but one of its arms stabbed into his chest, biting through his power armour and embedding itself in his fused ribcage.

Slashing with his chainsword, Marduk sheared through the tyranid's elbow joint and it fell dead at his feet, its forelimb still protruding from his chest. He had no time to remove it, as a wave of the tyranids swarmed out of the storm.

Shouting a warning, Marduk held his fire until the tyranids were closer. The creatures from several of the spore-pods must have banded together, for this brood numbered perhaps thirty individual aliens. However, they did not move as individuals; they moved as one single living organism, with synchronicity that could never have been matched by even the best drilled veteran coterie of the Legion.

Without any obvious form of communication, the swarm of aliens turned as one, angling towards the

Word Bearers, their movements precise and almost robotic. Marduk saw that these were a different sub-species from the leaping aliens, though they were similar.

More hunched, these ones scuttled forwards bearing what might have been projectile weapons in their fore-limbs, though in truth the weapons were merely extensions of their limbs, fused to them, as much a part of the creature as the rest of their vile bodies.

Bolters and heavy weapons roared, ripping the first of the creatures apart in bloody explosions, but they continued scuttling forwards, oblivious or uncaring of their fallen. Their bio-weapons pulsed, the fleshy projectile tubes contracting sharply with peristalsis. Marduk felt something splatter across his left arm plates, and hissed in pain.

Looking down, he saw a mass of fleshy grubs boring through his ceramite vambrace and into his flesh, and he swatted frantically at them, trying to dislodge them. He squashed dozens of them as they scrabbled for purchase on his armour, but several of them were already too deep for him to easily remove, burrowing into the muscle of his forearm, squirming within his body as they feasted on his flesh.

Focusing his mind, he pushed away the pain and discomfort, and killed two of the tyranids with his pistol. He saw one of the 13th coterie fall to the ground, screaming in agony as a mass of writhing flesh-worms burrowed through his helmet, clogging his respirator and boring through the lenses covering his eyes, gnawing their way through his skull and into his brain.

A flamer roared, bathing the tyranid brood in burning promethium, and they screamed in inhuman torment as their bodies were consumed. Bolters tore through the survivors, but still more clambered over the bodies of the dead to fire their living ammunition into the tight circle of Word Bearers. More snow was kicked up as another spore slammed down into the ice.

Marduk ducked his head as a stream of beetles was spat towards him. Several wriggling bugs struck his right shoulder pad, painted black in mourning for Jarulek, but he squashed the voracious feeder creatures before they could bury themselves in his armour and flesh.

A second putrid stream of voracious organisms spat past Marduk to engulf Darioq-Grendh'al. An orb of energy appeared around the corrupted magos, and the coruscating electricity of the potent conversion field fried the tiny creatures.

The magos turned heavily towards its attacker as the flickering energy field disappeared, and Marduk sensed anger surge through the daemon inhabiting the ex-priest's flesh. Darioq-Grendh'al planted his feet, bracing himself as the two servo-arms over his back stabbed forwards, their forms blurring as they were altered by the power of the warp. Metal re-formed and a pair of fleshy tentacles joined with the servo-arms, forming a cable, part organic and part mineral, pulsing with energy.

A pair of incandescent beams roared from the re-formed servo-arms, and the power of Chaos screamed in Marduk's ears.

The beams struck the tyranids, and half a dozen of them were engulfed in an inferno, hissing and writhing as their flesh mutated. Tentacles tipped with chitinous barbs burst from within the tyranids, ripping through their flesh and thrashing out through eye-sockets and mouths, turning the xenos beings inside out. Within moments, all that remained of the tyranids struck by Darioq-Grendh'al's fire was a thrashing mass of tentacles.

'Impressive,' said Marduk with a smile as Darioq-Grendh'al's servo-arms moulded back to their usual form.

'Two minutes,' shouted Kol Badar as yet another spore-pod slammed down, crushing a handful of tyranids beneath its impact. This pod was much larger than the others, and powerful forms larger even than an Astartes warrior struggled to free themselves from within it.

'To the north-west, move!' roared Kol Badar as a trio of giant tyranid beasts ripped free of the skin of the large spore-pod and reared up to their full height – easily twice that of a normal man – and another brood of smaller creatures swarmed from the howling winds, angling towards the Word Bearers. More pods slammed down from the heavens.

'Move, Grendh'al,' said Marduk, impelling the creature with his voice of command, and though the daemon resisted him, its will was overpowered, and it reluctantly turned to do as it was bid.

The Word Bearers carved through the hordes of lesser tyranids like a spear through water, smashing them aside as they drove forwards. A warrior stumbled as maggot-like organisms splattered across his armour, acidic life-fluids melting through his armour plates and burning into his flesh. Marduk lifted the warrior back to his feet, supporting him with one arm as he fired.

Spotlights tore through the darkness and the swirling snow, and the hulking shapes of Land Raiders appeared through the whitewash of fog and ice. Incandescent las-cannon beams stabbed from side-sponsons, scything through tyranid organisms that hurled themselves at the Word Bearers, symbiotic bio-weapons spitting. Heavy bolters scythed through dozens of the xenos beasts, ripping them apart with their high calibre rounds.

The Land Raiders came to a grinding halt before the warriors of the XVII Legion, growling like daemonic beasts, their hot breath steaming from exhaust stacks. The frontal assault ramps smashed down onto the ice, and the warriors of the XVII Legion stormed inside the gaping interiors of the immense steel beasts.

Sabtec relieved Marduk of the wounded warrior he was supporting. The warrior was reciting the Doxology of Revilement, focusing on the words to alleviate the pain of the bio-acid melting through his armour and flesh. As he passed the warrior into Sabtec's care, Marduk spun around standing in the door of the Land Raider as the last of the warriors of the Host stamped forwards.

The larger tyranid creatures they had seen clawing their way free of their spore-pod were stalking towards the Land Raiders, their tails thrashing. Each pair of upper arms ended in scything blades, and their secondary pairs of arms moulded into long-barrelled bio-cannons. A swarm of the lesser tyranids raced towards Marduk as the assault ramp began to close, and he fired into the pack, dropping two of them.

Lascannon beams made the air crackle with electrical energy as the twin-linked side-sponsons of the mighty Land Raiders fired, and one of the large tyranid creatures was vaporised. The other two lurched forwards, discharging their long-barrelled bio-weapons towards Marduk even as the swarming horde of lesser xenos raced towards him.

The bio-weapons ammunition splattered onto the assault ramp of the Land Raider as it rose, spraying acid across the thick metal that began to hiss and bubble. A drop splashed onto Marduk's chest plate, burning a hole through his armour and searing his flesh, but he ignored the wound and slashed with his chainsword as the lesser tyranids launched themselves onto the Land Raider's chassis.

Heavy bolter fire ripped two of them to shreds as the Land Raider lurched into reverse, but two of them hurled themselves through the closing aperture as the assault ramp hissed closed, and Marduk killed the first, impaling its head on his chainblade, the whirring teeth ripping its skull apart. Sabtec killed the second creature, slamming its bestial, xenos face into the side of the Land Raider again and again until it was an unrecognisable, bloody pulp.

More of the small tyranids scrabbled at the assault ramp as it closed, but then the assault ramp was sealed, severing several stabbing blade-arms that fell to the floor inside, leaking foul-smelling fluids.

Marduk slumped down into one of the seats, breathing hard.

Only then did he realise that he still had the bony blade-arm of one of the creatures protruding from his chest. He ripped it clear with a sharp movement, and tossed it to the floor alongside the pair of tyranid corpses.

The Doxology of Revilement was still being recited as Sabtec tore the melting breastplate from the warrior of his coterie who had been splashed with bio-acid, and the champion sprayed a black film over the wounds.

'First Acolyte,' said Kol Badar over a closed channel from the other Land Raider.

'Go ahead,' said Marduk.

'The tyranid invasion may have covered half this world already,' said the Coryphaus. 'I feel that it would be inadvisable to proceed to the drop-ship's location overland. We do not know the numbers of the xenos between here and there.'

'Agreed,' said Marduk.

'I suggest that we order the ship to launch, to meet us half way.'

'Understood. See that it is done,' said Marduk severing the connection.

Bloody and battered, Marduk pulled his helmet from his head and stowed it in the alcove above him.

At last they were leaving this doomed Imperial back-water planet, he thought, and he smiled, exposing his sharp teeth.

A month, maybe two, and he would be back on Sicarus, returning in glory.

The Land Raider rocked as tyranid bio-weapons struck its armoured hide, but still Marduk grinned.

Glory would be his.

CHAPTER FIFTEEN

DRACON ALITH DRAZJAER of the Black Heart Cabal strode down the dark corridor, his thin lips curled in distaste. He moved with the supple, arrogant grace of a born warrior. A pair of heavily armoured incubi bodyguards walked warily on either side of him, the sweeping blades of their punisher glaives lowered.

They passed dozens of cells, all crammed with wailing, wretched slaves, many of whom had already felt the ministrations of the haemonculus Rhakaeth, or soon would.

The wretched creatures were mostly human, but there were other lesser species packed into the crowded cells as well: tall, reptilian k'ith; kroot mercenaries; stony-faced demiurg; as well as eldar, either those of Drazjaer's dark kin that had fallen from his grace, warriors of his rivals, or his deluded craftworld cousins.

The cells closest to the haemonculus's operation chambers were filled with his experiments, and these blighted creatures filled the corridor with their sickly cries. Humans with their spines removed flopped impotently on the floors of cells, while others that had had their legs replaced with muscular arms whooped in insane rage, hurling themselves against the invisible barrier separating them from Drazjaer. They were thrown backwards as energy arced across the barrier, accompanied by the stink of ozone.

Other twisted monstrosities had insect-like eyes, more than one head, or random limbs sprouting from their bulbous stomachs. Some had leathery wings grafted to their backs, and others pulled themselves across the floor of their cells with flipper-like appendages where human hands had once been, their lower bodies shrunken and wasted, like the malformed legs of a foetus not yet reached its term.

Some of the abominations scratched at faces that were already torn to bloody ribbons, and all cried out for death. Still others flexed overgrown muscles, fan-like webs of skin opening up beneath their arms, while others appeared almost normal, with just minor enhancements, such as arms that ended in glittering blades, or had sharp ridges of bone running down their craniums.

A pair of Rhakaeth's grotesques guarded the door to the haemonculus's chambers: his altered ones, his companions, his twisted cortege; his more successful experiments. These eldar had come to the haemonculus willingly, desperate to experience new and varied sensations, and they had begged and backstabbed their way into Rhakaeth's favour in order to feel the touch of his razors.

One of the grotesques stood taller even than Drazjaer. Hundreds of quill-like spines had been surgically inserted into his flesh, running down his spine and across the backs of his arms. His mouth had been cut into a new form, a vertical slash bisecting his horizontal lips, and additional musculature added so that when it opened, its four corners peeled back independently. The abomination's eyes were those of some serpentine, alien species, and a dual pair of eyelids blinked as the grotesque looked towards the approaching dracon and his incubi. Its quills stood on end and began to shiver noisily. More spines flicked from within his forearms, and others slid forwards from the base of its palms.

The second of Rhakaeth's guards, a female eldar, was completely naked, though her flesh was covered in small metallic blue scales that shimmered and turned a dusky red as Drazjaer drew near. Her luscious, ruby lips parted and a forked tongue, pierced in a dozen places with metal studs, flicked out past sharpened teeth. The fingers of her left hand had been replaced with long knives, and parts of her body – and her companion's – bore scars and fresh wounds that had clearly been the result of her caresses.

Neither of the altered eldar warriors bore weapons, their enhanced bodies their instruments of death.

The incubi at Drazjaer's side levelled their glaives at the pair, and runes flickered with witch-light upon the blasters built into their sweeping tormentor helms. The potent weapons were neurally linked to the incubi's brain waves, and could be fired with a mere thought, leaving the warrior's hands free to wield their punisher glaives.

The grotesques hissed at the powerfully armoured incubi, the female creature flexing her fingers, and her male counterpart turning his upturned hands towards them. Drazjaer had seen that one fight before. It was capable of firing the spines from its palms, and the merest scratch of one of the quills would cause a slow and painful death. The haemonculus Rhakaeth had been particularly proud of that creation.

Drazjaer waved them aside with a languid, dismissive motion, and the pair of grotesques backed away from the portal, still hissing at the incubi.

'Stay here,' Drazjaer said to his bodyguards, in his soft, dangerous voice. The incubi bowed their helmeted heads in respect of his wishes and stood to attention, taking up a position opposite the grotesque body-guards, the ruby-red crystal lenses, hiding their eyes, glittering menacingly.

Drazjaer strode into Rhakaeth's chambers, the bladed arcs of the door slicing closed behind him, and gazed around.

He avoided the haemonculus's private chambers whenever possible, and it had been some years since he had last set foot in this part of his ship.

The only light within the room was a dull, pulsing glow that emanated from the floor and ceiling, throbbing like the beat of Khaine's heart; Rhakaeth's eyes were particularly sensitive to bright lights. The walls of the circular chamber were smooth and the colour of dried blood and bladed stands atop which was spread a veritable cornucopia of curios and torturous implements hovered above the floor.

There was no obvious order to the mess of objects strewn across the levitating stands. The hollowed skulls of eldar, carved with runes, lay alongside blades covered in rust-like flecks of dried blood, jars filled with blinking organic creatures that squirmed within their confinement, and decomposing severed limbs and organs left to rot.

Drazjaer moved to one of the hovering stands and lifted up a cube the size of a child's skull. Its sides were covered in stretched, flayed eldar skin, and as he held it, faces began to push from within, straining to escape. They opened their mouths wide in silent cries of torment.

'That was a gift to me from my old master,' said a hollow voice, and Drazjaer turned to see his haemonculus, Rhakaeth, ghost into the room, his impossibly thin, skeletal frame seeming to glide across the floor. Blood was splashed across one emaciated cheek, shockingly bright on his monotone countenance.

The haemonculus folded his wasted arms across his chest, skeletal fingers covered in blood scratching idly at the emaciated flesh of his upper arms.

'Before you killed him?' asked Drazjaer.

'Indeed. It is a crucible. The soul-spirits of an entire seer-council of our brothers of Ulthwé are housed within it,' said Rhakaeth.

'It's very nice,' said Drazjaer, placing the cube back upon the hovering stand.

'But you did not come here to admire my collection,' said the haemonculus, 'you came here to pay witness to my work. Please, my lord, come through.'

Drazjaer followed him through to a side room and gazed upon the two bloodied bodies that were held aloft by a multi-legged mechanism, their limbs pierced by the blade-arms of the machine.

The two figures were immense, as tall as eldar, but easily three times the weight, their bodies bulked out with thick slabs of muscle. Blood was everywhere in the circular room. It had sprayed across the walls and ceiling, was pooling on the floor, and covered the bodies and the mechanical arms that pinned them in place.

The dark red armour plates of the mon-keigh were scattered across the floor. Drazjaer moved one of them with his foot. It was heavy and inflexible, a brutal and crude form of armour for a brutal and crude race.

Returning his gaze to the two human bodies impaled upon the bladed arms of the mechanical apparatus that held them, Drazjaer saw that one of them was clearly lifeless, and anger blossomed within him. What good were they to him if they were dead?

As if feeling his master's anger bloom, Rhakaeth stepped away from the dracon, putting the bodies between them. The eyes of the still living human flicked towards the dracon, fires of rage in his lidless orbs. The man's flesh had been stripped from his body, and his chest cavity was open to the air, organs pulsing within.

'My lord dracon–' Rhakaeth began in his deep, hollow voice, but Drazjaer cut him off.

'I told you to keep them alive,' the dracon said, his voice low and deadly.

'This one did not die as a result of my ministrations, my lord dracon,' said Rhakaeth. 'The mandrake, Ja'harael, delivered it half-dead. It was all that I could do to keep it alive for as long as I did.'

'Ja'harael. It's all Ja'harael's fault,' said Drazjaer, sneering. 'I've heard that before, from the snivelling sybarite rotting in your cells. I do not wish to hear any of your excuses, haemonculus.'

'Whether you wish to hear me or not, my lord dracon, I speak the truth,' said the haemonculus, his voice devoid of fear. Indeed, Drazjaer had rarely heard any emotion in his servant's voice.

'And this one?' asked Drazjaer, leaning over the massive form of the still living human creature. It pulled at its restraints, massive muscles bulging as it stared at him in hatred. The dracon was unmoved, and peered with interest inside the figure's exposed torso.

'Living, and strong, my lord dracon. The potency of its soul-essence is worth a hundred, a thousand of the lesser mon-keigh breed.'

Drazjaer licked his thin lips. He had already gathered almost ten thousand souls for his lord and master, the dark lord Asdrubael Vect, but this did not yet meet the extortionate tribute the high lord of the Black Heart cabal had demanded of his vassal.

When Vect had butchered the cabal leaders of the Bleeding Talons, the Vipers and the Void Serpents in one dark night, Drazjaer had been cast adrift, vulnerable, now that his lord had been slaughtered in the murderous plot. He had been forced to kneel before Asdrubael Vect in chains, and had been asked if he would submit to his rule, if he would join the Black Heart. Only once he had sworn his warriors to the Black Heart over the soulfires of *Gaggamel* did Vect lay down his terms.

Drazjaer's time was running short. The Great Devourer hive fleet would overrun the system within the day, and his harvest would be over, his tribute not yet fulfilled. There was no running from Asdrubael Vect. No matter where Drazjaer went, no matter how far from Commoragh he fled, Vect would find him.

However, if he could gather more of these enhanced mon-keigh, these *Space Marines*, he mighty yet gain Vect's favour. Perhaps the dark lord would even raise him to the exalted status of archon, in command of an entire slave fleet.

'Their physical makeup is interesting,' the haemonculus was saying, 'clearly the result of gene-conditioning and surgical enhancement. It is offensively crude work, with little subtlety or grace, but I feel that I could harvest their organs to create a superior blend of eldar warrior.'

Drazjaer barely heard the sibilant hiss of Rhakaeth's voice, lost in his own thoughts of greed and desire.

'Do whatever pleases you, Rhakaeth,' he said. 'Just see that that one does not die. I believe that it is time to unleash Atherak and her wych cult upon the Imperial world.'

'The bitch's arrogance knows no bounds,' said the haemonculus.

'Indeed,' agreed Drazjaer. 'Let us see if her boastfulness is founded. Let us see if *she* can bring back more than two of these mon-keigh.'

'I will look forward to working upon more of these,' said the Rhakaeth, indicating the pair of altered humans strung up before him.

'Fine,' said Drazjaer, turning and striding from the haemonculus's chambers.

Outside, his incubi were still eyeing up the grotesque guards, and a third warrior had joined them, another of his sybarite captains.

'What is it?' asked Drazjaer.

'My lord dracon,' said the warrior, bowing. 'The traitor returns.'

SOLON MARCABUS KNEW that the end was near. They were running low on food, down to the last protein bar, and his strength was fading.

Dios seemed neither to tire nor despair, and he pressed on through the snow with grim determination while Solon often lagged behind, and it was Dios who rubbed warmth into Solon's frostbitten fingers and toes whenever they set up camp.

He was determined to see Dios on a shuttle away from Perdus Skylla, and though he had never been a pious man, Solon swore that he would devote his life to the Emperor if he only allowed the boy to survive this nightmare. Dios would have a future somewhere, on some distant planet, far from the threat of xenos incursions. Solon was fixated on the completion of what had become an epic pilgrimage towards the

Phorcys spaceport, and he would fight to his dying breath to see the boy safely off-planet.

Dios could have the life that Solon's son had been denied.

The ice crunched beneath his laboured steps. He could barely feel his arm, and though it was a relief to be free of the throbbing pain of his wound, he knew that it was a bad sign.

He heard a sound like thunder rolling towards them, over the blinding gale, but he gave it little thought; just more bad weather heading in their direction he thought grimly. He kept plodding along through the snow, putting one foot in front of the other.

The sound got louder, and Dios cried out. Solon lifted his head to see the boy gesturing wildly into the air.

A shuttle roared out of the banks of billowing snow and ice, flying low and fast through the storm. It was hit with a blast of wind and dropped metres through the air as it was buffeted to the side, and for a moment Solon thought it was going to crash, but the pilot compensated and the shuttle righted itself, engines screaming. Solon waved his arms above his head, attempting vainly to get the attention of the pilot, hoping and praying that the shuttle would stop. It passed low overhead, blocking out all sounds of the wind, and Solon stared up in awe and amazement as the shuttle screamed past, making the ground shudder with the power of its engines.

Then the shuttle was past them, its retro-burners blazing with blue flame. Solon whipped his head around as the shuttle roared over their heads. He could feel the heat from the plasma-core engines even through his exposure suit, and he relished the almost forgotten sensation. Stabiliser burners fired on the underside of the shuttle, lifting it over an outcrop of ice.

Dios was standing, staring, his eyes filled with wonder as he watched the shuttle disappear once more into the concealing storm.

Solon felt a sudden surge of hope. They had come for them! They *had* come looking for survivors! He was certain that he had sensed the shuttle slowing down. The pilot must have seen them!

'Hurry, Dios!' he shouted, filled with a sudden surge of energy, and he set off in pursuit of the shuttle, pounding through the snow and ice, his fatigue forgotten. They had come for them! They must have picked up the blinking distress beacon in Solon's exposure suit that he had activated as soon as the raiders, the ones that Dios called the ghosts, had departed.

Dios was falling behind, and Solon paused to wait for the boy to catch up, his heart thumping. Scooping the boy up in his arms, who whooped in excitement, Solon set off, pounding through the snow, running madly towards where the shuttle had disappeared.

Reality hit home like a punch in the guts. No one would be coming back. The shuttle was probably heading to Sholto guild to pick up rich merchants, or other high guilders of influence. No one would be coming to find an orphan and a lowly crawler mule.

He slowed his pace, feeling suddenly exhausted, and dropped Dios back down to the ground. The boy looked up at him in confusion. Solon avoided the boy's eye contact, hanging his head and putting his hands on his thighs, leaning forward as he strained to catch his breath.

Dios reached out to him, taking hold of his hand and urging him on. Solon angrily shook his hand free. Again, the boy reached for him, and Solon swatted his hand away.

'It's over, boy!' he shouted, suddenly enraged. 'Don't you get it? There is no salvation. No one is coming to help us! We are going to die out here, and no one is going to know. No one is going to care!'

Dios stared back at Solon blankly, and Solon fell forward to his hands and knees, tears welling in his eyes.

'No one is coming,' he said again, this time more softly as despair washed over him. 'No one is coming.'

Dios stepped alongside him, putting his arm around Solon's shoulders, and he felt all the tension and fear within him well up. The tears ran freely, and Solon was glad that the hood of his exposure suit hid them from the boy. After a few minutes, a calmness descended over Solon, and he took a deep breath.

He looked up at Dios, who was peering at him in concern, and he gave the boy a smile.

Solon pushed himself wearily to his feet and checked the digi-compass beneath a flap of canvas on his left arm, realigning himself with the direction of the Phorcys starport, which he guessed was still a day and half's hike away. Nodding to Dios, he set off again in that direction, but a tugging at his belt gave him pause.

Dios was gesturing in the direction that the shuttle had taken.

'No, Dios. It wasn't coming for us. I'm sorry, boy.'

Still, the orphan was insistent, gesturing more emphatically in the opposite direction that Solon had set off in.

With a sigh, he gave in, and turned back. Dios leapt forwards enthusiastically, grabbing hold of his hand and dragging him through the snow, into the billowing ice storm.

They had moved perhaps a kilometre through the snow when the wind changed direction, blowing the

banks of fog and ice away to the west, leaving the view
out in front suddenly clear. Solon could see further than
he had done for months, and he marvelled at the display of colour that danced across the heavens.

It was called the Aurealis Skyllian, and it was said
that the phenomenon occurred only under specific
atmospheric conditions. Solon had seen it only twice
before in his lifetime, once when he was a boy, a week
after his father had died in a mining accident, and
again on the first night he had spent on the foreign and
terrifying ice crawlers, just after he had been expelled
from the guild. Both times had been momentous occasions in his life, and this one would prove likewise, for
there, on the ice, a kilometre away, lit up by the eerie,
heavenly light in the dark sky overhead, was the shuttle.

It was settling on the ice flow, and Solon again felt
his spirits soar. They *were* stopping for them! Even if
they had not actually seen the two refugees tramping
across the ice, it didn't matter. What mattered was
that the shuttle was landing, and it was within their
reach.

A desperate fear that the shuttle would leave again
before they reached it filled Solon, and again he
scooped up Dios in his arms, and began to plough his
way through the snow.

Salvation had come, at last.

Thank the Emperor, thought Solon.

'THE IDOLATOR IS inbound,' said Kol Badar's voice,
'touching down over the ridge to the north.'

'Good,' said Marduk.

The Land Raiders had outrun the downpour of xenos
spores, and there had been no enemy contact for almost
an hour. Nevertheless, sensors indicated that the waves

of inbound spores were intensifying, and their spread widening.

'Be ready for disembarkation,' Marduk snapped at the warriors in the Land Raider. 'Two minutes and counting.'

CHAPTER SIXTEEN

'BARANOV,' SAID EUSTENOV, the pilot of the *Rapture*, 'they are pulling us in. Five minutes.'

The smuggler, rogue trader and sometimes blockade-runner leant forward over the back of his pilot, peering into the blackness of space ahead, on the shadow-side of the doomed planet Perdus Skylla. The sleek shape of the ship that the *Rapture* was to dock with could barely be seen, even at this distance, and he shook his head, marvelling at the technology that concealed it. It was merely a part of the surrounding darkness, though the bladed vales that protruded from its length like the fins of a fish gleamed sharply as the forward lights of the *Rapture* swept across them.

Patting the clearly nervous pilot on the shoulder, Baranov turned and stalked towards the rear compartment of his trading vessel, where members of the wealthy elite of Perdus Skylla were housed. He took a deep breath, gathering himself, and wiped the sweat from his brow. Then, with a casual, relaxed smile on his face, he placed his palm on the register panel beside the door-frame. The portal slid silently aside and he strode confidently through.

The gathered nobles and upper guild officials were lounging on the low, cushioned couches within, sipping from glasses filled with the finest amasec that Baranov could obtain. Each bottle had cost him a small fortune, but it mattered not when compared with the price the Perdus Skyllans had already paid him, and the wealth that he was promised from his employers.

Surgically enhanced beauties, the courtesans and mistresses of these fine, upstanding gentlemen, were laughing gaily as they sipped from their high glasses, and gave each other venomous glances behind their masters' backs. The men were gathered in small groups, talking earnestly about whatever they talked about, probably their latest guild takeover moves, or their strategies for the future.

No one paid any mind to Baranov as he stood before them. He was as invisible as a servant, and he cleared his throat to gain their attention.

'How far are we from the Imperial fleet, Baranov?' huffed a heavily jowled guild senator, and the rogue trader held up a hand to forestall him.

'My most esteemed companions,' he said with a broad smile, his voice raised over the din of chatter, 'I come to inform you that we are nearing our destination. I hope that you have been comfortable on your journey, and I apologise for any inconvenience that the turbulence we experienced earlier caused you. Alas, it was a necessary inconvenience. It was as if the loathsome xenos were determined to make your lives less comfortable, abominable creatures, all of them.'

Baranov raised a hand as murmuring rippled across the gathered group, and gasps came from several of the courtesans.

'Have no fear, ladies and gentlemen, the bulk of the xenos fleet is attacking Perdus Skylla from galactic east, on the far side of the planet. You were in little real danger, and my pilot, dear Eustenov, is the finest pilot in the eastern quadrant. Only the best for such vaunted company,' he said, bowing with a flourish.

The lie came easily to Baranov's lips. In truth, the *Rapture* was lucky to have avoided destruction, as several of the spores launched from the still distant tyranid hive fleets had come perilously close to colliding with his ship. It had taken more luck than skill to avoid them.

'We will be docking in around two minutes,' said Baranov, checking the time on his wrist-piece. 'It has been a pleasure to have such esteemed guests aboard the *Rapture*. Never before has such a fine group of individuals graced its humble decks, and I shall look back upon the service I was able to perform with pleasure for many years to come.'

Many of the nobles refused even to look at him, but Baranov didn't care.

'Many years to come indeed,' he said again, more softly, and bowing with a flourish, he returned to the shuttle's cockpit, thinking of what he would do with his new-found wealth.

'HURRY, DIOS,' SAID Solon as he raced through the snow towards the landed shuttle. The effort of carrying the boy had all but exhausted him, and now the boy was running along behind him, his eyes wide with excitement and hope.

They were no more than fifty metres from the shuttle, and he could see the embarkation deck at the rear of the fuselage lowering to the ground, beckoning him.

Salvation!

With a burst of speed, Dios overtook him, laughing as he ran, but then the boy stopped short, freezing in place. Laughing, Solon drew to a halt next to the boy, a smile on his lips.

'Isn't it the most wonderful sight you've ever seen?' he breathed, his heart pumping from the exertion.

Dios's eyes were locked on something in the distance, something moving fast. Squinting through the darkness, Solon could see four shapes moving rapidly across the ice flow, a white backwash kicking up behind them.

'Interdiction forces?' said Solon, but the vehicles were not the uniform white of the moon's military forces. They were the colour of congealed blood, and a shiver ran down Solon's spine as he looked upon them. They were larger than any Interdiction vehicle he had ever seen, for even without landmarks for reference to give the vehicles scale, he could see that they were massive.

Solon began to walk slowly towards the waiting shuttle, but a sudden wave of fear struck him, and he dropped to his belly, dragging Dios down into the snow with him. Sponson-mounted weaponry on the vehicles, which could only have been battle tanks, turned in their direction.

Solon and Dios watched with growing panic as the four battle tanks drew nearer, and they could see that their hulls were covered in chains, spikes and blasphemous runes. Skulls were rammed onto sharpened metal stakes that ran in ridges down the flanks of the massive machines, and strips of parchment were plastered to their sides, half obscured by snow and ice.

The first of the tanks ground to a halt before the shuttle, and dark smoke rose from its exhaust stacks. An assault ramp at the front of the vehicle slammed down on to the ice, and giants dressed in red plate armour emerged.

Solon had only heard stories about the blessed Space Marines that protected humanity, and he had never dreamed in his wildest fantasies that he would ever get a chance to lay eyes on the nigh-on mythical warriors of the Emperor. They were the Emperor's chosen, biologically enhanced warriors that were as strong as ten men, armed with the most advanced weaponry the Adeptus Mechanicus could provide, and armoured in heavy plate that could withstand a direct hit from a Leman Russ battle tank, so it was said. They were the finest fighting force that the galaxy had ever seen, and it was said that nothing could stand against them. Looking upon the divine warriors, Solon could well believe it, though these warriors looked more like bloodthirsty butchers than holy protectors of humanity.

'Angels of death,' he whispered.

In his childhood dreams he had pictured them armoured in faultless golden plate, with angelic countenances and noble bearing. While such beliefs were clearly childish, Solon knew that there was something horribly wrong here. He was desperate to believe that salvation had come to Perdus Skylla, that the Emperor had dispatched his finest warriors to free the moon from alien invasion, but these Space Marines filled him with dread.

The other monstrous tanks disgorged their cargo of Space Marines, and two of the massive vehicles backed under the shuttle's stubby wings. Locking clamps descended like umbilical cords, latching onto the immense tanks and lifting them up beneath its wings while the other pair manoeuvred into position behind.

The first warriors stamped up the embarkation deck into the belly of the shuttle. One of them paused on the ramp, consulting a hand-held tech-device. It turned in their direction, and Solon sank down lower into the snow, barely daring to breathe.

A warrior with a helmet fashioned like a grinning death's head spun to face them, and a fresh wave of panic gripped Solon as he realised that they had been spotted. Other warriors turned in their direction, and, raising their weapons before them, they began to march towards their position.

Sick with panic, Solon staggered to his feet, his heart thumping. He lifted his hands up before him, to show that he was unarmed.

The Space Marines halted, though they did not lower their weapons. One of them, a lean warrior whose head was bare to the elements, turned to the skull-helmed one, speaking something that Solon could not hear. The warrior appeared to approve, nodding his head almost imperceptibly before turning away and striding up the embarkation ramp towards the interior of the shuttle.

The barefaced warrior turned back towards Solon with a cold smile upon his noble face, and Solon licked his lips uneasily. The other Space Marines turned away, but this one warrior remained staring at them. Solon felt as if he was transfixed by the Space Marine's gaze.

Then the man turned into a monster, and Solon felt his sanity fray.

'No,' he whispered, as the warrior grew, his shoulders bulking out and his hands extending into talons. The warrior's image flickered like a faulty pict screen, and for a moment Solon could see the image of two beings overlapping each other, both inhabiting the same space. Although he knew such a thing was impossible, and his rational mind baulked at what he was seeing, he could not refute what he saw with his own eyes. The warrior was still there, lean and striding towards them with an easy, relaxed grace, but there was something else... something horrific.

It was a hulking daemon from the pits of hell, and its hateful features overlaid the classically handsome face of the Space Marine. Its eyes burnt with malice and the promise of pain, and its lips curled back to expose hundreds of sharp teeth, arrayed in serried layers, one behind the other, all the way to the back of its throat. Tall horns rose from its brow, and the air was thick and cloying where it exhaled.

The two images became one, a bastard hybrid, and Solon, horrified beyond reason, began to back away even as the daemonic hybrid creature began loping towards them.

'Run!' Solon roared, his paralysis giving way to abject terror.

Glancing over his shoulder, Solon saw that the hellish creature was gaining on them rapidly, covering the ground with tremendous leaps, using its arms to steady itself with each landing.

These were not the Emperor's divine angels, he thought; they couldn't be. They were the flip side of everything he had ever heard about them, and they were going to butcher him and Dios, after all they that had struggled through.

Solon glanced back to see the daemon close behind them, its powerful legs bunched beneath it as it prepared to launch itself upon them. Solon shoved Dios to the side as the creature leapt. It would not get them both at once, but he knew that he was only delaying the inevitable, for neither of them could hope to stand against such a creature.

Solon spun around to face the monster as it lunged towards him, staggering backwards in the snow, raising his hands futilely to ward off its attacks.

A beam of pure darkness stabbed through the air and slammed into the daemon's body, smashing it to the ice, and it roared in fury and pain.

The daemon writhed on the ground. A searing hole had punched through its side just above the hip, passing clean through its body, and as it thrashed around, hot blood splashed across the ice and snow, causing steam to rise where it landed.

Solon spun to see where the blast had come from, and blinked as he saw several dark vehicles gliding smoothly across the ice. They looked similar to the skiffs that the first colonists on Perdus Skylla were said to have used, long thin boats with blades on their undersides that had used the power of the winds to propel them across the ice flow. These were not touching the ground at all, but hovered two metres above the ground, and slid forward with phenomenal speed.

Another lance of dark light stabbed from one of the vehicles, striking one of the daemonic Space Marines' battle tanks, which exploded spectacularly, the immense fireball throwing the shattered vehicle high into the air.

Dark figures leapt from the sides of the skiffs. Somersaulting from the decks and landing effortlessly on the ground, they began running lightly towards the Space Marines.

'Ghosts,' breathed Dios, his eyes wide with fear and panic.

Grabbing the boy around the waist, Solon lifted him and ran.

BURIAS-DRAK'SHAL PUSHED himself to his knees, growling and spitting. The shot had gone clear through him, passing between his hip and the base of his fused ribcage, leaving a gaping aperture of weeping flesh and internal organs exposed to the air. Already his enhanced, daemonically infused physiology was sealing the wound, his blood flow clotting and his flesh beginning to re-knit, but it would take some time before he was fully healed, and no amount of healing could repair his sundered power armour.

Pushing himself to his feet, Burias-Drak'shal hissed in pain and staggered, falling back to his knees before once again rising. All thought of the pair of humans was gone, and he scanned the landscape, focusing on the dark shapes of the eldar as they darted towards his comrades.

Wincing in pain, the icon bearer began to stagger back towards the shuttle, when his enhanced senses picked up a familiar scent on the air. He threw himself forward into a roll as he registered the appearance of the shadow-eldar behind him, and came up facing the being, teeth bared.

That the creature was of eldar origin was clear, for its frame was tall and slight, its limbs long and elegant, but that was where the similarities ended. Its skin was as black as the night, and runes of twisted eldar design were inscribed into its flesh. These runes glowed with cold light, pulsing brightly as the creature entered fully into the material realm.

Burias-Drak'shal felt the power of the warp within the creature, but it was not possessed in the same manner as he was. It was almost as if the daemon within the eldar shade was at once there and not there, its will and individuality gone, but its strength tapped.

The shadow-eldar hissed at him, elegant, alien features contorting to reveal an array of small, sharp teeth, and its milky, elongated eyes, shockingly white against its black skin, flashed its murderous intent a fraction before it moved.

The creature disappeared, leaving a smoky outline in its wake, before it reappeared beside Burias-Drak'shal, the blades emerging from the back of its forearms slashing towards his wounded side.

Burias-Drak'shal was ready for it this time, swinging his arm around in a brutal arc that would have decapitated the slender eldar had its reflexes been less than preternatural. It swayed backwards from the blow, the possessed Word Bearer's talons passing just centimetres from its face.

Burias-Drak'shal pushed his advantage, throwing a stabbing blow towards the eldar's torso, seeking to rip its heart from its chest. The shade threw itself backwards and disappeared again, only to reappear to the icon bearer's left, and the twin blades protruding from the back of its arm stabbed deep into his body. The blades of its other arm slashed across his pauldron, slicing monomolecular cuts through his power armour and drawing blood from his bicep.

Burias-Drak'shal snarled and spun, lashing out at the shadow-eldar, but his claws merely passed through a dark mist as the creature leapt away once more. It reentered the material plane to his other side, its blades flashing again, and the icon bearer felt hot blood begin to flow from another trio of wounds.

His anger grew as the eldar continued to prey upon him, taunting him with its speed, and Burias-Drak'shal roared in frustration as once again his claws found nothing but air.

For all his anger he could sense that there was a pattern forming in the creature's attacks. It attacked and jumped away, always moving, and always attacking from a different angle.

As the shade disappeared once more, Burias-Drak'shal spun around on the spot, anticipating where its next attack would come from and lashing out. The eldar appeared where he had expected, and even its alien speed and reflexes were not up to avoiding the icon bearer's pre-emptive strike.

Burias-Drak'shal's talons closed around the slender eldar neck, and he pulled the creature sharply towards him, throwing it off balance.

'Got you,' growled Burias-Drak'shal, pulling the alien straight onto his rising knee, which thundered into the creature's sternum.

Burias-Drak'shal grinned as he felt the bones and tendons under his grip strain, and he clubbed the creature in the back of its head as it bent over double. It was slammed to the ground, and Burias-Drak'shal followed it down, driving his knee into the small of the eldar's back.

Burias-Drak'shal pulled his right hand back, and thrust down with all his enhanced might, seeking to drive his talons through the back of the creature's skull.

It disappeared from beneath him, his talons spearing deep into the ice, and the icon bearer snarled in frustration.

Flicking his head to the side, he saw that his brother warriors had been engaged by the bulk of the eldar raiding force, and with a hiss he began loping painfully towards the escalating battle.

BARANOV COULD BARELY contain his satisfaction as he hauled the bay doors of the *Rapture* open and the pompous, condescending elite of Perdus Skylla gaped in horror.

Eldar warriors were standing just outside the bay doors of the *Rapture*. Several of the courtesans screamed, while others whimpered in terror or merely gaped and soiled themselves. Baranov grinned, and stepped to the side.

A screaming woman was dragged from the shuttle by her hair, and the remaining high-ranking guilders shrank back, only to be pushed forward by Baranov's burly crew members.

Chuckling, Baranov swung away from the spectacle. For a moment, his gaze was drawn towards the shimmering integrity field that covered the yawning docking bay. It was almost imperceptible to the naked eye, looking as though nothing separated the inside of the ship and the vacuum of space, and it always made him feel slightly uneasy, as if he would be sucked out into the void at any moment.

Ikorus Baranov stepped back alongside the dark eldar lord's proxy, his arms folded across his chest as the wailing, weeping guilders and their lovers were led away in glimmering manacles that crackled with energy. He had never learnt the name of the eldar pirate, nor that of his representative. Not that it mattered, he thought. He would be unlikely to be able to pronounce it anyway.

'You have done well for me these past months,' said the eldar, his voice as smooth as velvet. The eldar spoke a curious form of Low Gothic, his pronunciation pitch perfect, but with a strangely singsong inflection.

'I am glad that your lord has been pleased with my deliveries,' replied Baranov, trying to keep his voice calm. In truth, the eldar terrified him, but they paid well. 'That will be the last of them, I'm afraid. I won't risk another run, not with the tyranids so close.'

Baranov flashed a glance at the eldar's face, trying to read him. Normally a good judge of character, he found it galling that he could not gauge the eldar's emotions in the slightest. Never again will I work with xenos, he thought, though he knew as soon as he thought it that it was a lie.

'The... what do you call them? Tyranids?' said the eldar. Baranov nodded.

'Your pronunciation is perfect,' commented Baranov. The eldar stared at him for a moment, and he felt himself shrink under his unfathomable gaze.

'The *tyranids* might well exterminate all of the lesser races, in time,' said the eldar casually.

'They are a menace,' agreed Baranov, unsure where the conversation was leading, and uncomfortable making small talk with the deadly eldar lord.

'If all of your kind are eradicated, where then will my lord find such slaves?' asked the eldar, gesturing towards the guilders being dragged away. 'Your race breeds like vermin. Your race *is* vermin, but you have your uses, don't you, Ikorus Baranov?'

'I... I believe we do, my lord. Or at least some of us do.'

'I am glad that you believe so,' said the eldar. He gestured more of his warriors forward, and they began to surround Baranov and his crewmembers.

'Ah,' said Baranov, 'I think we should part ways now, honoured lord. I won't press you for the payment for this last group. Consider it a gift, a gift to honour the friendship between us.'

'Friendship?' said the eldar slowly, as if savouring the word. 'A curious, irrelevant mon-keigh concept. And honour? Where is the honour in betraying your own kind? Delivering them to an enemy, albeit superior, race? That is honourable in your eyes?'

Baranov felt the sweat running down his back, and his throat was suddenly dry. He flinched as the eldar walked behind him, but he felt rooted to the spot, unable to think, unable to move.

'You are a detestable race,' said the eldar. 'Your very stench offends me, and yet, you have your uses. Your soul-fires burn so bright, and your fear... your fear is delectable.'

The eldar spun away from the petrified mon-keigh worm.

'Enslave them,' he said in the eldar tongue.

MARDUK TOOK CAREFUL aim at one of the frenzied eldar wyches as it darted towards him. Squeezing the trigger, the eldar's head disappeared in a mist of blood. The eldar warriors were almost naked, their flesh covered only by totemic war paint and ritual piercings, and they moved like deadly dancers as they cut into the warriors of the XVII Legion. Their strangely fashioned weapons wove dazzling patterns through the air, their movements at once enthralling and deadly.

A score of them had died as they approached, ripped apart by the murderous swathe of fire that the Word Bearers had laid down. More had perished when one of their hovering skiffs had been shot from the air, the fragile vehicle tipping onto its side, throwing its occupants onto the ice before it smashed down upon them, impaling several on its bladed sides and crushing more beneath its weight.

Now the wyches had engaged them in melee combat, and the odds were tipping towards the greater numbers of the eldar warriors.

Parallel beams of incandescent light speared through the night as a Land Raider fired upon the knife-like shapes of the dark skiffs that circled the battle, searing a pair of holes through one of its barbed, sail-like uprights. The raider vehicle veered to the side, moving with remarkable speed and grace as it avoided another pair of shots directed towards it, and another of the vehicles returned fire, a beam of darkness stabbing into the front of the Land Raider, which was rocked by the blow.

Jetbikes streamed out of the night, screaming low through the fight, peppering the Word Bearers with splinter fire. Marduk spun, his chainsword roaring, and cut the arm from one of the jetbikers as the vehicle screamed past him. Blood pumped from the wound and the rider lost control of his jetbike, which flipped into a sudden dive, skidding into the ice and smashing headlong into Kol Badar.

The Coryphaus saw it coming out of the corner of his vision and braced himself, leaning his shoulder into the careering jetbike. It shattered against him, breaking apart as it knocked him back a step, and the rider was catapulted over the handlebars, blood spraying in a wide arc from the stump of his arm.

Marduk fired his pistol into the chest of another of the wyches as it closed on him, and the painted figure was hurled backwards by the force of the shot. He spun, targeting matrices lighting up around him, and saw another of the wyches, her gaudy dyed red hair swinging behind her as she ducked under a swinging blow from one of Sabtec's coterie brothers and slashed a blade through the warrior's leg, cutting it off at the knee.

Marduk judged that this was the leader of the wych troop. She moved with exquisite, savage grace, her serpentine whip writhing with a life of its own. The whip cracked out, and its multiple barbed tips lashed around the arm of another warrior brother. Energy coursed up the length of the whip and the warrior of the XVII Legion dropped to the ground, his body convulsing.

Marduk levelled his bolt pistol at the wych's head, but before he could fire, a net of fine, razor-sharp wire wrapped around his arm, pulling his aim off target and slicing through his vambraces. A tri-forked spear stabbed towards Marduk's chest, but the First Acolyte swatted it aside with his chainsword and hacked into the eldar's neck, ripping his chainblade through flesh.

Untangling himself from the wire net that had cut half-through his vambrace, Marduk turned and staggered back from the furious assault of another of the wyches. It danced towards him with a pair of long-bladed swords weaving before it. Each of the swords had a guard that protected the wielder's hands, and they had curving blades for pommels.

The blades moved faster than Marduk could follow, and he was losing ground before their flashing advance. Snarling, he leapt forwards, his hatred fuelling his servo-enhanced strength.

One of the blades slashed for his neck, and Marduk blocked the attack with his forearm, while the other sword slashed up towards his groin. He met the blow with one of his own, and for a moment the two combatants were locked together. Then the eldar flipped backwards, first one foot and then the other cannoning into the base of Marduk's helmet, snapping his head backwards.

The two blades stabbed towards Marduk's heart, but he twisted at the last moment, and they scraped a pair of furrows across his chest. The First Acolyte grabbed one of the eldar's wrists, pinning it in place, and smashed the spiked guard of his chainsword into the wych's face, pulverising its skull.

Dropping the lifeless corpse to the ground, Marduk surveyed the battle. The eldar were everywhere, darting in and out of the melee, blades flashing and pistols spitting razor-sharp splinters. Another of the Land Raiders was destroyed, its blackened hull smoking and lifeless, and jetbikes screamed around the outside of the battle, banking sharply before gunning their engines and cutting like knives through the combat. Shadowy figures appeared on the outskirts, preying upon the unwary, blinking into existence behind warrior brothers engaged in combat, and cutting them down.

His warriors were acquitting themselves well, and the ice was strewn with the eldar dead, but he knew instinctively that this was not a battle he could win. The notion of retreating was repellent to him, but he had to keep things in perspective. He had what he needed. The knowledge was locked inside the explorator's brain, housed in the body of Darioq-Grendh'al. He had only to get away from this damnable moon, and return to Sicarus. Everything else was meaningless.

Marduk had ordered the warriors of the Host to protect Darioq-Grendh'al, but he saw now that such precautions were unnecessary. The corrupted magos was killing anything that came near him, and the first Acolyte smiled at the daemon's bloodlust as it overcame any resistance left within its host body.

A mass of writhing, daemonic tentacles, black and oily, burst from the magos's body to join his mechadendrites, each appearing to move with their own will and sentience. They coiled around the legs of those eldar that closed in around the magos, effortlessly hurling them through the air, while other sucker-tipped tentacles drew victims in close, where they were dismembered by Darioq's toothed servo-arms.

Snapping mouths upon the tips of mechadendrites burrowed into xenos bodies, and fresh mutations appeared upon the magos's flesh. More spines and horny protrusions pushed out along the ridges of his servo-arms, and from his knee-joints, metal merged seamlessly into bone and horn.

'We are leaving!' roared Marduk, and Kol Badar instantly set about ordering the evacuation.

An arc of black light struck the side of the shuttle, and Marduk felt a stab of unease. It was not a feeling that he was used to, and it served only to feed his anger. If the eldar immobilised the shuttle, there would be no getting off the moon.

'Move!' roared Marduk, stepping back towards the embarkation ramp of the *Idolator*, holding his chainsword in both hands. His bolt pistol was gone, but it mattered not. All that mattered now was getting off this cursed world.

The Word Bearers formed a retreating arc, closing together and backing towards the shuttle, bolters blazing and chainswords roaring, and the engines of the *Idolator* roared to life.

MARDUK STOOD WITH Kol Badar and Sabtec at the top of the embarkation ramp as the engines of the *Idolator* fired.

'Here he comes,' remarked Kol Badar as Burias-Drak'shal leapt through the press of dark eldar, crushing the skull of one of the wyches as he came. He was bleeding from dozens of wounds, the largest a gaping hole in his side, and his armour was peppered with splinters that protruded from his armoured plates like bizarre decorations.

The icon bearer staggered up the ramp, and Marduk stepped aside to let him pass.

'One minute more and we would have left,' barked Kol Badar, snapping off shots with his combi-bolter.

The daemon left Burias, his natural form returning, and he slumped forward unconscious, sprawling face first out on the deck, blood running freely from his wounds.

'Somebody see to him,' barked Marduk.

The engines roared as the plasma core came into full power, and the ramp began to close. Splinters spat up at the trio standing guard atop the ramp, and Sabtec and Marduk ducked back to avoid the deadly projectiles. A line of the fine shards struck Marduk across the side of his helmet, their tips just penetrating far enough to graze his cheek. He ripped his helmet off and tossed it into the shuttle's interior. Kol Badar merely endured the barrage of fire, for the splinters had not the power to penetrate his thick Terminator armour.

The eldar wyches made a last charge, leaping lightly onto the ramp as it rose past horizontal. Kol Badar killed three of them, firing his combi-bolter on full auto, and Sabtec took down another two, his bolter ripping the slender warriors in half. Marduk's chainsword killed another, the toothed blade ripping it from groin to heart.

Behind them was another wych, the tall, elegant and sneering female with flowing hair that Marduk had seen take down at least three of his warriors, and as Kol Badar and Sabtec gunned down her companions, her sinuous, serpent-like whip lashed out, its barbed tips whipping around Marduk's throat.

Debilitating energy coursed through the length of the whip, rendering Marduk's enhanced physiology all put paralysed, and his muscles twitched spasmodically. Fighting the energy coursing through him, Marduk dropped his chainsword and reached up to the strangling whip wrapped around his neck, trying to pry it loose. With a powerful wrench, the eldar warrior hauled Marduk towards her.

Sabtec cried out and reached for the First Acolyte, but Marduk was already falling. Kol Badar's combi-bolter roared, but the wych back-flipped from the ramp that was now more vertical than horizontal, and the bolts missed their mark. Marduk was dragged from the ramp behind the wych.

Kol Badar's power talons lashed out, grabbing Marduk around the wrist as he fell. The Coryphaus leant his shoulder against the closing ramp, and its motors strained against him as he held it open.

Debilitating energy was coursing through Marduk's body from the whip lashed around his neck, but he looked up at Kol Badar with fiery eyes.

'Don't... let... go,' he hissed.

Kol Badar stared into the First Acolyte's eyes, his entire body straining to hold the shuttle's ramp open.

Then the Coryphaus's talons opened, and Marduk fell to the ground below.

'No!' gasped Sabtec as the ramp slammed closed and the shuttle lifted from the ice. 'We must go back!'

'Be silent,' barked Kol Badar. 'He's gone.'

BOOK THREE: SHE WHO THIRSTS

*'And so from decadence, wantonness and
depravity a new power was birthed into the
darkness. In darkness it resides and in darkness
it hungers, now and for all time.'*

– Ravings of the Shalleigha,
Flagellantaie Diabolicus

Then searing pain exploded through Marduk's body, his every nerve ending on fire as needles stabbed into his flesh. He resisted it as long as he was able, and a further set of needles stabbed into him. Still, he fought his captors, struggling and roaring his anger. A third set of needles plunged into his neck, and at last he was overcome, and everything had gone black.

Glancing down, Marduk saw that his arms and legs were spread-eagled out to either side. His blessed armour had been stripped from his upper body, and his pallid skin was puckered with tens of thousands of tiny pinpricks of dried blood. His armour had been slowly fusing to his body, and the inside of their plates were covered with thousands of tiny barbs that were growing into his flesh. Removing the armour plating was a painful and oddly distressing procedure, for it was as much a part of him as his limbs, and he had only twice removed his breastplate since the blessed Warmaster had perished.

That was an age ago, a lifetime in the past. Once his armour had been granite grey, as had the armour of all the warriors of the XVII Legion, the colour they had worn since the Legion's inception, but he had long ago stained it the deep red adopted by all of his brethren at Lorgar's decree.

Marduk gazed blearily down upon his naked torso for the first time in untold millennia. It looked like the body of a stranger. His pectorals were thick and slab-like, and the muscles of his abdomen rippled as he strained against his restraints. Dozens of scars marred his perfect form and blue veins could be seen clearly through his translucent, pale flesh.

Marduk turned his head groggily to the side, looking along the length of his outstretched arms. His powerful limbs had been stripped of his power armour, exposing passages from the *Book of Lorgar* that ran in spirals of tiny script around his forearms. Just looking upon the tiny, archaic script gave him comfort, even though his eyes still could not focus on the individual words and characters.

Casting his gaze further along his arms, Marduk saw what was constricting his movements. A slender, tapering blade had pierced his wrists, passing through his flesh and between his bones, protruding a metre out the other side.

Marduk pulled against the restraints, trying to slide his limbs off the impaling blades, but jolting pain accompanied his efforts, making his body shudder and contort in agony. He could feel the needles, the long shards of metal that had been inserted between his vertebrae, piercing his central nervous system. They ran from the base of his spine to his skull, a slender needle inserted into every gap between the bones. Marduk ceased his struggles, and the pain instantly receded.

He was suspended, upright and hanging upon the blades piercing his wrists and lower legs. The blades shifted slightly, angling upwards, and Marduk hissed in pain as he slid further back along their lengths, the spikes grinding against bone.

As his vision cleared, Marduk took in the details of the room. It was circular in shape, and the ceiling was low. It was dim, the only light coming from the featureless floor and low roof, fading in and out in rhythmic pulses. There was a single exit from the room, semi-transparent strips of plas-like material blocking his vision of the room beyond.

Marduk registered the presence of another being in the centre of the room. He had thought he was alone, but his vision focused on the back of a tall, unearthly thin individual. Marduk glared at the creature hatefully, remembering its touch.

Its emaciated upper body was garbed in a tight-fitting, glossy black bodysuit, and its legs were concealed beneath an apron of similar material. The figure was leaning over something, a body perhaps, and appeared engrossed in its work. Dozens of blades, hooks and other less easily recognisable implements hung from its waist, and its hairless head was strangely elongated, its skull extending back further than was normal. Dozens of needles and tubes entered the flesh of its skull, flowing backwards like a mockery of hair.

Hovering above the table on which the death-like eldar worked was an immense spider, a dozen slim limbs extending from its body. The long, multi-jointed limbs were akin to the blades that pierced his own body, their surface black and reflective, and he wondered if it was a similar creature that held him. Its legs moved with swift, precise movements, each one easily four metres long and elongated to sharp points. Marduk decided that his first impression had been wrong. This was not a living creature at all. It was a machine.

As the machine spider rotated slightly in the air, its long legs moving rapidly and independent of each other, Marduk saw that his assumption was not quite correct. The thing *was* alive, or at least part of it was. In the dull light that pulsed from the ceiling and floor, he could see that there was an eldar figure at the heart of the spider-machine, or at least what must have once been one of the decadent xenos beings. Its face was obscured beneath a shiny black, featureless mask, and the spider-like limbs were attached to its torso, protruding from its spine. The eldar's humanoid upper arms merged into another pair of long spider limbs, though they were shorter than the others and ended in cruel

barbs. Where its two legs ought to have been there was
instead a bulbous, glossy black abdomen that hung low,
bloated and obscene. From the tip of this abdomen, a
pair of spinnerets exuded a sticky substance.

As Marduk's eyes became used to the dim lighting, he
saw that the spider-eldar was not hovering at all, but
was attached to the ceiling via a series of coiled cables.
A black substance moved within those cables in rhythmic spurts, like blood behind pumped through arteries
by a beating heart.

The tall, black-clad humanoid, that Marduk took to
be a sub-species of the eldar race, was talking to itself
in a hissing voice. The First Acolyte could not understand its words, for it spoke in the foul eldar tongue,
but he sensed that the creature was pleased. As it
moved to the side, he saw what was occupying the creature's attention. A fellow warrior of the XVII Legion:
Sarondel, one of the 13th coterie was pinned down
upon a bladed slab, his chest sliced open to expose his
internal organs.

Anger roiled up within Marduk to see one of his
sacred brothers of the Word so violated. The tall, skele-
tally thin eldar was removing the warrior's organs one
by one, and placing them in shallow dishes that hovered alongside the slab. The eldar's long fingers ended
in scalpel blades, and he saw a cruel smile on the creature's face as he got his first look at his captor's visage.

Its cheeks were hollow and sunken, emphasising its
sharp, high cheekbones and thin mouth, and its
almond-shaped eyes were black and dead. Its movements were crisp and sure as at sliced through
Sarondel's flesh, and the warrior growled, gritting his
teeth against the pain as his blood began to flow anew.

Marduk felt savage pride as the warrior of the 13th
coterie spat a wad of blood and phlegm up into the

twisted surgeon's face. The eldar was unconcerned, and wiped its face with the back of one hand.

'The dark gods of Chaos will feast on your soul come the end,' said Marduk. 'You are already lost, you just don't know it yet.'

The eldar straightened, dead eyes fixing on Marduk. It ghosted across the floor to stand before him.

'In the end we are all lost,' it said, lifting a bladed fingertip to Marduk's cheek.

The First Acolyte did not flinch beneath its touch, though he felt hot blood running down his face. Instead, he grinned, his blazing eyes holding the eldar's gaze.

'Your time will come sooner than you think,' he said.

'That is your prediction? You are a prophet then, human?'

'I am far beyond humanity. I am Marduk, First Acolyte of the 34th Grand Host of the XVII Legion, the Word Bearers, blessed of Lorgar. I make no predictions, xenos filth. I make you a promise.'

Marduk's eyes rolled back into his head as he sought to draw the power of the warp into his body, to call the daemons of the immaterium to him and unleash their fury upon this wretch that dared to defile the sacred forms of Lorgar's angels of the Word... but nothing happened. Silence and emptiness was all that greeted him, vast, cold and empty, and he screamed his fury.

Marduk tried to fly free of his mortal body, to rise above his earthly shell and become as one with the blessed ether, but it felt as if shackles held him locked into his body, imprisoning him within the cage of his flesh.

Had the gods of the ether forsaken him? Had they withdrawn their favour from him? The thought was more terrifying than any pain or horror that this being could ever heap upon him.

The eldar sneered at him, dead eyes watching him with keen interest.

'You can bring none of your taint here, slave,' it said, its voice mocking. 'Your gods have turned their backs on you.'

Marduk gritted his teeth and threw himself forward, muscles straining as he sought to rip the eldar limb from limb, but he was jerked backwards. The bladed limbs that impaled him hauled him back, and shooting pain blossomed up his spine.

Marduk thrashed and roared, and fresh blood began to run from his wounds as he fought to tear himself loose. The eldar merely gave a dry, cruel laugh, and turned away from him, and Marduk stared venomously at the retreating figure as it strode from the room, parting the hanging partition with a wave of its hand.

You can bring none of your taint here, slave, his captor had said, and Marduk could well believe the truth in the words. The feeling of isolation was staggering.

Did a null-field containment force keep his link with the warp at bay? Or had the gods truly forsaken him?

He had experienced a similar sensation of being cut off from the powers that be, once before, deep within the xenos pyramid on the Imperial world of Tanakreg, in that hellish otherworld that was not truly part of the material universe, but something else entirely. He had experienced a similar sensation there, and there he had won out, defeating his former master and escaping with his prize.

Escaping? The doubt came unbidden to his mind. Had he truly escaped? Or had he merely been *allowed* to escape? Surely such a being as powerful as the Undying One would never had allowed him to flee its realm had it not wished it to be so.

'My lord,' said a cracked voice, and Marduk glanced over towards the mutilated figure of Sarondel, stretched backwards upon the surgeon's slab, his chest ripped open. The monstrous spider creature was still poised over him, and it sprayed a liquid film over the exposed organs from the tip of its vile, bulbous, segmented abdomen.

'The gods... have they deserted us?' breathed Sarondel, echoing Marduk's thoughts. 'I cannot feel their touch.'

'Speak not such heresies,' growled Marduk. 'This is a test of our faith. The xenos filth will be punished for what they have done to you, brother. I promise you that.'

Sarondel groaned something indecipherable in response, and Marduk strained again to pull his limbs from the spikes impaling them. His efforts were hopeless. His muscles bulged with all his hyper-enhanced strength, but he was powerless against the slender blades that held his crucified form.

What if the gods *had* deserted them, thought Marduk with a stab of terror?

Silence such thoughts, Marduk raged. Such doubts are poison. Fortify your soul, he reminded himself, your faith will be rewarded.

Patience, he told himself.

His time would come, and he would be ready.

'You LEFT HIM behind,' said Burias flatly, his eyes glinting dangerously.

'Am I going to have a problem with you, Burias?' growled Kol Badar.

Burias pursed his lips, not taking his eyes off the Coryphaus. He took a deep breath, repressing his violent urge to leap across the shuttle cabin and tear the older warrior's head from his shoulders.

He had always fought at Marduk's side. Even as an acolyte, Burias had recognised that Marduk was destined for great things, and he was honest enough to admit that that he had befriended him in the hope that he would be dragged up the chain of command with him. Burias had never made any secret of this fact, and he had enjoyed the success he had achieved, and the privilege he had gained, as Marduk had risen to First Acolyte. With Jarulek dead and gone, it was surely just a formality before Marduk became a Dark Apostle, and then Burias's position would become even more influential. He was Marduk's confidant, his brother, his friend, and he would have had the ear of a Dark Apostle at his disposal.

In one swift, opportunistic move, Kol Badar had eliminated that future, and for that Burias would dearly love to rip his hearts from his chest.

'You think he is dead?' asked Burias in a low voice.

'He's gone,' said Kol Badar. 'The dark eldar took him. There is no coming back.'

Burias scowled, all his years of comradeship with Marduk, wasted. Once again, he let his eyes roll back into his head and the deafening tumult that was the immaterium screamed into him. Drak'shal had a bond with the First Acolyte, stronger than any bond between Burias and Marduk, a bond of servitude, a bond of command. It was, after all, Marduk who had first summoned Drak'shal into the icon bearer's flesh.

Drak'shal reached out at Burias's urging, searching for Marduk's soul-fire, for some hint of its existence. The daemon found nothing. Of course, it would take days, weeks even, to properly scour the turbulence of the empyrean, despite the bond the First Acolyte and the daemon shared, but a shadow presence should have been simple to locate. It was as if everything that Marduk was had been snuffed out. Slowly, Burias opened his eyes.

'He is truly gone,' he muttered in disbelief.

'As I said,' said Kol Badar.

This changed everything. If Marduk truly was dead, and what other explanation could there be, then Burias would have to quickly reassess his position. Without the First Acolyte's backing and favour, his position within the Host was tenuous. Kol Badar, as Coryphaus, was the most powerful individual within the Host, and would, as protocol demanded, take over the leadership role. Burias would be foolish to take that lightly. Without the First Acolyte to shield him, Kol Badar could do with him as his wished with impunity.

'What of the Council?' asked Burias, his mind whirring. 'The life of a Coryphaus that has allowed his Dark Apostle to die is a tenuous thing, but a Coryphaus that has allowed his Dark Apostle *and* First Acolyte to fall? You'll be made to suffer, and I have no wish to fall with you.'

'Walk with me,' commanded the Coryphaus, releasing the harness clamping him into his seat, and making his way towards the control cabin of the *Idolator*, fighting the angle of the ship's assent and the G-forces that pushed against his massive frame. Clearly, Kol Badar wished to continue the discussion out of the earshot of the other warrior brothers of the Host, which made Burias at once both suspicious and intrigued.

Burias threw off his harness and stood up unsteadily. Using the rail-holds above his head he hauled himself hand over hand towards the front of the shuttle. Once inside the control cabin, Kol Badar punched a blister-rune and the hatch was sealed behind them.

The crew of the *Idolator* had long been fused with their controls, and what remained of their flesh was covered in runes and sigils of binding. They stared ahead with sightless eyes, their entire existence dedicated to serving their infernal masters. They would not repeat what words were spoken in their presence even were they capable of speech.

'The Council need not know all the details,' said Kol Badar slowly, his eyes intense.

'They will need to be told something,' Burias hissed, 'unless we do not return to Sicarus at all.'

'No, that is not an option. No warrior of Lorgar has ever turned from the XVII Legion. No, we tell the Council the truth.'

'The truth?' asked Burias.

'Yes, that the Dark Apostle Jarulek was treacherously cut down by the traitor Marduk, who was envious and covetous of his hallowed role,' said Kol Badar, 'and that Marduk was subsequently slain for his misdeed.'

'You wish to lie to the Council?' asked Burias, his voice incredulous.

Kol Badar did not have a chance to answer, as warning lights lit up across the consoles of the shuttle. The Coryphaus moved swiftly towards the pict screens flashing with a stream of data, and swore.

'What is it?' asked Burias in alarm.

'A tyranid spore shower,' answered the Coryphaus.

It was heading right towards them.

'ADMIRAL,' SAID GIDEON Cortez, flag-lieutenant of the *Hammer of Righteousness*. 'The master of ordnance has a firing solution. Request approval to launch torpedoes.'

'Approved,' said Admiral Rutger Augustine.

He was standing at the forward observation deck with his hands on his hips, watching the battle unfold before him. The strategy of maintaining a blockade in front of the encroaching tyranid menace and decimating any world, inhabited or not, in its path still rankled with Augustine, but such were his orders.

Most of the enemy hive ships were still tens of thousands of kilometres away, but he could see them: immense, sentient creatures kilometres long with skin thick enough to endure living in deep space, their vile bodies armoured in segmented carapace easily as strong as the hull of the mighty Retribution-class battleship he stood in. It almost defied logic that creatures as large as this could exist in the universe. The largest of the bio-ships was easily a match for the *Hammer of Righteousness*, and rivalled her for size, and there were hundreds of smaller living ships that shoaled around the largest organisms. The smaller creatures ranged from the size of light cruisers all the way down to the size of attack craft and interceptors. The smallest bio-ships flew in dense clouds around the large hive ships, like swarms of angry bees around their mother-hive, and several Cobra-class escorts had already been destroyed by them when they had ventured too close.

The tyranid fleet was a terrifying prospect to face at close range, and Augustine had decreed that no Imperial vessel approach within six thousand kilometres of it. Even so, the xenos bio-ships were capable of startling bursts of speed that had at first taken the Imperials by surprise, and Augustine had lost the light cruiser *Dominae Noctus* and its entourage of frigates and escorts due to this unexpected trait.

A pair of hive ships had swung towards the Dauntless-class light cruiser as she had been turning to starboard to make a strafing run across the flank of the hive fleet, breaking from the formation of bio-ships.

Though the commander of the *Dominae Noctus* had seen the danger, he had been powerless to pull away fast enough. The cruiser had desperately unleashed the fury of a full broadside into the two bio-ships training in on him. Augustine had watched the destruction unleashed

on the living organisms on one of his flickering pict
screens, and had seen the carapaced hides of the beasts
rupture beneath the barrage, spilling bio-fluids into
space. Still, the bio-ships had continued on, spitting
streams of acid that melted the side of the Dauntless light
cruiser and launching swarms of smaller creatures, exhaling them from gill-like rents in their sides.

A trio of Sword frigates had nobly moved into the path
of the behemoths, seeking to draw them away from the
floundering light cruiser, and two of them were overwhelmed as boarding chrysalides were excreted from the
hive ships, clamping onto and cutting through their hulls
before overrunning their decks with swarms of warrior
organisms.

One of the bio-ships was drawn by the bait, and turned
on the last remaining Sword frigate, while its twin closed
on the doomed *Dominae Noctus.* The rest of the fleet had
watched in growing horror as immense hooked tentacles
shot forth from the prow of the bio-ships, locking onto
the hulls of the light cruiser and the frigate, drawing them
into the immense living beasts. More tentacles wrapped
around their hulls. The Sword frigate was crushed utterly
beneath the pressure and ripped in half. The *Dominae
Noctus* lasted little longer, for the tentacles drew it in close
to the hive ship, and its hull was rent by the immense,
bony beak concealed at the heart of the mass of tentacles.
For an hour, the creature gorged upon the light cruiser, its
hull almost entirely obscured by the tentacles that
wrapped around it, and Augustine had listened in stoic
silence to the screams of the dying as bio-acid and feeder
organisms had been spewed into the interior of the compromised ship.

Augustine had no intention of losing any more of his
fleet to the xenos fleet, and the Imperials were engaging the tyranids only at medium to long range.

The *Hammer of Righteousness's* dorsal lance batteries had taken a heavy toll on the advancing tyranid fleet, but the xenos ships continued on relentlessly, absorbing the casualties they suffered and pushing ever forwards. The bio-ships mortally wounded by the long distance barrages were devoured by the other hive-ships, who would doubtless use the genetic material to spawn more of their foul kind.

Augustine felt a shudder beneath his feet as the prow torpedo tubes fired, and he watched with satisfaction as the six immense, plasma-core projectiles, each almost eighty metres long, powered through the gulf of space towards the largest of the hive organisms.

Lance batteries from the rest of the fleet stabbed into the closest bio-ships, and other torpedoes impacted with fleshy bodies several kilometres in length. Tentacles flailed in death-spasms, and thousands of tiny organisms flew into the mighty wounds in the hides of the immense beasts, latching onto flesh and each other and excreting a cement-like substance over themselves to form a living bandage, sealing up wounds even as they were caused.

The largest of the hive ships veered to avoid the flagship's torpedoes, but its immense bulk turned slowly, and it was clear that it could not avoid the impacts. Smaller bio-ships interposed themselves, and three torpedoes exploded prematurely as they slammed into the sides of the lesser vessels. The last three plasma torpedoes hit their target, and gobbets of flesh the size of city blocks were blasted from the behemoth's flank.

'Order the *Valkyrie* to pull back,' said Augustine to one of his aides. 'She is getting too close.'

'Yes, admiral,' came the response, and the order was quickly passed on.

'Ground invasions have commenced on both the Perdus moons,' said Gideon Cortez, Augustine's trusty flag-lieutenant, his face grim.

Augustine sighed wearily. He didn't know how long it had been since he had slept. *Plenty of time to sleep when you are dead,* he thought.

He had already ordered the destruction of six inhabited Imperial worlds in this sector, but at least those worlds had been successfully evacuated before he had been forced to order their destruction.

Trying to give the citizens of the two moons as much time to evacuate as possible, Augustine had moved the blockade forward, so that the fleet could hold back the tyranid advance for as long as possible. Now, he looked down upon the twin moons, orbiting the gaseous giant nearby, and he cursed that he could buy them little more time.

'Percentage of the populations evacuated?' he asked, already dreading the answer.

It had been estimated that the twin moons of Perdus Skylla and Perdus Kharybdis would require three journeys of the bulk transport ships available, at the minimum, for a complete evacuation. As far as he was aware, only one journey had been completed.

'Less than thirty per cent,' replied Gideon.

'How many are left?' asked Augustine. He didn't really want to know the answer, but felt that he ought to know how many people he was condemning to death.

'On Perdus Kharybdis, around eighty million,' said Gideon in a quiet voice.

'Eighty million,' said Admiral Augustine in a weary voice, 'and Perdus Skylla?'

'No more than twenty million.'

'The evacuations were more successful there?'

'No,' admitted Gideon Cortez, shaking his head. 'The population of Perdus Skylla is but a fraction of its twin, mostly labourers and mine workers.'

'One hundred million loyal souls, and we are going to eradicate them, like that,' said Augustine, clicking his fingers together.

'Some might say it is a blessing, sir,' said Gideon, 'better than being devoured by the xenos.'

'Yes, you are quite right,' snapped Augustine. 'They should be thanking us.'

Gideon gave him a hurt look, and the admiral sighed.

'I'm sorry, Gideon,' he said quickly, 'that was unfair. How long would it take to do one final evacuation run?'

'The carriers are already en route for a final pickup,' said Gideon, 'though they will need an escort. Six hours, they'll need, according to the logistics reports.'

'Order the left flanks to close up, with the *Cypra Mordatis* at the fore,' said Augustine after a moment of deliberation. 'We can buy them six hours.'

Feeling Gideon still hovering behind him, Augustine turned to face his flag-lieutenant, one eyebrow raised.

'You have something to say, Gideon?'

'Can we really hold them for another six hours?' asked the flag-lieutenant, his voice low to avoid any of the other crew members overhearing his words.

'I don't know,' admitted Augustine, 'but we owe it to those people to try.'

Gideon still did not look happy.

'You can't save them all,' he said.

'No,' agreed Augustine, shaking his head, 'I cannot.'

THE IDOLATOR BANKED and jinked from side to side as hundreds of mycetic spores, fired by the hive fleet still some ten thousand kilometres from Perdus Skylla streamed down towards the surface of the moon. Each

of the cyst-like chrysalis organisms was filled with a
deadly warrior cargo, which would scour all life from
the doomed world. They fell like a meteor shower
through the atmosphere, their shell-like exteriors glowing hot as they descended at phenomenal speeds.

One of the spores passed within metres of the shuttle,
which was pulled to the side by the rush of air, but the
guidance systems of the ship hauled it back on course,
narrowly being struck by another pair of mycetic spores
as they roared down towards the surface of Perdus
Skylla.

Each of the spores was the size of a Rhino transport
vehicle, and a direct hit would cause tremendous damage to the unshielded *Idolator*. Engines roared as the
shuttle veered sharply to avoid a collision, but its movement took it into the path of another descending spore,
which clipped the side of the ship, sending it into a
spin.

The *Idolator* rolled through the air, dropping hundreds of metres and narrowly avoiding being struck by
more of the spores, but it came back under control,
pulling out of its death spin and shooting once more
skywards, pulling free of the descending shower of
ohrysalides.

Burias and Kol Badar picked themselves up, the
Coryphaus reading the damage reports that spewed
from the mouth of a graven, daemonic face. He swore.

'We are not going to make it to the *Infidus Diabolus*,'
he said, scrunching the thin strips of mnemo-paper in
his fist. 'Guidance systems are damaged, and the aft
engines are at quarter power.'

Burias was silent while the Coryphaus muttered, his
strategic mind working to solve the problem.

'Do we have enough power to break from the moon's
gravity?' he ventured.

'Yes,' snapped the Coryphaus, 'but we'd be drifting. We'll conserve our power once we have broken the atmosphere, and fire the engines to take us past the Imperial blockade. We'll order the *Infidus Diabolus* to break from its mooring and come to meet us half way.'

'The Imperial fleet will be aware of its presence as soon as it pulls out of the radiation of the sun,' said Burias. 'If they turn their fleet…'

'Then we must pray that they do not. Let us hope that the cursed Imperials are too occupied by the xenos to swing their blockade.'

'And if they don't?'

'Then we are dead.'

CHAPTER EIGHTEEN

'YOU ARE WASTING your time,' growled Marduk, blood
and spittle dripping from his lips. His head was held
immobile by bladed callipers that had emerged from
the floating slab on which he lay, making any movement of his head or neck impossible. He glared at the
eldar tormentor out of the corner of his left eye, his daemonic right eye rendered useless.

'I won't break,' snarled Marduk. 'You will have to kill
me first.'

His torturer did not look up, his utterly black eyes
focused on the incisions that he had cut into Marduk's
neck. He was gazing into them, prodding and poking
around the area where one of his progenoid glands,
those sacred glands that contained the essence of his
enhanced gene-seed, had been surgically removed thousands of years previously. As if satisfied, the eldar closed
up the wound, and lifted what looked like a spike-
tipped handgun from a pad that hovered at his side.

Marduk tensed, thinking momentarily that perhaps the eldar *was* going to kill him. The eldar ran the spiked tip of the pistol along the edge of the incision at his neck, and Marduk hissed in pain, feeling a searing laser melting his flesh. The eldar replaced the strange implement back on its floating platform, and Marduk realised that the wound in his neck was sealed.

The First Acolyte stared at the spiked pistol-like piece of apparatus for a moment, and then flexed his neck from side to side as the callipers retracted from their clamped position around his cranium. The bladed lengths slid away soundlessly, and came to rest around his head like a razor-sharp halo, leaving him free of their constriction, but still protruding from the hovering slab, just centimetres from his head.

Marduk hissed as fresh pain seared across his abdomen. Two long cuts bisected his flesh, and snarling, he leant forwards to watch the monstrous eldar surgeon at work. Doubtless that was the reason his head restraints had been retracted, so that he could witness the surgery being performed upon him. His skin was sliced, and the thick black carapace beneath, the implant that allowed his holy armour to be plugged directly into his body, was cut open with laser-tipped tools.

The biomechanical creature hovering on the pulsing ceiling reached out with four slender limbs, each of them piercing one corner of his flesh, painfully drawing his sliced black carapace apart to expose the stomach cavity. The wraith-like eldar began to probe his organs with his slender fingers. Marduk's chest had not yet been cut open, but he knew that it was just a matter of time. He had witnessed two of his brother Space Marines have their organs removed, though Marduk had noted that the eldar was careful to leave his victims alive, using inferior substitute organs to keep them going. It had taken some time to cut through the black carapace beneath the flesh of the warriors' chests, but the tools of the twisted creature were powerful.

'I have no interest in your death,' intoned his torturer, still engrossed in his work. Marduk could feel the fingers probing within him, handling his enhanced organs. The feeling was uncomfortable, but he pushed the sensation away, focusing his mind.

'If your intention is not to kill me, what then is to be my fate?' asked Marduk, feigning weakness in his voice.

The twisted surgeon did not pause in his work, and for a moment Marduk thought he would not get an answer, but at last the eldar spoke.

'Upon reaching Commoragh,' said the eldar, though Marduk did not recognise the word, 'your s*avayaethoth*, your… soul-flame… will be drained from your body. This soul-essence will be delivered to Lord Vect, for him to do with as he pleases. Your s*avayaethoth* burns brighter than those of your comrades. Most likely, the Lord Vect will take it into himself. All that you are will be consumed, utterly and completely, and She Who Thirsts will be denied her claim upon him a little longer.

'The soul-extraction,' continued the eldar torturer, 'is excruciatingly painful. What you have experienced thus far is nothing beside it, and I have been known to prolong the process for a week or more.'

'What will happen to you if I die beneath your scalpel before then?' asked Marduk.

'My master would be displeased,' said the eldar simply, as if he were talking to an imbecile.

'Your master is going to be very displeased, then,' said Marduk, and his primary heart stopped beating.

* * *

ADMIRAL RUTGER AUGUSTINE stared at the blinking icon in disbelief. Scans had picked up the telltale sign of a ship moving towards the rear of the Imperial blockade, emerging from within the radiation field of the system's dying sun.

'It's an Adeptus Astartes cruiser, sir,' said his aide in awe. 'And it's big'

'Yes, I can see that,' snapped Augustine, 'but is it friend or foe?'

'You think it may be renegade, sir?' asked the man, looking at him in shock.

'I don't know. I have received no information of a Chapter of Astartes coming to our aid, though it would be welcome. That they have not intervened thus far does not bode well.'

'Initial hails have been ignored,' said the aide. 'The archives are being scoured as we speak to identify the vessel.'

'Fine,' snapped Augustine, waving the man away.

'Trouble?' asked his flag-lieutenant, Gideon Cortez, as he strode to the admiral's side.

'Possibly,' replied Augustine. 'Damn it, I need more ships.'

'We could always order the Exterminatus of the Perdus moons now,' said Gideon in a low voice. 'Pull back, and swing to face this strike cruiser.'

'No,' said Augustine. 'I want that last convoy secured before I make the order.'

'Are the lives of those people down there worth risking the fleet for?' asked Gideon.

Augustine clenched his fists. Then he sighed.

'I'll give it one hour,' he said. 'Order the *Implacable* to disengage and swing around to the rear, with its full escort. Order them to stand off, though. Let the Astartes make their move.'

* * *

GLOWING RUNES FLASHED, appearing in the air above Marduk's still chest, and the haemonculus's pitch-black eyes flashed towards them in alarm.

With a flick of his bloody fingers he banished the runes and brought another set up before him, swiftly acknowledging the diagnostic reports. The mon-keigh's secondary heart had failed to pick up where its larger organ had failed. His subject was dead.

No! This could not be, he railed. There was no possible way that the subject's heart could have stopped, unless the creature had control of its functions, but such a thing was surely impossible in one as lowly as this lesser being.

More glowing runes appeared, hovering in the air above the mon-keigh's body, and Rhakaeth frowned deeply as he pulsed a swift mnemo-command to the lesser talos-artifice hovering above him. The creature's spider limbs were twitching nervously, sensing the displeasure of it master. His subject was not breathing.

Rhakaeth stabbed a needle into the Space Marine's neck before dropping the syringe to a waiting hoverpad, and summoning a breath-regulator to his side with a wave of his hand. Above, the lesser talos-artifice sank low above the table at Rhakaeth's mnemo-command, rubbing its forelegs together. Blue electricity jumped between the two bladed limbs, and at Rhakaeth's command, it touched the tips of the blades to the subject's chest.

The subject jolted, his body arching as power surged through him, and the runic projectors informed Rhakaeth that its twin hearts had recommenced their regular beat. Two heartbeats later, they had stopped again, however, and the haemonculus realised that the being was resisting his attempts to revive it.

Rhakaeth gestured, and additional hardware emerged from the underside of the operating slab, hovering up to his side. It mattered not that the creature was attempting to kill itself. It had no choice in the matter. He would keep it alive whether it wished it or not.

Leaning down low over the subject's lifeless face, Rhakaeth hissed in the crude, human tongue.

'You will not escape me so easily,' he hissed, 'and I shall make you pay for such disrespect.'

The subject's dead eyes flickered suddenly, its primary heart lurching back into life. Rhakaeth tried to pull back, realising that he had been tricked, but he was too slow, and the subject's teeth flashed for his throat.

IT HAD NOT been hard to fool his torturer. The eldar were an arrogant race and Marduk had guessed, correctly, that his captor would have no real understanding of Astartes physiology or what it was capable of.

It had been a simple matter to activate his sus-an membrane and begin the process of entering suspended animation, though it had taken more control to halt his primary heart completely.

Marduk bit into the eldar's neck, his teeth gripping the jugular tight. The eldar's flesh was dry, like a desiccated cadaver's. It would have been so easy to rip out its throat in one sharp movement, but that would achieve nothing other than fleeting satisfaction. Instead, he turned his head to the side, pulling the eldar across him, dragging its face towards one of the recurved, protruding calliper blades positioned to the side of his face.

Bladed spider limbs stabbed into his flesh, straining to pull its master free, and he felt the scalpel fingers of the eldar slashing frantically against his face and neck, but Marduk had no intention of relinquishing his hold. With relentless strength, he pulled the eldar towards the blade, careful not to tear its throat out. Still, the eldar resisted, but its body was weak in comparison to Marduk's, even restrained as he was, and the thick muscles of his neck bulged as he pulled the haemonculus onto the point of the blade. The tip of the calliper pierced the dry, wasted skin of its cheek, and a trickle of blood ran from the wound down the blade.

The eldar uttered something in its sharp language, and the blade-restraints were instantly retracted, ensuring that the torturer was not impaled, but also freeing Marduk's limbs.

The First Acolyte surged upright, tearing a chunk of dry flesh from the eldar's throat. The haemonculus fell backwards, gasping, hands trying to stem the blood flow gushing from the wound, and Marduk swung his legs from the bladed slab hovering just off the floor.

His stomach was still sliced open, and four of the spider-like legs of the eldar-machine hovering above him still pierced his skin. They slid from his flesh, and all twelve of the slender, powerful limbs descended towards him, stabbing and cutting. Marduk grabbed the spiked, gun-like instrument from the floating tray to his side, and with one hand holding his organs in place, he rolled himself off the bladed slab.

Marduk hit the ground hard, his intestines bulging from between his fingers. He rolled under the hovering slab, narrowly avoiding the stabbing legs of the spider-being that smashed down to impale him.

The haemonculus was crawling away, one hand clasped to his throat, blood gushing across the floor. He was trying to call for aid, but all that came from his mouth was a gargle of blood and froth.

Praying to the gods of Chaos that it would work, Marduk pulled the flaps of skin across his abdomen and pressed the bladed tip of the surgical instrument against the join. Its trigger was too small for his large fingers to easily operate, and they slipped off the slender trigger rune twice. The spider-creature wrapped its limbs around the bladed, hovering slab under which Marduk lay, and with a surge of power it hurled the table aside, throwing it into the wall, which shuddered and cracked beneath the impact.

Marduk managed finally to squeeze the trigger, and with a swift, painful movement, he roughly sealed the incisions. A pair of glossy black spider-limbs stabbed into his shoulders, and he howled with pain as the slender limbs passed through him, impaling his body on their lengths, and the wound-sealing implement fell with a clatter from his hands.

The First Acolyte was lifted into the air, still impaled on the two limbs, and was hurled away from the frenzied spider-creature. He struck the wall heavily, sending a ripple of cracks arcing out across its surface, and slid to the ground.

The spider-being disengaged from the ceiling, dragging its cabling and wires with it, and hit the ground, its bladed, slender limbs scrabbling for purchase. It launched itself at the First Acolyte, its forelegs rising to impale him once again.

Rolling beneath the stabbing limbs, which smacked into the wall behind him with colossal force, Marduk came up underneath the vile creature. He threw his body against the joint of one of the beast's back legs, which buckled under his sudden weight, and it stumbled.

Marduk grasped the slender limb with both hands and pushed his knee against the joint, grunting with the effort. The muscles of his arms and back strained, and he felt the limb bending beneath his force, until with a final, sickening crack, he sheared the limb in two.

Black fluid ran from the hollow limb, and the creature sprang away from him, scrabbling and sliding on the smooth floor.

Holding the bladed limb in both hands like a sword, Marduk waited for the creature to spring. He risked a glance behind him, and could see no sight of the haemonculus, though a telltale trail of blood was smeared across the floor and past the strips that led into an adjoining room.

Sensing movement, Marduk ducked and rolled to his right, narrowly avoiding being impaled on two barbed forelimbs. He slashed with the hollow limb, shearing through two of the creature's legs, which dropped to the floor, and more hissing, black fluid seeped from the creature's wounds. It spun to face him and thrust the rear of its bloated abdomen forwards, stabbing it towards him from beneath its body. Liquid squirted from its grotesque spinnerets, and although Marduk managed to avoid the worst of it, a line of the foul substance sprayed across his right shoulder. His flesh began to hiss and bubble, but he stood before the creature with his makeshift blade in both hands, ignoring the pain.

The creature's eldar torso writhed in obvious torment as ichor dripped from its severed limbs. Its blank face snapped towards Marduk, and it launched itself at him once more, bladed limbs flailing frenziedly.

The First Acolyte leapt to meet the beast, spinning the bladed limb around in his grasp so that he held it over his head like a spear. With a roar of animalistic fury, Marduk slammed the blade into the twisted eldar, the tip of the weapon piercing the flesh of its throat and driving on into its body behind its ribcage.

Bladed limbs hacked at his arms, tearing bloody strips of flesh from his bones, but the force of the creature's momentum was its death, for it continued to push forward, impaling itself further onto its own bladed limb.

Its front legs collapsed beneath it, and Marduk stepped back, breathing heavily, blood running down his arms. The loathsome creature fell headfirst into the floor, its greyish lifeblood running from its wounds. It tried piteously to lift itself up again, but its legs gave way beneath it, and it crumpled in a heap on the floor at Marduk's feet. He spat down onto the dying beast, and wrenched the bladed limb from its neck. Reaching down, he retrieved another of the creature's severed, razor sharp limbs from the floor, and so armed, he followed the trail of blood left by the haemonculus.

With the tip of one blade, Marduk parted the strips of heavy, semi-transparent material that hung from the doorway leading from the circular room that had been his entire world for the gods knew how long. He moved cautiously forwards, eyes darting around him, seeking any threat or movement.

This room was larger than the first, and circular, and half a dozen chambers led off it, each partially hidden behind hanging, translucent strips. He could hear groans and muffled shouts from within those rooms, voices crying out from raw throats whose owners had clearly heard the sound of Marduk's escape. Some of them sounded familiar, but Marduk ignored them, focusing his senses on finding the whereabouts of his twisted captor.

The centre of the room was bare except for a torturous bladed slab akin to the one he had just escaped from, with pale, thin lights shining down upon it. This table had a score of bladed arms extending from beneath it, but they appeared lifeless, or at least dormant. The room had dozens of hovering shelves and tables around its circumference, each one with strange perverse implements and objects arrayed upon it. The light was dim, pulsing faintly from the floor and the ceiling, but he could see the trail of blood on the floor clearly, and he quickly saw his wasted torturer crawling away from him, one hand still clamped around its bloody throat.

With a roar, Marduk leapt forwards, ignoring the pain in his tortured limbs. One of the eldar's wasted, skeletal hands was reaching up towards a flickering rune that hovered before what Marduk took to be a sealed, circular portal, but before it could activate the doorway, Marduk stabbed one of the slender blades down into the back of its thigh and dragged it backwards. It gave a wet, gargling cry of pain as it struggled futilely against him.

Marduk knelt over his eldar tormentor, twisting the blade ruthlessly, feeling it grinding against the bone, and smiled.

'How do you like the feel of that, xenos filth?' he snarled.

The eldar did not answer, but the bladed arcs of the circular portal slid aside soundlessly, and Marduk shifted his attention to the new threat, leaping forwards and spinning the twin blades in his hands before he even saw what was coming.

There were two creatures, vaguely eldar in appearance but altered, like mutant versions of the slender xenos. One was a woman, her body covered in tiny scales that flushed an angry red, and the other was almost reptilian in appearance, with hundreds of shivering quills inserted into its flesh.

The first blade struck the woman in the side of the neck before she could react, nigh on decapitating her, and his second blade stabbed towards the other creature's gut. Spines emerged from its wrists and it deflected the blow with a circular sweep of its arms. Then it threw its arms towards Marduk.

The First Acolyte swayed backwards, moving his body out of range of the creature's touch, but the spines in its wrists shot forward. Marduk twisted, but even so one of the spines sliced a shallow graze across his side, shooting pain blossoming from the scratch.

The female creature was on its knees, holding its head in place so that it did not flop to the side. Its scaled body was covered in rich, hot blood.

Marduk backed towards the centre of the room, stepping over the prone form of the haemonculus, which had managed to knock a surgical implant to the floor and seal its neck wound with a spray of a synthetic skin.

The spined abomination, enraged by the harm done to what Marduk guessed was its mate, threw itself towards him wildly. Marduk's blade swung up, swatting aside a pair of spines that were shot towards him. He rammed his weapon deep into the creature's side, wrenching the blade up under the ribs to pierce the heart. It slumped to the ground, hissing in hatred and scrabbling at his flesh as it died.

Moving to his torturer, which stared up at him venomously, Marduk hauled it to its feet. Holding it upright by the scruff of its thin neck, Marduk moved towards the circular portal, intending to step into the corridor beyond.

Claws dug into his shoulders as the female creature, its horrific neck wound all but healed with astonishing swiftness, landed on his back. It bit deeply into his neck, and Marduk dropped both his captor and his weapon.

Reaching over his back, his hands brushing past something cold and smooth attached to the back of his neck, he grabbed the feral creature in his crushing grip, and threw it over his head towards the wall. It tore a chunk from his neck as he hurled it away from him, and he cursed as blood gushed from the wound. The creature spun in the air like a cat, and landed on the circular wall on all fours. It did not fall, but rather remained stuck there, staring at him with hate-filled eyes.

It skittered up the sheer wall and onto the ceiling, and raced across it towards him. When it was three metres from him it launched itself from the ceiling, reaching for him with outstretched claws.

Marduk stepped into the creature as it flew towards him, and slammed his fist square into its face. Its skull crumpled beneath the blow, and its limbs went limp as it flopped to the ground. Having seen its regenerative powers already, Marduk gave it no chance to recover, and ripping the blade from the gut of its dying companion, he hacked completely through the creature's neck and tossed its head to the far corner of the room.

Swaying with blood-loss that his enhanced physiology struggled to stem, the result of the torturous wounds covering his body, Marduk dropped to one knee. His hands reached up behind his neck, towards the alien device that he had felt attached to the base of his skull when he had hurled the she-bitch monstrosity from his back.

His hands closed around a smooth, coldly metallic artifice embedded in his flesh. His fingers gripped the device around its edges, and his agonised muscles strained as he sought to rip it away from his flesh. The pain was intense, and it felt as if he might rip a part of his mind away with it, but Marduk ripped the alien device from his neck with a powerful surge of adrenaline.

The force of Chaos hit Marduk like a roaring tidal wave, staggering in its power. The full force of the warp rushed to fill the emptiness of his soul as the null-field generator that kept the power of the immaterium at bay was ripped clear, and his body was suffused with the power of the dark gods once more.

His vision swam, and blood dripped down his back as Marduk stared dumbly at the black thing in his hands. Synthetic claws with patches of skin and hair still clinging to them rimmed the ovular shape.

Understanding came to him. The gods had not deserted him. This foul device had merely cut him off from its blessed presence. It was a form of null-field generator. Marduk hurled it away in disgust.

BURIAS STOOD ALONGSIDE the Coryphaus, Kol Badar, on the foredeck of the *Infidus Diabolus*. The *Idolator* had docked with the mighty strike cruiser less than twenty minutes earlier, and Kol Badar had straight away ordered the warp engines of the ancient ship fired up, preparing to jump into the roiling ether and leave this cursed system behind.

It had been a tense flight from Perdus Skylla, for the damage done to the *Idolator* had meant that they had drifted, powerless, through the Imperial armada. At any moment, Burias had expected them to drift into the path of a broadside, and for the fragile shuttle to have been blasted to smithereens. Once clear of the blockade, they had drifted for tens of thousands of kilometres, until at last they had been drawn into one of the strike cruiser's immense docking bays.

There had been unease as they had disembarked from the shuttle and it became clear to the waiting warriors that Marduk was not accompanying them. Refusing to address the Host yet, Kol Badar had ordered Darioq-Grendh'al confined to his spartan quarters, and stalked to the strike cruiser's foredeck in preparation for warp jump.

Flickering screens of red light showed the relative position of the Imperial and tyranid fleets, and though the Imperials must have been aware of their presence, for the

Infidus Diabolus had left the surging radiation of the system's sun to come to meet the damaged *Idolator*, they had made little move to break their blockade to intercept them. A single cruiser with a host of escorts had formed a rearguard behind the bulk of the cordon, though it had made no hostile move towards them as yet.

Indeed, there was only one ship nearing weapon range, but the blinking screens relayed that this was nothing more than a passenger freighter, and scans had come back negative for weapon sweeps. It was of no consequence to the powerful strike cruiser.

Burias felt Drak'shal stir within him, and his eyes rolled back as he ventured inwards, to witness what had roused the daemon from its slumber.

'Jump on my mark,' said Kol Badar, instructing the daemon-symbiotes that acted as the strike cruiser's command personnel.

Burias blinked as he came back to himself, and turned towards the Coryphaus, disbelief and dawning horror plastered on his face.

'What is it?' asked Kol Badar, seeing the icon bearer's face pale.

'Marduk,' gasped Burias. 'He is alive!'

'Where?' growled Kol Badar.

Burias's eyes settled on the insignificant Imperial freighter.

'There,' he said, stabbing a finger towards the blip.

Kol Badar swore. The bladed fingers of his power talons clenched.

'Hold jump routine,' the Coryphaus said at last.

'What are you going to do?' asked Burias in a neutral tone. Kol Badar stared at him.

'Bring us to heading L4.86,' said the Coryphaus, holding the gaze of the icon bearer. 'Order the starboard gunnery crew to prepare weapons for firing.'

Burias raised an eyebrow

'Is there a problem, icon bearer?' rumbled the Coryphaus.

Burias licked his lips.

'No problem, my Coryphaus,' he said at last.

WITH FRESH ENERGY coursing through his body, Marduk rose to his feet, his eyes burning with the fire of devotion and belief. He stalked towards the pathetic figure of his torturer, who was vainly trying to crawl to safety, and lifted the skeletal eldar into the air.

Hefting him like a rag doll, Marduk stepped through the bladed portal doors.

The corridor was long and lined with hundreds upon hundreds of cells, each filled with piteous slaves. Many of them lay on their backs, with blank masks pulled over their heads that plugged into sockets in the walls behind them. They groaned and twitched as a barrage of terror was sent into their brains, while others were hooked up to all manner of torturous devices, while their cellmates looked on in horror. Marduk saw a naked human stretched backwards across a rotating wheel-like device, his hands and ankles bound and a slender blade poised in the air above. With each turn of the wheel, the man was brought fractionally closer to the blade, cutting into his flesh in a line from chin to groin. Other figures hung from insubstantial chains of light, bizarre apparatus attached to their heads by biting metal claws and their eyelids held forcibly open by tiny, black legs. A parade of horror passed before their eyes, and they thrashed around trying to escape their torment, but unable to look away as every debauched and horrific act imaginable was flashed directly into their retinas.

None of the cells appeared to have bars. Indeed, nothing appeared to hold them within their confinement at all, and Marduk moved warily along the corridor, eyeing the tortured humanoid forms to either side of him. Few registered his passing, and those that did stared at him with hollow, despairing eyes.

Marduk saw other cells filled with what could only have been the haemonculus's experiments, wretched eldar grotesques that had been twisted and surgically altered into whatever form pleased the perverted creature. He saw some with additional limbs grafted to their bodies, others with feathers that protruded where hair ought to have grown, and others bent over backwards and walking on all fours. One of them saw him holding the torturer before him, and it screeched in outrage, frill-like flaps of skin flaring up on either sides of its neck and a tri-pronged tongue darting from its mouth. Others turned to see what had enraged it, and as one they wailed, gnashed their teeth and whimpered to see their master laid low.

One monstrous grotesque opened its gaping mouth, the aperture spreading in four quarters that peeled back from its neck to its cheeks. It threw itself at Marduk, who spun towards it, but it slammed into an invisible barrier of energy that let off a stink of ozone and hurled it backwards.

More of the inmates began to turn in Marduk's direction, and he saw the hatred in the eyes of many of them as they looked upon the skeletal form of the haemonculus, helpless in Marduk's grasp. They rose to their feet to witness his passing, lining up to form a twisted honour guard for him.

One of the inmates, a human male, started calling to him, but Marduk ignored its cries, even as more of the wretched slaves began to holler, whoop and cheer, speaking a thousand tongues, both human and xenos.

This one human was particularly insistent, running alongside Marduk within the confines of his dark cell, begging and pleading.

Marduk paused, seeing a troop of eldar warriors moving towards him in the distance, clearly alerted by the ruckus.

'Release me, I beg you, my lord,' cried the man, no more than a metre from Marduk, but separated by the invisible wall of power. Marduk glanced down at the wretch. The man had obviously not been in his confinement for long. He bore no obvious injuries, and his skin was relatively clean, in stark contrast to the filth-encrusted masses. More than that, his eyes did not yet have the hollow look of hopelessness within them.

'Why?' asked Marduk simply, which gave the man pause. He licked his lips, and Marduk swung his head back the way he had come, seeing another troop of dark eldar warriors running lightly towards him.

'I have a ship docked on this vessel! We could escape, you and I together!' cried the man as Marduk made to move on. He paused, and swung back towards the wretch.

'What guarantee do you have that your ship is still here?' he asked quickly.

'None,' admitted the man, matching Marduk's fearsome gaze without faltering, 'but how were you planning on getting off-ship?'

Marduk swung his gaze around once more, seeing the eldar warriors drawing nearer from both quarters. The ones to his right were closer, and he saw several of them drop to their knees, raising weapons to their shoulders. Marduk lifted the haemonculus up in front of him for them to see, placing the blade of the spider-eldar's limb upon its already blood-drenched throat. That gave the warriors pause, though they did not lower their weapons.

'Things are not looking so good for you, friend,' said the man in the cell.

'I am not the one in a cell,' said Marduk.

'True,' said the man. 'The cell controls for this section are behind you.'

Marduk swung his head around to see a blank wall panel, though even as he looked upon it, glimmering runes of xenos origin flickered into being, hovering in the air a few centimetres from the wall.

'Touch the middle one, the one that looks like a serpent,' said the man. 'No, not that one, the one next to it. That's the door release. I've seen the guards use it.'

Marduk paused, indecision staying his hand. The man might be lying.

'What have you got to lose?' asked the man, as if reading his mind.

Marduk backed up to the control panel, his eyes flicking between the two groups of eldar warriors that had begun to edge forwards once more, just waiting for an opportunity to fire without hitting the haemonculus. His eyes drifted down to the eldar runes flickering in the air in front of the panel.

'Release him,' Marduk growled into the haemonculus's ear, tightening his grip on the skeletal creature. The eldar made no move, and Marduk pushed the blade more forcefully against its throat, drawing blood.

The eldar reached out a long, bony finger, moving it towards the glowing runes.

'No tricks,' said Marduk, 'or I'll have my own torture fun with you before anybody comes to save you.'

The haemonculus's finger paused just before it pierced the holographic image of a rune that resembled a jagged blade. Then it moved to the side and passed through the serpent-like rune, the one that the man had indicated.

There was a descending hum, and the man reached out a tentative hand. There was no surge of power and no stink of ozone, and the man exhaled deeply, flashing Marduk a grin.

'Thank you friend,' said the man. 'My name is Ikorus Baranov.'

Marduk ignored him. He was less than nothing to him, but the puny human's words were enticing. *How were you planning on getting off-ship?*

'Now the rest of them,' said Marduk. The haemonculus faltered, gargling something from its shattered throat, and Marduk pushed the blade deeper.

Instantly, the haemonculus's hand flickered over a series of rune images, and all the cell doors in the section powered down.

At first, nothing happened. Then a hulking two-metre beast covered in matted fur staggered into the corridor. Throwing its head back, it gave a blood-curdling roar. The dark eldar guards fired, knocking it back a step. It roared again, and lurched towards the group of warriors. Barbed prongs that shimmered with arcane powers were fired into its flesh, and it fell to its knees as agony seared through its body.

More and more of the slaves staggered from their cells, blinking their eyes heavily, as if believing that this was just another part of their torture. A broad shouldered, four-legged, centaur-like creature with a reptilian head lurched from its cell, which was barely large enough to hold its massive form. It hurled itself into one of the groups of eldar warriors, and two of them died instantly as it slammed their heads together, crushing their fragile skulls.

Eldar warriors began firing as more slaves spilled from their confinement, and crackling electro-whips lashed out. Slaves shuddered and screamed as the whips struck them, sending shooting pains through their nervous systems, and others fell, their fears, terrors and nightmares coming to life before their eyes as hallucinatory venom surged through their veins.

Other slaves fell upon each other, fists cracking against skulls and hands wrapping around throats as racial enmities surged to the fore and individuals driven out of their minds by their torments sought to slake their insane bloodlust.

All was chaos along the corridor, and Marduk smiled broadly, relishing the surge of hatred, fear and anger that washed over him.

'Which way?' he said.

CHAPTER NINETEEN

DRACON ALITH DRAZJAER stared at the curved, three-dimensional observation screen projected before him, watching as the hive fleet of the Great Devourer drew ever nearer. The bridge of his corsair flagship was dark. Reclining upon his throne, with its razor-sharp barbs rising around him, he scowled at the holographic images appearing before him.

He saw the twin moons orbiting the giant gas planet, with the flickering ghost-image of his bladed ship pulling away from them. His ship was as one with the darkness, and had the voracious organism-ships of the Great Devourer not been encroaching, Drazjaer was confident that he could have preyed upon this system for years to come without detection.

As the moons had finally completed their long arc around the gas giant and emerged into the light of the system's dying star, the dark eldar ship had slipped unseen through the mon-keigh blockade. It was likely that none had even registered his ship's presence, and those that had would have seen nothing more suspicious than a passenger freighter of their own design.

He had plied his trade in this system for two months, relying on the mimic engines and shadow fields of his slave-ship to confuse the mon-keigh scanners, while his warriors raided the evacuating populations. Within visual range, the mimic engines would no longer be able to fool even the pitiful scanners of the mon-keigh, but still his ship would be almost impossible to pinpoint, thanks to the shadow fields that cloaked its presence, and it was easy to keep out of the visual range of the lumbering mon-keigh ships.

It had proved a profitable and successful hunt, and thousands of souls were held in the torture decks below, ready for delivery to Commoragh. Still, it was not enough, and for the thousandth time Drazjaer cursed the very existence of the black-hearted lord of the Black Heart cabal, Asdrubael Vect. The tribute he demanded was extortionate. Drazjaer had hoped that raiding this one sector would have provided enough souls to please the vicious lord, and it had come close, but his time here was done.

Within the day, the tyranids would have overrun the prey-moons. The mimic engines would not fool the hivemind. It was time to move on, to continue his raids elsewhere, for to return to Commoragh without his full tribute was out of the question.

Dismissing the observation screen with a thought, Drazjaer swung away from the console, which retracted smoothly into the floor behind him. He saw one of his Incubi guards waiting for him, head bowed.

'What is it?' the dracon asked.

'There is a problem on *antitherea* deck, lord dracon,' murmured one of the incubi, his voice distorted by his tormentor helm.

With his screens down and completely confident that his mimic engines and shadow fields would be able to fool any of the mon-keigh vessels, Drazjaer did not see the Astartes strike cruiser turning towards his ship.

MARDUK HACKED A path through the press of inmates, slashing with the blade-limb and sending them reeling away from him, blood pumping from severed limbs. Those who fell were crushed in the rush to escape, and the man, Baranov, kept close behind him.

The First Acolyte had the skeletal form of the haemonculus in a headlock, using his body as a shield in front of him, and he hacked the blade through the neck of another inmate, who turned towards him, froth spilling from his mouth. The guards were being over-whelmed by the surge of slaves and paid Marduk no mind as they fought for their lives, weapons spitting and torturous electro-whips snapping.

'This way, I'm sure of it!' shouted Baranov, directing Marduk down a side corridor. The slave deck was a labyrinth of side-tunnels and holding cells, and every-where was chaos as the slaves set upon their captors and each other with insane fury. Marduk had sworn that he would make the xenos scum suffer for the ignoble suf-ferings that had been committed upon his flesh, and he smiled to see the mayhem he had wrought.

Marduk moved past dozens of cells. The wretched inmates still cowered within many of them, crouching in the corners, rocking back and forth, their heads in their hands, but it did not matter. Enough of the slaves were hell-bent on overcoming their captors to provide an adequate distraction.

'There!' shouted Baranov, pointing towards what looked like a dead end. 'That is where they brought me from.'

Marduk swung down the corridor. A group of eldar warriors was backed up against its end, a circular, closed aperture behind them. A slave, a human, launched itself at Marduk, hands clawing for him, but the First Acolyte slashed his blade across its face.

With the haemonculus held in a brutal headlock, Marduk broke into a run, dropping his shoulder and barging his way through the crowd towards the far end of the corridor. Baranov struggled to keep up, running in his destructive wake.

With a swat of his arm, Marduk slammed the first of the guards back into the wall, and slashed his blade across the neck of the second, blood gushing from the wound.

Something stabbed into Marduk's unarmoured back, and his body was jolted as his pain receptors flared, and his muscles twitched uncontrollably. He lost his grip on the haemonculus, who slumped to the ground in a bloody heap, and twisted around to see a trident sparking with energy jabbed into his flesh, held in the grasp of a blade-helmeted dark eldar warrior. He grabbed the haft of the weapon, sending flaring pain up his arm, and swung it upwards, sending the warrior wielding the weapon smashing into the low roof. The warrior released its hold on the trident, and Marduk turned and impaled another of its dark kin on its points.

'Get the doors open,' he barked, spinning and decapitating another warrior with a sweep of his blade.

'I'm trying,' shouted Baranov, his fingers flickering over the glowing rune of a side-panel.

'Try harder,' roared Marduk, just before he was slammed back against the wall as a coruscating arc of dark energy struck him square in the chest, fired from the snub-nosed rifle of another enemy.

The eldar warrior was about to fire on him again, but stumbled as another slave slammed into his back, knocking the eldar off-balance and towards Marduk. The First Acolyte reared up with a growl, the flesh of his chest blistered and smoking, and slammed his fist up into the eldar's chin, throwing his full force behind the blow.

The warrior's neck snapped backwards with an audible crack, and Marduk positioned himself in a protective position in front of Baranov, ensuring that no one came near him. He saw the haemonculus clawing away from him on the floor, and at a whim he placed his still-armoured foot upon the skeletal eldar's elongated cranium, pinning it to the floor.

'It's not opening,' said Baranov desperately. 'It's been locked down, or something.'

'You can open it for me,' Marduk said to the haemonculus, exerting more pressure on the creature's skull. It gurgled something, and Marduk bent down and picked it up by the scruff of its neck. His fingers completely encircling its neck, he held it half a metre above the ground. He pushed Baranov roughly aside.

'Open it,' Marduk growled, and slammed the haemonculus's head into the control panel for emphasis. Its nose broke, and blood splattered across the black panel.

The eldar gargled something, but its voice was unintelligible, and Marduk slammed its face into the panel again.

'Open it,' he hissed again, before slamming its head into the panel once more. Its face was a bloody ruin, its nose smashed, and blood and mucus was smeared across the deathly visage.

'You'll kill it,' warned Baranov, but the haemonculus lifted one of its claw-like hands, reaching blearily towards the panel.

The eldar's fingers stabbed at a series of runes and blade-arcs of the circular door slid open.

An armed group of eldar warriors stood beyond the doors, a hundred slender rifles lowered towards him. At the centre stood a tall figure in glistening black, barbed and segmented armour, its pale xenos face staring at him with noble arrogance. He saw the long-haired bitch that had ensnared him at its side, and a milky-eyed creature, glowing blue runes carved upon its ebony flesh.

'You... lose,' gargled the haemonculus, looking up at him in triumph.

'I don't think so,' said Marduk, and slammed the haemonculus's head into the control panel once more, this time with fatal force. Its skull crumpled.

He flicked his glance towards Baranov, whose face was pale as he stared out at the horde of enemy warriors before them.

'Stay close to me,' hissed Marduk.

Letting the dead figure of the haemonculus slump to the ground, leaving a smear of brainmatter across the control panel's surface, Marduk lifted his head high and stared defiantly at the eldar, awaiting his fate as a warrior of Lorgar.

Blood covering his heavily scarred, naked torso, Marduk locked his eyes on the central eldar figure. This one was clearly the leader of the dark kin, and if he had any hope of escape, it lay in him. The arrogant bastard stood with his arms folded across his chest, blades gleaming down its forearms, a look of utter contempt and sardonic humour on his xenos face. Surrounded by over a hundred of his warriors, all with weapons lowered, the haughty eldar lord sneered down his nose at Marduk.

'This is the prey-slave that has caused all this disturbance?' he asked, enunciating the words in a perfect, old form of Low Gothic. 'I am disappointed. It does not look like much.'

'I've still got the strength to rip your heathen head from its shoulders, xenos filth,' growled Marduk. 'Come, face me alone, if you have the nerve.'

'Face you alone?' laughed the dark eldar lord. 'We are far beyond any mon-keigh notions of honour, fool.'

'Coward,' snapped Marduk. 'Even unarmoured you fear to face one of the blessed warriors of Lorgar.'

The fiery-haired wych that had ensnared Marduk stood alongside the eldar lord, and said something sharp in the twisted eldar tongue, her eyes flashing and her hand darting towards one of the blades strapped to her slim waist. Her intent was clear: she wished to face Marduk in her lord's stead.

'Let your lapdog bitch fight,' urged Marduk, fixing his hate-filled gaze upon the wych. 'I'll tear her beating heart from her chest and laugh as I watch the life drain from her eyes.'

The dark lord snapped something sharp as the wych took a step towards him, sneering, and she paused.

'I have no wish to see you dead, prey-slave,' said the dark lord, 'and I fear that Atherak will not hold a killing blow. You are less than nothing to me, one of a race that exists merely to be preyed upon. You have no right of challenge.'

Marduk's muscles tensed in anger.

Having been stripped of his blessed armour, and with his flesh covered in the hellish wounds inflicted on him by the ministrations of the haemonculus, Marduk was but a shadow of his former self, but still his bulk and strength were impressive to behold. He advanced towards the arc of enemy warriors with his head held high, determined to face his fate defiant and proud to the end.

Marduk grinned, as he called the darkness forth.

* * *

NEVER BEFORE HAD Marduk felt such power as coursed through him now, and he felt the presence of the darkling god of Chaos, Slaanesh, surge into his being, almost shattering Marduk's sanity with the full force of its potency.

Marduk had always honoured Chaos in all its guises, and had reproached those within his flock who had strayed too close to the worship of any of the infinitesimal deities of the immaterium in isolation. He had never felt the attentions of any single god upon him like he did now, and he struggled to maintain control as the Prince of Pleasure exerted its will upon him. He fell to one knee, clenching his eyes closed tightly, struggling not to be overwhelmed by the surging power that threatened to tear him apart.

Do not fight me, whispered a seductive voice in his mind, its power staggering. The voice was silken, though behind its whisper Marduk could hear a billion souls screaming in torment and ecstasy. The power of the words ripped through his soul, and a tortured groan escaped his lips.

It is not for you that I come.

In an instant, Marduk lowered his defences, allowing the full potency of Slaanesh to manifest within him.

'Get it out of my sight,' said the dark eldar lord, unaware of the power growing within Marduk. Arrogant fool, thought the First Acolyte, he still believes me to be contained by the null-field device.

Marduk's face snapped up, his eyes a milky, pale blue with narrow slits in place of his pupils.

'*I know what it is that you fear,*' Marduk hissed in a voice that was not his own, and the dark eldar lord recoiled as if physically struck. '*Your souls are mine!*'

'The Great Enemy,' breathed the dracon in horror, speaking in the eldar tongue, though Marduk found that he could understand its words.

The First Acolyte pushed himself to his feet, feeling immeasurable power suffusing his body, and he lifted his arms out wide to either side, palms upwards. He could feel the panic and fear flow from the gathered eldar warriors, washing over him in a tantalising, delicious wave.

Marduk exhaled, and a pink mist rolled from his throat, filling the air with its heady, musky aroma.

'Kill it! Kill it now!' screamed the eldar lord, and a hundred weapons fired, as if his words had snapped his warriors from their horrified paralysis.

The air was filled with thousands of barbed splinters, lances of dark matter and coruscating arcs of energy.

None of the shots struck his flesh as Marduk continued to exhale, the mist curling and billowing from his mouth. Splinters slowed as they came within centimetres of his flesh, dropping to the floor in their hundreds with a musical ring, and beams of dark matter fizzled and dissipated as they seared towards him. Arcs of energy flowed around his body, leaving his flesh unscathed.

The pale mist rolled across the floor, and the eldar recoiled, continuing to fire their weapons as they backed away.

'*Come to me, my handmaidens,*' hissed the voice speaking through Marduk.

CHAPTER TWENTY

BARANOV THREW HIMSELF backwards as the eldar began to fire, and stray shots sliced through the air around him as he scrambled back behind the doors leading into the slave deck. His heart beating wildly, he pushed himself backwards with his feet, so that he came to rest with his back up against the wall alongside the dead figure of the haemonculus. He stared down at the crumpled, unrecognisable face of the eldar.

Several slaves had been cut down by stray fire, and lay bleeding on the floor. One of them, a young woman, reached piteously towards Baranov for help, blood bubbling from her mouth like foam. Baranov kicked at her hand to keep her away. Behind her, the other slaves were streaming away from the open portal as more stray shots pinged off the walls. A splinter ricocheted off a wall panel and struck the woman in the eye, killing her instantly.

The Space Marine spoke, and Baranov reeled in horror, doubling over in pain. It felt like *things* were clawing inside him, and an intrusive stabbing pain gripped his guts. He vomited, emptying his stomach as the utter *wrongness* of the voice clawed at his sanity, and tears ran down his face as he spat yellow bile onto the floor.

Baranov sank to the floor, oblivious to the vomit and drool on his chin and down the front of his chest, his limbs shaking. The Space Marine spoke with the voice of a daemon, a voice of madness. Its words were alien and horrific to Baranov, like a deafening cacophony of screams and guttural snarls.

A sudden compulsion made him crawl forwards on his hands and knees to peer around the corner of the circular doorway, and though he fought the urge, his soul screaming, he could no more stop his movements than he could stop his heart from beating. With tears running down his face, and shaking his head in denial, Baranov looked around the corner.

The Space Marine was standing with his arms spread wide, his head thrown back, and pink mist was seeping from within him, billowing from the cuts upon his body and spilling from his eyes, nostrils and mouth. The mist rolled out across the floor before him, and the black-armoured xenos warriors continued to blaze away at the daemonic figure as they backed away from its touch, though their weapons did nothing.

Baranov thought he saw shapes within the mist, sensuous bodies wrapped around each other in ecstasy, but he blinked his eyes and they were gone, nothing but contorting shapes formed by the roiling, pink smoke.

The mist coiled around Baranov's legs, and he felt hands caressing his skin, which was at once arousing and repulsive. The musk entered his lungs and he felt instantly light-headed, as if his mind was addled with opiates, and his flesh tingled with sensation.

He saw that his first impression had been correct. There *were* figures in the mist, and they were rising like serpents, their bodies unfurling as they stood, their every movement fluid and supple beyond human capacity.

There were dozens of them: tall, slender figures not unlike the eldar in proportion, though the similarities ended there. They were neither male nor female, or rather, they were both simultaneously, and they moved with inhuman grace and suppleness, their bodies twisting and writhing. Baranov found that his breath was coming in husky gasps as he looked upon their unnatural forms.

The figures solidified, and Baranov was paralysed in horrified rapture. His soul screamed within him of the utter wrongness of what he was seeing, yet his body was responding to the hellish allure of the figures. He saw their faces, and they were angels, beings of incomparable beauty. Their hair writhed like nests of vipers, and their eyes gleamed with the promise of pleasure... and pain.

The daemon's faces changed suddenly, the facade of beauty sloughing off as they opened luscious mouths, exposing needle-like teeth. Their eyes were as black as night and too large for their hellish faces, and Baranov realised that the daemon's slender arms ended not in hands, but in elongated, serrated claws.

Then the killing began.

The daemonettes moved with impossible grace, matching and surpassing that of the eldar. Every sharp movement of the daemons ended in a spurt of blood, a killing thrust, a severed limb. Bladed arms slashed across jugulars, and slender claws snapped bones. Elongated, tri-forked tongues lapped lasciviously at spilled blood, and the daemonettes spun and pirouetted through the carnage, killing with every graceful, savage movement.

Baranov breathed deeply of the intoxicating musk as he began to hyperventilate, and his irises swelled into wide, staring discs.

A daemonette appeared out of the mist alongside him, running a slender claw along the inside of his thigh, drawing blood. A stinging tongue caressed his neck, and Baranov moaned.

MARDUK LAUGHED ALOUD, hacking left and right with his blade, severing limbs from bodies and relishing the unabashed terror of the eldar.

The daemonettes were tearing through the eldar, carving a bloody swathe through their panicked ranks. Dozens of the daemons were snuffed out of existence as their physical bodies were torn apart by the frantically fired weapons of the eldar, but more of them continued to appear from the heady musk, taking shape even as their sisters were cut down.

Marduk fought his way towards the eldar lord, who was backing away frantically, his guards closing around him in a tight-knit circle. The heavily armoured warriors slashed around them with curved-bladed glaives, scything through daemonettes screeching like banshees, their voices raised in piercing cries that were at once hauntingly beautiful and horrific.

One of the incubi was dragged down, bladed arms stabbing into its stomach and head simultaneously, and a pair of daemonettes danced towards the dark eldar lord, claws slashing towards him.

The dark eldar lord moved with blinding speed, catching the blows on his bladed forearms, turning them aside and snapping one of the claws clean off with a deft twist. The daemonette hissed as milky ichor dripped from the wound, and the eldar lord stepped in close, slashing the blades across its face, tearing its unholy flesh from ear to ear.

The eldar lord swayed back from a sweeping blow from the other daemonette, before leaping into air, spinning, and slamming first one foot and then the other into the daemonette's face. Blades in his boots sliced through infernal skin, spilling more steaming ichor, and the lord stepped back as his incubi body-guards finished the injured creatures, ripping them in two with powerful blows of their punisher glaives.

'*I come for you!*' roared Marduk, his voice still that of the daemon, as he slashed a path towards the dark eldar lord.

'IT'S MOVING A little fast for a freighter, don't you think?' commented Burias, looking with narrowed eyes at the flickering vid-screens on which the positions of the fleets blinked.

The Imperial vessel that Marduk was located aboard had moved swiftly as the *Infidus Diabolus* had swung towards it, altering its trajectory with a speed and manoeuvrability that seemed far beyond that of a simple freighter; indeed it came about to a new heading with a swiftness that was far beyond any Imperial ship. Despite its surprising swiftness, the sudden movement of the *Infidus Diabolus* would surely allow at least one barrage upon it before it slipped out of range.

'Targeting matrices locked on,' croaked seven daemon-servitor symbiotes in unison.

'Fire,' barked Kol Badar.

A moment later, Burias felt the reverberations through the *Infidus Diabolus* as a full broadside salvo was launched upon the curious Imperial freighter.

* * *

THE ELDAR VESSEL veered to starboard as hundreds of cannon batteries unleashed their devastating fusillade, displaying a speed of manoeuvrability that a strike craft a tenth of its size would have envied. That brutal salvo would have torn through the void shields of any Imperial ship in seconds, and smashed apart its hull armour within moments, but the bulk of the shots went screaming past the shadowy outline of the dark eldar ship. Its mimic engines projected an outline that was vastly different to its actual proportions, fooling the targeting arrays of the *Infidus Diabolus*, and hundreds of tonnes of heavy duty ordnance roared past the ship, screaming wide of the mark.

Even with the naked eye, its exact position was impossible to discern thanks to it shadow fields, all light refracting and curving around its hull so that it seemed barely there at all.

Still, the weight of cannon fire was heavy and indiscriminate, and it tore through the bladed membranes of the back-swept vanes that rose like a ridge across the back of the dark eldar ship. Several barrages also slammed into its hull proper, wreaking terrible damage.

Even as the ship dived away from the *Infidus Diabolus*, slicing through the void like a knife, it returned fire, and stabbing lances of dark matter slammed into the Word Bearers' strike cruiser.

A dozen broadside cannon batteries were destroyed instantly, and tens of hundreds of indentured slaves, chained together in long worker gangs, whose sole existence was to load and prepare the mighty weapons for firing, were dragged into the emptiness of space, where their organs imploded. Fire blossomed across the strike cruiser as its hull was compromised in a handful of places, though the flames almost instantly died as bulkheads isolated the crippled areas and the air within was sucked into space.

The Astartes cruiser fired again, correcting its aim now that the mimic engines of the dark eldar vessel had been nullified.

'ADMIRAL!' SHOUTED THE flag-captain of the *Hammer of Righteousness*.

'What?' snapped Admiral Rutger Augustine. His knuckles were white as he clenched the railing before his view screen on the bridge of his flag-ship.

'That rogue freighter…' began his second in command, Gideon Cortez.

'What about it, Gideon? We are fighting a damn engagement here.'

'It's… it's not an Imperial vessel, lord.'

'What are you talking about?'

'The scans, they've been wrong. It's a xenos vessel, sir. Eldar. They must have been transmitting a false signal that's been fooling our sensors.'

Augustine swore. He had his hands full already with more than half his fleet engaged with the tyranids. The last thing he needed was for an eldar fleet to turn up. One never knew what their intentions were. Were they here to fight the tyranids for their own benefit? Or would they attack the Imperial fleet while it was engaged with the xenos foe?

'Is its disposition hostile?' he asked.

'Negative, sir, it is moving away from the fleet.'

'Well that is something at least. Ignore it. I have no wish to incur the wrath of the eldar. Not here.'

'There is something else, Rutger,' said Gideon, and Augustine could hear the reticence in his friend's voice. It must be bad, he thought with a sigh.

'Go ahead,' he said wearily.

'The Adeptus Astartes cruiser has been identified. Its signature has been pulled from the archive banks of command central. It is the *Infidus Diabolus*, lord. Word Bearers Legion.'

'Traitors,' said Augustine. He cast his gaze heavenwards, and barked a humourless laugh. 'Tyranids, eldar, and now traitor Space Marines. Perfect.'

'There is some good news, sir,' said Gideon.

'Oh?' replied Augustine.

'It would appear that the eldar and Chaos ships are engaging each other.'

Augustine shook his head.

'The Emperor works in mysterious ways,' he said.

Eldar were one thing, as often friends as foes, but a cruiser of traitor Space Marines? They were the enemy, and must be eliminated.

'Order the *Implacable* to move up in support of the eldar vessel,' order Augustine. 'Order them to engage and destroy the *Infidus Diabolus*.'

MARDUK STUMBLED AS the entire xenos ship was rocked by a second series of impacts, and he cursed. He had to get off the ship.

He saw the female, flame-haired wych that had captured him cartwheel through the melee, her whip crackling through the air behind her, and three of the daemonettes screamed in fury as their earthly bodies were slain, disappearing into mist.

Another daemonette reared up behind her and rammed its claws through her slender, tattooed body. Marduk plunged his blade into the wych's face, spitting her head on its length. Face to face with the daemonette, Marduk grinned. The daemon licked its teeth at him in response, and ripping its claws from the wych's body, it spun lightly on its heel, claws singing through the air to decapitate another eldar, sending its head flying.

Marduk whipped the blade free, spraying blood in a wide arc and spun to his right, slashing it across the helmet of another warrior, the slender xenos limb slicing through the armour with consummate ease.

Another barrage struck the eldar ship and Marduk stumbled again, cursing.

Darts spat into Marduk's chest, and he hissed as debilitating pain wracked his body for a moment, before the power of the warp within him surged, and he felt the pain recede. One of the dark lord's guardians stood before him, and more darts were fired from the tip of its backwards-curving helmet, which resembled a scorpion's tail.

Marduk lifted a hand, the movement guided by the power of Slaanesh surging within him, and the darts were halted in mid-air. With a quick motion, Marduk sent them slicing off to the side, where they took an eldar in the face.

The bodyguard darted towards Marduk, swinging its glaive with surprising swiftness, forcing him to leap backwards to avoid being cut in two. There was no time to launch a riposte, for the eldar danced after him, its return blow striking towards his neck.

Marduk met the blow with one of his own, but the glaive sheared through his blade as if it were not there, and though Marduk swayed to the side at the last moment to avoid the killing blow, the blade smashed into his shoulder, sinking deep into his flesh.

Grabbing the blade with one hand, keeping the eldar from pulling it clear, the First Acolyte and the eldar were momentarily locked together. Marduk stood half a head taller than the slender warrior, and over twice his weight, but the eldar was swift, despite its heavy armour.

The eldar's foot snapped out, hitting Marduk squarely in the throat. Again, the eldar snapped a kick to his neck, but this time the Word Bearer met its force with his arm, clubbing down hard on the leg as it rose towards him.

The eldar gave a reptilian hiss of pain as its leg was broken, its armour crushed beneath the blow. Instantly, Marduk ripped the glaive from his shoulder and whirled it through the air. He hit the eldar in the back as it fell away from him, severing its spinal column.

The weapon was phenomenally light in his hands, and he slashed it to the right, cleaving the arm from another of the eldar lord's bodyguard as it despatched another daemonette.

There was no order to the battle. The eldar were completely overrun by the daemons of Slaanesh. The musk had a powerful, intoxicating effect, and everything was brighter, more alive, and more intense than in any battle Marduk had experienced before. He heard every groan, scream and gasp, and every splatter of blood as it struck the flooring. The blood being spilled was the most entrancing, vivid colour imaginable, and he felt a savage joy at the play of light across the armour of the eldar warriors, the alluring smell of death, and the feel of the xenos weapon beneath his hands.

He saw the guards of the eldar lord fall one by one, dragged down into the mist, until the black-armoured figure stood alone, defiant and savage, yet hopelessly overwhelmed. This one moved well, and Marduk longed to test his strength against him, but it was not to be.

The daemonettes circled in around the eldar lord, snarling and hissing, closing off any chance of escape, and Marduk had no wish to come between the daemons and their prey.

Another series of detonations rocked the eldar ship, and Marduk swung away from the doomed eldar lord, leaving him to his fate.

'THAT ONE IS MINE,' said a voice, and Baranov looked up to see the Space Marine that had released him from his imprisonment striding towards him through the pink mist, eyes blazing with dominating power as he glared at the daemonette that held Baranov in its thrall.

The daemonette hissed in anger, but obediently spun away from Baranov, who cried out in desire and pain as it relinquished its hold on him. Bloody, stinging welts covered Baranov's body, and his eyes lingered on the fey creature as it spun away on one clawed foot and slashed its arm across the neck of a slave, who was standing nearby, mouth agape. Blood fountained from the mortal wound, yet the man moaned in pleasure, and the daemonette bore it to the ground in its embrace, the pair disappearing into the knee-high mist.

Baranov was insensible, shaking and gibbering from the horrors he had witnessed as the Space Marine hauled him brutally to his feet.

'Take me to your ship,' growled the immense figure, eyes blazing with fury and power.

'My ship,' muttered Baranov, his sanity in tatters, but he was brought back into reality as the Space Marine slapped him across the side of the head. His brain was rattled inside his skull by the force of the blow. The immense figure grabbed Baranov by the front of his shirt and pulled him towards his snarling, bloody face.

'Take me to you ship, or I'll gut you here,' he growled.

DRACON ALITH DRAZJAER turned on the spot, his eyes darting between the encircling daemonettes. All his long centuries of decadent life, avoiding the claim that

She Who Thirsts had over his soul, and it had come to this. Anger, bitterness, desperation and fathomless terror flowed through him in equal measure, but his body had been well trained in the death-cult temples of Commoragh, and he reacted instinctively as the daemonettes closed in on him.

He spun towards one of them, catching the daemonette's blow in one hand and slashing his bladed forearm across its neck with his other arm. He spun the daemonette into the path of one of its companions, and ducked beneath the slashing claws of the third daemonette, coming up inside its guard and ripping its abhorrent body apart with twin swipes of his arms.

Turning swiftly, he swayed beneath a swinging claw that would have ripped his head from his shoulders, and slammed a kick into the daemonette's perverted, backwards jointed knee, shattering it. As it fell, he rammed his elbow into its face, spitting it on the blade that jutted from his armoured plates.

He caught a blade on one forearm, and then another on his other arm, and snapped a kick into the daemonette's leering face. Blades snapped forwards from his knuckles and he stepped in close and punched the bitch daemon in the throat twice, hissing fluid spraying from the wound even as the infernal lesser daemon returned to smoke.

Drazjaer felt the presence of the mandrake, Ja'harael, materialise at his side.

'Save me, half-breed, and all that is mine will be yours,' Drazjaer hissed in desperation.

The mandrake stepped in close behind him and rammed blades into the dracon's unprotected back.

'You have failed Lord Vect, dracon,' hissed the mandrake in his ear. 'Your path is your own.'

The daemonettes closed in once more, licking their lips seductively.

'Goodbye, lord dracon,' said Ja'harael, and his form turned to shadow, even as the graceful claws of a daemonette slashed towards him. The daemonic blade-limbs sliced harmlessly through his insubstantial body, and he disappeared, retreating into the refuge of the webway.

Drazjaer screamed, his earthly voice and that of his damned soul joined together in union.

Delicate claws snapped closed, and Drazjaer's body was shorn into a dozen pieces. His soul was sent screaming to feed the insatiable hunger of the daemonettes' master.

SCREAMS AND SCREECHING inhuman cries echoed in the distance, and Baranov was pulled sharply into the darkness of a side-passage as yet another troop of eldar soldiers ran past, heading towards the escalating mayhem of the battle underway within the heart of the eldar vessel.

'There,' whispered Baranov, unable to stop his body shaking. He pointed across the open dock towards his ship, the *Rapture*, which was, thankfully, still where he had left it. The yawning expanse of space could be seen beyond, held at bay by an invisible integrity field.

Another explosion rocked the ship, and Baranov fell to his knees, though his companion yanked him back to his feet instantly.

'Keep behind me,' boomed his immense, bloodied benefactor, who broke into a run towards the *Rapture*. Baranov had no time to think, and he bolted from cover after the towering, terrifying Space Marine.

There was a shout, and Baranov saw a pair of eldar move to intercept the hulking Space Marine. Pistols spat shards of death towards the immense figure, but they barely slowed him, and he thundered into the pair, his halberd swinging in lethal arcs. Two slices and the fight was over, and two eldar bodies fell to the floor with mortal wounds.

The Space Marine reached the *Rapture* some ten paces ahead of Baranov, and swung around, his hellish eyes scanning for the enemy. Baranov ran underneath the landing gear of his prized shuttle and keyed the entrance code. The gangway ramp lowered towards the floor with a satisfying hiss. He ran up the ramp and bolted towards the control cabin, throwing himself into the pilot's seat. Flicking levers and turning dials, the *Rapture's* engines roared as they made ready for flight, and Baranov ran through a hasty diagnostics check.

'Are you in?' he called out over his shoulder.

'Go,' came the roared reply, and Baranov heard the sound of weapons fire.

'Hold on,' he shouted, and he gunned the engines.

The *Rapture* lifted from the deck, and her landing gear folded up beneath her as she turned on the spot, aiming towards the gaping docking bay doors and the refuge of space beyond. Weapon fire struck the hull, and Baranov swore as he saw a flashing damage report register on one of his pict screens. Then he slammed the two propulsion levers flat to the console, and the *Rapture* filled the dock with the flames of her engines. The rogue trader vessel speared out through the gaping bay doors, shooting free of the eldar vessel that had so nearly claimed his life and soul.

CHAPTER TWENTY-ONE

SOLON PUSHED THROUGH the bustling crowds with growing desperation and fierceness, shoving people brutally out his way, ignoring their curses and cries of anger as he fought his way towards gate D5, one of more than fifty that was still taking passengers. He dragged Dios through the press, determined not to release his grip on the boy now that they were so close.

They had seen the mass transport from some two kilometres distance as it descended through the atmosphere, hundreds of massive retro engines roaring to slow its vertical descent. The storms that had raged over the moon had been rolling away to the south for the past six hours, and for the first time in almost three months Solon had seen the stars overhead from horizon to horizon.

The angry red glow of the Eye of Terror dominated the sky, a circular corona of hellish light that peered down on Perdus Skylla with evil intent, gloating over its fate.

Flashes of light sparked in the heavens, like a hundred stars being born and dying again instantly, and it took Solon some time to realise what the flashes were.

'An Imperial armada is fighting for us, Dios,' he had said in awe when realisation had finally come to him, and he marvelled at the spectacle, trying to imagine the colossal battle raging overhead.

It had taken them almost four days to close towards the Phorcys starport, and they had met thousands of refugees, joining their convoys as they gravitated towards their last hope of salvation. Burning streaks of fire could be seen in the distance as hundreds of alien spores descended on the ice world, each one filled with xenos warriors intent on slaughter, and Solon knew that the final death of the world drew near.

With grim determination he pushed on through the crowd, elbowing his way forward, struggling along with more than a hundred thousand other desperate souls to pass through gate D5 and secure a berth upon the last of the mass transports.

It was like a form of hell, with so many thousands of people straining to push into the narrow defile leading to the boarding gate, and the stink of humanity was heavy. People screamed as the breath was crushed from their lungs by the press, and others cried out as they fell, to be trampled to death underfoot.

Women wailed as children were swept away from them in the surging crowd, and thousands of voices rose, yelling out in desperation to loved ones lost in the press. Other voices lifted desperate pleas to the Emperor, crying out for aid, for salvation, for forgiveness.

Wild-eyed priests had climbed up radial spires along with gaggles of frenzied supporters, and they raved and screamed their sermons over the heads of the crowds that rippled like a living sea beneath them.

A form of mass hysteria and mania gripped the flood of humanity, and fights broke out in isolated pockets of madness within the sea of bodies, with men clubbing each other to the ground, their faces twisted in rage and fear, only to be trampled en masse as the crowds surged back and forth.

A woman that had scratched a bloody aquila into her forehead screamed that the time of repentance had come, calling out for others to join her in joyous suicide, so that their souls might join with the Emperor in glory. She grabbed Dios by the arm, pulling him towards her, but Solon smashed his fist into her face, and she disappeared into the crowd once more.

Other desperate Imperial citizens, knowing that they had no chance of getting on board the mass transport and driven mad with despair and terror, hurled themselves to their deaths from the upper levels of the starport, screaming for the Emperor to draw their souls to Him. They plummeted down into the crowds, creating momentary gaps as they crushed those beneath them, before the gaps were instantly filled with more desperate people, clambering over each other towards the boarding gate.

Solon was nearing the vast gateway that led towards the immense transport ship, and was being carried along with the crowd down the centre of the vestibule area that angled into the gate. Those on the outer edges of the crowd were pressed against the rockcrete walls as they angled inwards, the weight of bodies behind them surging into the narrowing defile crushing the life out of them.

Someone stumbled in front of Solon, and soon dozens of citizens were pulled down, screaming and roaring. Dragging Dios behind him, Solon clambered over the morass of bodies, uncaring of who he stamped underfoot in his desperation to get to the gates.

A wailing roar rose from the crowd as the immense gates began to close, grinding in from either side, and Solon pushed on with added fury, smashing people aside as he strove towards the front.

He was only fifteen metres from the gates, and he surged forwards, pulling those in front down and clambering over them in desperation. Skyllan Interdiction Forces were screaming out over the crowd on loudhailers, ordering them back, but no one listened to their words. The gates continued to close, the press unbearable, and Solon was pushed back further from the gates, crying in anguish.

Once again, the crowd surged, and more people fell to the ground. A gap opened up, and Solon stumbled forwards, pulling Dios behind him, towards the closing gate.

The Skyllan Interdiction soldiers opened fire into the crowd to force them back, laslocks stabbing into the crowd. People screamed, but there was nowhere to flee, and the sickening stink of burnt human flesh caught in the back of Solon's throat, making him gag. Soldiers roared, ordering the crowd back, but it was an impossibility, and again they fired into the crowd, indiscriminately spraying las-fire into the mass of humanity.

Solon was struck a glancing blow high in the shoulder that spun him around, and he almost fell. Dios shouted something that was lost in the deafening roar around them and leapt forwards, trying to pull him to his feet. Knowing that to fall was to die, Solon grabbed at those around him, scrabbling for purchase. Hands punched down at him, trying to dislodge his grip, and boots kicked him in the ribs, and trampled on his legs. With a burst of energy, he dragged one man down, scrambling to his feet as he condemned the man to death, crushed to pulp beneath the surging crowd.

Five metres.

The gates were grinding closed, but Solon was so close it was painful. He pressed forward once more, and made good progress, battling his way towards the gates. He reached the front just as the gates slammed shut with a resounding crash. The sound struck Solon like a death knell, and he reached forwards and grabbed the bars of the gate, crying out in anguish.

The soldiers on the other side of the gates were backing away, eyeing the crowd nervously.

Hundreds of people threw themselves on the barred gates, clambering up onto support struts, calling after the soldiers or the last citizens that had made it through.

'Open the gates,' shouted scores of voices. Those behind, not yet realising that the gates had been sealed, that all hope had evaporated, continued to press forwards, crushing those at the front against the thick bars.

'Just take the boy!' roared Solon, his voice hoarse. One of the soldiers heard him, but shrugged his shoulders and turned away.

'Squeeze through, Dios,' urged Solon as they were hammered from behind and drove into the gate with crushing force. Dios cried out as his small body was pressed against the bars.

'Push through, damn it!' shouted Solon, and Dios squeezed one arm and leg through the narrow gap between the bars. He cried out as he got stuck, and looked around frantically for Solon.

'Breathe out, boy,' said Solon. 'You can make it.'

Dios exhaled all his breath, and Solon gave him a push. The boy was stuck tight, and he feared that his skull or hipbones would break if he pushed any harder, but the alternative was no more appealing. Another few minutes in this crush and the boy would be dead anyway.

'Breathe out, Dios!' he shouted again and gave the boy another shove. Dios cried out in obvious pain, but then his head passed through the bars and he fell to his knees on the other side. His head was bloody, and Solon realised that it was the blood that had saved the boy's life, for it had probably made the bars more slippery.

Dios picked himself up, and looked through the bars at Solon, his face fearful.

'Go!' screamed Solon, pointing behind Dios, where the lucky ones who had managed to pass through the gates were streaming into the expansive open holds of the mass transport, being herded by soldiers.

Dios turned and looked towards the ship, and then back at Solon. Solon saw that his face was an even more unhealthy shade of blue, and his eyes still burned with feverish light.

'Go, Dios!' Solon roared. The press behind him was intolerable, and he clambered up the bars, stamping on faces behind him.

'Go!' shouted Solon again, and the boy gave him one last look before he turned and ran towards the waiting mass transport.

Solon remained clinging to the bars until he saw Dios board the ship safely, and the transport's massive bay doors were locked and closed behind him. He felt strangely numb, and impossibly weary. The crowds were dissipating, wandering aimlessly, staring around with hollow eyes. Some sat down, numb with shock, while others gathered in small groups to pray. Others set about looting and destroying anything that they could, while some merely lay down on the ground to wait for the end.

Solon walked through the crowd, feeling hollow and empty. He took comfort in the fact that he had got Dios to safety, though he knew it was but a displacement of the guilt he harboured for not having been able to save his son.

He avoided the frenzied priests screaming of the end times, though hundreds flocked to hear their impassioned, doom-laden sermons.

With no real destination in mind, Solon wandered through the spaceport, seeing misery, fear and resignation everywhere he looked. After perhaps an hour he found himself at the windows of a viewing station, and watched the mass transport rise from its dock, as the flower-petal segments of the dome overhead parted to the heavens.

Solon watched the mass transport as it lifted up and rose from the dome, and he breathed out deeply, content in the knowledge that Dios was safely aboard.

He had no way of knowing that the boy had been infected by a genestealer and was, even now, taking that taint further into the heart of the Imperium.

Solon found a place that overlooked the ice flows, and settled down to watch the world die.

'ENEMY FIGHTERS LAUNCHED,' croaked the daemon-servitor, and Kol Badar glared at the pict screens that showed the flock of Fury interceptors and Starhawk bombers being disgorged by the closing Imperial Dictator-class cruiser. Sword frigates and destroyers were moving towards the *Infidus Diabolus* in a flanking formation, and the Coryphaus slammed his fist down on the pict screen. The plasglass screen shattered, its image distorting as hundreds of spider-web cracks appeared across its surface.

The eldar ship was slipping out of range of the *Infidus Diabolus's* batteries, and Kol Badar reluctantly ordered the Word Bearers' ship to pull off its pursuit, and to swing around to face the new threats. He watched with angry eyes as the eldar vessel darted away, taking the whoreson bastard Marduk with it. He would have felt much more comfortable knowing that the First Acolyte was dead, but he would have to content himself with the fact that the eldar had probably already killed him.

'Launch Thunderhawks and Stormbirds to intercept the enemy fighters,' said Kol Badar, 'and come to new heading, CV19. This is not a fight we can win.'

IKORUS BARANOV THREW the *Rapture* into a spiral as a formation of Imperial attack craft screamed past the front of the shuttle, their forward-mounted lascannons stabbing through the darkness.

The boxy shapes of larger assault craft the colour of congealed blood roared into view, battle cannons blasting at the swiftly moving formations of Imperial ships. As Baranov hauled on his controls, he saw several of the Fury interceptors explode beneath the barrage while those caught on the edge of the detonations spun crazily, wing thrusters destroyed.

Larger vessels that resembled immense birds of prey swept through the chaotic space battle, weapons flashing, and more of the interceptors were destroyed. The birds of prey were slower than the darting Furies, however, and as Baranov threw the *Rapture* to starboard to avoid a flurry of lascannon fire, he saw one of them explode in a fireball as numerous strafing runs from the smaller fighters peppered its dark red hull.

Behind the streaking, smaller ships, Baranov saw the distinctive, heavily armoured prow of an Imperial cruiser in the distance, a flotilla of frigates and destroyers fanning out to its sides. Swearing, Baranov dragged on the controls of his labouring ship, and an immense shape hove into view.

This ship was far closer than the Imperial vessels, and its deep red hull was powerful and bristling with weaponry and launch bays. It lurched as it turned to face the Imperial battle group, and Baranov dragged on his controls, not wanting to be caught between them when they began firing.

'THERE,' SAID MARDUK, stabbing a finger towards the familiar shape of the *Infidus Diabolus*. 'Take us there.'

He saw the human wretch, Baranov, give him a sidelong glance, and bared his sharpened teeth at the man. Baranov paled, and dutifully swung the *Rapture* towards the mighty vessel.

Attack craft sliced across the nose of the rogue trader's ship, pursued by the powerful, boxy forms of Thunderhawks, and defence turrets on the sides of the *Infidus Diabolus* spread a blanket of fire out towards the slower moving enemy bombers as they began an attack run against the strike cruiser.

Baranov dived the *Rapture* down towards the underside of the *Infidus Diabolus*, taking them out of the danger zone as the defence turrets increased the weight of their fire against the incoming bombers.

'Towards the lower launch decks,' said Marduk, pointing. 'There are fewer defence batteries there, and they have already locked onto the Sunfires. We should be able to enter the hangar bays unmolested.'

Marduk knew that the enemy bombers and interceptors would take precedence over an unarmed shuttle, and that the automated guidance systems of the *Infidus Diabolus* would probably not fire upon them while being assailed by other more pressing targets.

'That's it,' said Marduk as they drew ever closer.

A Fury wove across their bow, pursued by a Thunder-hawk displaying the leering daemon face of the Latros Sanctum splashed across its hull, and Baranov hauled on his controls. A bank of lascannons aimed at the interceptor struck the *Rapture* in its port thrusters, send-ing the shuttle careering off course. Warning lights flashed up, and fire roared through the rear cabins. The air within the shuttle was suddenly sucked from the ship, and only the safety bulkheads slamming closed, sealing the control cabin from the rest of the ship, stopped Marduk and Baranov from being dragged out into space.

'Take it in, fast,' shouted Marduk, and Baranov dragged the damaged shuttle back under his control, aiming it towards the gaping launch bay that was loom-ing up before them, filling their vision.

Assault batteries alongside the launch bay pivoted towards the *Rapture* as she screamed towards the ship, and they began to fire. The shuttle was struck twice, shearing one of her wings off in an explosion of sparks and flame, and then the *Rapture* was inside the Word Bearers' launch bay.

Indentured workers scurried from their path as the *Rapture* slammed down onto the launch bay landing zone, and a shower of sparks rose as the shuttle skidded and spun across the metal flooring. It smashed into a wall and ricocheted off, shearing its left side completely away before coming to a screeching halt.

'Nice landing,' said Marduk.

Two full coteries of Word Bearers Space Marines stood with bolters trained on them as Marduk and Baranov stumbled from the twisted wreckage of the *Rapture*. Marduk grinned and slapped Baranov on the back heav-ily, knocking the man to his knees.

'It's good to be home,' he said.

The First Acolyte was still naked from the waist up and his flesh was a tattered ruin, hanging from his body in bloody strips. The gathered warrior brothers stood with bolters levelled at Marduk, for a moment, not recognising him, before they dropped to their knees, bowing their heads to the ground before him.

'THE TRAITOR ASTARTES are attempting to disengage, admiral,' said Gideon Cortez, flag-lieutenant of the *Hammer of Retribution*.

'How many have we lost?' asked Admiral Rutger Augustine.

'Two frigates and a destroyer. Another two destroyers have taken severe damage. The captain of the *Implacable* wishes to pursue.'

'Order him to disengage,' said Augustine, somewhat reluctantly. 'We need those ships to protect the line.'

'The mass transports have pulled free of the Perdus moons' atmospheres,' said Gideon, reading the communiqué from a data-wafer that was passed to him from a subordinate.

'Finally,' said Augustine. He looked out towards the moons. A fierce battle was underway, as the bulk of the tyranid fleet converged on the doomed worlds, moving into firing range of the main blockade line.

'Your order, admiral?' asked Gideon.

Augustine sighed.

'Exterminatus,' he said wearily.

SOLON WATCHED THE rays of dawn lift above the horizon for the first time in over five months, relishing the sensation of natural light upon his face. The storms had all but cleared, and from his position he had a clear view across the ice flows. The white glare was almost painful, even through the tinted windows of the spaceport, and he was awed by the sublime view.

For the past hour he had watched the alien chrysalides falling from the sky. The xenos enemy could be seen now, approaching Phorcys like a living tide. People were screaming in panic, but Solon did not bother himself. There was no army here to face the enemy for it had long evacuated the moon, and there was nowhere left to run.

Above the living carpet of the enemy, trails of fire were roaring down from the sky, as if the burning tears of the Emperor were falling from the heavens to smite the never-ending xenos horde.

The cyclonic torpedoes, fired by more than a score of battleships in high orbit, slammed into the surface of Perdus Skylla, and the moon was instantly engulfed in flames.

Solon and all those who had not managed to secure passage off-world died instantly, and more than eight million tyranid organisms perished in the hellish con-flagration.

'THE EMPEROR'S WILL be done,' said Admiral Rutger Augustine as he watched the moon ignite from the bridge of the *Hammer of Righteousness*.

CHAPTER TWENTY-TWO

Beneath a sky of fire and blood, the Basilica of the Word rose impossibly high into the air, hundreds of barbed spires piercing the roiling heavens. Each spire was more than five kilometres high, and studded with jutting, rusted spikes. Ten or more living sacrifices were impaled on each spike, and they moaned in agony and torment as their flesh was torn from their bones by skinless daemons. Thousands more kathartes circled the basilica, filling the air with their screeches and deathly cries.

The sound of the daemons mingled with the morbid chanting of countless millions of proselytes within the basilica, their voices accompanied by braying daemonic choirs and the pounding of industry. Lurid flames burst forth from daemon-headed gargoyles as an endless stream of sacrifices were slain in the blood-chambers deep within, and the deep baritone of Astartes voices lifted in morbid cantillation.

Outside the temple, the lines of sacrifices, ten million strong, shuffled forwards, a never-ending stream of humanity that wound its way through the blood-soaked avenues. Deathly cherubs with skeletal wings growing from their bloated, childish bodies swooped low over the masses, and foul-smelling incense billowed from the censors hanging from the chains that pulled at their skin. Ever more penitents were constantly added to the lines, slaves and odalisques taken from a hundred thousand worlds on which the Word Bearers had fought, bringing the holy word of Lorgar to all, willing or not. Most were already utterly corrupted to the worship of dark gods and went to their deaths willingly, eagerly, yet twisted, black-clad minions of the Word Bearers continued to stalk the lines, stabbing their needle-like fingers into any that shuffled forward too slowly, urging them on.

Discords floated along the lines, mechanical tentacles waving gently, and the rapturous blare of Chaos in all its insanity assaulted the eardrums of the condemned from their grilled speakers. Relentless mechanical pounding boomed from the discords, overlaid with daemonic bellows and roars, voices whispering of death and the glory of Chaos, weeping of children and hate-filled screams.

Eight immense gehemahnet towers surrounded the monstrous temple, and the doleful tolling of their bells resounded across the hellish landscape. Hundreds of thousands of rapturous voices rose in glorifying chants as the colossal bells pealed, the sound torn from raw throats.

For as far as the eye could see, from horizon to horizon, towering shrines and temples to the dark gods rose from the blood soaked earth of Sicarus, daemon home world of the XVII Legion and seat of power of the

Primarch Lorgar. Kilometre-high obelisks hanging with thousands of lifeless bodies and daubed with infernal runes had been erected in every quarter, and grand mausoleums, cathedrals, and giant statues surrounded by squares teeming with worshippers spread out around the basilica.

Spider-legged cranes picked their way across the horizon, each one accompanied by half a million slave-workers that toiled to raise ever more impressive structures of devotion and worship to the gods of Chaos, constructing new temples, fanes and sacrariums atop older, crumbling edifices and cathedrals. The work was constant, level built upon level, so that the majority of the buildings were subterranean, an impossibly deep, labyrinthine warren of interconnected structures, all devoted to the worship of Chaos in all its guises. Indeed, millions of slaves toiled below ground, never seeing the surface at all, carving out more caverns of worship, crypts and deep, hidden sanctums many kilometres beneath the surface of the daemon world.

The rogue trader, Ikorus Baranov, was down there somewhere, thought Marduk in amusement, if he was not already dead. He had enjoyed the look of horror and betrayal on the weakling mortal's face when he had ordered him to be taken into the slave gangs. The human had served its purpose, and was less than nothing to Marduk.

Two moons hung low in the burning skies, their jet-black surfaces wreathed in hellfire, like the eyes of the gods staring down upon Marduk.

He stood on a high balcony constructed from human bones, staring down upon the glory of the Host, arrayed below him on one of the immense terraces that extended down the sides of the basilica: *his* Host.

It was gathered in all its might, standing in serried ranks, and Marduk felt pride as he looked upon them. Pennants of flayed human flesh fluttered from back-banners, and all within the Host had repainted their left shoulder pads, the ones that had previously been stained black in mourning for Jarulek, Dark Apostle of the Host. They were no longer in mourning, Marduk thought with a smile.

At the front of the power armoured bulk of the warrior brethren stood the Anointed, the warrior elite of the Host, and armoured divisions interspersed the ranks. Rhinos, Land Raiders, Predators, Vindicators, all had had their battle-scarred hulls repainted, and fresh sigils to the ruinous powers and litanies of the true word had been daubed and inscribed upon their ancient, armoured skins. Hundreds of slaves and chirumeks worked upon the hulls of these armoured divisions, patching damage and sanctifying their hulls anew in the blood of unbelievers.

Daemon engines and Dreadnoughts clawed at the flagstones of the terrace to the side of the bulk of the Host, each titanic amalgamation of machine and daemon kept in place by chains held in the hands of hundreds of straining slave-proselytes.

This is my Host, thought Marduk with pride and satisfaction. *Mine.*

MARDUK STOOD WITH his eyes lowered as he awaited the judgement of the Council. None but the Dark Apostles were allowed to look upon the sacred members of the Council when it was in session, and he kept his eyes dutifully cast down as he awaited the outcome that would determine his fate, for now and forever.

The wounds he had suffered under the knives of the eldar haemonculus had long since healed, leaving just faint scars upon his flesh, joining those that he had earned from fighting on a thousand worlds. His body was armoured in archaic plate, a holy relic that had been chosen from the armoury of the *Infidus Diabolus*. Marduk had spent long hours in solitude scrimshawing the litanies of Lorgar upon their surfaces.

He held his skull-faced helmet under one arm, the helm that had been worn by the blessed Warmonger before him, and over his armour he wore an unadorned robe the colour of bone, as the ritual required. His face was sunken and pale, for he had partaken of neither food nor water for a month, just one part of the arduous tests that he had been subjected to in order to prove his suitability.

He had been on Sicarus for almost three months, and since the commencement of the rituals of testing and purification, he had not spoken to a living soul, though his days were filled with acts of penitence, recitation of the Great Works and communion. He had endured all manner of ritual debasement, as his soul was stripped bare and he was reborn into the dark faith.

He was subjected to solitary confinement for weeks on end, sealed within the ossuary sepulchre deep beneath the Basilica of the Word, interred within a crawl-space little larger than his body, walled in with bricks and blood mortar. Hallucinogenic smoke coiled around him in the tomb, and as he breathed the fumes in deeply and his body passed into a catatonic state nearing death, his spirit had soared free. Garbing himself in armour of the soul, he had fought an endless army of daemons that sought to test his resolve, armed with a gleaming sword in one ethereal hand, a shield of darkness strapped across his other. How long the infernal gods had directed their minions against him he knew not, but finally he was brought back to the land of the living, his imprisonment shattered. He awoke a new warrior, weak in the body from his confinement, but strong in faith and spirit.

Endless days of ritual torment and study followed, when every aspect of his mind, faith and body were tested to breaking point, but through it all Marduk remained strong, refusing to succumb to the daemonic whispers that taunted him, telling him that he had already failed, that his soul would be consumed by the ether and his name forgotten by history.

All that was behind him, and he stood before the Council, proud and noble, as he awaited their final word.

'Kneel,' came a growled command, and Marduk fell to the ground, impelled by the sheer dominance of the voice.

A figure moved before him, and a hand was placed upon the crown of his head, pushing it backwards to expose his throat.

I have failed, thought Marduk, though he could not believe it.

A serrated khantanka knife was drawn and its cold blade placed against the carotid artery of his neck, but he did not flinch. He would face death with pride, though still he refused to believe that such was his fate.

The knife slashed the artery, and Marduk gasped as blood fountained from his neck. Bright blood pumped from the wound, spraying out around him. It gushed over his breastplate, running down over his torso and onto the floor, pooling around his knees.

Marduk swayed, still shocked that it had come to this, and all colour drained from his face as the pool around his knees spread outwards.

His pristine skull helmet dropped from numb fingers, splashing into the pool of warm blood, and he fell forwards. He threw a hand out to catch himself, but his strength was fading, and it was all he could do to stop himself from sprawling face-first into the already congealing pool of his lifeblood. Anger swept through him.

Marduk used the anger swelling through him to give him strength, and he pushed himself up off the floor. If he was to die, he would not die scrabbling on the floor like a dog. Even as more blood pumped from his neck, he retrieved his blood-smeared helmet from the floor and shoved it back under his arm.

He blinked, staring at the pool of blood in which he knelt. There was so much blood that he was amazed that there was any within him at all, and his vision wavered.

This is the end, he thought.

The mark of Lorgar on his forehead began to burn, smoke rising from his skin as the searing rune blistered his flesh.

A hand was placed against his neck, and the wound was closed as warmth suffused him.

'Arise, Marduk,' said the domineering voice, and Marduk felt hands on his shoulders, helping him to his feet. He was weak with loss of blood, and did not realise that he had passed the final test, and had received Lorgar's blessing.

Lifting his gaze, he stared into the impossibly dark eyes of none other than Erebus, he who had been first Chaplain of the Word Bearers when Horus had lived, he who had brought the true faith to so many.

'Welcome, brother,' said Erebus.

Other than Lorgar, and arguably the Keeper of the Faith, Kor Phaeron, Erebus was the most powerful, revered and influential member of the XVII Legion, and at his word countless millions had perished.

Erebus's head was shaved smooth, and covered in intricate script, his flesh a living Book of Lorgar, and

Marduk stared at him in confusion and wonder, still not understanding what was taking place.

The other seven Council members stepped forwards, surrounding Marduk, and he gazed around at their hallowed, revered faces in awe. He knew them all by name and reputation: the Dark Apostle Ekodas, the craggy-faced holy leader of the 7th Company Host, who had led a holy crusade of retribution upon the Black Consuls, almost wiping the Cursed Chapter, a successor of the hated Ultramarines, from the galaxy; at his side was the Dark Apostle Paristur, shrewd and savage, who had killed the Blood Angels Chaplain Aristedes in single combat on the walls of the Emperor's palace. Mighty heroes of legend all, the Council members closed ranks around Marduk, touching their fingertips upon the already congealing blood and daubing unholy symbols upon his armoured plates. Erebus dipped his thumb in the blood and marked Marduk's cheek, and he felt his skin blistering beneath the touch.

One of the Dark Apostles, Mothac, encased in ensorcelled daemon armour, a gift from Lorgar, held a thick book in his arms, its weight immense. The book was bound in the skin of Ultramarines, and Marduk gasped as he looked upon it.

'The Dark Creed,' he murmured, overcome with awe. These were the holy writings of the daemon primarch of the Legion.

Finally, realisation dawned on him. He had succeeded!

Mothac's face was solemn, and the Dark Apostles gave him some room as he hefted it before him.

'Swear your undying allegiance upon the Dark Creed and you will be one with us, Brother Marduk,' said Erebus.

Marduk placed a bloody hand upon the hallowed book, his eyes blazing with faith.

'I swear it,' he intoned.

* * *

'DARK APOSTLE,' SAID Burias, and Marduk, standing on the balcony overlooking his Host, turned towards his icon bearer with a smile.

The newly appointed Dark Apostle wore a cloak of flayed flesh, and his right hand leant upon the butt of the mighty crozius arcanum that had been wielded by Jarulek before him. It felt good to wear the deadly weapon, the icon that represented his new-found position.

'That will take some getting used to,' he said.

Burias smiled savagely at Marduk, and inclined his head towards the archway leading from the bone balcony.

'The sorcerer comes,' said Burias, a note of distaste in his voice.

The archway led into his private shrine within the immensity of the Bastion of the Word. All Dark Apostles had their own quarters within the immense structure. This one had belonged to Jarulek, and it now belonged to him.

With a glare of warning to Burias, Marduk turned to receive the Black Legion sorcerer.

Kol Badar stood by Marduk's side, immense and strong, his face unreadable. Only the clenching and unclenching of his mighty power talons gave away a hint of the Coryphaus's thoughts, and Marduk smiled. Kol Badar had not taken Marduk's ascension well, but he had knelt before Marduk, as had all of the Host, and sworn his life and soul to him.

Darioq-Grendh'al stood at his other side, garbed in robes of black, his face hidden beneath a deep cowl. The fallen magos was still changing, though his corruption was all but complete, and Marduk marvelled at how far he had fallen. He was truly a creature of Chaos, both in body and in spirit, and his mighty servo-limbs quivered as if beneath a mirage, their form subtly changing from one second to the next.

Burias stood alongside the champions Sabtec and Khalaxis. Burias was tense and eager to be away, and Marduk sensed too that Khalaxis was yearning to battle once more. Soon, he thought. Sabtec's face was set in his usual stoic expression. Marduk had been impressed by his skill, and knew that he would achieve great victories in his name.

To the side, dwarfing them all, was the immense bulk of the Warmonger, standing immobile, his heavy weaponry held at the ready.

These are my warrior faithful, thought Marduk, my officers and advisors. He knew they would serve him well, and if they didn't, he would sacrifice them, and none would be able to question his actions, for he was their Dark Apostle and he held their lives in the palm of his hand.

Marduk turned his attention to the new arrival, Inshabael Kharesh, sorcerer of the Black Legion. His gaze met piercing blue eyes that glinted with hidden secrets and knowledge, and Marduk affected a feigned smile of welcome. The Dark Apostle did not like the man, for he saw sorcery as a weakness – the only true power lay in faith, not conjurer's tricks and magic – but he was not one to argue with the will of the Council.

'You will extend him all the courtesies that such an esteemed envoy demands in the coming crusade,' Lord Erebus had said. 'He is the emissary of the Warmaster, and though Abaddon is but a pale shadow of Horus, we must show the requisite respect. This sorcerer could be a great ally for the XVII Legion. See that he is treated with courtesy.'

'It will be as the Council demands, my lord,' Marduk had replied, bowing.

'The… artefact is ready to be tested upon the warriors of the false Emperor?'

'It is, my lord.'

'Do not fail me, Marduk. Should this crusade falter I will be *most* displeased,' said Erebus, his voice soft, yet carrying a potent weight of menace.

The sorcerer nodded his head in respect to Marduk, dipping his staff, which bore the unblinking eye of Horus, low to the ground.

'Welcome, Inshabael,' said Marduk smoothly. 'I am honoured that you will be joining us for this crusade. It is always good to fight alongside our brothers of the Black Legion, and I am sure that your wise council will be invaluable in the coming days of blood.'

'I extend my gratitude to you for your kind words, Dark Apostle Marduk,' replied the sorcerer, his Cthonian accent harsh. 'The Warmaster is keenly interested in your… xenos curio.'

Marduk bowed his head, a pale smile on his lips. Abaddon had clearly sent the sorcerer to watch over the Word Bearers, but Marduk did not allow his anger to be reflected on his face.

The sorcerer's eyes drifted skywards, towards where the *Infidus Diabolus* hung in low orbit, and Marduk followed his gaze. The battleship was but one of many there, hovering motionless in the burning skies of the daemon world. There were thirteen battleships in all, and again Marduk felt his breath stolen by their awesome sight.

Thirteen battleships of the Word Bearers: five full Hosts, each led by a Dark Apostle.

The Thunderhawks and Stormbirds of the other Hosts were already flocking skywards, each one filled with bloodthirsty, zealous warriors. Heavier shuttles rose ponderously towards the waiting battleships, battle tanks and screaming daemon engines looked within their holds or hanging beneath them from metre-thick cables and locking clamps.

Immense transports lifted from the surface of Sicarus, emerging from beneath the parade grounds around the basilica, which slid aside to reveal gaping, subterranean crypt-holds below. The giant tubular vessels were powered by roaring engines that scorched the buildings below them as they rose into the air, defying the powers of gravity that strained to pull them back to earth. Kathartes swirled around the behemoths, filling the air with their piercing screams, for the daemons knew what was held within, and were hungry for them to be awoken. God-machines worshipped as physical representations of the powers that be, the titans of the dark Mechanicus rose towards the battleships, and Marduk relished the time that would soon come when the demi-legion of immeasurably destructive war machines would be unleashed. Long had it been since he had marched to war with the immense forms of titans striding behind him, each step covering fifty metres of ground, and their weapons laying waste to entire Imperial cities.

'An impressive sight,' said the sorcerer.

'Indeed,' agreed Marduk, a satisfied smile on his face. 'Once more the Imperium will tremble.'

The Dark Apostle lifted his skull-faced helmet from under his arm and pulled it over his head. It connected with a hiss, and he breathed deeply of the acrid, recycled air.

'The Black Legion are keeping their eye on us?' growled Kol Badar in a low voice across a closed circuit vox that none bar Marduk could hear.

'Something like that,' said Marduk, replying across the closed circuit. He glanced towards the hulking Coryphaus.

'Don't think for a moment that I don't know what you tried to do, Kol Badar: your little attempt to usurp me,' said Marduk mildly, his voice oozing menace.

The Coryphaus stiffened, but made no response.

'I am your Dark Apostle, with the full backing and confidence of the Council,' continued Marduk calmly. 'I will no longer tolerate or indulge *any* insubordination. I will warn you only once.'

Then he turned to his comrades and broke off the closed communications.

'Come, my brothers,' he said, his voice booming. 'It is time.'

'We go to war?' inquired the Warmonger, its voice booming, sepulchral and eager.

'To war,' confirmed Marduk.

EPILOGUE

MARDUK STOOD WITH his arms folded across his chest as he watched Darioq-Grendh'al at work.

A series of dark metal rings, each as tall as a man and inscribed with Chaotic runes of power, were aligned above a pentangle of blood, held in mid-air by the servo-arms of the magos. There were three rings in total, each fractionally smaller than the last, and they were aligned to form a single, large circle. Mechadendrite tentacles steadied the rings, holding them motionless with snapping, barbed claws and daemonic mouths. Another tentacle, black and smooth, emerged from within the ex-priest of the Machine-God's body, squirming from a bloody rent that opened up on his metal chest, reaching towards a control column that rose beside the magos.

A blinking eye appeared at the tip of the tentacle, and it peered down at the controls. Then the eye melted back into the fleshy tip of the tentacle, and it keyed in a sequence of buttons on the console.

A red light rose from the centre of the pentangle, and a similar light stabbed down from the ceiling above, where a similar daemonic symbol had been daubed. The two beams of light met, passing through angular holes within the sides of the dark metal rings, and Darioq-Grendh'al released his grip on them.

Marduk half-expected the metal rings to fall to the ground, but they hung in place, perfectly motionless as the magos stepped away. A pair of black-robed chirumeks, their wasted flesh augmented with mechanics, stepped forwards and presented the magos with a featureless stasis box. Mechadendrites stabbed a series of buttons, and the lid of the stasis box slid aside, smoke rising from within.

Then, with delicate care, the magos brought forth a perfect, silver sphere from within the box. The chirumeks scurried back into the darkness, and Darioq-Grendh'al moved back towards the rings hanging suspended in mid-air.

The magos extended his mechadendrites, reaching towards the joined beams of red light, and placed the silver sphere in their centre, where they had joined. It hung there, caught between the two beams, and Darioq-Grendh'al retreated once more.

The dark metal rings began to rotate, three rings moving in separate arcs that rolled around one another, moving smoothly and with increasing speed. The sound of air being displaced by the spinning rings got louder as they rotated faster, and soon the sound became a solid hum. The red light of the twin beams became diffuse, filling the sphere created by the rotating rings as they spun ever faster.

Marduk's eyes were locked on the silver sphere, the Nexus Arrangement that hung motionless in the centre of the rapidly spinning rings. At first nothing happened, but then glowing green, xenos hieroglyphs appeared across the perfect silver sphere. They glowed with intense light, and the sphere appeared to melt, its faultless, seamless exterior becoming seven rings that began to rotate around a centre of glowing green light.

The rings began to turn, mirroring the movements of the larger rings constructed by Darioq-Grendh'al, though their movements were slower.

Turning a dial, the red beams of light began to intensify and thicken, turning the green light at the centre of the xenos sphere a daemonic, bruised purple colour.

'It works,' said Marduk, with a grin. It was his to command.

GREEN LIGHTNING FLICKERED across the tip of the black pyramid as the prison of the ancient being known as the Undying One was shattered. A billowing cloud of dust rose from the ground as the immense pyramid began to rise, green hieroglyphs glowing into life upon its sides. Larger than any battleship, it lifted towards the dark sky, powered by engines far beyond human comprehension, for it was created by beings that had been in existence before the stars had been formed.

The majority of its bulk had been hidden beneath the rock, and it shattered the earth as it rose to the heavens, casting a shadow over the continent below. It rose higher into the air, green lightning still crackling across its sheer sides.

Directed by the Undying One's immortal will, it turned towards the angry red blemish that scarred the night sky, towards the Eye of Terror, towards the one that had released it from its imprisonment.

ABOUT THE AUTHOR

After finishing university **Anthony Reynolds** set sail from his homeland Australia and ventured forth to foreign climes. He ended up settling in the UK, and managed to blag his way into Games Workshop's hallowed Design Studio. There he worked for four years as a games developer and two years as part of the management team. He now resides back in his hometown of Sydney, overlooking the beach and enjoying the sun and the surf, though he finds that to capture the true darkness and horror of *Warhammer* and *Warhammer 40,000* he has taken to writing in what could be described as a darkened cave.

WARHAMMER 40,000

Dark Apostle

ANTHONY REYNOLDS

Blistering SF action set in the nightmare future of the 41st millennium

ISBN 978-1-84416-507-0